The Road to Ladysmith

The Last Imperial War

By

Nigel Seed

The Second Book in the Michael McGuire
Trilogy

www.nigelseedauthor.com

ISBN-13: 978-1725773431

ISBN-10: 1725773430

This book is for John Fine who has helped
me by reading all my books in the early
stages and advising me based on his own
military service

This book is a work of fiction and is not intended to be a history of the Boer War. I have placed my characters into the real events as far as I could to make my story work. There are a few places where my hero has stolen the actions of real people who fought this difficult campaign, in others he has interacted with real people. In the final chapter I have detailed the real events, places and people that actually existed so that you, the reader, can judge whether I have done them justice. In one or two places I have moved events in time to make my story work; I hope those of you, who know this piece of history well, will forgive me. If you find this campaign interesting I have also listed some useful books that you may wish to investigate. This book is intended to be the second in a trilogy that takes my hero through an interesting time period that was the beginning of the end for the British Empire. I hope you enjoy it and the book that follows, if you do, an honest review on Amazon, or any other of the good book websites, would be very much appreciated.

Acknowledgments

We are all travellers in the wilderness of this world and the best that we can find in our travels is an honest friend.
-Robert Louis Stevenson

I have been blessed with a number of honest friends who have helped me by reading my book at the embryonic stages and giving me useful criticism. They know who they are, but they deserve a mention for putting up with me. My grateful thanks to Pam and John Fine, Glenn Wood, Brian Luckham and Peter Durant.

The biggest debt though is to my wife who has lived this project with me and been supportive throughout, especially when I was struggling

From – Book 1 – No Road to Khartoum

Michael McGuire is a Captain in the Royal Irish Fusiliers, stationed in Cairo in 1898. He didn't start out that way. He was arrested in his native Dublin for stealing a loaf of bread to feed his starving mother and sister. Found guilty, he was given the choice of the 'Queen's Hard Bargain', go to prison or join the army. McGuire chooses the army and joins the Grenadier Guards in Dublin Castle. He finds that he likes the life and becomes a useful soldier. He is selected to join the Gordon Relief Expedition to march to the relief of Khartoum.

For his courage during that campaign he is rewarded with a field commission and joins the Royal Irish Fusiliers, to be close to the woman he rescued in the deserts of the Sudan. As he joins his new regiment he is tasked with forming a small group of men to be the advance eyes of the regiment when it is on the move.

His reconnaissance team comes to the notice of the headquarters in Cairo and he and they are used for some deep penetration tasks to gather intelligence in the Sudan. When the reconquest of the Sudan begins, McGuire is ordered to increase the size of his small unit to become the Reconnaissance Troop working directly with the head of intelligence.

He and his troop rapidly become very valuable to General Herbert Kitchener during this war and he is promoted to Captain and awarded the DSO. He and his men take part in most of the battles of that campaign, including the massive battle of Omdurman, after which he is sent home to his wife in Cairo to nurse his wounds and to recover from the arduous campaign.

Uncommon Words

There are a number of words used in this book that are peculiar to the region and may puzzle some readers. I have listed the most relevant below to increase your enjoyment.

Donga – a steep-sided gulley or dry watercourse

Kopje – a rocky hill, often steep and rising up out of the plain around it

Drift – a ford across a river

Kaffir – a term used to describe the native Africans. It has, in recent times, become a racial epithet, but at the time was just a general term for the Africans who came from many different tribes and nations.

Spruit - a stream or watercourse

Boer – a citizen of one of the two republics of the Orange Free State and the Transvaal. Mainly of Dutch descent, these people resisted the expansion of the British Empire into their territory.

Outspan – to make camp at the end of a trek or journey

Inspan – to prepare the wagons of a trek to move on again

Khakis – a nickname that the Boers gave to the British based on the colour of their uniforms

Sanger – a rudimentary shelter for protection from enemy fire. Commonly built of local materials such as stones. Still used today where the ground does not allow trenches to be dug.

Chapter 1
A Rude Awakening

Michael McGuire sat contentedly, leaning against the side of the sailing boat and watched his two children competently handling the lateen sail and steering a course between the other boats. He looked forward and could see his wife Emma standing on the terrace of the white villa that looked out across the Nile. The boat slid effortlessly alongside the small dock they had built and he stepped ashore. He made a point of not offering to help as he knew that Richard and Eleanor liked to be trusted.

He walked up the short flight of stone steps onto the terrace and sat down with Emma as she poured the tea. He was watching the sun dip towards the horizon and turn the river to bronze when he heard the gate behind the house open and then the sound of studded boots on the pathway.

He sighed and turned as the young soldier reached the end of the terrace and saluted. "Captain McGuire, sir?"

"That's right. What do you need?"

"Colonel's compliments, sir, and he apologises for disturbing your leave, but he needs you at an officers' conference first thing in the morning."

"I see. Which Colonel would that be and where is this conference?"

"Colonel Murphy, sir, and it's in the Officers' Mess at eight o'clock."

"Thank you. Please tell the Colonel I will be there. Dismissed."

He walked back and sat down heavily by the small table. He reached forward and took his tea.

"What do you think that's about?" Emma asked, sipping her own tea.

"No idea. Not sure why they want me there either. I'm still on detached duty at Headquarters with Colonel Wingate. Never mind, I'll find out in the morning. I would not be surprised if it's a mistake, with the Colonel being new to the regiment."

"I hope so. I'll get Bassem to press your uniform and polish your boots."

***

The other officers of the regiment were already in the mess anteroom when McGuire arrived. He nodded to those that he knew and took one of the coffee cups from the side table. As he found his chair the Colonel strode into the room.

"Sit down, gentlemen. No need to stand on ceremony this morning. I bring good news."

He waited until they had all settled again before he continued. "As most of you will be aware from the newspapers, the government have been having trouble with the Boer republics in South Africa. It appears that the way they are treating British and other people working in their domains leaves something to be desired. Milner, the governor of the Cape Colony, has requested troops be sent as a show of strength and to secure

12

the borders so we ensure the Boers do not get any silly ideas."

He took a sip from his coffee cup. "As usual the politicians have delayed and withheld the necessary funding, but now have decided to send a strong force under the command of General Redvers Buller. Since it is now such a rush they are dragging in regiments from all over and I am pleased to be able to tell you that we are going south."

He waited for the hubbub from the officers to settle. "We will sail from Alexandria on the 24th of this month on a ship called the *Avoca*. So there is little time for preparation. More details will emerge over the next few days, but for now I want you to parade your companies and tell them we are off. It is unlikely there will be any fighting and all the fuss should die down by Christmas. At least, that is what I have been told. Start your NCOs on preparing the men and getting all the equipment packed. Dismissed, gentlemen. Captain McGuire, would you remain behind, please."

McGuire waited while the other officers streamed out of the mess, all talking excitedly. The boredom of garrison duty in Egypt was to be livened up, if only for a few months.

Colonel Murphy walked across the room and took one of the leather armchairs opposite McGuire. "We haven't had a lot of time to get to know each other, with you being detached to Headquarters, Captain."

"No, sir. Colonel Wingate has been keeping my troop quite busy lately, working with one of the new battalions."

"Yes, I'd heard. Your reconnaissance troop seems to have quite the reputation. Especially after all you did during the reconquest of the Sudan."

"Good of you to say so, sir."

"Credit where it's due, Captain. Now let me see if I have your situation correctly. You joined the regiment on the personal recommendation of the Queen, even though there was no vacancy for you. My predecessor, Colonel O'Brian, created a post for you with your Reconnaissance and Intelligence unit."

"That's correct, sir. Only eight of us to start with, and I had to buy my own camels."

"You were asked to expand the unit for the reconquest of the Sudan?"

"I was, sir. We went up to thirty-one of us, drawn from various units in the garrison and organised into four-man patrols. Although I did lose some men during the war."

"So how many are you now?"

"Seventeen, including me. I have four patrols of four men each, two led by a Corporal and one each by my troop Sergeants, Donnelly and Parks."

"I take it you have recovered from your wound? So how would you feel about coming back to the regiment and coming south with us?"

"That would be up to Colonel Wingate, sir. If he agrees we would be delighted to join you.

14

Provided the parent units of some of my men agree as well."

Murphy smiled. "Wingate has already agreed, so that's settled. We don't know what the conditions are going to be like in South Africa, but an extra officer with a group of highly trained marksmen could be very useful to me. We won't be taking your camels, though, so you'd better make sure your men have good boots. You and I will get to know each other better on the journey so I can decide how best to use you."

"With your permission, sir, I'll go and instruct my men to start getting ready and then I think I will be having a rather frosty conversation with my wife."

Chapter 2
24th September 1899

McGuire and his men marched from the Alexandria railway station to the docks through the inevitable crowds of Arab tradesmen trying to sell them things at ridiculous prices. The rest of the battalion had already passed this way so the hawkers were not too hopeful and gave up after a few stern words in Arabic from Sergeant Donnelly. A harassed ship's officer stood at the head of the gangplank waiting for them and McGuire led the way onto the ship with his kitbag and rifle over his shoulder. Names were checked and the men were led away to their accommodation by one of the deckhands. McGuire was taken forward and up to the area allocated to the regiment's officers.

He was pleased to find that, as a Captain, he had a small cabin to himself with a porthole that looked forward over the bow of the ship. He dropped his kitbag on the bunk and stowed his rifle away, then went looking for the Colonel. He found him sitting in one of the lounge areas overlooking the dock and watching the loading.

"Captain McGuire, welcome aboard. All your men accounted for?"

"All present, sir. They are settling into their accommodation at the moment. I'll go down and see them shortly."

"Good. Now, I couldn't help but notice, as you came aboard, that you were carrying a rifle and did not seem to have your sword with you."

"That's right, sir. I carry a rifle when we are on active service so that I do not stand out from the men. No point in giving the snipers a helping hand."

Murphy chuckled. "I don't think we need to worry about snipers on this expedition, Captain. We are only going to show some force to a bunch of Boer farmers. It's not as if they even have an army."

"I hope you are right, sir. In any event, I can be much more effective with a rifle, if only to bring down some game to supplement our rations."

"Ah, now that is a good reason to take your rifle, but I would appreciate it if you could acquire a sword. The men expect it, you see."

"I'll see what I can do, sir, but now, if you don't mind, I'd like to check on my men."

McGuire went back to the gangplank and found the same ship's officer standing there with his list of people to check aboard. Even in what seemed to McGuire to be the cool of an Egyptian winter, the man was sweating through his white jacket. He checked his list and called a sailor across to lead McGuire down into the ship through the maze of passageways. His men came to attention as he entered the large cabin with bunks stacked three high around the bulkheads.

"Carry on with what you were doing. Sergeant Donnelly, any problems?"

"Not really, sir, but we do have a surprise for you." He turned and yelled across the cabin. "Fine, come here!"

McGuire's mouth dropped open just a little as he saw Corporal Fine walking towards him. "Fine, what are you doing here? You were unfit to sign on in the regiment again."

"I was, sir, but months of working as the manager in the warehouse for your good lady wife have let me recover and when I heard the reserves were being called up I couldn't stay away."

McGuire looked down to the sleeve of Fine's jacket and saw that he was wearing the red diamond patch with the yellow embroidered 'R' that distinguished his men from the rest of the regiment.

"I see you're wearing the Reconnaissance Troop badge. Does that mean you are back with me?"

"If you'll have me, sir."

McGuire smiled. "I'm delighted to have you back. All that training you joined in on before the Sudan campaign is about to pay off, I hope."

He turned to the big Sergeant waiting patiently beside him. "Sergeant, I think we will let the men relax for a day to get used to the ship and get over any sea sickness. You and I will work out a training regime and we'll start the next day."

While the rest of the regiment relaxed on the decks or sang songs around the piano in the saloon, McGuire had his men pounding around the same decks wearing full kit. The idlers shouted rude comments and the other officers watched with wry amusement. They took more notice when the reconnaissance troop was practising marksmanship from the ship's stern deck with their newly issued Lee Enfield rifles.

The targets were beer bottles with a cork in the neck to make sure they floated and very few of them escaped intact. After the ship coaled in Aden and sailed into warmer waters McGuire had his men strip to the waist for their physical training, known as 'bars and rings', using improvised obstacles from the ship's equipment.

After dinner one evening the Colonel called McGuire to one side. "Captain, I realise you train your men differently to the normal regimental procedure, but would you explain to me what you are doing?"

"Certainly, sir. Sitting on a ship for weeks enjoying a cruise is very pleasant, but since I expect my men to be used as forward scouts they need to be strong and fit."

"And why do you have them stripping off like that?"

"Sir, I found one of the ship's officers who is a colonist and I have been quizzing him about conditions we are likely to meet. He tells me that up on the border of the Boer republics there is an awful lot of wide-open ground. Veldt, he called it. Water can be hard to come by and it gets damned hot in the sun. I want my men acclimatised, with their skin already browned so they do not burn."

"Well, it seems to keep you and your men amused so I won't stop you, but it is completely unnecessary. We are just staging a show of force, not launching an all-out war. By the way, the ship's Captain tells me we should be in the harbour in two days. I'll tell the other officers in the morning over breakfast."

The ship's Captain was correct and they slid into the Durban harbour in the early hours of the morning, right on time. There was the customary confusion on the dockside, so McGuire held his men back until it subsided.

As they walked down the gangplank he turned to Donnelly. "Sergeant, I have been told that there will be water supply bowsers travelling with us wherever we march, so personal canteens are not important. You and I have had too much time in the desert to believe that, so at the first chance you get, I want every one of our men to have two canteens. Make sure they are full every morning and make sure it's water and nothing else."

Chapter 3
Moving Up

Once ashore, the men were marched rapidly to a waiting train. There was one carriage behind the steam engine and then a line of cattle cars. McGuire spotted one of the transport officers with his red armband and caught hold of his sleeve as he bustled past.

"What the devil is all the rush about? And why are my men being transported in open cattle trucks?"

The harassed officer sighed. "Your regiment is needed up at Ladysmith and we have been told to get you there as quickly as possible. These are the railway wagons we have available. The proper carriages won't be here for another two days."

"Two days won't make any difference, surely?"

The transport officer looked at McGuire and smiled. "You haven't heard then? The Boers declared war yesterday and General White wants all the available men up country."

"Very well. Thank you, Lieutenant."

McGuire turned to find Sergeant Donnelly waiting behind him. "Sergeant, you heard that? Right then, you'll have to make the best of it. See those big sheds over there? Send Corporal Macklin, our light-fingered friend, to see if he can find something suitable to give the men some shade on the journey. Make sure he doesn't miss the train and tell him not to get caught. And don't forget the extra water canteens if you get the chance."

As McGuire walked towards the officers' carriage he looked over his shoulder and saw Macklin with two of his men walking casually towards the sheds. He smiled as he recalled how Macklin and O'Leary had acquired the equipment he needed to set up his reconnaissance unit when he was first appointed. His smile faded as he remembered O'Leary's lonely grave in the deserts of the Sudan.

Reaching the carriage, he threw his kitbag inside and then followed it. Another transport officer checked his name and directed him to a compartment where three other captains were already installed. He stowed his bag and his rifle on the rack above the seats and sat down to wait for the confusion to be over.

The officer sitting opposite him leaned forward with his hand out. "We haven't been properly introduced. I'm McAllister. I saw you on the ship, of course, but you always seemed so busy."

"Michael McGuire. Pleased to meet you."

"I notice you have a rifle with you, but no sword. Isn't that a little odd?"

"Not really. My men and I are a reconnaissance unit. I expect to be operating forward of the main body of troops. I don't intend to make myself stand out from the crowd to be a target for a sniper."

The officer in the corner snorted. "Snipers? We are dealing with a bunch of farmers who have delusions about their military capability. Snipers, indeed."

McGuire leaned back in his seat and smiled faintly. "From your mouth to God's ears. I've talked to a colonist about these farmers. It seems they have modern Mauser rifles and most of them have been feeding their families by hunting for years. Not chasing foxes while wearing fancy jackets, but shooting them for food."

"And you think that makes them soldiers?"

"Maybe not, but I think some caution might be in order before we dismiss them entirely."

McAllister waved his hand languidly. "No point in arguing before we see what's what." He pointed at the officer in the corner. "That one is Davies, by the way, A Company, and our quiet friend here is Murray from C Company."

Murray nodded. "So which company have you been allocated to, McGuire?"

"I haven't been allocated to anything yet. No doubt the Colonel will decide where to use me when he is ready."

The brief conversation died out as the train pulled out of the station and away from the docks. In a few minutes they were clear of the town and McGuire stared out of the window to try and get an idea of the country they would be operating in. It might not be the desert he was used to, but it was wide open and he saw little sign of water.

The train rattled through the night and arrived near Ladysmith in the early morning. McGuire blinked himself awake as the brilliant sunshine came through the dusty windows of the carriage. He stood up and stretched before grabbing his rifle and kitbag and climbing down onto the platform. Ignoring the other officers milling around, he walked down the train to find his men.

He reached the cattle car as Sergeant Donnelly dropped to the ground. "Good morning, Sergeant. I hope your journey wasn't too bad?"

"Tolerable, sir, and that tarpaulin we acquired made it better. Kept some of the dust and cinders from the engine off us and made it a bit warmer in the night."

"Good. How are the men?"

Donnelly looked back towards the train car as the other men started to climb down. "A bit stiff and they could do with some breakfast, but apart from that they seem fine."

"Right then, make sure they don't leave their kit on the train and let them walk around a little to iron out the stiffness. I'll go and try to find out what our next move is."

Chapter 4
Ladysmith

"Right, gentlemen," Colonel Murphy said, standing before his officers. "General White has decided that we are to carry out outpost duty tonight, to give the other troops a break. If you look at the map here, you can see where each company is to take up position. I want all of your companies in place an hour before nightfall, so you know exactly what is in front of you. Any questions?"

Murphy looked around the assembled officers and nodded. "A word of caution. Captain McGuire and his men are going to be out in front of the outposts in an advanced position. Apparently the Boers have been sneaking around during previous nights, so McGuire's men can either give them a nasty surprise or give you advanced warning of any incursions. Make sure your men know our people are in front of them. I don't want any nasty incidents. Dismiss."

McGuire watched as the officers dispersed and then walked across to the Colonel. "Where would you like my men, sir?"

Murphy turned to the hand-drawn map pinned to the board behind him and pointed to a series of lines. "Out here, around a thousand yards in front of the outpost positions, are a series of dry gulleys. Apparently they are called 'dongas' by the locals. If you and your people take up position in them you should be able to move around unseen."

"Sounds good, sir. I think I will set up four positions. One for each of my patrols, with two men on watch at each one at any one time. With your permission, I will start now. I imagine the Boers will be watching when the outposts set up, but they may not be quite as vigilant at the moment."

"Very well. Another thing, Captain. I notice all your men are wearing two water bottles on their equipment. Doesn't that weigh them down for no good reason?"

"That was my idea, sir. It could be a long time between chances to fill water bottles in this area. I'd rather have them prepared for the worst."

McGuire and his men walked slowly forward. They were well spread out to make themselves less of a target to any concealed riflemen. As they reached the area of the dongas McGuire had them wander about, apparently without purpose. Then they dropped down into the steep-sided gulleys and waited. As the afternoon wore on they heard the rest of the battalion moving into position behind them. They stayed low until night fell and then, in each of the four locations, two men climbed up to the edge of the donga and watched while the other pair settled down to sleep.

There was no sleep for McGuire as he slowly and carefully made his way from one patrol to the next. At each one he lay next to the sentries and scanned ahead of them. Nothing moved and the night was silent.

As he reached the last position on his rounds he was met by Sergeant Donnelly. "Movement over to the right a little way, sir," he whispered.

"Can you see anything?"

"No, sir, too bloody dark. Should be moonrise any time now, though, so we may get lucky."

They waited at the edge of the donga, watching for any sign of an enemy approach. The moon heaved itself over the shoulder of a kopje and the silver light flooded across the plain. They watched for any movement and then it became clear that there was a small herd of gazelles, walking slowly across their front.

Donnelly smiled and raised himself up to watch them pass. "You don't see many of them walking down the Shankill Road, eh, sir?"

The bullet cracked past just above them and the two men dropped to the ground. "Where the hell did that come from? If it's some jumpy paddy behind us, I'll have his hide for that."

McGuire moved slowly back to the edge of the donga. "I don't think it's one of ours, Sergeant. That came from in front of us."

"Are you sure, sir?"

"Pretty sure, yes."

"So much for the Boers being a bunch of farmers. That sneaky bastard has moved in close and we never heard a thing."

McGuire smiled tightly to himself. Maybe this was the wake-up call the regiment needed. He had been with soldiers who had underestimated their enemies in the Sudan and was not about to make that mistake again.

All four of the patrol were now on the edge of the donga, scanning the area in front of them carefully. "Steady, lads. Watch and shoot only when you have a clear target. I don't want the outposts getting spooked behind us. Sergeant, take a walk along to the other patrols and make sure they are all awake, and for Christ's sake keep your head down."

McGuire turned back to watching though the sight of his Lee Enfield rifle. Then he saw the grass move and the dew reflected the moonlight. Now he knew where the enemy was he waited until the man tried another shot.

"Madine," he whispered, "put your helmet on your rifle barrel and raise it slowly. Make it look like someone is having a look round."

Private Madine dropped back to where his blanket and helmet lay. He moved back to the lip of the gulley and slowly raised his rifle with the helmet on the barrel. Nothing happened until he moved it slowly to the right as though scanning the plain.

McGuire saw the glint of light on the barrel of the enemy rifle as it swung to take aim at the helmet. He gently squeezed the trigger and was rewarded with a scream of pain as the weapon fired and his bullet flew. He waited to see if there would be any movement from other infiltrators before deciding to move forward himself. He slid forward on his belly through the damp grass and over the rough stones it concealed until he reached the sniper's position.

As he reached the edge of the donga he looked down to see the body lying in the bottom. He slid over the edge and down to the man he had shot. The man was moaning quietly with pain and the blood from his wound was black in the moonlight. Too much blood. McGuire realised the wound was mortal and his prey had little time to live. He lifted the man's head gently and gave him a drink from one of his canteens. The man nodded his thanks, then the gurgle in his throat and the sudden stiffening of his limbs told the tale.

McGuire laid the man down gently as Donnelly slid over the edge of the gulley. "Nice shot, sir."

"Not too good for him, Sergeant. He's gone."

"A shame that. It might have been nice if he'd told us where his friends are."

"Go through his pockets, will you? See if he has any maps or anything that might be of use."

Donnelly carried out a rapid search through the man's clothes. "Nothing much, sir. A bible and some dried meat. Seems like he travelled light. Just his rifle and a bandolier."

"All right, take those back with us when we go back in. At least we can try his rifle and see how good these Mausers are."

The Sergeant ran his hand over the Mauser rifle and then worked the bolt. A round was pulled from the chamber and ejected. It fell to the ground between Donnelly's boots. As he picked it up and examined it he whistled softly to himself.

"Problem?" McGuire asked.

"Maybe. Take a look at this." Donnelly said, as he tossed the bullet across to his commander.

McGuire snatched the brass round out of the air and looked down at it in the palm of his hand. "A dum-dum. They've been modifying their ammunition then."

"That's a nasty thing to do. It'll make a hell of a mess of anyone it hits. That shouldn't be allowed."

McGuire nodded as he looked at the bullet. "We can't really complain, though. We invented the damned things. Rounds like this were developed at the Dum-Dum armoury in India."

"Still, it might make the lads keep their heads down a bit if they know about these."

As the dawn broke McGuire and his patrols stayed in cover, to avoid any chance of being mistaken for the enemy by their own regiment. As the light reached down into the bottom of the donga Donnelly looked down at the dead Boer and sighed.

"Problem, Sergeant?"

The tough soldier from Belfast nodded at the body. "Just looking at our friend down there, sir. He's just a kid. Can't be more than fourteen or fifteen."

McGuire looked down. "You're right. Apparently the Boers have mobilised any man who can hold a rifle and is willing to join something called a commando. So we are going to be seeing youngsters like him, and old white beards as well."

"Doesn't seem fair somehow. They've got no chance against us."

"I hope you're right, Sergeant, but I have the feeling we may not find this as easy as some people believe."

Chapter 5
Advance to Contact

Colonel Murphy waited until all the officers could hear him before he spoke. "Good morning, gentlemen. It seems we are on the move again. General White wants to send supplies forward to Dundee by train and we are going along as escort. Have your men draw four hundred rounds each and then we will march to the station. The train leaves in two hours. Any questions?"

"I do, sir."

McGuire looked round and saw it was one of the captains he had shared a carriage with. "Why do we need a whole battalion to protect a supply train in our own territory, sir?"

"Strangely enough, Captain, a good question. Dundee is tactically weak. General White wanted to bring the garrison back to concentrate them here in Ladysmith. General Penn-Symons declined. So we are to ensure there is no interference with our supplies by the Boers, who are known to be in the area."

There were no more questions, so the group broke up to get the men on the move and on to the train. The short journey passed without incident and the battalion stood by while the train was unloaded by local black labour. For four days the regiment rested in Dundee until on the 19th October they heard that the rail line had been cut by the Boers.

The garrison was paraded at 5 a.m. on the morning of the 20th and was dismissed about 5.20 a.m. As the men walked away towards their breakfast they heard a voice call, "Look! There they are!" On the hill called Talana by the local Zulu tribesmen, they could see figures walking around wearing black waterproofs. Most of the men laughed, assuming it was the town guard as they knew the Boers were still some way off. An hour later they heard a heavy gun fire somewhere to the north and a shell fell between the town and the camp. After a flurry of activity from the staff officers, the order came down from the General that they were to attack Talana Hill, to the north.

Tactics were to be kept simple, just as they practised on field days around Aldershot. First the artillery would pound the hill, then the infantry would attack, with the cavalry held back to chase down the enemy as they inevitably retreated.

As the three battalions selected for the attack assembled, the Boer guns continued to fire. Luckily for the British, the Boers were using percussion fuses, most of which did not explode as they hit the sodden ground. The only casualties from this bombardment were Trumpeter Horn of the 69th Battery, whose head was taken off by a shell, and a grey mare belonging to the 60th Rifles that was directly hit.

The artillery batteries limbered up rapidly and drove forward to establish firing positions from where they began to shell the hill. As McGuire watched through his binoculars he could

33

see that the fire was being concentrated around a series of white farm buildings which had walls running between them. Below that there was a small area of woodland. As he watched the shrapnel bursts above the buildings he felt someone walk up alongside him.

He lowered the glasses and turned to find Colonel Murphy. "The gunners seem to be doing a thorough enough job, sir."

Murphy nodded and looked up at the hill. "I hope you're right, Captain. Those stone walls up there could be troublesome if the Boers are still there."

McGuire gave the Colonel a tight smile. "If they can use the Mauser rifles they've got properly, I fear you are right, sir. I tested one back in Ladysmith and it's a fine weapon."

"No doubt we will find out. In any event, I have a job for you and your small band."

"Yes, sir. What do you need?"

"It seems the Indians from Cape Colony have formed a group of stretcher-bearers and are to follow us into the attack. I want you to escort them. I don't want them running off if I have wounded to pick up."

"Do you think they might?"

"They are untested in battle. With you and your marksmen there, they might think twice about running off like scared rabbits."

"I was hoping you might use us as skirmishers ahead of the main body."

"I don't think we need you for that today. The tactics the General has decided on are pretty straightforward. No, you go and bring the Indians forward."

McGuire stifled his disappointment. "Very well, sir. Is there anyone in particular in charge of them?"

Murphy nodded. "Someone called Gandhi, I am told. You'll have to ask when you reach them."

McGuire saluted and went to collect his reconnaissance troop. Once they were ready they moved across to where the Indian stretcher-bearers were waiting for the advance to begin.

"Does anybody here know someone called Gandhi?"

The nearest man pointed across to where a lone tree stood, giving a little shade to a small man who was staring intently up the hill. "That is Mister Gandhi."

McGuire walked across towards the tree. "Hello, are you the one they call Gandhi?"

"I am Mohandas K Gandhi at your service, Captain. What can I do for you?"

"It's more what I can do for you, Mister Gandhi. I have been sent to provide escort for you and your people as the attack goes forward."

Gandhi gave McGuire a sad smile. "Escort? That is a nice way of putting it. Despite all my people being volunteers, your senior officers do not trust us. They think we will turn tail and run when the shooting starts, is that not true?"

McGuire looked at the smaller man. There was something in the eyes, a calm courage, maybe? In any event, he was convinced by this man that the stretcher-bearers scattered around did not need to be driven forward.

"That's true, Mister Gandhi, but I suppose you are about to prove them wrong?"

"I suppose we are, Captain. Maybe your people will then look down on us a little less?"

"Maybe they will. Going into battle with just a stretcher takes a rare kind of nerve. I would feel vulnerable without my rifle."

Gandhi smiled. "We have food prepared if you and your men would like to join us. Do you enjoy curry?"

"I've never tried it, but thank you for the invitation and we would love to join you. My men have learned to eat whenever they can when in action, as they don't know when the opportunity will arise again."

McGuire and his men settled down among the Indian stretcher-bearers and gratefully accepted the curry they were handed. Corporal Fine was the first to take a large spoonful and almost spat it back out.

"My Lord! What is that stuff?"

The Indians around him chuckled and Gandhi smiled. "I should have told you, it is a little spicy for European tastes. I promise you will like it when you get used to it."

McGuire tried his and Gandhi was right, it was very spicy, but interesting. "So, Mister

Gandhi, what did you and your people do for a living before all this started?"

"Many things. I am a lawyer with a practice in Cape Town. We have accountants, journalists, shop managers and many other trades represented here."

"It's good of you to come here to support us. I fear we will need you more than our senior officers think."

Gandhi nodded and pointed at the hill. "We will soon find out. Your infantry is starting their attack."

Chapter 6
Talana Hill

All around McGuire the Indians and the reconnaissance troop rose to their feet and watched as the lines of khaki moved to the attack. McGuire knew, from the briefing earlier in the day, that, as well as the Royal Irish Fusiliers, the King's Royal Rifle Corps and the Dublin Fusiliers were in those close-packed lines of men moving forward so confidently. Having tried out the Mauser, he had advised Colonel Murphy to move forward in open order, but the General insisted that his idea of close order formations were to be used to concentrate fire.

The Maxim guns of all three battalions had been set up at the corner of the small wooded area to give covering fire. The troops emerged from the treeline and started for the first of the white walls around Smith's Farm. The artillery bombardment ceased and there was a moment of peace before there came the sound of rifles from further up the slope. One or two at first, and then it became a continuous roar of the Mausers as the Boers rose from where they had been sheltering and took up firing positions. Even through his field glasses McGuire was hard-pressed to spot the enemy at this distance.

He could see that the intensive fire from further up the hill was having an effect as men in the assault force began to fall. The advance reached the first wall and stalled. Men who rose up to return fire were cut down by the accurate fire from above. The Maxim guns fired and swept the hillside, but had little effect on the stone walls that concealed the Boers and kept them safe.

Donnelly moved alongside McGuire. "Looks like we haven't learned much from Omdurman then, sir."

McGuire shook his head sadly. "No, it doesn't. Maybe we should have had some Dervishes to lecture at the annual training days in Aldershot. They know what it is like to face concentrated fire from modern rifles."

McGuire looked again through the field glasses, and then spoke to the smaller man standing with him. "Are your people ready, Mister Gandhi? It looks like there is quite a bit of work for them on that hillside."

"We are ready. I just hope the Boers respect these armbands we have been given. We shall see."

"Right then, please could you get your people on the move? Sergeant Donnelly, spread our people out to provide what protection we can for these men. If they start to be shot at then we provide covering fire if we can."

The two groups moved forward together. As they came closer they could see wounded men trying to drag themselves back down the hill, away from the incessant rain of bullets. Others, unable to move, writhed in agony. The stretcher-bearers reached the wooded area and, from there, they could see the wounded that needed them so badly.

The first two pairs of men carrying stretchers went forward out of the wood and made their way towards the men who seemed to need them most. Before they had gone fifty yards they were all cut down by accurate rifle fire.

McGuire cursed quietly and held up a hand to stop any others trying. "Mister Gandhi, keep your men back in the cover of the trees."

"But, Captain, these poor men need us."

"You're no good to them dead. Wait until the attack has gone further up the hill and the Boers are too busy to bother with you. Or wait until the battle is over." He turned and waved another of his men to him. "Sergeant Parks, stay with the stretcher-bearers and keep them here. Don't let them go forward until it's safe. Is that clear?"

"Yes, sir. Keep them safe until they have half a chance of surviving."

"Exactly that. Keep one of your men with you to stop them being too damned daring."

McGuire turned away to find Donnelly walking towards him. "Good timing, Sergeant. Parks plus one is staying here. The rest of us are going to move out to the left in wide arc. Once there, we are going to drop some enfilade fire on Brother Boer to try and help our people."

"Right you are, sir, but have you seen that?" Donnelly said, pointing out to the right.

There, walking through the wood, was General Penn-Symons. Close behind him walked a staff officer carrying the General's red pennant on a cavalry lance. The two men strode forward to a gap in the wall. They could see the General calling to the men either side of him to encourage them forward. The regimental officers took up the call and the men rose and dived over the low wall. As they did so McGuire saw the General stagger and then turn to walk calmly back down the hill. Through the binoculars he could see the stain of blood spreading across the man's stomach.

"A brave man that General, eh, sir?"

"True, but a badly wounded one now. He's taken a belly shot. All right, let's get moving. The troops have still got a long way to go and we can help."

Running fast and hard with their rifles at the low trail, the reconnaissance troop followed McGuire out of the wood and across the rear of the attacking force. This far behind the firing line they were unlikely to attract the attention of the Boer riflemen, but McGuire was taking no chances and forced them to move quickly.

Once clear of Smith's Farm and its stone walls, the troop continued well out to the left until they had a shoulder of rock between them and the battle. Here McGuire allowed them to pause and get their breath back. He stood and looked around to assess the situation before leading the rest of the men up the slope. They laboured up the steep incline, keeping the rock outcrop on their right until McGuire estimated they had passed the farm buildings. He stopped the men and then he and Donnelly climbed the outcrop to check their position.

As they reached the peak of the rock McGuire removed his pith helmet and peered over. Within seconds, two rifle rounds pinged off the rocks close to his head and whined away into the distance.

Dropping rapidly back into cover, McGuire turned to his Sergeant and grinned. "It seems our 'mere farmers' are not as foolish as our generals think. They have a group of riflemen covering their flank."

"So what do we do? We could rush them."

McGuire shook his head. "I think not. Clambering over this rock would be slow and we would be silhouetted against the skyline. We'd be easy targets. No, I think we move higher up the kopje until we are well behind them. Even if we can't do much damage, it will divert them from our troops. At least, I hope so."

The two men dropped down to the rest of the troop and continued the climb. As they reached the end of the outcropping Donnelly moved forward carefully and checked their position again. They were above and behind the farm buildings and could see the Boers concealed behind the stone wall. The flank guards were still concentrating on the area where they had seen McGuire. The Sergeant moved back to report what he had seen and then the troop moved forward, squirming on their bellies to take advantage of the low cover of rocks and scrubby bushes.

Once they were in position, in as wide a line as they could make, McGuire looked to see if they were all ready. He wished he had more men to make a real impact on the enemy below. There was nothing he could do to make that happen and returned to observing the enemy. The Boers were still pouring fire into the slowly advancing troops and the British were taking casualties, while the enemy was safe behind their wall.

"Reconnaissance troop, fire!"

The Lee Enfields fired in unison and McGuire could see the shock below him as the Boers realised they had been outflanked. With the soldiers moving up the hill and the rifles now covering them from behind, the position was obviously untenable. The Boers rose up at a command from a large man with a bushy beard and rapidly moved back from the wall. The troops below saw the movement and there was a yell all along the line as they pressed forwards.

The Boers made it over the top of the hill and McGuire heard their horses moving as they rode away. That was not his problem; the cavalry and mounted

infantry should be waiting to deal with them from here on.

McGuire and the troop stayed where they were and watched the sweating men of the assaulting battalions push on up the hill. As they reached the hill there was a pause as they stopped and watched the Boers riding away. Then the whistle of an artillery shell was heard, then another, and explosions blasted the hilltop. McGuire spun round, confused. Where the hell was the Boer gun? And then the awful truth dawned on him: they were being shelled by their own guns. He screamed at his stunned men and forced them to run back down the hill to get them away from the impact area, where men were dying under the rain of their own side's shells.

Once they were clear he stopped and took stock. None of his men had been hit and they could now return to help the stretcher-bearers recover the men who had not been so lucky.

Chapter 7
Action at Elandslaagte

Forty miles south of the action at Talana, the Gordon Highlanders were off duty in Ladysmith. They had heard of the victory the previous day and were relaxed, knowing that the Boers had retreated north. They thought it was a joke when Captain Buchanan ran down the lines calling the men to prepare to deploy. How could the enemy be nearby after being sent packing only the day before?

Yet only an hour later the battalion was marching, kilts swinging, down to the railway station in Ladysmith. Once at the station, they were piled into a series of cattle trucks drawn by two locomotives. The Devonshire Regiment were already on the move in another train that was to the north of them. As they pulled out of the station they could see the cavalry and mounted infantry riding alongside them, and on the other side the guns of the horse artillery kept pace.

Just beyond Modderspruit the trains stopped and the infantry climbed down from the cattle trucks and formed up ready to march towards the enemy. A weak commando of a thousand men commanded by Commandant Kock had cut the railway line at Elandslaagte and had taken up a position there. The mission was to attack the Boers and to regain control of the railway between Ladysmith and Dundee and to allow the troops from Dundee to withdraw to Ladysmith unhindered.

As the infantry marched forward, they could see the station at Elanslaagte some two miles away. To the left of the line was the blackened colliery and to the right a stony ridge. Beyond that they could see the white tents and the wagons of the Johannesburg commando. The horseshoe of ridges made this a natural strongpoint. Although the ridges were only three hundred feet high there was no cover to shield their approach, only the stones and anthills scattered across the open ground.

As they marched, they passed two generals standing on a small rise with their staffs behind them. The shorter man was General French, the cavalry commander. The second man was tall and looked a little effete with his hand hanging limp-wristed. This was Ian Hamilton, the infantry commander, and the limp wrist was caused by a bullet that had smashed his wrist bones during the battle of Majuba Hill in the first Boer war. He had refused to have the useless hand amputated so he could continue in the army.

Both men were keen to clear the Boers away as rapidly as possible to protect the lines of communication to the force at Dundee. General White had heard of the victory at Talana and the death of General Penn-Symons the previous day. With Boer forces moving in, he knew that the position at Dundee was tactically unsound and had ordered the troops to withdraw to Ladysmith.

The artillery wheeled into line and the fifteen-pounder guns began to shell the Boer position. French was a believer in standard cavalry tactics and was determined to hold his force back until the infantry had done their part in moving the Boers off their prepared positions. Hamilton, on the other hand, was less convinced by the infantry manual, having faced captured magazine rifles in North West India. Instead of the conventional shoulder-to-shoulder formation, he advanced his troops in exceptionally wide-open order, to make them a less easy target for the long-range Boer rifles.

The Devonshire regiment advanced directly at the Boers, while the Gordon Highlanders and the Manchester regiment swung round to take the enemy's left flank. The Devonshires advanced rapidly, but were eventually brought to a halt by fast, accurate rifle fire and were obliged to find what cover they could, behind rocks and anthills.

The Manchesters and the Gordons managed to get closer until they, too, were brought a halt by the all-too-accurate Mauser fire. The troops continued to edge forward into positions where they could see the Boers and fire on them. The fire from all three battalions was having an impact on the Boers and they began to withdraw.

Hamilton saw that white flags were raised over the Boers' laager and ordered the ceasefire. As his men rose to move forward and accept the surrender, the white flags dropped and the Boers started to fire again. The troops fell back until rallied by Hamilton. Angry now, they stormed forward and threw the Boers off the heights.

The enemy ran quickly to their waiting horses and trotted away. As they retreated, the British cavalry came into their own. The 5th Dragoon Guards drew their sabres and the 5th Lancers lowered the long bamboo lances as both regiments pursued the Boers in the gathering dusk. The sabres slashed and the lances stabbed into the fleeing enemy. In one case two Boers on one horse were run through with a single lance thrust. The cavalry passed through the now disorganised column of Afrikaners, then whirled and charged again.

They charged a third time and demoralised and terrified Boers began throwing themselves from their horses and cowering behind rocks while begging for mercy. The troopers had heard about the abuse of the white flag and were in no mood to grant mercy after such treacherous behaviour. Night brought an end to the slaughter and some three hundred Boers, including their commander, Kock ,were taken prisoner. Most of them were wounded and Kock was to die in the field hospital at Ladysmith a day or so later.

Losses among the British infantry had been heavy, but it was a victory and the way was now clear for the Dundee garrison to retire.

Chapter 8
Return to Ladysmith

McGuire watched as the last shovelfuls of earth were dropped onto the graves of the fallen soldiers. There were far too many of them for the gains that had been made. They had buried the Boer dead as well, but not so many of those. He turned and looked to where the wounded were being moved to the carts that would take them back to Ladysmith. The orders had come up by despatch rider and they were to march the forty miles back to the main force. With a large number of enemy moving towards them they were not to wait for the railway line to be repaired. They had to be gone from this place rather than risk being surrounded.

The march would be a risk in itself with no cavalry screen. Word had come that the cavalry, who had been detailed to chase down the Boers fleeing from Smith's Farm, had been surrounded and had surrendered. They were now being marched north, to a prisoner-of-war-camp he presumed. Their carbines, ammunition and horses would be a welcome gift for Brother Boer. He sighed and turned away from this place of death and disappointment. The victory had turned to ashes in his mouth, as it had for most of the British.

He walked across to where Sergeants Donnelly and Parks were getting the men ready to join the retreat. "Did the stretcher-bearers get buried properly?"

Parks looked up from where he was adjusting the contents of his pack. "They did, sir, and that Mister Gandhi said some nice words over them."

"Where is he now?"

"Him and the stretcher-bearers are down with the surgeons. Some of the wounded are too badly cut about to ride in the carts, so they are going to carry them to save them pain."

"For forty miles over rough tracks?"

"That's what Gandhi said, sir."

"Bloody hell, I wouldn't want to do that. Those Indians are pretty special."

Donnelly grinned. "Have you heard what the lads are calling them?"

"Calling them names after what they have done?"

"Not name-calling, just a nickname. They are calling them the body-snatchers. Good one, eh? Never seen anybody be so gentle with the wounded. Glad they are on our side."

"Good men, all of them. Right, let's get the troop moving and join the regiment. We wouldn't want to be left behind in this place."

McGuire stood quietly and watched the two Sergeants round the men up and get them moving. He watched the way the men of the small unit moved. Their heads were up and their rifles were clean. He smiled; these men did not feel beaten or down-hearted. With a regiment of men like this he could march to Pretoria on his own. Well, maybe with a few others to help, he thought.

As the units formed up for the march the rain came. Not the gentle rain of Ireland, but the pounding, lashing rain of Africa. In seconds every man was soaked to the skin. Their equipment got heavier as the rain soaked into their webbing packs and ammunition pouches. Men slung their rifles with the barrels pointing down to avoid filling them with water.

The long march commenced and in no time the rain had turned the rough tracks into a glutinous brown porridge that clung to their boots and plastered their legs. They could hardly see twenty yards through the teeming wall of water, but without tents or any shelter they had to move anyway. The men trudged forward, forcing themselves onwards. The wounded in the uncovered wagons suffered most of all.

McGuire and his small group of men had been flung out in front of the labouring column, and with white cloths slung around their waists, they acted as guides for the main body of troops. As night fell after the first day they had made fourteen miles from their starting point. Ordered to rest, they flung themselves down in the mud and slept.

At ten o'clock the next morning they resumed the march, with the Royal Irish Fusiliers in the lead. The rain had eased slightly and there was even a hint of sun through the clouds. Not enough to dry them, but enough so that McGuire and his men could usefully move out ahead and scout for the enemy. The main concern was the narrow pass out of the valley that was called Van Tonders Nek. Here a few determined men could hold them up almost indefinitely. McGuire and the reconnaissance troop moved forward and took positions on either side of the Nek. They were lucky: the Boers had not arrived yet.

By the Tuesday, the struggling column was through the Nek and out on to the flat plain that led down to Ladysmith. Caked in mud, exhausted after four days with virtually no sleep and pitiful rations, the men could relax a little as they continued on. As the sun warmed them the Irish began to sing and the mood of the imperturbable British Tommy lifted. The first war correspondent rode out from Ladysmith to meet them. They were safe.

Behind them the Boers took possession of Dundee. As they rode into the town they found a British military hospital still there. The wounded who were in too poor a condition to move had been left behind. The two army surgeons surrendered and their swords, pistols and horses were taken from them. Other than that, they, and the wounded, were treated civilly by the Boer officers.

The Boers' troops meanwhile looted the supplies that had also been abandoned and stole anything of value that had been left behind in the tents. The food stores were of particular value to them and they took possession of forty days' supply for five thousand men. The victory of

Talana Hill had turned into an ignominious rout for the British.

Unknown to the retreating column, intelligence had indicated that two strong Boer commandoes were moving to attack them. A brigade of four battalions from Ladysmith, including the Gloucestershire regiment, were sent forward to Rietfontein to hold back the enemy and to allow the column from Dundee to pass unmolested. The British were unable to make much headway against the entrenched enemy and were forced to withdraw. However the action did prevent the commandos from the Orange Free State and the Transvaal from linking up and destroying the Dundee column. During the action the Commanding Officer of the Gloucesters led a company and a Maxim gun forward. The company was effectively destroyed by accurate rifle fire and the Colonel was killed.

Although the British achieved their limited aim at Rietfontein, it was at the cost of one hundred and fourteen dead and wounded, while the Boers held their positions and suffered very little.

Chapter 9
Ladysmith

Colonel Murphy stood with his back to the sun looking at his assembled officers. "Good morning gentlemen. We've had a couple of days to recover from our ramble through the countryside and General White has a new task for us."

He waited for the muttering from the officers to subside. "I know you would like to give your troops longer to recuperate, as would I, but Brother Boer has other ideas. Intelligence tells us that the commandos are on the move towards us and it looks like we are going to be outnumbered. If we sit still we are going to be surrounded and that can't be allowed to happen. So we are to make a sortie to disrupt the enemy's plans."

The officers listened intently as they were given their instructions. McGuire waited to hear what his small unit was to do, but there was no mention of him. As the other officers rose to return to their companies he remained behind to speak to the Colonel.

"Ah, McGuire, I bet you think I've forgotten about you."

"I was beginning to wonder, sir."

The Colonel chuckled. "I imagine you were. Now then I have started to appreciate your odd bunch of roughnecks and their independent mind set. I think you can be more useful to me elsewhere than in this main adventure. Do you mind being sent off on your own to do a little reconnaissance?"

"That's what we were originally formed for, so I would be delighted, and I'm sure my men would as well."

"Good, now as you know, the regiment will be heading north, but I want you to go south. If the Boers do manage to surround us I want options. I need to know where we can march out of here if we have to. The maps we have are unreliable and the first thing the Boers are likely to do is to cut the railway line. So there is your mission: find me a way out and while you are about it, find me paths where small groups or even single soldiers can travel through undetected."

"Shouldn't the Intelligence people be doing this kind of thing already, sir? I don't want to tread on anyone's toes."

Murphy nodded. "They should, but there is an air of over confidence in the headquarters. There is still the view that we are facing just a bunch of farmers. You and I have had painful evidence that the Boers are more than that so, as I say, I want options."

"Fair enough, sir, I'll have my men on the move before you leave. One question, if I may: do the staff officers know about this?"

"Fair question, and the answer is no. This is for me and since I have you I want to use your talents."

McGuire stepped back and saluted. "Right, sir, I'll get on with it. Good luck with your sortie."

Thirty minutes later the reconnaissance troop was ready to move out. With all the regimental baggage still stuck somewhere near Durban they were obliged to travel light, which suited McGuire well. Using the rudimentary maps they had been issued, each four-man patrol was given a route to survey. They were to bring information back to allow Corporal Connolly to create one of his excellent maps. His skills as a forger and his experience of map making had not left him, and his expertise would be valuable if they needed to move the Ladysmith garrison southwards.

McGuire stood in front of his men; he could see they were keen to be on the move. "I know I've said this before, but I am going to say it again. Do not engage the Boers unless you have to. Keep out of sight. I don't want them to know what we are doing. We will meet up on the banks of the Tugela at Potgeiter's Drift and stay there for a day to let Corporal Connelly make his maps. Corporal Fine, you are with me. Move out."

He stood back and watched the men leave as Fine walked across to him. He adjusted the Lee Enfield rifle on his shoulder and then moved his heavy revolver to a more comfortable position on his belt, ready to start his own march south.

"Don't you wish you were going with the regiment, sir?"

"In one way, yes, I do. They'll be seeing some action very shortly, I suppose. But on the other hand, reconnaissance and intelligence is what we were formed for, so we'd better get it done."

The two men turned as they heard words of command being shouted behind them. The six companies of the regiment taking part were formed up and ready to move, as were the Gloucestershire Regiment who were to work alongside them under the overall command of Colonel Murphy. Accompanying them was a herd of army mules carrying their extra ammunition and the guns of the 10th Mountain Battery. They stood and watched as the lines of troops began to move towards the north.

"I hope the day goes well for them."

McGuire nodded. "From your mouth to God's ears. They should be all right; they're a good regiment and the Colonel knows his business."

Chapter 10
Nicholson's Nek

Lieutenant Colonel Murphy stood to the side of the track in the moonlight to watch the regiment trudge past. Behind his own men marched the Gloucesters and behind them the Artillery with their pack mules and mountain guns. They all seemed in good heart from what he could see.

He turned to the large man beside him who was also watching the troops intently. "Well, RSM, what are you thinking?"

"I'm thinking the men are holding up well, sir. They've been worked hard, but they are standing up to it. Only three have fallen out sick in the last week. That's pretty good."

"It could be something to do with a rumour I heard."

"Indeed, sir?"

"Oh yes. I heard the Regimental Sergeant Major had put the word around that anybody falling out would answer to him personally."

The RSM smiled behind his magnificent moustache. "It seems to be working don't you think, sir?"

Murphy chuckled. "It does indeed. Now, how about putting the fear of god into those artillery men? They are dawdling along."

"My pleasure, sir."

Murphy watched as the RSM strode towards the artillery men and their mules. He shook his head and smiled, then walked forward to the column and fell in alongside the C Company commander.

"Enjoying the evening stroll, John?"

"Yes thank you, sir, very pleasant."

As the RSM neared the artillery men and their laden pack mules the leading animal put its hoof down into a tuft of spiky grass. As it did so a snake reared up in fright. The mule leapt backwards and let out a bellow of fear. It bucked and the ammunition box on its left side was dislodged and fell to the ground. Even more surprised, the animal bucked again, braying loudly in the still night. The second ammunition box crashed noisily to the ground and the now terrified animal turned and stated to gallop back the way it had come through the rest of the mules. In moments all the other animals had taken fright and were stampeding back towards Ladysmith. Some of the handlers were dragged, others were kicked, but all lost control of their beasts.

The RSM stood stock still watching the guns and ammunition disappear into the darkness with loud braying from nearly two hundred animals rending the night. The artillerymen stood in the track staring after their pack mules until the RSM of the Fusiliers reached them.

"Don't just stand there! Get after them and get them back here! Now move!"

An artillery Major strode through the bemused men. "Thank you, RSM, but I will give the orders to my men, if you don't mind."

The RSM turned slowly and looked down at the smaller man. "Very good, sir, but maybe you'd like to give the order now, before the guns and ammunition reach bloody Cape Town?"

"That is insolence. I shall have you up on charges."

"Good for you, sir. May I suggest you do that after you have explained to the column commander why your men are still standing here, while we are advancing on the enemy?"

The Major adjusted his collar. "Ah, yes, I see your point." He turned to the bemused artillery men standing along the track. "You heard the RSM! Get moving and get those animals back here on the double!"

The RSM spun on his heel and marched smartly towards the front of the column until he reached Colonel Murphy.

"How bad is it, RSM?"

"Bad, sir. The mountain guns and the spare rifle ammunition are running hell for leather across the veldt with the artillery chasing them. All we have is the ammunition the men have in their bandoliers."

Murphy stroked his moustache. "Damn! If the Boers are where they are supposed to be we have no chance of holding out for two days. Nevertheless, we go on to our objective. If we don't the left flank of the attack on Pepworth is going to be exposed."

They walked on further while the Colonel considered the problem. "Right, RSM, we need to be at Nicholson's Nek before first light even more urgently now. I need the men to be in a decent defensive position with whatever cover we can construct. Get them moving and pass the word to the officers about what has happened."

As the dawn broke Murphy looked around him at the position they had established on a low rise that dominated the pass known as Nicholson's Nek. Men were working to construct low-walled sangers out of the rocks, while those few with entrenching tools tried to dig rifle pits in the unyielding ground. Without the mountain guns to keep the Boers at bay this was a dangerous position and he was under no illusion about how precarious his situation was.

He walked around the position talking to the men as they laboured and making sure that the officers were keeping them at it. He wished he could retreat, but no permission had come from General White in response to his message during the night. Until he was relieved he could not risk exposing the other two columns that were attacking Pepworth.

"Begging yer pardon, sir."

Murphy stopped and turned to the soldier who had spoken. "Yes. Owen, isn't it? How are you doing?"

"Just peachy, thank you, sir, but I wondered if you had seen those riders over there," he said, pointing along the Nek.

Murphy took out his field glasses and looked where Owen had pointed. There he could see a row of horsemen wending their way through the pass towards him. With their dark clothes and slouch hats he knew they were Boers. He looked left and right to see that others were fanning out of the pass across the slopes. He tried to count them, but gave up as more and more came into view.

He sighed and called to the Captain standing nearby. " Captain Miller! Pass the word to stand to. Brother Boer seems to be paying us a visit."

He continued watching the Boers deploy across a wide front, then turned to go back to his own position. He stopped and looked down at Owen in his shallow trench.

"Good work, Owen. Now, in a short while I will need your keen eye aiming a rifle at our friends over there."

"You'll have it, sir. I have a bet with my pal that I take down more of those spalpeens than he does."

Murphy chuckled. "Good for you. Find me later and tell me who won."

The Boers were dismounting now and while some of them took up positions on the slopes others started to move closer to the British. Accurate rifle fire from the Mausers started to fall on the defenders, forcing them to take what cover they could and preventing them interfering effectively with the men who crept and crawled towards them.

The rifle fire became more intense and the British were hard pressed to return fire from their exposed positions. As the advancing Boers crawled closer the casualties mounted and the shortage of ammunition stared to become a considerable problem. Murphy was considering his options when all around the Boers began to stand up and walk forward. What the devil were they doing? Then he saw it. Off to his left in one of the forward trenches, manned by the Gloucesters, a white flag had been raised.

"What the hell? I gave no such order."

The Major standing next to Murphy scanned around. "The Boers are coming in from all directions, sir. They seem to think we have surrendered."

"Oh bloody hell! Tell the men to cease fire and lay down their weapons."

"Sir?"

"We have no choice. It would be dishonourable to continue now we have apparently raised the white flag. And find out who the hell put that damned flag up. Find out what the devil he was playing at."

The men reluctantly laid down their weapons and stood up. Some of them were clearly furious and two officers deliberately broke their swords rather than hand them over. The Major returned from the trench where the white flag had been raised.

"Well?"

"It was an officer of the Gloucesters, sir. His men were out of ammunition and about to be slaughtered. He intended only to surrender his own position. He is mortified by what has happened and sends his apologies."

"Damn. Very well, let us go and meet Brother Boer."

As they walked forward to the man with the bushy black beard, who was clearly in charge of the Boers, Murphy could see that the enemy were already helping his wounded. Unwounded men were being herded into a group and rifles and anything else of use was being stockpiled.

An hour later the nine hundred and fifty-four men, mostly from the Royal Irish Fusiliers, were marching north into captivity. Unknown to them, the attack they had been protecting the flank of had failed and those men had already been recalled to Ladysmith.

General White was so broken by the debacle he was indecisive. He took little action and two days later the railway line to the south of Ladysmith was cut. The siege had begun.

Chapter 11
Orphans of the Storm

"How's the map making going, Corporal Connolly?"

Connolly lifted his head from his drawing and looked at McGuire. "Pretty well there, sir. The lads are giving me plenty of detail from their nature rambles through the hills."

McGuire smiled. "Good. How long do you think before you are finished?"

Connolly looked down at his map and then back up at his commander. "It's ready now if you like, sir, but I could make it better with another two or three hours."

"I don't think the Colonel will be in any rush for it, so take your time. Macklin took down some kind of buck and we might as well eat before we head back to the regiment and army rations."

McGuire leaned back on one elbow and looked down the sloping bank to the river below. The Tugela was flowing quickly and seemed to speed up as it reached the drift they were camped by. Across the river he could see the flat veldt stretching away before him while behind him were a series of rocky kopjes. It was attractive country to some, no doubt, but he had grown to love the wide open deserts of Egypt. That made him think of his family back home in Cairo; he really must write to them again soon.

"Riders, sir!"

McGuire rolled over and got to his feet. As he reached the top of the bank he looked where Sergeant Donnelly was pointing. The Sergeant handed him back the field glasses he had borrowed and McGuire lifted them to his eyes and scanned across the ground to the north. There was a single rider going hell for leather, and behind him a group of maybe twenty more, also galloping as hard as they could.

McGuire spun the focussing wheel and looked more carefully. "Sergeant, have the men stand to along the top of the bank. The first man is one of ours and by the look of them the following group are Boers."

He continued to watch the riders getting closer as Donnelly yelled at the men to get into positions. McGuire looked behind him to see the three men who had been bathing in the river scampering up the sandy bank stark naked except for a rifle and bandolier of ammunition. He smiled. His men knew that the order to stand to meant now and not when they were ready.

He looked through the binoculars again and then lowered them as he called to his line of marksmen. "Hold your fire until they are closer. Nobody shoots until I do. Make sure you don't hit our man and I don't want any of the Boers getting away."

"Sir, they're closing on our man. If we fire now it will probably stop them and he could get away without a problem."

"That's true, Sergeant, but they have things I want, so our man out there can do his part for us before we save his hide."

They could hear the thunder of hooves now as the riders came rapidly closer. The lone British rider had tried to angle away towards the iron railway bridge, but the Boers had spread out that way to head him off. He was now riding directly towards the reconnaissance troop, presumably trying to cross the river at the Potgieter's Drift that was behind them. He must have known that was hopeless. As soon as his horse slowed in the water the Boers would be on him and, with their accurate rifles, he did not stand a chance.

McGuire put down his field glasses and squinted through the sights of his rifle. He could make out their faces now. The British one red and anxious, while the Boers were clearly enjoying themselves. That would change in a few seconds. He picked his man, a small man with a bushy dark beard streaked with grey.

He gently squeezed the trigger of his Lee Enfield and felt it buck against his shoulder. He had time to see his target roll backwards out of the saddle before the roar of the rifles either side of him started to empty saddle after saddle. As the men continued pouring accurate rapid fire into the pursuers McGuire stood up and waved to the lone British rider. The relief on the man's face was amusing to watch as he adjusted the direction of his mad ride towards the troop.

As the rider reached McGuire he dropped down from his lathered horse and walked forward, gripping the reins. McGuire looked behind the rider to see that the Boer horses were without riders. Every one of them had been taken down by the fire from his men.

"Cease Fire! Double forward and deal with the wounded. Sergeant Parks, secure those horses. I want them all brought here. Corporal Macklin, make sure you get all the rifles and get me their jackets and hats while you're at it."

He turned to the breathless rider who stood before him and returned his salute. "What the hell are you doing out here on your own, man?"

"Despatch rider, sir. Taking the report from General White."

"Why not just put it on the train?"

"There is no train, sir. The Boers have cut the line south of Ladysmith. I only just got out. The town is surrounded. There must be thousands of the beggars."

"Ladysmith? The whole town surrounded?"

"That's right, sir. General White has settled in for a siege and that's why these despatches have to get out, to get him a relief."

"Well, damn me. Never mind, you can rest here for a while to let your horse recover. We were going to eat and you can join us. You can tell me what happened while we wait for the meat to cook."

The rider looked back at the three men slowly walking back towards them carrying Boer equipment. "Excuse me asking, sir, but your men seem to be wearing the colour flash of the Irish Fusiliers on their helmets."

McGuire nodded. "That's right. We're the reconnaissance troop."

"Troop? I thought you were all infantry?"

"We are, but it's the name this small unit picked up during the Sudan campaign."

"Well, forgive me, sir, but you're orphans now. The Royal Irish surrendered at Nicholson's Nek. They've all been marched off into captivity by the Boers."

"Are you certain?"

"Yes, sir. They were surrounded and ran out of ammunition. All their spare ammunition and the mountain guns were lost when the mules stampeded. There was nothing else they could do. The Boers would have slaughtered them."

"Christ! What a mess." McGuire paused and looked out across the veldt. "No matter, you take your horse down to the river and then make your way over to the fire. Get some rest."

As the man led his horse down the bank McGuire walked towards the area where the Boers had fallen. "How many, Donnelly?"

"Twenty altogether, sir. Seven wounded; the rest are finished."

"How badly wounded? Do you think we can move them?"

"They'll have to be on horses. They won't be able to walk."

McGuire nodded. "That's no problem. Parks and his men are rounding up the horses now. You and your men carry on dressing their wounds."

As they spoke Sergeant Parks walked up to them leading two horses by the reins. "How are we doing with the horses, Sergeant?"

"We've caught fifteen so far, sir, and I've sent two men who can ride after the others."

"Good. Any of them injured?"

"Just one, so far, with a minor wound on his neck. I'll put a dressing on that and he'll be as right as rain in a couple of days."

"That's a relief. Take them down out of sight by the river and don't let them wander off. I've got plans for these beasts."

Chapter 12
The Troop Rides Again

"How are the wounded doing, Corporal Macklin?"

Macklin looked up from where he was kneeling, changing the dressing on one of the wounded men. "Tell you the truth, sir, they need more than I can give them. They're in some pain and one of the youngsters is going to die if we don't get him to a surgeon soon."

"I thought that might be the case. Get them ready to travel as much as you can. We'll get them away within the hour."

McGuire strode away from the area where the wounded lay under the improvised shade his men had built for them. He spotted Parks on the far side of the river instructing the men how to ride and look after horses. Once again Parks' skill with animals was proving useful. The Sergeant mounted a horse and rode through the river to McGuire. He flung his leg over the horse's neck and dropped down in front of his Captain.

"Yes, sir?"

"I need you to choose the seven best riders we've got. We're going to ride towards the Boers and they'll be leading other horses with the wounded on them. Oh, and choose the calmest horses for the wounded to ride."

"Very good, sir. When do you need them?"

"When do I ever want anything?"

Parks grinned. "Right now then?"

McGuire nodded. "As quickly as you can. Macklin and his patrol are getting them ready to move. I will be leading with a big white flag to try and make sure we don't regret this. Donnelly and the rest will take a position here to cover us if we have to make a run for it."

Within the hour the wounded Boers were lifted as gently as possible on to the horses and the seven men selected to lead them mounted their own beasts. McGuire put his foot in the stirrup and lifted himself up onto the saddle of the black horse with the white blaze on its face. He was still deciding what to call it. His first camel in Egypt had been called Kathleen after his sister and she had not been pleased when she found out about it. He checked behind him that the men were ready to move and waved them forward.

As they rode slowly past him he looked down at Donnelly, who stood by him. "I don't know how long we are going to be, Sergeant. We'll ride until we come to our first group of Boers and just hope they respect a flag of truce."

"Well, sir, I'll remind you of the advice the chaplain gave us. 'Trust in God, but keep your rifle close.' Good advice, that was."

McGuire nodded and smiled. "It was indeed. I wonder if the chaplain was captured with the rest of the regiment."

"My guess would be yes. He's not the man to stay back in safety when his regiment was going to meet the enemy."

McGuire nodded again. "That's true. Now I know I don't have to remind you, but keep a good watch while we are gone and we'll get back here as soon as we are able."

Donnelly shaded his eyes and watched the small column of mounted men wend their way slowly northwards across the veldt. He stayed watching until they disappeared from view and then made his way back to the small campsite they had set up on the riverbank of the Tugela.

McGuire continued to lead the group forward, looking for the smoothest paths to try and save the wounded any more pain. As he rode he scanned the hilltops and across the plain, but saw no sign of the enemy. After an hour he called a halt to let the wounded rest and to give them water.

Parks called him across to where he stood by one of the wounded. "This man wants to speak to you, sir. His English is good."

McGuire knelt down next to where the wounded man lay on a rough army blanket. "What can I do for you?"

"Nothing. I wanted to thank you for what you are trying to do. I didn't expect a Rooinek to be so decent."

"Rooinek? What's that?"

The man chuckled. "In English it's Redneck. It's what some of us call you."

McGuire grinned and sat down cross-legged. "And what made you want to fight the Rednecks?"

"You're trying to take our country away. You left us alone until we found the gold and diamonds and now you English want to take over."

"Not really, my friend. A lot of people moved to your country to work in the mines and your people wouldn't even let them vote."

The man snorted. "*Uitlanders*. Why should we let them vote? They would just try to take over and make us change our ways. Why should we let our country change to suit foreigners?"

McGuire nodded slowly. "I see your point of view, but do many of your people feel that way?"

"Ask the thousands of men who now surround Ladysmith. We outnumber your people there and our big guns have a longer reach. The town will fall in days and your people will learn what it is to fight the Boers."

McGuire stood up and looked down at the man lying before him. In his rough jacket and his bushy beard he looked nothing like a soldier, but he was right that the British were learning what it was to fight these determined people.

"Time we got you on the move back to your people. They should be able to look after you better than we can."

Once again the wounded were lifted gently back onto the horses and the small group began to move forward. After another hour McGuire was about to call for a further rest stop when he saw a patrol of eight horsemen riding towards him. He lifted the white flag on its rough pole a little higher and spurred forward to meet them. The eight men spread out as he approached them and reined their horses to a standstill. McGuire rode on slowly until he was about twenty feet from them.

"Who is in charge here?"

A small man walked his horse forward a few steps. "I am. What do you want? Are you surrendering?"

McGuire shook his head slowly, keeping an eye on the men in front of him. "No, I'm not surrendering. I have some of your people with me. They are wounded and need better medical treatment than I can give them."

"What do you expect me to do?"

"Take them back to your lines and look after them."

The small man looked past McGuire to where the wounded were being lifted down to the ground. "Why are you taking them down from the horses?"

"I'm giving you your people back, but I have a use for their horses. You'll need to send for some to take them in. They can't walk that far in this heat."

"Then leave us the horses."

"I can't do that. I need them."

"Then we'll take them from you and take you prisoner at the same time."

McGuire smiled a little and shook his head. "No, you won't do that, my friend. Take another look behind me. Those seven men of mine are all marksmen and the rifles they carry are at least as good as yours. If you try to take them they have orders to empty your saddles without a word from me."

The small man looked beyond McGuire to see a line of seven soldiers kneeling with their rifles at the ready. He considered his options and looked around at his men, who waited for his order.

"So how do we do this?"

"Your wounded are on the ground over there. We will mount up and ride away. Then you can pick them up. I suggest you send one of your men now to get the horses they will need to take them in."

"What is your name, Englishman?"

"I'm Captain McGuire and I wish you people would stop calling me English. I'm as Irish as the morning dew."

The small man smiled for the first time. "Very well, my Irish friend. When we capture you I will see that this is remembered. Not all of you are villains, it seems."

McGuire nodded to acknowledge the compliment, then turned his horse and slowly rode away. He and three of his men led the horses away for two hundred yards, then dismounted and took up kneeling positions with their rifles while the remaining four men doubled across the flat plain to join them. They all mounted and trotted away leading the empty horses. They stopped at the top of a low ridge and looked back to see that the Boers had joined their wounded and were looking after them.

Content that he had done the decent thing, McGuire led the men away and back down to their camp by the Tugela. Now that he was unencumbered by the wounded and his troop was mounted again he could begin to patrol the area until the main British relief force arrived.

Chapter 13
Back To The Army

The troop packed up all their equipment and mounted the horses. With Parks in the lead they walked the animals into the Tugela River and across the drift. Each man kept checking upstream for any debris being washed down that might injure the horses. In the event, they crossed without difficulty, but McGuire did notice the water level and the current had increased over the days they had been by the river.

As they rode to the east the next day, they could see smoke rising in front of them and, as they breasted a rise, they could see that it came from the funnels of two locomotives. Even at this distance, they could see the troops leaving the trains and being marched to a tented camp. The neat lines of white bell tents stretched for quite some distance and they could see more tents being put up even as they approached.

Riding easily and slowly, they stopped when a cavalry patrol rode out to meet them. The cavalrymen were wary and had their carbines in their hands as they drew nearer. The officer in charge of the patrol rode forward and looked at McGuire's dirty uniform.

"And who are you people?"

"And good morning to you, too, Lieutenant. I am Captain McGuire and we are the reconnaissance troop of the Royal Irish Fusiliers."

The young Lieutenant looked again at McGuire and saw the badges of rank that had been painted black to be less obvious to any enemy sniper. He raised his hand in a reluctant salute which McGuire returned.

"Sorry, sir, but the General is concerned about Boers slipping into our lines and causing problems."

"So he should be. Now tell me which General are we talking about here? There seem to be so many of them."

"General Redvers Buller, sir. He arrived from Cape Town last night and is already making an impact. Increased cavalry patrols with orders to gather intelligence and double guards by the infantry."

McGuire nodded. "It sounds like he knows his business. Where can I find the General? I need to give him some useful information."

"He has taken up residence in that white farmhouse close to the station building. I doubt if the staff will let you in to see him, though. They are in a bit of a panic."

Signalling his men to follow him, McGuire spurred his mount forward. "I think he'll see me. I've just come from Ladysmith and we've been watching the Boers move into position on the hills. Thank you, Lieutenant."

With that the reconnaissance troop rode slowly through the cavalrymen and walked their horses towards the station buildings. As they got close, McGuire called a halt and turned to his two Sergeants, who rode up behind him.

"Keep the men here so I know where to find you. Don't get involved in all that chaos. I think we'll try to keep our distance from loud staff officers and their strange ideas."

As his men dropped down from their horses and removed the saddles, McGuire rode forward into the sort of chaos only an army can create. NCOs were shouting instructions that were immediately countermanded. Officers strutted through the mob of soldiers slapping their high boots with riding crops and getting more and more angry at the lack of progress. He rode on, skirting around the worst of the confusion until he found a place to ride across the iron rails to the house the Lieutenant had pointed out.

As he reached the house he dismounted and handed the reins of the horse to the orderly, who stepped forward to take them. Walking towards the front steps, he was stopped by a supercilious officer in an immaculate uniform. The man looked McGuire up and down and was clearly unimpressed with what he saw.

"What are you doing here, Captain? Shouldn't you be back unloading whatever dung cart you travelled in?"

"Sorry about my appearance, sir, but there hasn't been much opportunity for spit and polish between here and Ladysmith. I hear the General is seeking intelligence about the enemy and I have some useful information he will want to hear."

"I somehow doubt that. He is a busy man, you know."

McGuire sighed. He had run up against a few officers like this during the Sudan campaign. "Nevertheless, would you please tell him that Captain McGuire is here and that I have intelligence about the Boer positions that surround Ladysmith?"

"McGuire? What regiment?"

"The Royal Irish Fusiliers. We are the reconnaissance troop."

As they spoke a barrel-chested man came out onto the veranda of the farmhouse and looked down at them. "Who is this officer and what is he doing here?"

The staff officer came to attention. "Ah, General, this is Captain McGuire. I was just about to send him on his way. I told him you were too busy to see him."

Redvers Buller turned and looked at McGuire. He looked him up and down and noted the rifle on his shoulder. Then he noticed that his badges of rank had been obscured and lastly he noted the colour flash on his helmet.

"McGuire. I know that name. There was a McGuire who got into Khartoum during the Gordon Relief Expedition."

"Yes, sir, I'm glad you remember."

"Yes, that was quite an adventure. We didn't meet in the Sudan, did we?"

"No, sir. After the Khartoum visit I was sent back downriver to Cairo and beyond."

81

The General chuckled and then looked at the staff officer. "This is the man you were going to send away? I had a meeting with Her Majesty before I took ship out of England. She told me about your adventure in Khartoum and that she has told you to carry General Gordon's revolver. Do you still have it?"

McGuire patted the canvas holster attached to his web equipment. "Right here, sir. I wouldn't dare lose it."

"Come inside, Captain, and tell me what you have been doing. And you, Major, find us some decent tea. This dust is catching in the back of my throat."

Buller led McGuire into the small back room he was using as his personal office. Pushed against the wall was a camp cot with a sword and pith helmet lying on it. The general sat down heavily in one of the two chairs and waved his guest into the other one.

"Right then, young McGuire, you've been here longer than I, so what can you tell me?"

"A few things, I hope, sir. Firstly, when we arrived here most officers were disparaging about the bunch of ragged farmers we were to face. They are far more than that."

Buller leaned back in his chair. "I think you can safely say we have learned that lesson, but go on."

"Yes, sir. Next, they are deadly with their Mauser rifles. They take up well-hidden firing positions and use the weapon to good effect. They

82

seem to have no shortage of ammunition either. Some of our units advanced in close formation and were cut about quite badly. Wide-open order reduces casualties when facing accurate rifle fire."

McGuire paused and looked at the General, who said nothing but nodded for him to continue. "They also have heavy guns that we have christened the Long Tom. I think it's a Le Creusot and it outranges our field guns by quite a distance. Luckily they don't seem to have many of them or we would be in real trouble. Then, lastly, the maps we have been issued are something of a joke. They may be fine for people crossing the area by oxcart, but for planning military movements they are far too inaccurate. I have a map here that we have made ourselves over the last week or so, while looking for a route out of Ladysmith. It doesn't use all the conventions of a military map, but it is accurate."

The General stood up and took the rolled-up map that McGuire handed him. He walked to his desk and spread the paper out. He put various items at each corner to hold it flat, then stood silently and contemplated the drawing that Connolly had produced.

"You know, I spoke to General Kitchener in London last year. He told me about the maps you and your men produced for him in the Sudan. I can see why he was so impressed. You have done me a service, young man. Now I suggest you go and find some accommodation for you and your men. I may have a task for you quite soon."

83

McGuire saluted and left the office. As he opened the door he met the staff officer coming in, bearing a tray of tea. He stepped back and held the door to allow him to pass and then walked through and out of the farmhouse. As he walked towards his horse he heard someone call his name and turned to see a round-faced man walking towards him.

"It is McGuire, isn't it? I thought I recognised you."

McGuire looked hard at the man, but couldn't place him.

"Don't recognise me, eh? I don't blame you; we only met for a moment or two at Omdurman. You showed me the way to find Kitchener with a report about the Dervish movements. I'm Churchill. I was with the 21st Lancers at the time."

McGuire smiled. "Ah yes, I do remember you now. You made it through that mad charge then?"

"Indeed I did, and without a scratch to show for it. I'm here as the correspondent for the *Morning Post* this time. So tell me, what have you been doing? By the look of your uniform you haven't just arrived."

"I need to get back to my men and sort them out, or I would love to chat."

"Never mind, I'll ride with you and you can bring me up to date as we go. Give me one minute to borrow a horse."

As they rode out of the military confusion McGuire told the eager Churchill what had been going on around Ladysmith and what he had learned about the Boers. The reporter took it all in and made notes as he rode.

As they reached the place where McGuire's troop was waiting Sergeant Donnelly stood up and walked across to greet them.

"Don't your men salute you, Captain?"

McGuire turned in the saddle towards Churchill. "Not out here they don't. Any Boer sniper seeing me being saluted would identify me as the target he wanted. And for the same reason I don't carry a sword or wear a shiny Sam Browne belt. We lost quite a few officers who wanted to look the part."

"Interesting. Their men are that good with rifle, are they? I'll have to remember that. Now before I go, tomorrow morning I have been invited to go on one of the armoured train patrols up the line with Captain Haldane. Would you like to come with me? I'm sure Haldane won't mind."

McGuire shook his head. "A tempting offer, but I think I have to decline. General Buller may want me for a task in the near future."

Churchill leaned over and patted his arm. "Have you not seen the confusion at Estcourt? Buller will still be sorting himself out tomorrow so you can have a little fun."

Chapter 14
The Armoured Trains

Churchill and McGuire climbed up the metal sides of the railway wagon that was in front of the locomotive manned by half a company of the Dublin Fusiliers. Behind it there was another car with the rest of the company. McGuire was introduced to the train commander Haldane and invited to sit with him on a pile of sandbags that had been piled as extra protection.

McGuire looked round at the men peering out through the gun ports in the side of the rail car. "I'm surprised you don't have a roof on this for protection with all these hills around."

Haldane lowered his binoculars. "I would be happier myself with some overhead protection, but the railway people only have open trucks here and the General Staff do not feel it is necessary."

McGuire sighed. "And of course the General Staff won't be here to be worried about fire from above."

His companion grinned. "That's about the size of it. Anyway, it looks like we are setting off at last. Just a quick run along the track, to take a look at Colenso, and to see if we can see any Boer movement along the way."

"I was surprised to hear we had pulled back out of Colenso. We seem to be being a little timid, don't you think?"

"I suspect the powers that be were worried about ending up with another siege to deal with.

That wouldn't play well in the newspapers back home now, would it?"

The train pulled slowly forward and moved along the track to the north. Whenever they came across a native close to the track they stopped and asked if he had seen any sign of the Boers. The answers varied between none and thousands, depending on what the man thought the officers wanted to hear.

Eventually Colenso town came into view and the train stopped again. Through the field glasses the town appeared to be empty. There was no sign of any Boer occupation or any preparations being made outside the town for any sort of defence. The train moved forward until it was less than half a mile from the town. A junior officer and a sergeant went forward on foot, to check what could be seen. They came back and reported that the only sign of life was a dead horse lying in the road.

Haldane shrugged and waved to the engine driver. With a blast of steam the train started to retrace its route back to Estcourt. Churchill walked to the pile of sandbags and stood looking out across Colenso.

"I was really hoping to get my first glimpse of the Boers. Very disappointing for my readers back in England. I could have made it sound very interesting and dangerous."

"Why make it more than it really is?" McGuire asked.

"To sell more newspapers, of course. The readers don't want to read about the tedium of camp life. They want to hear about courageous officers and brave Tommies charging into enemy fire and overcoming the foe. Lots of waving flags and brandished swords. All rot, of course, but that's what they want from their army."

"And you don't mind writing that drivel?"

Churchill laughed. "Of course not. I intend to be a Member of Parliament some day and having my name on stories of heroism will help with that. Plus, of course, it encourages the man in the street to support the war."

They pulled into Estcourt as Churchill finished speaking. McGuire shook Haldane's hand and thanked him for the experience, then climbed down to the ground.

"Will you be coming with us again?" Churchill asked.

McGuire shook his head. "No, I'll leave the train heroics to you, for your readers, while I go and try and make myself useful with some less exciting soldiering."

Four days later McGuire saw Churchill riding towards him close to the headquarters building. "McGuire! Just the fellow. I've managed to wangle myself another run on the armoured train towards Colenso. Would you care to join me?"

"Not for me, thank you, Winston. I'm getting my men ready for a patrol later in the day."

"That's a shame. I had in mind a story for the *Post* about Gordon's revolver still being at the front, but now on your hip at the other end of Africa."

McGuire shook his head at the enthusiastic Churchill. "Even more reason for me not to go. I think I would rather stay out of the newspapers."

Churchill waved as he turned his horse towards the station where the armoured train waited. "Suit yourself, but a little bit of press attention can help an officer's career back in London." As McGuire rode away, Churchill reached the station and, dismounting, he tied the reins of his horse to a hitching post. He walked on to the platform and waved to the impatient train commander, Haldane. He climbed up the side of the car and dropped down in amongst the troops already inside. As soon as he was aboard, Haldane waved to the driver and, in a rush of steam, the train began to roll forward towards Colenso.

Churchill made his way to the front of the car to stand next to Haldane, who was looking forward. "Are we expecting any excitement this time, old man?"

"Not really. There have been a few reports of Boer movement around Colenso, but not in any great numbers. This is just a routine check."

"A shame. My readers would like to read about feats of daring and bravery against our enemy."

Haldane shook his head. "I'm sure such tales would be very exciting for the armchair warriors in their London clubs, but you know most of a soldier's life is boredom interspersed with the odd bit of abject terror."

Churchill grinned. "I do indeed, but that is not what my readers want over their breakfast."

"There'll be plenty of all that flag-waving rubbish for you, once General Buller has made his preparations to take back Ladysmith."

"Do you think that will be soon?"

"I've served under Buller before. He's a careful man. No shortage of daring, but he likes to make damned sure everything is prepared before he moves and then he will open the road to Ladysmith."

The train moved on through quiet countryside and the men stared to relax. As they reached the station at Chieveley around a hundred horsemen were seen riding south and then beyond the station they spotted a row of black dots along a low hill. The telegraphist on the train clipped his equipment on to the telegraph wires and sent a message back to Estcourt about what they were seeing. The train was ordered to return as far as Frere and to remain there in observation of the developing situation.

The order was obeyed and the train started back towards Frere. At a little under two miles from Frere the train rounded a bend and the troops saw that a hill that commanded the line from a distance of about six hundred yards was occupied by the Boers. The soldiers cocked their Lee Metford rifles and slid a round into the breach since it was clear that they would not be allowed to pass unmolested.

The Boers held their fire until the train reached the closest point to the hill they occupied.

The noise from the hilltop was intense, with bullets pinging off the armoured sides of the trucks. The khaki-clad men inside returned fire, secure in the knowledge that enemy's rifle bullets could not pass through the metal side panels. Then everything changed as three artillery pieces were wheeled forward into view. The Boer guns opened up and fired as fast as they were able. Two of these weapons were field guns and the third was a rapid firing Maxim gun that was firing small shells. The driver put on full steam in an attempt to get the train away from the heavy fire as quickly as possible.

The train accelerated forward as it ran the gauntlet of explosions from the three guns. It swung around the curve of the hill and reached a downward gradient. As the gradient began, the speed increased again and then further around the bend the driver saw the large boulder that had been rolled onto the track ahead of him. There was no time to brake. The first truck, which had been carrying repair materials for the track, was flung up into the air and turned to land upside down beside the track. What happened to the guard who was on that car was not known, but he was unlikely to have survived.

The next car held men of the Durban Light Infantry. It was derailed and ran forward for twenty yards or so before it tipped to one side and scattered the men across the rocky ground. The third car jumped the track and swivelled across to block the way forward. The rest of the train stayed on the rails with the locomotive clanking as its boiler started to cool. Other than that, there was a quiet moment as injured men from the front two cars struggled to sit up or move.

The quiet was not to last as the Boers changed their position and opened fire once again. Shells crashed around the train and bullets tapped like angry hailstones against the iron sides of the train. The train driver leapt out of his cab and started to run down the slope. As he reached the end of the wrecked train he realised there was no safe place to run to. He stopped and returned to the cab where there was at least a little cover.

Churchill ran forward and assessed the situation. Unless the tracks could be cleared it was only a matter of time before they were all slaughtered. He called for help and the uninjured men who had been thrown from the truck rallied and came to help him. By brute force alone they managed to tip the railway truck over and clear that part of the line. That left the truck that was skewed across the track. The same men took themselves to that one and forced it part of the way off the track, until it stuck fast and they could do no more.

Seeing the problem, Churchill ran back and instructed the train driver, who then started to move the train backward and forwards, hitting the obstructing car again and again. Eventually the way was cleared and they then found that the coupling to the cars behind had been smashed by a shell. Under fire, there was no way this could be repaired, so the men climbed rapidly out and took cover behind the engine.

The train driver started to slowly move the engine forward away from the Boers with the troops running alongside. As the gradient increased the locomotive began to move faster and, despite their best efforts, men were left behind. Some were hit by rifle fire and others who had been injured by the crash fell out and took cover as best they could.

Churchill was outpaced by the locomotive, but continued to run between the tracks with bullets pinging around him. He took cover in a ditch and was about to run further when he looked up to see a mounted Boer aiming a rifle at him. He looked down and realised his holster was empty. The pistol that he believed had saved his life at Omdurman in the Sudan was gone. He slowly raised his hands. He was a prisoner.

Chapter 15
Aftermath

General Buller looked at the short despatch in his hand again before tossing it onto his makeshift desk. "Get McGuire in here now."

McGuire had been waiting outside to receive the details of the reconnaissance task he was to complete. With the majority of British cavalry sealed up inside the Ladysmith perimeter, his men and their stolen horses were a valuable asset.

McGuire entered the General's office and saluted. "I hear you want me to go out towards Ladysmith, sir?"

Buller looked up. "Not any more. The armoured train has been ambushed just short of Chieveley. I want you to go and see what the situation is. The locomotive made it back with a few men clinging to it. I want to know where the rest are and what the devil the Boers are doing. When can you move?"

"Right away, sir. My men are standing by their horses already."

"Go, and don't let yourself get captured. I need information, not heroes."

McGuire left the farmhouse and strode across the road to where his troop were standing in the shade. "Have you all got those jackets and hats we took off the Boers?"

The men confirmed that they had and McGuire swung himself into the saddle of his black horse. Without ceremony he led the way towards the rail line with the troop following him. They rode north alongside the tracks until they came to Frere. The battered locomotive still stood there leaking steam from damaged pipes. McGuire looked around for anyone who had been involved in the incident, but none were in evidence.

They rode forward until they were a mile from the town and then McGuire led them off the track and behind a small rise. "All of you put the Boer jackets over your uniform and change your helmets for their slouch hats. As we move forward try and look like a farmer."

The men smiled at the joke as they put on the disguises. They rode forward again, looking far less like an army patrol. They came in sight of the wrecked train just as the last of the Boers left. They had been scouring the site for any weapons and ammunition that might be of use to them. McGuire waited and then led the troop slowly forward, scanning the hilltop as they moved.

The dead lay where they had fallen. But they had been stripped of their uniforms and equipment. The wounded that were too badly hurt to move had been made as comfortable as possible then left, but they, too, had been stripped of jackets and field helmets. McGuire looked around at the hilltops; although he could see no sign of the enemy he was wary.

"Patrol leaders to me now!" The four men rode forward and stopped by him. "Sergeant Parks, you and your men look to the wounded. Corporal Connolly, you and your men help with the wounded. Corporal Macklin, I want your men on the heights now, keeping a lookout. All of you stay alert in case the Boers come back. Sergeant Donnelly, ride as fast as possible to Frere, get me a locomotive and a car up here to pick these men up. If you can find any, bring medical staff with you. And Donnelly, don't take no for an answer. I will take Corporal Fine and Donnelly's patrol and we will go further up the line to see what is going on there. Off you go."

Donnelly wheeled his horse and rode swiftly south. The others moved to their tasks and McGuire led the way up the line to the top of the gradient. From here he could see across the plain and there were Boer horsemen moving towards Chieveley. The guns that had ambushed the train were being dragged away by horse teams and he could see other guns in the distance. It seemed that the Boers were getting ready for a fight.

McGuire led his men slowly back down to the site of the ambush. In the distance he could see a train puffing its way towards him. Donnelly had been persuasive. The train arrived and the orderlies from the flat car jumped down and began to move the wounded, helped by the men of the reconnaissance troop. As McGuire watched a young Lieutenant stomped towards him.

"Are you in charge here?"

"I am indeed. McGuire's the name."

"I want your Sergeant court-martialled for threatening an officer."

McGuire smiled slowly. "Do you now? And what threat did he make?"

"He told me that unless I got on that train he would beat seven shades of shit out of me. That cannot go unpunished."

McGuire nodded. "Ah that's a Belfast expression. So why would he feel the need to say something like that? Surely you were keen to join the train?"

"I was not. I was busy."

"I take it from your uniform you are a medical officer, so tell me, Lieutenant, what was more important than coming here to deal with wounded soldiers?"

"That's beside the point."

"Donnelly! Come here." McGuire paused as the big Sergeant rode up to him. "What do you mean by threatening this officer when he was busy?"

"Busy, sir? He was just sitting down to his lunch."

McGuire turned and looked coolly at the officer who stood before him. "Your lunch was more important than soldiers' lives? Lieutenant, you say one more word about my Sergeant and you will be standing in front of General Buller explaining that, and I will be delighted to testify at your court martial. Now get over there and do your damned job."

The Lieutenant scuttled away and McGuire turned to Donnelly. "Seven shades of shit? Really? You're not on the Falls Road now, Sergeant. You can moderate your language to an officer in future."

Donnelly grinned. "Yes, sir, but you have to admit I got his attention."

McGuire was forced to grin at his tough, effective Sergeant. "True, but now we need to get back and report. It looks to me as if our Boer friends are on the move or at least getting ready to move our way."

Chapter 16
Action at Willow Grange

"So then, Captain McGuire, from what you have just reported what is your appreciation of the Boers' intentions?"

The staff officer standing next to the General looked up from the map spread before them. "Really, sir, I don't think Captain McGuire is the person to interpret the Boers' intentions. He has no staff training and, at the moment, not even an official appointment."

Redvers Buller turned slowly and looked at the immaculately dressed Lieutenant Colonel. He looked him up and down from his gleaming riding boots to the knife-edge creases in his tunic.

"You didn't serve in the Sudan, did you, Colonel? Well, Captain McGuire did. He and his band of unconventional soldiers were scouting ahead of the army throughout the reconquest of that benighted country. You will be aware that General Kitchener is excessively sparing with praise, no doubt? Yet he praises this man at every turn. That DSO ribbon on his chest was hard-won, in some of the most difficult and dangerous conditions. Do you think that compares to your training at the staff college?"

The Colonel flushed a bright pink. "My error, General. Please continue Captain."

McGuire heard the politeness, but judging by the Colonel's face he had just made another enemy. He sighed inwardly and looked down at the map.

Putting his finger on the railway line he spoke quietly. "I was here, sir, as I told you." His fingers moved across the paper. "The Boers were here, here and here around Willow Grange, in various concentrations. I would have to be guessing, but from what I saw these two commandos looked like they were getting ready to advance to contact with us. This column, however, did not. My thinking is that these troops are going to bypass us and try to move around us to cause confusion in the rear of our lines."

The General nodded slowly. "Colonel, your opinion?"

The staff officer sucked the end of his pencil as he stared down at the map. "Obviously, I'm not sure that Captain McGuire is correct in his opinions, but whatever the enemy intends needs to be disrupted. They are clearly up to something and if this is a diversion to allow a commando to slip past us that has to be stopped. I suggest we throw a force forward as a matter of some urgency to meet them around here."

McGuire looked down and saw that the tip of the Colonel's pencil rested on a feature labelled Beacon Hill. Buller scanned around the other officers standing by and they all nodded agreement.

"McGuire?"

"I think the Colonel is correct, sir. Even if I am totally wrong, the Boers need to have their plans disrupted. I've seen that hill and it is remarkably steep, but a gun or two on there could dominate a lot of ground."

"Thank you, Captain McGuire. I think it's time my staff earned their salt and developed a plan. In the meantime, I would like you to go and find the naval detachment and escort them to Beacon Hill. Keep the Boers away while they get their gun up there."

McGuire saluted and went in search of the naval detachment. He found them camped close to the railway line with their gun sitting on its carriage nearby. As he approached he saw a naval officer coming towards him.

"Lieutenant, is that your gun?"

"It is indeed, sir. The troops seem to be stirring, so I'm on my way to headquarters to see if they have work for us."

McGuire smiled. "I can save you the walk. I've been tasked to escort you as you take that gun up on to Beacon Hill."

The Lieutenant pulled a map from his pocket. "Which one is that, sir?"

McGuire pointed out their objective. "And it's going to be a pig of a job to get that piece up there. By this afternoon you may wish you were back on your ship."

"Not to worry, sir, my tars can achieve miracles. It's why we were sent to support the army."

McGuire nodded and patted the Lieutenant's shoulder. "From your mouth to God's ears, my friend. Now get your men on the move while I round up my troop and we'll join you within fifteen minutes."

The reconnaissance troop formed a screen while the naval gun team trundled the heavy weapon along the track beside the railway, until they caught up with the Durham Light Infantry, who had preceded them. As they reached the bottom of Beacon Hill the storm started, and such a storm. The rain lashed down, causing streams to pour down the side of the steep hill, and then came the hailstones. Pieces of ice larger than any of the men had seen before smashed into them. Field helmets were punctured and men cried out as the hailstones struck their upper bodies with enough force to cause injury. To their credit, the naval team hunched their shoulders and carried on moving the gun up to the base of the hill. They attached ropes and started to pull the awkward load up over the rocks and slimy soil patches.

McGuire could see they had no chance of making it alone. "Donnelly, get the horses picketed and then get the men on those drag lines with the navy. I'm going to borrow some men from the Durhams over there."

With help from the Durhams and, with a lot of brute force and courage, the gun was dragged inch by inch up the steep and awkward slope. Thankfully, the hail stopped, but the rain continued to pelt down, making the slope extremely dangerous. Eventually the exhausted men dragged the heavy weapon onto the top of the hill and collapsed to draw breath while the naval team manoeuvred it into a suitable position among the rocks of the summit.

McGuire walked across to where the naval Lieutenant stood looking through his field glasses. "Nice job, Lieutenant. Well done."

"We couldn't have done it without your men and the Durhams, sir, but I'm wondering if it was a waste of time and effort. With this rain I can't see far enough to find a target."

"I shouldn't worry too much about that. These storms are violent, but they seem to end as quickly as they start."

"I certainly hope so. At least it gives my men time to rest before we start work."

McGuire walked away to the side of the hill and looked down the steep slope to where the infantry were assembling. At this distance he could not see who they were, but he could see that the numbers were building up appreciably. As he looked round he saw that some of the officers had moved around the shoulder of the hill to take a view out across the plain. From there they could see and be seen from the hill named Brynbella. The Boers on that hill were wide awake and saw their enemy. They opened fire with one of the guns they had positioned on that hill, and although they did no damage, it sent the officers scurrying back into cover.

The naval gun on the hilltop behind McGuire returned fire, even though it was probably out of range of the Boer position. Unfortunately, this let the Boers know that something big was building and they moved their riflemen into the already prepared trenches.

Across the plain, a stone wall led directly from the base of Beacon Hill to the north-eastern edge of Brynbella and as night fell two regiments moved forward using this as a guide. Halfway across there was confusion and a jumpy rifleman opened fire on the other regiment in the dark. This led to an exchange of fire between the two British regiments and a number of men were wounded by rifle and bayonet. On his hilltop McGuire could see the rifle flashes and swore quietly under his breath.

By 3.30 in the morning the West Yorkshire regiment had made their way onto the crest of Brynbella without being detected. A challenge from a sleepy sentry resulted in a volley and a loud cheer from the Yorkshire men. This gave the Boers time to rush to their horses and make a rapid retreat, leaving much of their paraphernalia and a number of horses behind.

As the dawn broke over the hills the West Yorkshires were occupying the ridge and the rest of the force was coming up to support them. The Boers in the meantime had occupied another ridge some 1500 yards back. The Boers had two field guns and a pom-pom. The British on Brybella had no such support and the naval gun on Beacon Hill was now way out of range.

The actions by the British were now completely uncoordinated, with infantry retiring away from the guns while other units were moving forward to support them. The 7th Artillery Battery were given no orders and stayed where they were. Realising the confusion, the force commander gave the order for a general withdrawal. The naval gun on top of Beacon Hill seemed to have been forgotten by the troops marching away and McGuire decided to remove it before any Boers could come forward and take it.

The journey down the hill with the heavy gun was if anything even more dangerous than it had been to take it up. Men slid and slipped down the rocky hillside, doing their best to jam the wheels to stop the heavy weapon rolling away. Men risked their lives putting wedges under the wheels and clinging to the ropes that held the gun back. Eventually the battered and exhausted men made it to the bottom of the hill and the gun was hitched up to be dragged back to Estcourt.

Mounting his horse, McGuire rode around the hill to observe the Boers. Although they had been left in command of the field, he could see no sign that they were advancing. Despite the poor performance of the British, there had been an effect. The Boer commander, General Joubert, had now decided not to move any further forward in the face of superior numbers. In fact, he decided to pull back across the Tugela to Colenso rather than risk being caught by the British with his back to the river. Joubert had now lost the initiative. Laden down with heavy wagons and hampered by the muddy conditions caused by the storm, the Boers were extremely vulnerable, but the British did nothing and the enemy melted away, destroying the bridges over the Tugela as they went.

Chapter 17
A New Task

"Sit down, Captain, make yourself comfortable. I've got a brandy and soda coming. Would care to join me?"

"That's very kind of you, sir. It's been a long day."

Buller waited until the orderly had poured the two drinks and then leaned back in the cane chair on the porch of his headquarters that had once been the stationmaster's house in Frere. He sipped the brandy and looked out over the mass of tents to the veldt beyond.

"Do you know why I asked you to come and speak with me?"

"Not really, sir," McGuire said as he sipped his own brandy.

Buller sipped again before he spoke. "I had a visit from my chief medical officer today. He told me your Sergeant threatened one of his young doctors with violence. Is that true?"

"Yes, sir, unfortunately it is. I'm afraid my Sergeant was a little incensed that the doctor in question declined to come and treat wounded soldiers because he wanted his lunch."

"I see. The good doctor missed that part out in his report to me. However, I think you may remember the CMO from the Sudan. He tells me you put the barrel of a Webley revolver in his face because he wasn't treating one of your men. Is that also true?"

"Absolutely true, sir. He and a number of other surgeons were cluttered round one bed and ignoring my man who was bleeding to death from a gunshot wound."

"Hmm, again the good doctor missed that detail out of his report. He did tell me that Kitchener sent him away with a flea in his ear when he reported your actions. It seems that despite his harsh exterior Kitchener cares as much for the men under his command as I do."

McGuire nodded. "I think he does, sir. That wound to his face makes him look over-stern, but, as you probably know, it's something of an act."

Buller paused for a moment or two. "All right, your Sergeant is off the hook this time, but never again, is that clear?"

"Clear as day, sir. Is that all?"

"No, it's not. You realise that in the near future I intend to advance across the Tugela to relieve Ladysmith. It's no secret; even Brother Boer knows and is getting ready to receive us, I imagine."

"I would bet on it, sir. The Boers are no fools."

Buller nodded slowly and sipped again. "No, they're not. Now, what I want from you and your band of ruffians is information. How many Boers are we facing, where are they, what artillery do they have and what preparations have they made to delay us? I say 'delay' because there is no chance that we will not relieve Ladysmith."

"I'm sure the Ladysmith garrison will be glad to see you, sir."

"No doubt. Now then, with the railway bridge blown to the north of us towards Colenso, I intend to make my thrust out to the west. Looking at the map you gave me, Potgieter's Drift is where the main body will cross. With my shortage of cavalry, that will be the infantry first with field guns in support. The guns will initially be south of the Tugela and will cross once we have a position established on the north bank. Is that all clear?"

McGuire leaned back in his wicker chair. "Crystal clear, sir. One thing you should know, though, is that the north bank is steep. The men will be slow climbing it and the guns will struggle unless we put ox teams over to drag them."

"Yes, your map shows that. I want you to take an engineer officer with you to assess the drift and he will then use native labour to improve it, once we can secure the far side to guard the native labourers."

McGuire put his glass down carefully on the small table. "How long do I have for this reconnaissance, sir?"

As he walked away from the headquarters McGuire saw an officer standing by a horse, watching him approach. As he got nearer he could see the colour flash of the Royal Engineers on the side of his field helmet.

"Captain McGuire?"

"That's me."

"Good afternoon. I'm Rogers. I've been told I am coming with you, to take a look at a potential crossing place for the army."

"All right then. If you have everything you need, mount up, and we'll go out and collect my men."

"Out? Aren't they in the lines with the rest of the troops?"

"No, I've got them out on the veldt doing some training. They'll have all their equipment with them, so there won't be a delay."

They rode out of the lines of white bell tents with the inevitable smells from the camp kitchens and then out onto the wide veldt. After a mile or so they came in view of a wide donga that cut through the flat land. Coming to the edge, they looked down to see the reconnaissance troop sitting in a circle with two men inside the rough ring facing off against each other.

Rogers turned and looked at McGuire. "We seem to have trouble. Do you want me to help you stop it?"

McGuire chuckled, then pulled a whistle out of his pocket and blew it. The men below all looked up and the two in the centre of the ring stopped circling and stood upright. The two officers rode down the slope and as they reached the ring McGuire dismounted.

Rogers sat still on his horse and looked around. "Don't your men salute you, Captain? You seem to have a discipline problem."

"Discipline is just fine, thank you. Get down and I'll introduce you."

The engineer paused, then dismounted and walked to where McGuire stood waiting for him. "Men, we have been given a task and this is Captain Rogers. He's an engineer who is coming with us at least part of the way."

The men looked at Rogers and some nodded, but none stood and none saluted him. He was nonplussed by such behaviour and wondered whether to make something of it.

"Now then, Captain, you thought the men were fighting, did you not?" McGuire said. "Well, you're half right. I teach my men to fight without weapons. You see we operate out on our own and if we get into trouble there is the possibility we might run out of bullets before we run out of Boers. We practise our skills so that even then we can ruin the enemy's day for him."

"Oh, I see. I was taught to box myself while I was at school. I just haven't seen it done like this since I joined the army."

Sergeant Donnelly stood up from where he sat close by. "This isn't boxing, sir. This is no sport. I teach the men to win, to kill and survive."

Rogers looked down his nose a little at the Sergeant. "Boxing is a fine manly sport, Sergeant."

McGuire knew what was coming next and nodded slightly to the big man from Belfast. "Right you are, sir," said Donnelly with an evil grin. "Maybe you'd like to give us a demonstration? Private Madine, come here."

111

The smallest man in the troop stood up and walked to where the two officers stood with the Sergeant. "Nice to meet you, sir."

"Would you care to match your boxing skills against Private Madine, sir? I'm sure the troop would love to learn from you."

Rogers turned to McGuire. "Is this serious? Is your man really suggesting that I fight a Private?"

"Not fight him, oh no, that would be wrong: this would be a demonstration of your skills at unarmed warfare. If you could teach the men something that would be very useful."

The Captain sniffed and looked at Madine. "I can't fight him, he's far too small."

McGuire patted Madine on the shoulder. "Private Madine here is the smallest man in the troop; he's also the lightest and quickest."

Madine nodded. "Excuse me, sir, you missed out 'and the best-looking'."

"I beg your pardon, Mister Madine. Are you suggesting that you are better looking than your troop commander?"

"Ah, sir, we would need a lady here to judge that, but it would be a close-run thing and I am younger."

Rogers stood open-mouthed at this exchange. "You have a very strange idea of how to run men, Captain. However, I'm prepared to enter into the spirit of this thing. Come along, Private. I'll show you how to box."

With that Rogers strode confidently to the centre of the ring of men. As Madine went to follow him McGuire tapped him on the shoulder and he stopped.

"Remember he's on our side. Don't damage him."

Madine nodded and walked after the engineer Captain. By the time he reached him Rogers had removed his shiny leather Sam Browne belt and laid it on the ground with his pith helmet and jacket. He turned to face the young soldier and put his fists up in the approved manner. Madine stood and looked at him with his head cocked slightly on one side.

"Very well. Madine, is it? Put up your fists and we'll begin."

"No, that's fine, sir. You start and I'll watch how it's done, if it please your honour."

Roger shrugged, then aimed a rapid straight right at the smaller man's jaw. Madine's head was no longer there. He had dropped to the sand and his right leg swept around and kicked the officer's legs out from under him. The engineer landed flat on his back and the breath was knocked from his body.

"Good grief, that's cheating!"

McGuire stepped forward and, extending his hand, helped Rogers to his feet. "No, that's fighting. We don't treat it as a sport. The only purpose is to survive."

"So there are no rules?"

"Just one: win at all costs."

Rogers walked back towards Madine, who stood calmly waiting for him. "Now that I know the rules, let's start again."

Without waiting for an answer the officer swung his foot, intending to drive his boot up between the soldier's legs. Madine took half a pace backwards, grabbed the shiny riding boot and heaved up. Again the officer landed on his back.

McGuire walked forward and looked down at the irate Captain on the ground. "Now if you weren't on our side Madine here would have dropped down onto your stomach and then cut your throat. That's what he has been trained to do, but I told him not to hurt you."

Rogers raised himself on one elbow and looked around at the men. None were laughing at him which surprised him. He held up his hand and McGuire pulled him to his feet.

As he dusted himself down he looked up at McGuire. "I have a confession to make. I attended a lecture given by General Kitchener about his campaign in the Sudan. He told us about you and your band of ruffians and he mentioned your odd training methods. I wanted to see for myself, and it seems he was right about you."

"So did we pass the test?"

The engineer grinned. "So far, yes. I'm interested to try one of these desert stews Kitchener spoke about."

McGuire smiled back. "We'll be having one of those tonight if we can drop some game on the way." He turned to Donnelly. "Get the troop

114

mounted, Sergeant. We are off back to Potgieter's."

Chapter 18
Reconnaissance

Captain Rogers turned in the saddle and looked back at the troop who were following them. "You don't ride like the rest of the army either?"

McGuire looked over his shoulder at his men, then smiled. "No, we try not to. All that column of twos stuff is fine if you don't mind being identified from a long way off. We like to keep the Boers guessing for as long as we can."

"Any other cunning techniques I should know about?"

"Yes, as it happens, and you're just about to see one."

McGuire led the way down into another donga that cut across the flat plain. Once all the troop was down inside the valley, and out of sight of any watchers, he reined in and dismounted. Rogers did the same and watched in amazement as, without a word, the members of the troop dropped to the ground and unrolled their blankets from behind their saddles. In moments they had all removed their distinctive field helmets and were shrugging into dark jackets. Then they slapped scruffy slouch hats on their heads and stood ready to move.

As Rogers turned to question McGuire he was handed a jacket and hat by one of the troop. He looked at the clothing in his hand and then at McGuire.

"Disguise?"

"That's right. We spent most of the Sudan campaign dressed as Dervish warriors so we could try and pass unnoticed in the desert."

"And now you want to look like Boers?"

"Now we are far enough from the army, so that some nervous sentry doesn't try and take a shot at us, we try and look like the enemy. It should work from a distance. Up close it would be different, but we hope not to try that out."

The men mounted and rode along the donga, to emerge as far as possible from where they had entered. McGuire looked around and then they started riding off towards Potgieter's Drift. As they rode Sergeant Parks peeled off to the left, where he had seen a small herd of gazelle. He fired from the saddle and dropped one of the animals before slinging it across his saddle and riding back to the troop.

McGuire turned to Rogers, who was watching all this with wide eyes. "You wanted to try one of our field stews. So Parks has just got us the main ingredient. The rest of the men carry anything else they find along the way that we might like."

"Where do they get it from?"

McGuire grinned at the engineer. "I make a point of not asking."

"Are your people all criminals?"

McGuire laughed. "Not all of them, but they are all the sort of men who were misfits in their original units. They are the ones the army doesn't like to deal with. Men with independent thought and initiative. That is reserved for officers in a normal regiment. But in this small unit that is exactly what I went looking for."

"Were you a misfit as well?" Rogers asked quietly.

"Me? Absolutely. I was a Private soldier, given the choice of jail or joining the army. I did some useful work during the Gordon Relief Expedition in the Sudan and was given a field commission, but I was never fully accepted by my fellow officers. So this kind of unconventional role, that keeps me away from the officers' mess, is just up my alley."

They rode on in silence with Rogers wondering how to respond and coming up with nothing. As night fell the troop made camp within the confines of yet another deep donga. A small cooking fire was set inside a pit dug at the bottom of the dry watercourse and the men sat around waiting while the evening meal was prepared.

"When do we reach the drift? I'm anxious to get a look at it to see what I need to do to make it a viable crossing place for the army."

McGuire leaned back against the saddle that lay behind him. "I thought maybe you wanted to get away from my small troop of criminals! The drift is about two miles away over to the north. We'll leave here before dawn and be waiting there as it gets light."

Rogers took the metal plate of stew that Madine handed to him and turned to McGuire. "I'm actually quite enjoying being with this troop.

Going back to the real army is going to be a bore after this. Why so early?"

"We don't know where the Boers are and if we ride up they could open fire with their remarkably accurate rifles. We could lose men. So we picket the horses and crawl the last few yards into a hidden position on the river bank. Then we wait and see who is moving about before we do anything."

***

It was still dark when Rogers heard the troop moving around quietly in the night. He rolled over under his thin blanket and sat up. He saw a dim shape moving towards him and a mug of hot tea was thrust into his hand.

"There you go, sir, gunfire to set you up for the day."

"Gunfire? I didn't hear anything."

The figure chuckled. "No, sir. Tea with a tot of rum in it. We call it gunfire. Drink up while it's warm. Your horse will be saddled when you're ready."

Rogers sipped the brew as he watched the men moving around him. There was no shouting as each man seemed to know what he was supposed to do without orders. The rum in the tea was certainly welcome in the chill of the early morning. He stood up and walked over to the horses with the blanket around his shoulders still drinking his tea.

"Ready to go?" McGuire asked.

"Yes. Do we get any breakfast on top of this rum?"

"We do once we get to where we are going, but it will only be cold bully beef and hard tack this morning. Can't risk a fire so close to the river."

The troop rode silently out of the donga and towards the river. As they got closer they could hear the sound of the water through the still air and the horses were picketed behind a low ridge with two of the men detailed to guard them. The rest then made their way on foot to the river bank and lay down in the scrubby grass. They were still there when the dawn broke across the tops of the kopjes on the north side of the Tugela. They watched as the light marched down the hillsides and illuminated the valley floor.

Even through his field glasses, McGuire could see no sign of movement, although there were signs of recent digging in various places. He carried on scanning slowly backwards and forwards and was rewarded with the sight of a Boer climbing out of his trench to go and drop his trousers beneath a tree on the hillside.

"Brother Boer is over there all right. Halfway up the kopje to the left of that big jagged boulder, squatting under a tree."

Rogers swung his own binoculars around and soon found the man. "More of them coming out of the trenches now. Sensible people. Having dung in the trench you are going to fight in would not be pleasant, especially in this climate."

"Ah, then, take a look at the base of the slope. The Boers seem to be driving a column of local people along. Looks like a work party with all those spades and picks they are carrying."

The engineer studied the approaching group of natives. "Kaffirs. Is that what they call them? Is that a tribe or something?"

McGuire shook his head. "The Boers do call the natives Kaffirs. I think it is just a term for all black people, but the way the Boers use it sounds pretty dismissive to me. Rather like the way our army called the Dervishes fuzzy-wuzzies. I never cared for that either."

The two officers continued to watch the Boer lines and noticed more and more of the enemy moving around. Obviously they felt secure in their trenches and were unworried about being observed.

"Corporal Macklin, take your patrol across the river. Check the depth and strength of the current. Then set yourself up at the top of the far bank to cover the Captain here while he examines the drift."

Macklin and his three men moved rapidly down the bank and into the river. Holding their rifles above the water they pushed through towards the other side. They were around halfway across when Macklin fell forward with a cry. He struggled back to his feet and turned towards McGuire. He forced his way back through the quickly flowing water and walked up the bank.

McGuire saw the blood flowing down both of Macklin's shins. "What the devil did you fall over out there?"

"Barbed wire, sir. There are strands of barbed wire under the water all across there. It's tight, so they haven't just thrown it in. It must be secured to posts somewhere."

"Hell, that would have made a mess of any horse we tried to take across here," Rogers said. "We'll have to clear that before we try anything else."

"How do we do that?"

"Wire cutters. There's a railway workshop just south of Estcourt. If I get back there, I can have my sappers manufacture them from any scrap iron they have around the place."

Corporal Macklin rolled his trouser legs back down as he finished checking the tears in his skin. "I'll go back across to join the lads now, sir. If you decide to come over, be careful; it bloody hurts."

Rogers moved forward. "I'll come over with you and then you can show me where the wire is."

Together the two men slid down the bank and into the water. They waded across carefully to avoid further damage from the spikes of the barbed wire. As they reached the other side, McGuire could see Macklin climbing the bank to join his three men, while Rogers examined the slope and the condition of the bank from down below.

A single rifle shot echoed across the veldt and Private Madine rolled backwards from the top of the bank and lay on his back with his head towards the river. The hole punched through his forehead was clearly visible even from across the water. Macklin and his remaining two men worked the bolts of their rifles to chamber a round in each of them and then started to look for who had fired. As they raised their heads just above the bank edge they were greeted by a barrage of rifle fire and they slid down into cover. McGuire scanned the enemy trenches through his field glasses, but, even with their help, he was hard-pressed to spot those firing at his men.

"Donnelly, Parks, get the men up here and prepare to lay down rapid fire on my command. If we can make the Boers take cover the lads can get back over here."

He knew that his men were unlikely to hit anyone, but a trained marksman could fire the Lee Enfield remarkably rapidly and he hoped to convince the Boers they had been seen. In moments the men were lined up along the southern bank with their rifles at the ready and their extra ammunition, in stripper clips, laid out next to them.

McGuire made a last assessment of where he though the enemy fire was coming from. "All of you, the trench to the right of that large grey-barked tree. Independent rapid fire. Now!"

The men lay in the grass and fired as rapidly as they were able. As the magazine of ten rounds was exhausted the stripper clip was slotted into the top of the rifle and with a single thumb press the rifle was charged again. McGuire yelled for

Macklin and his men to get back across the river and they ran down the bank past Captain Rogers. The engineer officer scrambled up the bank and heaved Madine's body over his shoulder before he, too, made for the river's edge.

Initially the four men were covered behind the far bank of the river, but, as they reached the middle, bullets started to raise small waterspouts all around them. They did not pause, but pushed on as fast as possible. One man yelled as he was hit and fell face down into the water. He was up again in seconds and moving forward. The last man across was Rogers with his sorry load. As he dropped down into cover Madine's lifeless corpse rolled to the bottom of the low ditch they were sheltering in.

"Cease fire! Conserve your ammunition. Now keep watch. If they think we've gone they might show themselves and then you can take a shot."

McGuire slid down next to Madine's body, where Rogers was trying to get his breath back. "That was damned risky, but thank you for it. The men would not have been happy leaving Madine over there on his own."

Rogers nodded, but said nothing. There was nothing to say.

Chapter 19
Escape

The State Model Schools in Pretoria had been turned into a prison camp for captured British officers. Here, Churchill was forced to sit and wait with growing frustration. He applied to be released on the ground that he was a civilian journalist, but the Boers denied that claim. The prison was surrounded by a mix of walls and fencing at least ten feet high with powerful electric lights shining through the night. Every fifty yards stood an armed sentry and the Boers had proved entirely immune to bribery. However, there was a weakness in that once past the lights a man would be difficult to see in the relative darkness beyond and Churchill had a plan.

On the 12th December, as the dinner bell rang, Churchill took advantage of the movement of people and slipped into the office building and hid. He watched though a chink in the curtains for an opportunity, but the sentries were on watch and alert. As the camp quieted down for the night, the sentries relaxed a little and the one opposite Churchill's hiding place turned and walked across to talk to the next sentry. With their backs turned to him this was Churchill's chance and he took it. He ran to the wall and heaved himself up onto the flat top of it. Here he paused to ensure the movement had not attracted the attention of the sentry. Then, as quietly as he was able, he dropped down into the garden that was at the other side of the wall and hid in the bushes.

He waited for the officer who was supposed to join him in the escape. After an hour he heard voices from beyond the wall and heard his name amongst the inconsequential chatter. He crawled back to the wall and hissed that he was there.

From the other side of the wall his intended companion spoke. "Can't get out. The sentry suspects something. Can you get back again?"

Churchill did not answer for fear of being heard. Then he leaned against the wall to consider his options. He could not face climbing back into the tedium of the camp and decided to make the attempt to escape. He knew he would be captured, but at least for a while he could be a damned nuisance to the Boers.

Once his mind was made up, bravado was the course he chose. He slapped his hat on his head and, standing up, strolled to the garden gate, making no attempt to hide himself. He strolled past the sentry and tipped his hat in greeting, making sure that it covered his well-known face. The sentry nodded back and returned to his watch without recognising the escaping prisoner. Churchill walked on for another hundred yards, expecting a rifle shot at any second. When the shot did not come he realised he had made it and was at large in the enemy capital.

Audacity seemed to be the best course to take, so Churchill walked along in the main street rather than skulking in the shadows. With his hands in his pockets and whistling a tune, he looked as though he belonged there and went unchallenged. He made his way to the railway station, intending to stow away on a train heading towards Portuguese territory. Without a compass he was unable to tell which lines ran to the east, and in any case, all the trains standing there were guarded.

His only chance of boarding a train was to jump aboard once it had left the station, preferably when it was moving slowly. Making sure he was not being observed, he chose a track and started to walk along beside it. As he cleared the town he saw a bridge ahead of him with a small campfire and sentries sitting beside it. A swing out to the side and then a scramble across a dry river bed in the dark got him past this bridge and the three that followed it.

As the sky started to lighten he saw a small cluster of houses and a station ahead of him. Beyond that was the gradient he had been hoping for and he made his way past the buildings to reach it. He settled himself in the undergrowth beside the track and waited. As he had anticipated, the next train along the line stopped at the station before pulling out and heading towards him. It was going alarmingly quickly by the time it reached him, but he decided to risk it and rose from his hiding place, once the locomotive was past him.

He ran alongside the track and in the half-light managed to grab hold of a metal bar to swing himself up onto the side of the open-topped box car. He climbed up the side and fell into the car onto a stack of filthy sacks covered in coal dust. No matter, he was now moving away from his prison at a useful twenty miles an hour.

As the day dawned he kept watch on his progress and was delighted to see the sun rise ahead of the train. He was heading due east, as he had hoped. He heard the hiss of the steam valves as the train began to slow and raised his head to see a station approaching. He could see the armed Boers on the platform and decided this was the time to leave the train. He climbed down onto the couplings between the cars so as not to be seen and when a suitable area of bushes approached he made his leap. As he landed he stumbled and fell to the ground before rolling down the slight embankment. Unhurt, he was now in the bushes and had not been seen. From his vantage point he watched the Boers climb into the cars and search through the sacks.

Churchill stayed in hiding until nightfall and then walked on beside the tracks, skirting around any places that might contain enemies. As he walked the lack of water and food began to tell and the oppressive heat during the day, coupled with the cold of night, started to wear him down. By the time he came in sight of a mine with a number of small houses scattered around it he was exhausted and ready to quit.

He picked a small house at random and stumbled onto the veranda before knocking on the door. After a short pause the door swung inwards and the man standing there raised the lantern to look at him.

"Good grief! Get inside quickly before anyone sees you."

Churchill walked forward and slumped into the wooden chair by a rough-hewn table. He looked at the house owner, who had turned after closing the door. The man raised the lantern again and stared at him in obvious amazement.

"Well, Mister Churchill, I wasn't expecting to see you tonight! You have no idea how lucky you are."

Churchill cleared his dusty throat. "How do you know me?"

The man walked across to a small desk and came back with a tattered handbill that he gave to Churchill. "Those have been handed out to everyone, with promises of a reward to anyone who catches you."

Churchill looked down at his own photograph, taken when he had first arrived at the prison camp. "Why do you say I am lucky?"

"Because, my friend, you have knocked on the door of the only Englishman for twenty miles. Everyone else at this mine is a Boer and you would have been on your way back to prison in quick time."

"Won't my being here put you at risk?"

"It would if anyone saw you, so we'll have to make sure they don't. Now, I guess you need food and water by the look of you and then I'll make you up a place to sleep."

"You live here alone?"

"That's right. My wife stayed at home in Oldham to look after her old mother."

Churchill smiled a little. "I stood for election as a Member of Parliament in Oldham not long ago. I got beaten, though."

"I know. I voted for the other fella, but you watch, if you get away with this you'll make it next time. Now let's get you fed and into a bed before you pass out."

"I think I should know your name before you put me to bed."

"Sorry, I should have said. I'm John Howard. I'm the mine manager here."

"Your house seems too small for me to hide in, John."

Howard nodded as he started to bring bread and cheese to the table. "You're right, but just behind us here is a disused mine and I'm going to set you up in there. As long as you stay in there during daylight you should be fine until I can get you on to a train out of here."

Churchill was dozing on the blankets that had been set down in the mine for him when Howard came along the tunnel. "Churchill, time to go."

Churchill raised himself on one elbow and squinted at the shape in the dim light. "Where to?"

"Into the house first for something to eat and then off to the coal train later. I've got food and water for you to take for the journey."

"Do you think I'll make it over the border?"

"With luck, yes. Provided you burrow down under the sacks of coal the border guards shouldn't find you. They check the trains going through, but they're not likely to unload tons of coal by hand."

The two men walked out of the mine together. They paused at the entrance to make sure they were alone before walking through the kitchen door of the small house. The meal was plain but wholesome and once it was finished Howard went to collect the small burlap sack of supplies.

"Be careful with the water. Only drink when you have to so that it lasts. It would be unfortunate if you were driven out of hiding by thirst."

Churchill took the bag and held out his hand for Howard to shake it. "Even if this fails, I want you to know how grateful I am for your help. Is there anything I can do for you in return?"

Howard smiled. "When you get back to Oldham tell my wife that I'm fine and tell my brother I said he should vote for you."

Churchill nodded. "That's a promise."

"Good. Now let's go. The train is due in about twenty minutes. It slows as it climbs the gradient and you should be able to climb on. Let me go first, to check there is nobody around."

They walked briskly through the night until they came to the rail track. In the distance behind them Churchill could see the headlight of the approaching coal train and hear the rattle of the cars. Howard had been right, the train was slowing as it climbed the gradient and the two men ducked into the cover of a large bush to make sure they were not seen by the train crew.

Once the locomotive was past they rose up and moved quickly alongside the slow-moving railcars. In the light of the moon Churchill saw the metal bars that would serve as his way up. He grabbed on and heaved himself aboard. He turned to see Howard trotting beside him and reached down for the sack of supplies. He tossed the sack into the car and climbed in after it. He sat on the steel wall of the car and waved his thanks to his saviour.

Burrowing down through the filthy coal sacks, Churchill made himself a nest low down in the load, leaving just a small gap to make sure he could breathe. He slept fitfully, but came awake as the cars juddered to a halt. He heard Boer voices shouting as the men inspected the load in each railcar. He heard a couple of sacks being heaved to one side, and then blessed silence until the train juddered forward again.

He pushed his way up out of the sacks and risked peeping over the edge of the car. He saw that the last of the railcars was just passing a small wayside station. It would have been nondescript, but for the two flags that flew there. The Boer flag was at the far end with the Portuguese flag nearest to him. He was over the border.

Safe now, he could relax on top of the coal sacks and enjoy the sunshine. As the train pulled in to Lourenço Marques Churchill jumped down and walked into the town. His filthy clothes gained him a few strange looks before he found his way to the British Consul. The next day he was escorted to the small steamer *Induna* by armed men to prevent any Boers from snatching him back and on this coaster he made his way to Durban.

Chapter 20
A Change Of Plans

McGuire and the Reconnaissance Troop rode wearily back to the British main encampment. The men turned off to find the tents they had left days before while the two officers rode on to Buller's headquarters. As they rode up, Buller came out onto the shaded veranda and watched them dismount.

They saluted as they walked towards him. "You look tired, gentlemen. Can I offer you a brandy and soda as a remedy?"

"You can, sir, you surely can," Rogers said. "My throat feels like half the dust in Africa is coating it."

Buller smiled and waved them forward. "Come through into my office and tell me what your visit revealed, while I get my batman to bring us all a drink."

Once their drinks had arrived Rogers and McGuire briefed the general on their findings. They showed him the new map that Connolly had drawn up and told him about the obstructions below the water of the drift.

"Clever. A good thing you found out about the barbed wire. I can't afford to lose any cavalry making a crossing. I have little enough as it is. So your reconnaissance has been valuable, even though my plans have changed. We are not going to cross at Potgieter's Drift. I have decided to make a more direct approach to Colenso. There are a number of other drifts we will be using. McGuire, can you get your men down to them to deal with any wire that has been strung across them, once Captain Rogers has made his wire cutters?"

"Certainly, sir. If you can give me a couple of days to find it all."

Buller nodded. "Good man. I'm still getting the army ready to move, so you'll have your time."

"We'll start as soon as we have the cutters then."

Rogers stood up. "If there's nothing else for me, sir, I'll trot along to the workshop and get them started on making them."

As he left the room Buller turned to McGuire. "Are your men fit for this task? They've had quite a ride over the last few days."

"A good night's sleep tonight and a slow day tomorrow will have them ready to start as soon as it gets dark."

"Then let me show you on your own map."

At the table Buller rested his finger on the river. "We must cross the Tugela and, as you know, I have a number of options. I intend to make a demonstration towards Colenso to get the Boers' attention and hopefully to get them to move men to meet it. Then, I intend to throw a force across the river at Bridle Drift, there. The intelligence people tell me that the enemy has his defences set back from the river there, so that we can form up before advancing. I then intend to have that force swing around to the east to roll up the Boers as they move."

"So where would you like me, sir?" McGuire asked.

"Two places. I want you to quietly reconnoitre Bridle Drift for me. Clear any obstructions that you can and confirm the intelligence report. Next, I want you to go to Punt Drift. Make sure you are seen by the Boers. I want them to think that is where we are looking. They aren't stupid, so they must know we will be looking for alternatives."

McGuire stood and looked down at the crude map with the believed Boer positions marked. He ran his finger along the side of his nose as he considered the problem. He looked up to see the General watching him quietly.

"Do you need more men?"

McGuire shook his head. "No, thank you, sir. It's tricky enough to control even my small troop in the dark and I know I can trust them. New men would be an encumbrance, I'm afraid."

"Well then, good luck and report back to me the morning after, to tell me what you see."

McGuire saluted and left the room still thinking through the task he had been given. He knew his men were up to the job, but he also knew there were serious risks. He turned and walked to his horse before mounting up and riding slowly through the lines to where he had been billeted.

Chapter 21
Night Reconnaissance

"Right, are we all clear on what we have to do tonight?" McGuire looked around at his men and saw them all nod. "Just the same, I'm going to tell you again. Sergeant Donnelly's party at the Bridle Drift must be silent and make sure you are not seen. My group with Sergeant Parks is going to make noise to attract the Boers' attention. Once the shooting starts, which I'm sure it will, we get the hell out of there. All clear?"

Once again he saw the men nodding and two or three smiled. Sergeant Donnelly stepped up and ordered his men to mount up before turning to McGuire.

"Don't worry, sir, they know their business. They'll be fine."

"From your mouth to God's ears. Let's hope so. This is hellish risky and I don't want to lose any of them. We've come too far together."

Donnelly nodded. "They know that. That's why we're the best damned small unit in the army. Listen, sir, why don't you let me take the Punt Drift? We can't afford to have you getting hit."

McGuire chuckled quietly. "Thank you for the offer. Trying to save my life again, eh? But no, the risky one is my place. You just make sure you don't go too far forward when you are scouting the Boer positions."

"I had to ask, sir. Good luck."

"And you. Now you'd better get going. You've got a decent walk to get to the river after you leave the horses."

McGuire watched the first party ride away towards the west to get to the Bridle Drift before he turned to the rest of his men, who were waiting patiently. "All ready, Sergeant Parks?"

"Ready as we'll ever be, sir."

As he mounted McGuire thought about the man Parks had been when he first joined the reconnaissance troop. A farm boy who should never have been in the army, he'd cried when the drill sergeants screamed at him. Now, though, there was a calm courage about him and his men were confident he would not let them down. The campaign in the deserts of the Sudan had changed him, even more than it had changed the rest of the troop.

They rode towards the area known as the loop until they came to the donga where the horses were to be picketed. Dismounting, they hammered the pegs into the unforgiving earth and tied the reins to them. They waited until it was fully dark before they started the walk to the drift. Ahead of them McGuire could see the cooking fires of the small African village close to the river. He knew that the drift would be somewhere close to that.

As they neared the village a couple of dogs barked, but nobody came to investigate and they passed by. The slope down the river bank showed where the drift was and the men stripped down to just trousers and boots before they entered the water. Feeling forward with their feet, they moved slowly towards the far bank. Parks was the first to feel the barbed wire under the surface and ducked down to cut through it. He surfaced with the two ends in his hands and the cutters held in his teeth. Men either side of him took hold of the jagged wire and pulled it away to the sides.

They moved on, with the water reaching chest deep in places. Each time they found a wire they cut through it and dragged it away from the path any following troops might use. Reaching the far bank, McGuire climbed slowly until his head was above the edge. He could see no sentry fires to tell him where the Boers might be. He waited until he heard the low voices of the enemy in their hidden rifle pits. They were close, very close, and he slipped back down the slope to the river's edge.

"Move back across the river," McGuire hissed.

He waited until he could see by the light of the thin moon that all of the men were on the move before he entered the water to follow them. He caught up with them as they struggled back into their tunics on the south bank of the river and picked up their equipment.

"You want the noise now, sir?" Sergeant Parks asked.

"Not yet. Just by that village up there I saw a stone wall. If we get behind that before we annoy Brother Boer we should get away without any casualties if we're lucky."

The men scrambled up the last of the river bank and took up positions behind the wall. McGuire could see their teeth reflecting the light as they grinned. By God, he was proud of these men.

"Corporal Fine, will you do the honours?"

"Certainly, sir, my pleasure."

Fine lifted his rifle and cocked it before firing a single shot into the air. Before the echo died McGuire shouted at him.

"Who the hell fired that shot? Sergeant, take that man's name and take that bloody rifle off him."

Parks played his part. "Right, you miserable creatures, who fired that?"

Before they had a chance to play out the rest of the pantomime the first rifle shots cracked over their heads. As the firing continued, they were glad of the stone wall when the rounds struck it and whined off into the night. The fire increased and McGuire could tell it was coming at them from three directions. They had certainly stirred up a hornets' nest. He guessed the sentries had been dozing and were firing in alarm.

The fire slackened and McGuire could hear someone with the voice of authority ordering the Boers to cease fire. They waited for an hour behind the wall to let the Boers settle down again before they slipped silently away from the river and made it back to their horses. They sat around the donga, then one of the men lit a fire to brew tea while they waited for Donnelly's party to join them. Just before dawn they heard the horses coming along the dry watercourse and Donnelly's men dropped from their saddles to sit by the fire for their tea.

"Any problems, Sergeant?"

Donnelly sat down heavily next to McGuire. "No, sir. We thought the Boers had seen us when they opened fire, but it was you they were aiming at. Any of the lads get hit?"

McGuire took a mouthful of tea. "No, we got away with it this time. As soon as it's light we'll ride back and I can report to the General. I take it the Boer positions were where the intelligence report said they were?"

"They are, and damned difficult to see as well. If they hadn't started yelling when the shooting started over your way we might have missed them."

"A good night's work. We'll let the men sleep when we get back to the camp, but for now I think it's light enough for us to make a move out of here."

Chapter 22
The Battle of Colenso (The Loop)

"Captain McGuire. To me, if you please."

McGuire rode forward and dismounted next to General Buller as he stood on the rise that had been named Gun Hill. "Sir?"

"You've been down to the river. Does it seem to you that the column General Hart is leading is marching in the right direction?"

McGuire raised his field glasses and scanned the ground towards the Tugela. He could clearly see the close-packed khaki column marching north towards the river. He swung left and right to check the landmarks he knew from his previous reconnaissance.

"It depends, sir. Unless you have changed the orders they appear to be heading too far to the east. Bridle Drift is over to the left there. They seem to be marching into the loop of the river and towards the Punt Drift."

"Your opinion from being down there, Captain?"

McGuire cleared his throat. "I don't like to criticize a senior officer, sir, but that looks to me like they are walking into a trap of their own making. As they get deep into the loop there will be riflemen on three sides of them and damned little cover on that flat ground."

Buller looked again through his binoculars. "I thought so too. Is your horse fresh?"

"Yes, sir."

"Very well then. I want you to ride down to that column, find the commander and, with my compliments, tell him he is off course. Don't delay. The further they get into that loop the more risk of casualties."

McGuire saluted and flung himself into the saddle. He hauled his horse's head around and dug in with his heels. The animal responded well and they cantered down the slope towards the marching column. As they neared the rear ranks he kicked the horse into a gallop to overtake them and reach the commander.

At the head of the column he reined in the horse next to the tall, aristocratic Hart and saluted.

"Good morning, sir. General Buller's compliments and he is concerned that you are marching in the wrong direction. Your objective, Bridle Drift, is over to the west."

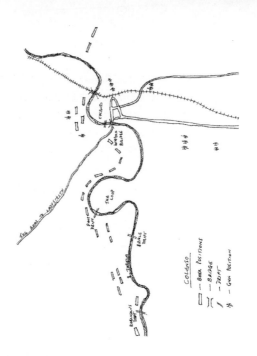

The tall man's head came around slowly and he looked down his nose at the panting Captain. "I know exactly where I am and you are incorrect. Rather than rely on a scruffy, hand-drawn map, I have obtained the services of an African guide who actually lives here."

McGuire swallowed. "With respect, sir, it was my troop that drew that map and it is accurate, I assure you. I think your African must be confused."

The commander looked forward to where the native guide waited. "I shall rely on local knowledge. You may return to General Buller and assure him that everything is under control. I shall take the objective he has given me without fail."

"Sir, I must insist. You are in the wrong place and very shortly you are going to find that you have Boers in concealed rifle pits on three sides of you. With your men marching in close column of fours you are a dream target for modern rifles."

"What is your name, Captain?"

"McGuire, sir. Royal Irish Fusiliers, Reconnaissance Troop."

The commander nodded. "Yes, I've heard about you. Well, sir, you are insolent and we will speak more of this when the battle is over. A mere Captain does not advise me on how to handle my troops. I have been controlling soldiers since before you even joined the army and I think I know my business by now. A column of fours avoids straggling and gives the men confidence. Now get out of my way. I have a battle to win."

McGuire opened his mouth to speak, then thought better of it. This officer was not going to listen, that was clear to him. He saluted and turned his horse back towards Gun Hill. As he reached the slope up to the General's position he heard the crackle of rifle fire beginning behind him. He reined in and turned to look back the way he had come. Even at this distance he could see that men were down and the rest were scattering. He couldn't believe it; the officers were driving the men back into their densely packed column and continuing to advance. Madness, utter madness.

He rode back to General Buller and dismounted. "I'm sorry, sir, the column commander has a native guide and has chosen to trust him rather than the map or my information."

Buller said nothing, but raised his field glasses and watched the disaster starting to unfold.

Major General Hart looked back at the four battalions of the Irish Brigade following him. They were marching in a soldierly fashion in column of fours as he had ordered. The Dublin Fusiliers had tried to move into open order, but he had soon put a stop to that nonsense.

He marched onwards at the head of his column, with the native guide showing him the way to the drift. He was still seething about the galloper who had tried to tell him how to handle his men. An insolent officer could not be tolerated and he would have to be dealt with later. Hart could hardly believe what the man had tried to do.

From somewhere in front of him he heard the thump of an artillery shell being fired and almost immediately the whistle of an approaching shell. The howitzer shell plunged into the ground behind, just ahead of the Dublins. The second landed behind the brigade. If that was the worst they could do it was laughable. The third shell just missed the Connaught Rangers, but the fourth landed right in amongst that battalion, throwing men to the ground with blood, equipment and body parts scattered in all directions.

At that moment, a perfect storm of rifle fire from the hidden Boers lashed the column. Hart looked for the native guide, but he had vanished as soon as the firing started. The four thousand men now massed in the salient of the loop threw themselves to the ground. Here and there officers managed to get small groups to their feet to make short advances, but in the hail of Mauser bullets they soon threw themselves down again.

In the loop of the river the accurate and concentrated fire from the Boers' Mauser rifles was chopping men down left and right. With them packed so closely together the Boers hardly had to aim to hit the soldiers in front of them.

Officers shouted encouragement, but order and cohesion had been lost. The Boers in their rifle pits, using smokeless ammunition, were invisible to the troops and gave them nothing to fire at. Nobody now knew where the drift was and there was confusion everywhere.

To his credit, Hart displayed remarkable courage walking among his men trying to get them to move forward. Some rose to follow him, but again were driven to the ground by accurate fire from their hidden enemy.

Away to the left the Inniskillings were working their way towards the proper objective of Bridle Drift. Had they reached it and crossed they might have relieved the pressure on the rest of the Brigade. Hart saw what they were doing and ordered them to move back into the loop. It was his last major mistake: the brigade was now trapped, and the ambush was turning rapidly into a disaster for the British.

The Boer artillery continued to pound the flat area inside the loop. They did little damage, but they kept the men lying flat and unable to move forward or backwards. The British artillery tried to pound the Boer positions, but their lyddite shells were ineffective against dispersed troops as the blast was too concentrated.

In the face of the effective Boer fire, the troops could only stay where they were under the blazing African sun. Their canteens had been left behind with the wagons to lighten their load and now the need for water was becoming a serious problem.

Chapter 23
The Battle of Colenso (The Artillery)

Standing on Gun Hill with his staff, General Buller watched the debacle of Hart's column through his field glasses. He lowered them as a staff officer touched his arm.

"What is it?"

The staff officer pointed. "To the right, sir. The artillery are moving into position by Colenso village."

Buller raised his field glasses again and sucked air between his teeth. "Bring me the large telescope."

As the staff officer moved quickly to comply, Buller turned back to the Colonel who stood at the other side of him. "Remind me, Colonel, did I or did I not make it clear the guns were not to go too far forward and were to ensure they had infantry support?"

The Colonel nodded. "You were very clear on that, sir, and Colonel Long confirmed your order."

"Then what the hell is that bloody man Long doing down there? And where the devil is his infantry support?"

Around Buller the staff officers raised their binoculars and swung to find the guns advancing on Colenso. Twelve fifteen pounders, each drawn by a team of six horses, were cantering forward in column. Some way behind them the slower naval guns were moving forward. As they watched the field guns swung around and the men jumped down from the ammunition limbers to uncouple the guns. In moments, the twelve guns were lined up with their crews adopting the approved position around them.

Buller lowered his telescope. "Dear God, what is Long thinking? He's acting like this is a demonstration in Hyde Park."

Buller was not alone in his amazement. Across the Tugela, Louis Botha, the Boer commander, lay in his concealed trench and watched the guns wheel into line, well within range of his massed Mauser rifles. As he had ordered, his men spread out around the veldt in their trenches held their fire. He looked left and right to try and work out how the British were trying to trap him. Surely having these guns move so close was bait to tempt him into some rash action?

The British opened fire and Botha watched as the officers strode behind the gun line to ensure that the firing was at regular intervals. The shells howled overhead, aiming for the empty trenches the Boers had created further back and up the sides of the kopjes. Botha's plan was working. He licked his dry lips and rolled to one side to give the order to open fire. In seconds, the whole of the Boer commando was pouring carefully aimed rifle fire into the artillery position in front of them.

One of the first to fall was Colonel Long, shot through the liver. The second-in-command was hit seconds later, as were other officers. The men manning the guns continued to fire in a slow methodical way as they had been taught during training on the Aldershot heath. Men fell and ammunition was expended. The second line of ammunition wagons were brought forward to just behind the gun line. Drivers fell as they, too, came into range of the deadly rifle fire.

The gunners could take no more and they retreated on foot, dragging their wounded with them. They retired to the shelter of a deep donga they had crossed as they advanced, and took cover. The twelve artillery pieces stood in a neat row out on the open veldt with the ammunition wagons behind them. The firing from the invisible Boer trenches died away and the guns stood alone and silent.

On both sides of the river the opposing commanders could hardly credit what had just happened. Botha knew he could not advance with the river in front of him and remained where he was. On Gun Hill, Buller stood aghast at the sight of the guns out on the plain.

"Captain McGuire, is your troop ready to ride?"

"Always, sir. What do you need?"

"I need your band of marksmen down there to help me get those guns back. Mount up and follow me."

Buller strode to his horse, followed by some of his staff, and mounted. He hauled the head of the horse around and set off down the slope at a brisk canter. McGuire ran to his troop, who were waiting behind the hill. In seconds, they were mounted and chasing after the General.

Sergeant Donnelly rode alongside McGuire as they closed on the General's party. "Didn't expect to see a General riding towards the Boers like this today."

McGuire looked over his shoulder at the tough soldier. "That's why the troops like him so well. The man has courage."

"I hope he knows what he's doing and we don't get caught the way the gunners did."

"If anyone knows his business, it's Buller. More than you can say for some of his senior officers, though."

They caught up with the General just as he rode down into the deep donga. As they came to where the shattered gunners were sheltering, Buller dismounted and walked between them, stopping to talk to the men as he did so. He knelt beside the wounded men and touched them to reassure them. Then he walked forward to the lip of the donga and lay down to observe the position.

Before him the guns stood in a forlorn line. Horses were still in their traces, some alive and some dead, and some thrashing the ground in pain. Even from here he could see no sign of the concealed Boer positions. He slid down the slope at the edge of the donga and waved his officers forward.

"Lieutenant, get back from here and find the surgeons. Bring them forward and help these men.

Move now." He stood and walked to where the gunners lay. "Now, lads, will you take a chance to save the guns?"

After a moment one bombardier and six men got up and volunteered. Buller turned to his staff. "Some of you go and help. McGuire, I want your men to give covering fire from here. Don't let any Boer show himself without consequence and keep their heads down. As best you can."

Three staff officers stepped forward, one of them Lieutenant Freddy Roberts, the only son of Field Marshal Roberts. McGuire spread his men out along the edge of the donga as the three officers and the seven gunners got ready for the wild ride to come. He watched to make sure they did not ride forward until his men had opened fire. The last man into the saddle was Freddy Roberts, who grinned at McGuire, then slapped the rump of his horse and yelled for the gunners to follow him.

McGuire spun round as the horses leapt forward. "Open fire! Keep their heads down, even if you can't see the buggers."

The men fired low across the flat veldt in front of them to ensure their rounds would be skimming across the trenches. One of the inexperienced Boers raised his head to see what was going on and a snap shot from Corporal Fine caught him in the forehead and threw him back in a whirl of flying blood and brain tissue. The men paused as the riders thundered across in front of them on their way to the guns.

As they arrived where the guns stood in their neat forlorn row, the gunners leapt from their horses and went to work to cut the dead and dying horses out of the traces. Lieutenant Roberts held the head of a panicking animal while its companions were cut loose. The two live horses from that team were led to the nearest gun and the traces were coupled to it. Then Roberts, and the three men with him, leapt into the saddles and urged the frightened beasts into a run back towards the safety of the donga. The second team was right behind them as they raced back towards Buller.

McGuire was forced to admire their almost suicidal bravery as he urged his men to continue firing. Bullets from the Mausers were throwing up fountains of earth all across the dusty ground and others were flying over the heads of his men with the characteristic crack as they passed. The two teams made it into the donga, but as McGuire looked he saw that two of the gunners and Lieutenant Roberts were missing.

"Cease fire! Three men down. Did anyone see where they fell?"

Corporal Fine pointed out to the right. "One of them went down there, sir. I think it was the Lieutenant. The gunners fell near the guns."

McGuire risked raising his head to look where Fine was pointing. He was right: there was a khaki-clad body lying in the dust. As he watched, McGuire saw the man move. Only wounded, but with all the rounds flying by that would not last long. He tossed his rifle to Fine and set off running along the donga, crossing behind his spread-out men.

Once he was close enough he ran out of the donga and straight to where Roberts lay. He heaved him over his shoulder and staggered back to the shelter of the dry watercourse. Every second he expected to feel the Boers' bullets rip into him, but there was nothing. He realised the enemy had stopped firing and was allowing him to recover the wounded officer.

McGuire laid Roberts down as gently as he was able next to the nearest surgeon and his medical assistant. The doctor glanced down at the young Lieutenant lying in the scrubby grass and shook his head slowly. He looked up at McGuire.

"He's badly hurt. It's going to be touch and go and I need to get him into surgery now if he is to have any chance at all."

McGuire looked around for stretcher-bearers to see two of the Indian 'body snatchers' already running towards him. They laid the stretcher down next to the wounded man and with remarkable compassion lifted him gently onto the dull green canvas of their stretcher. Then they were gone, carrying Roberts away as quickly as they could without hurting him.

Around him McGuire could see another party preparing to race to the guns to try and save more of them. The Boers were ready for them and as they moved they were met by a hail of accurate rifle fire and were forced to recoil into the donga.

General Buller walked through the exhausted men. "That's enough for today, men. We can get more guns, but I need you."

McGuire smiled to himself. No wonder the men loved this old warhorse. No matter what the armchair warriors said, this was an officer who cared for his men.

Chapter 24
The Aftermath

"I expect you're wondering why I didn't send more men forward to recover the guns, Captain?"

"I was surprised, sir," McGuire said.

"I think my staff officers were as well. They don't seem to take the wider view. If I had sent the infantry forward the losses would have been extreme and they would probably have failed. The damned gunners put their guns in an impossible position. If I am to relieve Ladysmith, I cannot afford to destroy my army for the sake of a few guns, even though the armchair warriors in London will curse me for it."

"And are we still going to relieve Ladysmith, sir?"

Buller sighed. "We are. I have my instructions from London. That bloody man White should never have let himself get bottled up in there, but now it has become a matter of honour to get him out."

"I see, sir, and how can I help?"

Buller shifted in his chair before answering. "You made quite a reputation for yourself in the Sudan campaign by sneaking around behind enemy lines. Could you do the same here?"

"Where do you want me to go, sir?" McGuire asked.

"Ladysmith. I get messages from White by heliograph, but if I am to make my plans I need to know the state of the garrison, and frankly, I need to know what state General White is in."

"I'm not sure that I'm the right man to make an assessment of a General, sir."

"Do you want me to send one of my senior staff officers with you?"

McGuire looked around at the staff officers working or idling nearby. "No, thank you, sir. I have more chance of being successful without them."

Buller chuckled. "I have to agree with you. Had I been allowed to choose my own staff it might have been different. There are far too many here who are happy with a desk in the War Office."

"When do you need your answers, sir?"

"That rather depends on you, Captain. How long to get in, how long to make your appraisal and how long to get back out. If you can get me my report as soon as you can without taking excessive risks, that will be fine."

"I'll leave tonight, sir. That way I can be a long way from here before any of the Boer spies see us and I turn towards Ladysmith."

"You think the Boers have spies watching us?"

"They'd be fools if they didn't and I think they have proved they are not foolish."

"Very well, Captain, I wish you luck, and before you go would you find the surgeons and see how Lieutenant Roberts is progressing? I need to write to his father."

McGuire stood and saluted before walking through the staff officers to his horse. He rode back down the hill towards the lines of white tents where he knew the field hospital had been set up.

As he rode towards the large flag with the Red Cross emblazoned on it, he looked to either side where wounded men from the loop and Colenso were waiting their turn. They seemed to be remarkably cheerful while anticipating the surgeon's knife. As he dismounted and walked towards the largest of the tents he saw arms and legs being tossed into metal bins beside the tent. He stopped an orderly to enquire where he might find the chief surgeon and walked on to find him.

He found the commander of the field hospital sitting on a packing case wearing a blood-spattered apron and with his arms reddened by gore. The man looked up with tired eyes.

"How can I help you, Captain?"

"Sir, I've been sent by General Buller to enquire about Lieutenant Roberts. Do you know where he is?"

The surgeon nodded and stood up wearily. He beckoned for McGuire to follow him and walked slowly to the rear of the main tent. As they came around the corner of the tent McGuire could see lines of blanket-covered mounds, each with a pair of boots protruding from it.

"Roberts is one of those. He was just too badly wounded for us to save him. Please give the General my regrets, but there was nothing we could do."

"Oh God, so many. And Roberts was the Field Marshal's son."

"They were all somebody's son, Captain. The pain is the same, no matter what the rank."

McGuire rode back to where his troop was camped. They were cleaning weapons and restocking their ammunition bandoliers as he arrived. Sergeant Donnelly walked across to meet him as he tied his horse alongside the others.

"You look troubled, sir."

McGuire nodded. "You've known me too long. I've just had to tell General Buller that the Field Marshal's son is dead. However, we have a new task. You and I, along with Corporal Fine, are going to Ladysmith. We have to sneak through the Boer lines and then get back with a report."

Donnelly smiled grimly. "Just like old times in the Sudan then."

"I don't think so. In the Sudan we had a lot of wide-open desert to choose from for our route. I think getting past the Boers will be a little more difficult."

"What about the rest of the men?"

"We'll take them part way with us. We may need them and Sergeant Parks at some point."

Chapter 25
A Chance Encounter

"Are you sure we needed to ride in such a big circle to get here, sir?" Corporal Fine asked.

"If you want to get back to Cairo one day, then yes. The Boer scouts will have seen us leave the army and will have noted the direction we rode in. I'm hoping that our long circuit will have allayed any suspicions."

Corporal Fine did not reply. He trusted McGuire's judgement and hoped he was right this time as well.

"Sergeant Parks, are you clear about your part in this expedition?"

"Yes, sir. I am to keep the troop here out of sight, but to watch for any heliograph signals. If you need a distraction to help you through the lines, then we are it."

"Good. I just hope I don't need you. With just a small amount of luck we should be in and out with the Boers no wiser."

"Be lucky, sir."

McGuire nodded and walked across to where Donnelly and Fine now waited with the horses in the gathering twilight. As he neared them he looked them over once again. With their borrowed Boer clothes and slouch hats they looked the part while riding the captured Boer horses and carrying Mauser rifles. As long as they could keep clear of the patrols they should pass muster from a distance.

"Right then, let's go. Try and ride like a Dutchman and if they see us show no signs of alarm. They must be expecting small patrols to be wandering about."

Donnelly grinned. "We know the drill, sir. Not too much different from doing this in the Sudan."

"Except there we spoke the language. Here we need to avoid contact with the enemy if we possibly can."

They rode out across the veldt towards the Tugela river. They had been told about a drift here to the west of the Potgieter's. Taking that would put them way beyond the normal operating area of the army. Still, they kept watch as they rode through the weak moonlight.

The drift was where they had been told it was and they rode their horses through the tumbling water and up the bank the other side. From here they followed a faint track towards the base of the nearest kopje. They could see no sign of guard fires and on a cold night like this McGuire guessed that was a good sign.

They found a narrow ravine that cut back into the hillside just as the dawn was breaking and here they set themselves up to sleep through the day, each taking turns to keep watch at the narrow entrance while the others slept or cooked. Fine had seen a patrol of seven men pass by, but over half a mile away and there had been no danger. As dusk came on they saddled the horses and made ready to move closer to their objective.

McGuire led the way out of the steep-sided ravine and onto the level ground that ran around the base of the kopje. They rode slowly to avoid the sound of hoofbeats or jangling harnesses. After half a mile McGuire reined in and behind him his men did the same. He stood in the stirrups to confirm what he had seen and there, just beyond the shoulder of the hill, was a small fire. He dismounted and handed the reins to Donnelly before walking carefully forward to take a look at the enemy sentry.

McGuire dropped to his belly and crawled the last few yards to peer over the low ridge at the man sitting by the fire. The firelight reflected off the blade of the spear that lay by the man's side and showed that his skin was black. McGuire could see only the one person and the small herd of cattle standing patiently to one side.

Making his mind up, McGuire stood up and walked over the ridge and down towards the fire. As he went he eased the Webley revolver hidden under his jacket. He kicked over a pebble and the man by the fire spun round with the spear in his hands.

"Don't worry, I'm not here to rob you. I thought a weary traveller might share your fire."

The tall, broad-shouldered man by the fire lowered the spear and stepped backward behind the fire. "Come then and sit. Do the others come forward as well, baas?"

"What others?"

The man chuckled. "The ones hiding in the dark and holding your horses."

"You have good ears, my friend. Can I bring them to your fire?"

The man nodded and waited while McGuire called his companions forward. The two men walked out of the night leading the three horses. They tied the reins to a thorn bush and came to sit by the fire.

"Will you share my food? It is not much."

McGuire looked at the blackened pot hanging over the flames. "What are you cooking?"

"Sadsa. You call it mealie meal. It is better with the sauce we call sitchevu, but I do not have any this night."

"Maybe we can share our food with you. We have the food the English eat. They call it bully beef."

The black man looked at the three men across the fire from him in turn. "You say 'they' eat it, but you are not Afrikaners. Are you uitlanders?"

"What are uitlanders?"

"They are the ones who come across the sea to work in the mines and take the gold. If you do not know this then you must be the English who fight the Afrikaners."

McGuire thought for a moment, then reached forward and took the can of ration meat that Fine held out for him. He opened it as he thought, and then passed it across to the herdsman.

"So, my friend, you know of the war. Have you decided who you want to win?"

"This is a white man's war. The Africans will gain nothing but more misery from it. Already the Afrikaners are forcing my people to work for their war. We dig holes in the ground for them to fight from and some of us are sent to collect food and bring it for them, like these beasts."

"So you work for the Boers? Yet you speak our language well."

"I was taught by the missionaries near the town you call Ladysmith. Then the ones you call the Boers came and they make us work."

"What is your name, my friend?"

"My name is difficult for white men, so the missionaries called me Samuel. It is a name from their holy book."

"Well, Samuel, I am McGuire and this one is Fine. The one at the end is Donnelly. Shall we share our food now?"

They ate in silence and McGuire was amused to see the grimaces on the faces of his men as they tried the mealie meal. It definitely needed something to make it good to eat. Samuel, on the other hand, seemed to relish the bully beef.

"Samuel, you must know this country well?"

"It is my home. I know every rock and donga."

"We need to get into Ladysmith to speak to the soldiers there. Are there many Boers between here and there?"

"Many, and they watch the roads day and night."

"Is there a way they do not know? Where they do not watch?"

Samuel nodded. "There is a way."

"Samuel, will you show us that way to meet with our friends?"

"If the Afrikaners catch us they will whip me till I die. They have the big whips called sjambok. I do not want to die that way."

"And we have rifles. We can protect you."

"Why would you do that? I am only a black man. You do not care about me."

McGuire sat back and looked the African in the eye. "These men will tell you if I speak the truth. We fought in a war in the deserts of the north and people of that land fought alongside us. They were our brothers. If you work with us you become our brother and we eat, sleep and die together."

Samuel looked at Corporal Fine, who nodded, and then he turned to Donnelly. The big man from Belfast put down the tin plate he held and looked at the African across the fire.

"He speaks the truth. I swear by my God and all that is holy."

"You swear a powerful oath. I will lead you past the Afrikaners and into the town. Then what will you do?"

"We will speak to the people there, so that we may take information back to the army. Then we will ask you to lead us safely out again."

"And then?"

"And then I will give you this gold coin."

Chapter 26
Into Ladysmith

True to his word, Samuel led them by a roundabout route towards the town. As they got closer they found a hidden valley with a small spring tricking down the rock walls where they left the horses. From here they would cross the last two miles on foot through the encircling Boer lines.

The route that Samuel followed took them close enough to Boer watch fires that they could hear the sentries speaking to each other in low tones. Once they had to throw themselves to the ground and lie as still as rocks while one of the sentries walked from the fire to relieve himself against a bush. With his night vision affected by looking into the flickering watch fire, he did not see the four men stretched out on the veldt.

As they came closer to the British defence lines Samuel cautioned them to be quieter yet. The sentries here might be more alert and were certain to be more nervous. They crawled closer until McGuire saw the glow of a pipe beside a rock. He left his men behind and crawled closer before he spoke quietly.

"Sentry. You really shouldn't be smoking on watch."

The pipe dropped to the ground and McGuire heard the sound of the rifle bolt as the sentry chambered a round.

"Halt! Who goes there?"

"Captain McGuire, Royal Irish Fusiliers. Call your guard commander and do it quietly."

"Stay where you are or I fire. Corporal, Corporal Beatty to me."

McGuire lay still and heard the sound of studded army boots moving across the rocky ground. A new voice spoke from the darkness.

"Who goes there?"

"Captain McGuire, Royal Irish Fusiliers and three men. Come from General Buller's headquarters with a message for General White."

There was a pause. "Advance one and be recognised. Nobody else moves."

"That's fine, we know the drill. I'm coming forward now."

McGuire stood up and moved carefully forward. He reached the guard position and stopped.

"Your alertness does you credit, Corporal. As I said, I am Captain McGuire."

"Dressed like that you don't look like any Captain I know."

"How would you like me to dress to try and come through enemy lines? Maybe I should have brought a brass band and marched through? Now call the duty officer and let's get on. My men are at risk while you think about it."

The Corporal stiffened. "Very good, sir. If you follow me, I'll take you to my officer. He's inside the redoubt over here."

The young officer proved easier to convince than the Corporal and McGuire's men were allowed inside the siege lines. As they walked out of the dark the officer looked oddly at McGuire.

"The Kaffir is with you? He'll need to stay here. Can't have him wandering about in the town."

"Lieutenant, the Kaffir, as you call him, is with me. He guided us through the Boer lines and I have sworn he will be protected. He stays with me and my men. Now give me a guide to take me to General White's headquarters."

As they walked along with the guide that the Lieutenant had provided, McGuire took the opportunity to begin his mission. "So then, what's it been like during the siege?"

"Boring, sir. Damned boring. And the short rations don't make it any better."

"Why boring?"

"Nothing to do, sir. We sit around each day and wait for the Boer Long Toms to send a shell or two into us. They don't hit much and we can see them firing, so we have time to get into the shelter trenches."

"And the rations?"

"We've been on half rations for a while now and a week ago that was cut back again. They say we'll be eating the cavalry horses soon."

McGuire looked around as he walked. There did not seem to have been many defences constructed. That seemed strange given the number of Boers surrounding them.

"Have the Boers attacked?"

"Not really, sir. Once in a while a patrol comes too close and we fire a couple of rounds at them. Most of the time we just sit and look out while they look in. So there's just the Boer artillery to worry about. They usually stop when the naval guns fire back."

The building they were approaching had a sentry outside and a large flag on the pole outside it.

"Here's the headquarters, sir. I'll leave you now, if I may? I need to get back to my platoon or they'll eat my rations."

"Dismissed and thank you. We'll find our way from here."

The guide saluted and hurried back the way they had come. McGuire watched him go before he spoke.

"Well, you two. What did you make of that?"

"Truthfully," Donnelly said, "I was surprised at the way he spoke. They seem to have given up trying. It's almost as if they don't care. Maybe he's just like that, but if the rest of the garrison feel the same they are not going to be a lot of use."

Fine nodded in agreement. "And the guard post was sloppy. Only one man on watch and he wasn't alert. The duty officer fast asleep on the front line. Doesn't look too clever to me either, sir."

"No, I agree, but I'll see what the headquarters officers are like. Maybe that's just a poor example we've seen. You three stay around here and I'll see if the General is awake yet."

McGuire walked towards the sentry, who lowered his rifle so that the bayonet pointed at McGuire's chest. "And where do you think you're going, mate?"

McGuire sighed. "I'm Captain McGuire of the Royal Irish Fusiliers and I'm here to bring General White a message from General Buller."

The sentry looked McGuire up and down, from his floppy Boer bush hat to his scruffy riding boots and then smiled. "Yes, and I'm the Queen of Sheba. Now get on your way. The General has more important things to do than talk to the likes of you."

"Very well, call the duty officer and I'll explain to him."

"I've told you once. Be on your way before I get angry."

McGuire considered his options before stepping forward towards the path that led into the headquarters building. The sentry growled and lunged forward with his bayonet-tipped rifle. McGuire flipped his left arm up, knocking the rifle to one side, then took a pace forward and gripped the weapon with his right hand before twisting it out of the startled soldier's grasp. In less than a second he had spun the rifle over and the bayonet was up under the sentry's chin.

"Now, shall we start again? My name is Captain McGuire. I am in disguise to allow me to travel through the Boer lines and you are going to call the duty officer."

The shaken man licked his lips. "Yes, sir. If you wait here I'll go and get him for you."

"That's very good of you. I'll keep hold of your rifle for you, shall I?"

As the soldier ran up the pathway McGuire inspected the rifle. The rear sight had dirt in it and the foresight had rust on it. He slid open the bolt and peered down the barrel. That, too, was dirty. No regiment in the military that was ready to fight would have allowed such sloppiness. He handed the rifle to Donnelly as he heard the footsteps coming down the path towards him.

"Who the hell are you and why have you got my sentry's rifle?"

"And you are?"

"Lieutenant Maltravers. Duty officer of the day."

"Well, Lieutenant, as I told your sentry, I am Captain McGuire, come from General Buller to see General White. As you can see, I and my men are in disguise to let us traverse the Boer lines. It has been a long night and is likely to be a longer day, so I would appreciate it if you people would stop playing silly beggars and let me pass."

The Lieutenant seemed confused. He ran his finger around inside the grubby collar of his shirt before speaking. "Very well, sir, if you would come with me I will see what I can do. Who are these other people?"

"They are my men and would appreciate a place to wait in the shade with a cool glass of water."

"Of course. Bring them this way. Not the Kaffir, though."

"Lieutenant, these are all my men and they stay together. Do you understand me?"

"Indeed, sir. Please bring them all this way."

Donnelly suppressed a smile as the three men followed McGuire up the path. He stopped and turned back to the sentry before thrusting the rifle into his hands.

"And you get that bloody rifle cleaned. You're a damned disgrace."

As they approached the veranda of the white-painted building, an officer wearing the red collar tabs of the staff came out of the door and stretched. He looked at McGuire following the young officer towards him and smiled.

"McGuire! My dear fellow. I wasn't expecting to see you today."

McGuire raised a hand in greeting. "Good morning, Major Turner. Nice to see you again."

Turner shook McGuire's hand. "We thought we'd lost you when you didn't come back from the reconnaissance. Where on earth have you been?"

"My men and I couldn't get back in through the Boers. They were thicker than fleas on a tinker's dog. We rode east and joined up with the relief force under General Buller."

"And why are you back here?"

"I need to speak to General White so that I can report back to Buller on the real situation in Ladysmith."

At that moment the bugles blew one after the other. Turner took McGuire by the elbow and steered him towards a trench carved in the lawn of the house.

"Long Tom must have fired. The bugles give us time to take cover, but in truth there is little danger."

McGuire dropped down into the trench next to Turner. "Long Tom?"

"It's one of the Boer 'Le Creusot' guns. Mounted on top of one of the kopjes. Has a far longer range than most of our field pieces, but luckily the naval gun can reach it. We'll pop off a shell or two in reply and then we settle down again. Here it comes."

McGuire listened to the whistle of the shell as it approached, then heard the explosion as it impacted. "Is that it?"

"Usually, unless the Boers are feeling frisky, and then we might get three or four shells in the day. None on Sunday, of course. The Boers don't like to fight on the Sabbath. Shall we go and see where it landed and then we'll try and get you in to see the General?"

Chapter 27
Long Tom

McGuire came back out into the sunshine and stood on the veranda. The interview with General White had been depressing. The man seemed to have aged and lost any fire he might have once had in his belly. He was waiting for relief by Buller, but saw no way he could sortie from Ladysmith to help.

Major Turner had been waiting for him. "So now you've seen the General, what next?"

McGuire put his slouch hat back on and looked around him. "Walk with me, would you?"

They walked through the neat gardens until they were well clear of the headquarters building and could not be overheard. McGuire looked around again before he spoke.

"Is he always like that?"

"Like what, precisely?"

McGuire searched for the right word. "Beaten. He seems to ooze hopelessness. He has no plans to help Buller and no plans for the defence, except for the troops to sit in their positions and wait."

Turner nodded sadly. "Beaten? A good word for it, I think, and it seems to be getting worse, if anything. A number of officers have put forward plans to sortie against the Boers to disrupt their lines, but all have been turned down."

"I think I may have changed that a little. He showed me a plan that had been put forward to send a party to sabotage the Boer gun. What did you call it – 'Long Tom'? I volunteered to join the attack with my two men as scouts. He said he would consider my offer."

"I hope he accepts your support. Sitting here and taking it from the enemy is sapping the troops' morale. A knock back would cheer them up. It might make them forget the short rations for a while."

"What about the rest of the officers? Are they in a better frame of mind?"

"It varies. Some are active, keeping their men on their toes and improving defences. Others seem to have sunk into the same sort of lethargy as the General. The main worry is that the lethargy will spread as time goes on."

McGuire looked around to see where his men were waiting. "I think I'd better get on with my visit. I'll take a walk round the garrison ready to report back to General Buller."

"Good," Turner said. "It will cheer the men to know that Buller has sent someone in to look them over. Now this evening you must come and dine with me. We're having horsemeat again. You can tell me what happened at Colenso. We only got the briefest of messages over the heliograph. And then, my friend, you can join the sortie we are planning later tonight? I think you might rather enjoy it."

* * *

Samuel reined his horse in and dropped from the saddle. "This is close enough, baas. From here we walk or they will hear us."

McGuire dropped down next to his own horse and looked up at the looming Lombard's Kop. He could see the glow of a Boer watch fire halfway up the slope, where he knew the guns they were going to attack must be located. If Samuel was right, the fire was set behind a thick wall of sandbags and the watchmen made a habit of hunkering down around it. Their overconfidence would work in favour of the British attackers.

Samuel moved forward into the darkness to check around while McGuire and his men waited for the soldiers of the Imperial Light Horse and the Natal Carbineers to reach them. The horses came silently out of the night, with sacking around their hooves to deaden any sound. As the soldiers reached the small scouting party they dismounted and grouped into their troops.

Samuel came back and his broad smile showed that the Boers were where they were expected to be. The African turned around and led the way silently back up the hill towards the gun position. The attack got to within twenty yards of the sandbagged emplacement and then halted at a signal from McGuire. The men spread out to give themselves room to fire if they needed to.

General Hunter came forward and crouched down next to McGuire. "What do you see?"

"The fire is on the other side of the sandbags. You can see the glow. Nobody has seen us, so they must be sitting around it as my man predicted. The surprise is yours, General."

"So it is. Well, here goes nothing. Fix bayonets and charge the buggers!"

The troopers rose up and dashed forward yelling. The threat of bayonets was enough for the Boer sentries and they made a rapid retreat up the hillside with around half the troopers still chasing them. The two artillerymen they had brought with them ran to the guns and started to remove the breech blocks while the engineers attached gun cotton charges to strategic places.

As McGuire stood and watched the troops around him, Samuel came out of the dark with a cooking pot in one hand and a spoon in the other. "That Afrikaner is a good cook. You want some, baas?"

McGuire grinned. "No thanks. You enjoy it. You've earned it."

Before the Boers could recover and send a force to protect the guns, the men were brought back together and set off down the slope to their horses. As they got clear they were rewarded by a series of very satisfying explosions from behind them as the guns were blown off their carriages. The men mounted and rode back to Ladysmith in high spirits, carrying the breech blocks as trophies.

As the raiding party rode through the British lines McGuire found himself beside General Hunter once again. "Nicely done, McGuire. Led us right to where I wanted to be."

"Thank you, sir, but do you mind if I ask you a question? I thought the Imperial Light Horse didn't carry bayonets?"

Hunter grinned happily. "They don't, but the Boers don't know that and our Dutch friends are bloody terrified of bayonets."

Chapter 28
Back To The Army

"Right then, Sergeant, time for us to leave. Have you seen enough to have an opinion yet?"

"Yes, sir, but you aren't going to like it."

"Go ahead," McGuire said. "Surprise me."

"Well, sir, judging from most of the men I've spoken to over the last couple of days most of the troops are still ready to fight. They're weak from the short rations and they're unfit from sitting on their arses all day long, but they want to have a go at the Boers."

"But?"

Donnelly paused. "This is the bit you won't like. The problem is the officers. Mostly the senior officers on the staff. They seem to have given in and they're really not trying, if you take my meaning."

"I see, and what about you, Corporal Fine? What do you think?"

Fine continued packing the haversack he had before him. "Much the same, in truth, sir. The leadership that should be making sure the Boers are not having it easy is missing."

"I see. I'll take your opinions into account when I report to General Buller, but for now are you ready to move once it gets dark?"

Both men nodded. "Just hope the horses are still there when we get back to them," Fine said.

"They should be. They had water and food and that rope across the ravine entrance should have stopped them wandering."

McGuire looked across to where their African guide was sitting on his haunches, waiting patiently. "What about you, Samuel? Are you ready to lead us to safety?"

"No problem with that, baas. Just need to wait till it gets really dark out there. Moon won't rise till late this night."

The men sat down with Samuel to wait until he judged it safe to make their move. The sentries covering the part of the line where they would cross had been warned to expect them and would not challenge them as they went. Everything they carried had been checked twice to ensure it made no noise, so now all they could do was wait.

"It's time, baas. We go now and we'll be by your horses by moonrise, or dead."

Fine chuckled. "You had to say the last bit? Never mind, Sammy, mate, the Captain has the Devil's own luck. We'll get through."

"I'd rather you called it my incredible soldiering skill than giving the Devil the credit, if you don't mind."

Fine grinned. "Just as long as it works, sir, your skill or 'old hob' makes no difference to me."

McGuire smiled. As long as his men were making jokes he knew they were ready. He only worried when they became serious and quiet.

Samuel led the way into a donga that ran in the direction they needed. As they passed the last sentry the man raised a hand to them in farewell. His outline was just visible against the starlit sky. Two hundred yards farther on the donga petered out and they moved out onto the flat veldt. Samuel dropped to one knee and took a slow look around. McGuire and the others followed suit and waited for him to move on. With a quiet clicking noise at the back of his throat he stood and moved on with the soldiers close behind him.

Away to left and right McGuire could see the small watch fires glowing in the night and knew that somewhere close by the Boer sentries watched. They walked silently forward, aiming for an area of darkness between the fires. As they came abreast of the watchers McGuire was beginning to relax a little when Samuel dropped to his belly. McGuire dropped next to him and the others did the same a few feet behind.

McGuire looked to where Samuel was silently pointing. For a moment he could see nothing and then a patch of darkness moved as the Boer turned to scan across the flat plain. The lay silently waiting for the man to move on, but he seemed to be in no hurry and the moonrise was coming. They could not afford to stay here much longer.

Behind him McGuire felt rather than heard movement. He looked over his shoulder carefully to see Donnelly rising from the ground. The faint stars glinted off the blade in his hand. There was silence for three then four minutes and still the sentry did not move.

Donnelly crept up behind the watcher, then lunged forward. His left hand snaked around and covered the man's mouth while his right hand plunged the knife into the man's back. The blade thrust upwards and then twisted, ripping the organs within the sentry's body. A low grunt in the dark signalled the end of the Boer. The Irishman lowered the body to the ground, catching the rifle as it fell. He hissed and the others rose up to join him.

Samuel stood and looked down at the body of the Boer. The blood that stained his clothes and Donnelly's was black in the feeble light. He raised his head and stared into the Irishman's eyes before he turned silently away.

Moving onwards, they saw no other Boers and reached the ravine where the horses had been left. They were still there and the men moved quickly to calm them before they made any noise. Samuel sat silently while the three soldiers saddled their horses. Then McGuire walked across to him and squatted down.

"Samuel, I owe you thanks. You have kept your promise and led us safely. The work we do is important and you have helped. I promised I would pay you a gold coin and here it is with another to give you my thanks."

The African took the two gold guineas and slipped them into the pouch he wore on a leather cord around his neck. "Baas, the moon will rise soon. You should be gone from here and on the track like the Afrikaners before they see you."

McGuire nodded. "We are ready to go now, but I have a question. Will you go with us?"

"Why would I go with you?"

"Samuel, I lead a special group of men. All of them are good hunters with the rifle. They can fight with their hands and feet. They ride long distances and they are the eyes of the army. It would help us if we could have a man who knows this country better than we do. Will you join us and be one of my soldiers?"

"Will there be more of that meat in the metal box?"

"There will, and more beside."

"Then I will join you."

"We have no horse for you to ride tonight, but you can climb up behind Fine."

"There is no need. I am a Zulu. I can run beside a horse until the horse is tired and must rest. Now we must go or the moon will see us."

Chapter 29
The Interview

"Captain McGuire, the General can see you now, sir."

McGuire rose from the camp chair he had been sitting in for the last two hours and dusted himself down. He straightened his jacket and followed the young subaltern into the shade of the headquarters building. Before being an army headquarters it had been the station master's office and the walls still bore the timetables and railway notices of peacetime.

"I'm sorry you had to wait for so long, sir, but the General has been extremely busy with the senior staff officers."

McGuire grunted. "Another push across the Tugela soon?"

"I really couldn't say, sir, but I rather imagine it will be something like that."

The younger man knocked on the door and then swung it wide for McGuire to walk through. Buller was sitting at his desk with a large map before him as McGuire came to attention and saluted. The General rose and pointed to the two more comfortable chairs by the empty fireplace.

"Sit down, young McGuire. Lieutenant, see if you can make yourself useful and bring us two brandies and soda. I take it you haven't had a brandy for a while?"

McGuire smiled. "No, sir. Supplies in Ladysmith are a little thin on the ground at present."

"I imagine they are. So tell me what condition is the garrison in? Can they be relied on to sortie and support me when the relief gets close enough?"

"I hope you want me to be frank, sir?"

"Of course. Tell me exactly what you found."

They paused as the drinks Buller had ordered were brought in. They waited until the Lieutenant had left the room and closed the door.

"That was quick," McGuire said.

"They know my habits and I enjoy a brandy or two after a long, hard staff meeting. It will have been waiting for me."

Both men took a swallow of the drink before McGuire spoke again. "To be brutally honest with you, sir, I don't think you should rely on any help from the garrison."

"Why not?"

McGuire paused again, balancing his words; making derogatory statements about senior officers was never a good idea.

"The men are weakened by being on short rations for so long. They are short of artillery ammunition and they are physically unfit though being inactive."

"There's more, isn't there?"

"Sadly, there is, sir. Some, and only some, of the senior commanders and staff officers seem to have lost heart. They are not encouraging the troops and they are not allowing offensive action against the besiegers. There was a successful sortie against a Boer gun position while I was there, but that was unusual. It cheered the men immensely."

"And General White?"

McGuire looked down into his drink, then raised his head and looked at Buller. "I'm afraid the General is one of those who have lost heart, sir. I spoke to him and I have to say he seems a beaten man. He knows getting trapped in Ladysmith was his fault and he regrets it hugely. He seldom leaves his headquarters and has not visited the defence lines at all."

"I see. That is what I feared and you have confirmed those fears for me. Nevertheless, I am going to relieve that town, but my plans will need to change now. Unless Lord Roberts overrules me."

"Why would he do that, sir?"

Buller put down his glass. "Ah, you've been out of touch. I have been superseded as the Commander in Chief. After our failure at Colenso, and other failures in the Eastern theatre, Field Marshal Lord Roberts has been appointed to take over. Apparently he is bringing Kitchener out with him as Chief of Staff. I may not be here much longer, it appears."

McGuire shook his head slowly. "I hope we don't lose you, sir. The men have faith in you. More than I have seen for any other senior officer during my time here."

"Thank you, Captain, that is encouraging. Now tell me, in your travels around the army you have seen things go wrong. I get little chance to speak to frontline officers, so give me your opinion. In your opinion, why are we failing against our Boer opponents?"

"Are you sure I am the one to pass comment, sir? Would the officers on your staff not be more qualified?"

"Captain, I have made some enquiries about you. You formed a small elite unit that served Kitchener well during the Sudan campaign. You are unconventional and so are your men. So let me hear your views."

McGuire leaned back in his chair and considered the question. "This army has been successful in small wars all around the empire, but during most of those we were fighting tribesmen who had great courage, but little tactical awareness. The Boers are a different kettle of fish. They see no glory in standing in the firing line and facing our troops. They dig trenches and take cover in them. They use modern magazine-fed rifles that use smokeless propellants. Both of those things make them difficult to see. Our troops, on the other hand, are handled as if this was a field training day in Aldershot. They are marched towards the Boers in close-packed columns of four, so that even the Boers, who are poor shots, can hardly miss. They don't take cover until an officer orders them to. Their courage and discipline are working against them. Then, even when we get close to the Boers, they jump on their horses and ride away to fight another day, while our troops plod on through the dust and heat."

Buller looked over the rim of the glass at McGuire. "And what is your solution?"

"Sir, your senior officers grew up in the days of the single shot rifle like the Martini Henry. They need to understand that the modern magazine rifle can slaughter their men at almost a mile. They need to train their men to fight in open order so they are a more difficult target and, most of all, these men need to be allowed to take cover and return fire."

"You want me to retrain the army in the middle of a war?"

"To be honest, sir, I don't think you have much choice. The losses you are suffering in these attacks will only get worse unless something changes."

"Captain, your thoughts reflect my own. I think I have a lot of work to do and making these changes to an army in the field is not going to be a quick process. Thank you, Captain. You should get some rest now. You look tired."

McGuire stood up and saluted before turning towards the door. He stopped as Buller spoke again.

"My staff tell me you have brought a black man back from Ladysmith and are trying to enlist him. Is that correct?"

"Yes, sir. Samuel is a brave man and a fine tracker. He could be very useful to my reconnaissance troop."

Buller nodded. "Very well. You have my authority to sign him up. If anyone is difficult about it, refer them to me. If nothing else, it should irritate the Boers."

Chapter 30
Thunder

The sound of thunder rolling across the veldt woke McGuire just at dawn. He lay in his field cot and looked at the canvas of his tent roof. No rain yet, at least. Another rumble of thunder and he rolled out of his narrow bed. He tapped his boots and emptied them to make sure no scorpions had made a nest in there during the night before slipping them on and throwing back the tent flaps on his way out.

The sky was a clear blue. No sign of thunder clouds at all. All around him, other officers were standing outside their own tents and shielding their eyes as they stared towards the north-west. McGuire turned and looked out towards Ladysmith. It wasn't thunder. The Boer heavy guns on the hill tops were firing into the town. This wasn't the normal desultory shelling they had become used to. This was something else.

"Fancy a ride across there to have a look, McGuire?"

"You're up and about early, Churchill," McGuire said as the round-faced man walked towards him.

"Can't afford to miss any excitement. My readers expect me to thrill them over their breakfast tables. So then, are you riding with me?"

McGuire shook his head and smiled. "Some of us have to stay around in case the General wants to do something about it. But enjoy your ride."

He watched as Churchill waved a hand and walked away to find his horse. McGuire smiled to himself again. That man was a law unto himself, but he couldn't help liking him.

He ducked back into the tent and slipped on his jacket before buckling the pistol belt around his waist and picking up his rifle. He left the tent again and strode through the lines to where the reconnaissance troop was billeted. By the time he reached them Donnelly and Parks had the men up and dressed. The men were saddling horses as he arrived.

The two Sergeants saluted. "Good morning, sir. Any idea what's happening?" Parks asked.

"Not a clue. Glad to see you've got the men ready to move. I guess we may well get sent forward to see what's what."

Donnelly smiled. "Looking around at all the confusion it may be a while before they get to us. Breakfast, sir?"

"What have we got?"

"Fried bully beef and eggs with some pretty decent bread."

"Where the hell did you find eggs?"

"Macklin went for a walk last night and they followed him home."

McGuire grinned. "Best we eat them before anybody comes looking for them."

* * *

Lieutenant Digby-Jones and his mixed working party of sappers and naval gunners were completing the new gun position in the Ladysmith defence perimeter for one of the long range naval guns as the dawn raced across the veldt. Around them, the escort of soldiers from the Gordon Highlanders were sitting on the hard ground idly chatting and dozing. The night had been strangely silent, with just the odd sound of hymn singing floating across from the Boer positions.

Without warning, bullets started to ping off the stone sanger around the position and fly off into the air with their characteristic whine. Sappers grabbed their rifles and dashed into the sanger. Others who could not find their weapons turned to run.

Digby-Jones drew his heavy Webley revolver and stood his ground as the stampeding men ran towards him. "The first man that passes me, I'll shoot him dead!"

The men slid to a stop, confronted by the young officer, and then returned to the shelter of the sanger or the nearby field gun positions. The Gordons took positions rapidly and promptly opened fire on the Imperial Light Horse, who caused confusion by wearing the same slouch hats as the Boers. The Light Horsemen rapidly withdrew to a small fort they had constructed. Only twenty feet around, this stone-walled fort had been loopholed and provided a sound defence against the attacking Boers.

The rapid fire from the small fort and the gun positions drove the Boers to earth and the attack stalled before descending into a two-way hail of ineffective rifle fire.

Around the perimeter the attacks came hard and fast, supported by the long-range artillery fire. In 'C' sector little effort had been made to develop defences and the Boers took the ridge line as well as getting behind a picket line of the Manchester Regiment and cutting them down in swathes. Elsewhere the line held against the Boer attack, but only with difficulty.

Six companies of the Rifle Brigade formed the mobile reserve and reacted quickly alongside the artillery's field guns to throw the Boers back out of the positions they had overrun. Despite the courage of the riflemen, the cost was heavy and charges by small group of British soldiers led by gallant officers were cut down by the Boer rifles. The power of modern magazine rifles and the inability of British officers to appreciate it was fully demonstrated.

Staff officers finally took control and ordered these suicidal attacks to cease. The lines held and the Boers were slowly driven back until at about 11 a.m. the Boers melted away into dead ground leaving their dead behind them. More British soldiers died in these few short hours than at Colenso and it was believed that Boer losses had been higher.

Ladysmith still held out, but the poor performance by the senior officers was writ large.

Chapter 31
Spy Hill

McGuire had watched the fresh-faced young Lieutenant wending his way through the mass of white bell tents. The fingers pointing his way seemed to indicate the man was looking for him, but he decided to let the younger man find him rather than call him over.

"Are you Captain McGuire, by any chance, sir?"

"I am, by every chance. How can I help you?"

"Sir, General Buller would like to see you. He told me to tell you he has a job that would suit your rogues well. Does that make sense?"

McGuire nodded. "It does indeed. Now when would he like to see me?"

"Well now, sir. It's taken me quite a while to find you, so it might be wise to hurry, sir."

"Really? You've been slow, so now I have to rush to compensate for you. Is that how you see it, Lieutenant? I think you are going to make an ideal staff officer with that mind-set."

"I'm sure I don't know what you mean, sir."

McGuire ignored the hurt feelings of the younger officer as he slung his rifle over his shoulder and set off towards the headquarters building. As he walked he could see that there was something in the wind. All around him men were repacking their equipment, cleaning weapons and collecting ammunition. This had all happened before, of course, but this time it looked more urgent.

As he neared the house doing duty as the headquarters he saw General Warren leaving with his senior staff officers trailing in his wake. He saluted as they went by, then walked up onto the shaded veranda.

"Ah, McGuire, perfect timing. The General can see you now."

McGuire followed the Major into Buller's meeting room to find the General staring down at a large map. The bull-necked Buller looked up as he came in and gave him one of his rare smiles before waving him to a chair on the other side of the briefing table.

"Good morning, sir. You sent for me."

"I did, young McGuire. I've had a message about you from Lord Roberts."

"Unusual for a Field Marshal to bother about a mere Captain, sir. What have I done to annoy him?"

"Nothing, unfortunately. You may not be aware of the bigger picture. Roberts has left me in charge of the West, with instructions to go onto the defensive, while he and Kitchener concentrate on the East and thrust towards Pretoria. I'm not going to do that. I have said I will relieve Ladysmith and by God I'm going to do it. However, it seems that Kitchener remembers your valuable service to him in the Sudan and wants you back with him."

"That's gratifying, sir, but I had hoped to be part of the relief of General White."

Buller nodded. "I'm glad to hear you say that, as it is my intention to retain you here as long as I can. You probably saw General Warren leaving as you arrived?"

"I did, sir. He seemed to be in quite a hurry."

"So he should be. He is going to turn the key in the lock that will give me Ladysmith. I have given him two-thirds of the army and with it he will march west and cross the Tugela at the Trikhardts Drift. The enemy defences there are weak, so he will push through and then take the range of hills. I will then take the rest of the army across Potgieter's and we will form a pincer movement against the Boer positions. Once we command those heights, Ladysmith is ours."

McGuire considered the map on the table. "I see, sir, and what do you need from me?"

"As always, information. I want you to scout the Boer positions and report back to me. Pay particular attention to this hill. It is the key to commanding the whole area."

McGuire looked to where Buller's finger rested on the map. "Spion Kop?"

"That's what the Boers call it. It means Spy Hill and it is well-named. Scout that one in particular. I intend that it will be attacked in the dark and you and your rogues are going to be the guides to make sure the advance does not go astray."

"Very good, sir. Who do I report to?"

"Both to General Warren and myself. He is leading the attack, but I need to know what is going on. And then once we have Ladysmith, you and your men will be heading east to join Kitchener for whatever tasks he has for you."

***

McGuire and his troop rode far to the west and changed into their Boer disguises. A brief reconnaissance across the Tugela had confirmed that the north bank was lightly defended and the troops should have no trouble brushing the defenders aside as they advanced. Still, there were defenders and they were watching the drift carefully.

McGuire hatched a plan to get his troop across without provoking the Boers into firing on them. Just after dawn they rode at the drift as fast as they could. Half a mile behind them a squadron of cavalry emerged from a donga and chased them towards the Boer lines. The reconnaissance troop breasted through the water and rode up the far bank before leaping from their horses and taking cover. As the pursuing British got closer they opened fire, taking care not to actually hit any of the cavalrymen. The British made a great show of reining in and spinning round to ride quickly back into the shelter of the donga.

The troop remounted and cantered away from the river, acknowledging the cheers from the concealed Boer trenches as they rode quickly past. Once clear of the defence lines they found an area of dead ground and stopped to regroup. McGuire looked around at his grinning men. They had thoroughly enjoyed the escapade, but now there was work to do.

The patrol leaders gathered around McGuire and studied the hand-drawn map spread out on the ground. He allocated each one an area to observe and gave himself the problem of Spion Kop. Dressed as Boers they should be able to move around looking like a patrol, provided they never came close enough to the positions to be challenged.

The troop split up and rode away to their allocated areas. McGuire took Corporal Fine's patrol and Samuel to find the best route up to the top of Spion Kop. As they came closer to the hill he could see that the approach was steep and rocky. This was not going to be a quick attack. Just the approach and the climb would take most of a night and the risk of detection by Boer sentries on the hilltop would be ever present.

The patrol rested in the shelter of a deep donga while McGuire and Fine surveyed the climb through field glasses. They knew the Boers had positions on the hill, but could see nothing of them. Their strength and where they had actually constructed their defences were both unknowns.

"Any ideas, Corporal?"

"I don't suppose riding like hell in the other direction would do?"

McGuire chuckled. "I can't see the General being too thrilled with that."

"Maybe not, sir, but that is a bare-arsed climb to attempt in the daylight, with our friends sitting up top somewhere."

"I agree, but in the dark I wonder how much detail we are going to be able to see."

McGuire rolled to one side and looked behind him as Samuel wormed his way between them. "Baas, if you walk up that hill I don't think you walk down again."

"Do you have a better idea?"

The broad smile crossed the African's face. "I think I do. See there, about halfway up?"

"What am I looking at?"

"Goats, baas. Running wild on the hillside. That's just not right. If I get out of this uniform I can go up there and get my goats back."

"Your goats? Oh, I see what you mean. What happens if the Boers see you?"

Samuel smiled again. "They just see a stupid Kaffir chasing his goats. They'll believe that. They like to think my people are stupid."

McGuire paused and thought. "What do you think, Corporal?"

Fine slid back into the shallow donga. "If you're asking me, sir, I think it's bloody risky, but maybe not as risky as us going up there for a look round. Maybe if we set up the patrol here we can cover him in case the Boers rumble what's going on?"

McGuire picked up the binoculars and surveyed the steep slope again. He put them down again and sighed.

"Are you sure you want to do this, Samuel? I would hate to lose you."

"I'll do it, baas. You just tell me what to look for."

McGuire pushed himself down the short slope he was lying on and motioned for the two men to follow him. He led the way into the deep donga where the rest of the patrol waited with the horses. He was pleased to see that the sentry was alert and keeping a careful watch.

"Right then, Samuel. What I need from you is the location of any paths up the hillside and also any places where it would be difficult to get by, so that we can avoid those. Don't go so high up the hill that we can't see you from down here. If the Boers get interested in you we won't do anything unless they try to get you, then we will open fire. Is that all right for you?"

Samuel paused as he was pulling off his uniform jacket and looked at McGuire for a second before he nodded. "I'll find you the way up that hill, baas. Just don't shoot too soon. I can fool the Afrikaners. I've been doing it for years."

***

Samuel walked quickly up the side of Spion Kop. Freed from the heavy army boots he had been given, he felt lighter and more at home. He looked down to where he knew the rest of the patrol were waiting and covering him, but could see no sign of them. Away in the distance he could see the line of the Tugela and the dust clouds being raised by the army as it moved.

Using his spear for support, he pressed on, making sure that his approach sent the goats wandering further up the hill.

"Hey, Kaffir what you doing here?"

Samuel looked up to find two of the Boers looking down from the crest of the hill with their rifles at the ready. "Goats, baas." Samuel pointed. "These devil goats ran off and I need to get them back."

The rifles lowered slightly as the Boers looked down and saw the goats wandering the hillside. "Did you see any khakis down below?"

Samuel pointed out towards the river with his broad-bladed spear. "Over there, baas. Many men and many bullock carts going to cross the river, I think."

"We can see them, you dumb Kaffir. What about nearer to here? Any khaki patrols near here?"

"I didn't see any, baas. Just the big crowd of them over there. I think some of them are across the river. I saw your people moving away from them and going up the hills."

"We know about that. Now get your goats and get out of here unless you want to get shot."

"No, baas, I don't want that. Thank you, baas. I go now."

The two Boers moved back and disappeared from view as Samuel rounded up the goats and sent them trotting down the hill. He smiled as he walked behind them, but didn't forget to look around him as he went. He didn't see McGuire and the rest of the men until he was almost on top of them and then he dropped down into the donga beside them.

"Well, Samuel, is there a way up there?"

"Oh yes, baas. It will be steep for men in these boots and carrying guns, but the way is there."

"Good. We'll go back and join the others now. You sit down with Corporal Connolly and tell him all you have seen, then he will draw it for the rest of the army. You've done well. I thought we were going to lose you when the Boers appeared."

"Oh no, baas. They wouldn't shoot a simple goatherd like me."

Chapter 32
A Change of Plan

Samuel went and found Connolly as soon as the patrols linked up again. McGuire called Parks and Donnelly to him.

"Well then, what progress while we have been split up?"

Parks looked at Donnelly before speaking. "We've given the damned Boers a gift. The army are still crossing the bloody river. I've never seen so many bullock carts and they're moving so slowly it's ridiculous."

"I'm sure General Warren knows what he is doing, Sergeant."

Donnelly grunted. "Are you, sir? When we first moved across here we reckoned there were somewhere around six hundred Boers in these positions. We've been watching their reinforcements pour in ever since. There must be ten times as many now and they've brought their African servants with them to dig trenches further back from the river."

"So what has the army been doing about that?"

"Virtually nothing. They established defensive positions and then sat down to wait for the baggage train to catch them up. There's been some patrolling by the cavalry, but that's about it. They're now being shelled from the hills and our guns don't have the range to reply."

McGuire looked at the huge train of carts struggling across the drift and sighed. "Have you reported the build-up of Boer numbers to the staff?"

"We have, sir. I went when we saw it first and Parks went yesterday. The staff officers seem remarkably unconcerned. Maybe they have a plan we don't know about?"

"Maybe, but General Buller said nothing about it when he tasked me. Never mind, once we get the map Connolly is making with Samuel I'll take it in to General Warren's headquarters and see if I can get some attention to the build-up. I want you to take a copy to General Buller with a report of what is happening here, though I guess he already knows that part."

With the hand-drawn map completed and a copy made, McGuire mounted up and rode for General Warren's headquarters. He found it in a tent close to the Tugela where he could see the bullock carts struggling through the drift. He reported to a staff officer and sat down in the shade of a tree to wait.

He was dozing when a young officer woke him with a touch on the shoulder. "The General can see you now, sir. If you'd follow me, please?"

McGuire climbed to his feet and dusted himself down before slinging the rifle across his back and adjusting his pistol belt. He noticed that the young officer shook his head slightly, no doubt at the scruffy appearance of one about to see a General. McGuire saw the gesture and smiled.

"Don't worry, young man, the dust of the veldt doesn't stick to staff officers. You're in no danger."

Warren and two other officers were waiting as McGuire entered the tent and saluted. "Well, Captain, I hope you are bringing me some good news?"

"I hope so too, sir. As you know I was tasked with reconnoitring the slopes of Spion Kop to confirm whether an assault is feasible."

"And?"

McGuire unrolled the map and laid it across the field table in front of Warren. "If you look here, sir, you can see that I have marked a route up the hillside that is possible. It is steep and it will tire the men, but it can be done. I was unable to get on top of the kopje, so I don't have information on their strength, but I can confirm the Boers are up there keeping watch."

Warren and the two Colonels wearing the red collar tabs of staff officers looked down at the map and studied the route McGuire had proposed. The larger of the Colonels stroked his fierce moustache as he looked up from the table.

"Can this be done at night, Captain?"

"It can, sir, with difficulty. I suggest I put my troop in position to act as guides to get the assault force up the hill."

Warren rubbed his left ear before he spoke. "Very well, gentlemen. I have decided that the planned attack on the Rangeworthy Hills is not justifiable with the Boer numbers that we know are positioned there. Spion Kop is the best alternative. From there we can dominate the area once we get artillery up onto the top."

The two staff Colonels nodded, while McGuire held his tongue. Warren paused for a moment or two before he continued.

"We shall use the Lancashire Brigade. They are fully across the river and can be ready to move by dusk. McGuire, get your men into position without being seen. As night falls get them up the hill to provide guidance. Colonel Thomas, I want orders prepared for the infantry, and Colonel James, you will ensure that the artillery and support troops are ready and moving in behind the assault brigade. Captain, you have your orders and thank you for your assistance. You may go now, while we work out the details."

McGuire saluted and left the tent. He looked out across the river at the mass of bullock carts still crossing and wondered what the devil was in them that needed so much transport. The Boers seemed to manage very well with whatever they could carry on the backs of their own horses.

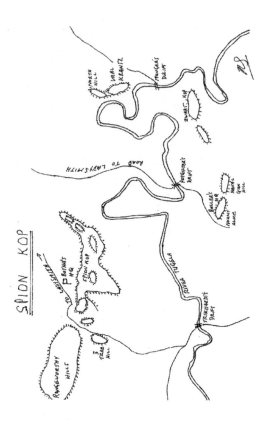

He mounted up and rode through the soldiers who would soon be climbing that steep slope. A night attack was always difficult, with the danger of the troops losing touch and going astray. He hoped his troop would be able to stop that tonight. How many Boers would they meet on the hilltop and would the tired and winded men be able to fight effectively after that climb?

Chapter 33
Spion Kop

The sound of boots coming across the veldt was muffled. There was no other sound. No talking, no clinking of equipment, nothing. The Lancashire brigade had prepared well. As they emerged from the darkness McGuire walked forward and fell in beside the commander at the front of the column.

"Good evening, sir. Nice evening for a stroll. A shame there's no moonlight."

Colonel Woodgate grinned at McGuire. "Although romantic, I think moonlight might spoil our surprise party, don't you think?"

"Indeed, sir. Now, in about a hundred yards or so we should see the first of my men. They are spread out to each side of the viable path up the hill. Samuel and I will stay with you as he is the only one who has walked the whole of the track."

"Samuel?"

"My African tracker, sir. He's just up ahead. For this attack he has insisted on carrying his assegai. He says the blade is better than a bayonet."

"Not too sure about trusting my command to the guidance of a native. Is he sound?"

"I've trusted my life to him before, sir. He's a good man."

"I hope you're right."

"I am, sir," McGuire whispered. "And here he is."

Samuel rose from the ground where he had been squatting to wait for the column. Without a word he pointed up the hill with his assegai and the faint starlight caught the broad metal blade.

"Very well, Captain, lead on and we'll get this hill taken before dawn."

Samuel took the lead with McGuire close behind him. It was a stiff climb, but the Lancashire men kept up and kept silent. Then, from nowhere, a small white dog appeared, probably somebody's mascot. One bark from the animal could bring disaster.

"Kill the bloody thing," Woodgate hissed.

McGuire walked to where the dog was sitting on a rock and wagging its tail happily. He scooped the animal up and walked back to the first line of soldiers. He spotted a younger solider, probably one of the drummer boys, and handed the dog to him.

"Now take that dog down the hill and keep it quiet. Don't come back until you hear gunfire. Now move."

As the drummer stumbled back down the hill carrying the wriggling dog, McGuire returned to the Colonel. "Dealt with, sir, no harm done."

They carried on climbing until they could see the hilltop dimly outlined by the stars. The climb had been harder than even McGuire had anticipated and the dawn was fast approaching as they neared the objective. With the change in temperature a thick mist descended and hid them from view, but also hid any sign of Boers. A man slipped on a loose rock and grunted as he fell. The rock rolled downwards, crashing against others as it went.

From above and just in front of them came the challenge. "*Werda?*"

The challenge was followed instantly by a flurry of rifle shots. The British threw themselves flat until the rattle of rifle bolts signalled that the Mauser rifles they faced were empty. The men charged forward over the lip of the hill and on to the small Boer picket. Bayonets flashed in the early dawn light and the Boers fled, leaving their boots and one dead comrade behind them.

The hill was theirs and in the mist they started to prepare a defence position. It was then that they found that only twenty picks and shovels had been carried up the hill and the soldiers started to build a low rock wall from the stony ground they had captured.

"Captain McGuire!"

"Here, sir."

"Captain, if I am going to fortify and hold this hill I need to copy the Boers and get my men into trenches. Once this damned fog clears, their guns on the other hills are going to play hell with us. I need you and your troop to get down this hill and find me some sappers with a decent number of entrenching tools and get them up here quick time. While you are at it, find out what the hell has happened to the artillery. I know it's going to be tough getting the guns up here, but we should have heard from them by now. And McGuire."

"Yes, sir?"

"Make it as quick as you can. I don't want to have to rely on this shallow depression and a few rocks thrown up round the edge."

McGuire collected his men and they set off down the way they had climbed through the sheltering mist. At the bottom they found the mules that had been carrying the water for the brigade, but no sappers and no sign of the artillery.

***

At the far side of the Kop the Boer piquet arrived at their commander's tent, breathless, shoeless and confused. Botha sat on his camp stool and remained calm. The khakis had taken the Kop, in which case the Boers must take it back. He sent orderlies racing to the artillery positions on the nearby hills with orders to turn their guns and bring them into action against the British on Spion Kop. He knew that his five field guns and two pom-poms were unlikely to dislodge the British on their own. He needed troops up there as well.

The Boer commandoes did not have the fierce discipline of the British and Botha knew that not all of his burghers would storm the hill. Some would skulk among the rocks at the bottom. He could only hope that he could motivate sufficient men of courage to make the attempt. He sent word around to the commando leaders and waited.

The burghers of the Carolina Commando, under their leader Henrik Pinsloo, were the first to respond and climb the kop through the mist, fanning out as they went. Botha stood and watched them climb. Could they hold out until the rest of the men he had sent for arrived? Would they respond?

The Carolina men took their positions on the Conical Hill and Aloe Knoll high points and waited for the mist to clear. In front of them they could hear the British moving rocks, but had no idea what they were facing. As the mist began to clear three or four hundred men were climbing the hill to join them. The Pretoria Commando had arrived. The Boers took up their positions, loaded their Mauser rifles and waited.

The mist cleared and there were the British still working to try and create a defence position in the rocky ground of the hilltop. Then first of the Boer artillery shells screamed over them and exploded among the soldiers. The khakis dropped to the ground behind their improvised earthworks and vanished. The pom-poms started to throw their two-pound high explosive shells now and from the hidden British came the occasional cry of a wounded man. Still the Boer riflemen waited.

Any head that appeared from behind the low wall of rocks was an instant target for the accurate Mausers and the Boers saw helmets and blood fly up as a soldier's head was pierced by multiple high velocity bullets. The British were trapped in a grave of their own making.

***

As the mist cleared that morning the British realised they were not at the top of Spion Kop as they had imagined. Theirs was a position on a false peak and there was a higher ridge in front of them. As realisation dawned, the Boer artillery and riflemen opened fire and they were pinned down. Any man who raised his head was risking death. They tried to return fire by raising their rifles and firing unaimed shots, but these were mostly ineffective. They had no answer to the artillery rounds that flew in from the Boer positions on other hills and exploded above them, showering them in red-hot shrapnel.

Officers rallied small groups of men to leap up and charge towards the Boers. These were cut down by the merciless rifle fire and eventually the soldiers hugged the ground and prayed for night or reinforcements. The mules carrying the water and spare ammunition were still at the bottom of the hill and unable to make the steep climb. The relentless sun across the mens' backs made the lack of water a torture beyond endurance and now the ammunition was running low.

After five hours of this torture some men of the Lancashire Fusiliers threw down their rifles and put up their hands. The Boers ceased fire and started to come forward. White handkerchiefs were fluttering and then the Boers saw a large red-faced man rise up out of the inadequate trench and shout across the hilltop.

"I'm the commandant here. Take your men back to hell, sir! I allow no surrenders."

This was Colonel Thorneycroft. He had just been informed that he had been promoted to

Brigadier General and was in command of the troops on the Kop. For some reason Warren never told other officers, including at least one who was senior as a Colonel to Thorneycroft. As he dropped back into cover he saw the first of the reinforcements arriving. A company of the Middlesex Regiment was advancing up the hill with fixed bayonets. Thorneycroft ordered them to charge the Boer positions and managed to get at least some of the exhausted defenders to move as well.

The sudden charge took the Boers by surprise and despite heavy casualties the British were able to occupy the highest part of Spion Kop. Artillery and rifle fire from the nearby hills continued to pound into them and again they were forced to take what cover they could. Further reinforcements were on the way across the veldt, but much too slowly.

With the night there came no respite. The Boer guns continued to pound the top of the hill, even though the burghers themselves were withdrawing to lick their wounds. Thorneycroft knew his men could take no more and decided to withdraw. Had the reinforcements he had begged for arrived, he might have held the hill, but that chance was gone as far as he knew. He gave the order and the men who could move stumbled out of their shallow trench and onto the downward slope. Behind them they left only the dead and the dying.

***

McGuire had tried all day to hurry the reinforcements to the hill with no success. Now he was returning with his small troop in the hope that his marksmen could be of some use. As he reached the base of the hill a horseman cantered up alongside him and dismounted.

"McGuire! I might know you'd be somewhere in the thick of it. How has it been here?"

"Churchill. Do you ever do any soldiering? Or do you just ride around doing your work for the *Morning Post*?"

Churchill laughed. "My readers expect me to be there for them, to tell them of the glorious deeds of our troops."

McGuire shrugged tiredly. "Nothing glorious here for them. It's been another shambles, as far as I can see."

"Never mind. I can gloss over that. For now, can I join you on the way up here?"

"Please do. You can tell me what has been happening elsewhere on the field."

Churchill grinned at him, but the grin fell away as he looked up the path they were following. "Who are these men? What's happening?"

In front of them, men in tattered and blood stained uniforms were stumbling down the hill. The wounded were supported by comrades in not much better shape. The Indian stretcher-bearers ran up the hill and helped the men in the worst condition to lie on their canvas stretchers before carrying them away to the field dressing station.

Churchill stared aghast at the horrendous injuries that the bursting shrapnel had caused. Arms and legs were torn and stomachs had been ripped open. How these men could still live and how they had managed to make it this far down the hill was unfathomable to him.

The rearguard led by Thorneycroft stumbled to the end of the hill track. The men appeared disorientated, even drunk, although they had had no alcohol. Here they met the reinforcements they had waited for throughout the day. Sappers to dig emplacements and trenches with gunners to bring up the field guns.

Thorneycroft looked at them with dull eyes. "I have done all I can," he said. "I am not going back."

Spion Kop was left to the dead and dying of both sides. In the British trench the bodies lay three deep in places. Tossed around like rag dolls by the incessant artillery fire, the dead did not care anymore.

At dawn the next day Botha was amazed when he looked up at the hill to see two Boers waving their hats and rifles from the summit. Despite having abandoned the hill in despair, they had won. It seemed impossible, but it was true. The mighty British army had retreated again.

Chapter 34
A New Plan

"Rider coming, sir."

McGuire turned around and raised his field glasses at Donnelly's words. It took him a moment to find the horseman in the morning haze. As the lone rider walked his horse towards them McGuire was surprised to recognise General Buller. He tracked the binoculars left and right, but could see no sign of any staff officers.

He walked the last three paces to the top of the donga and waited. As the General rode up to him McGuire took the reins and held them as the large man dismounted.

Buller looked at him quizzically. "I'd heard that you and your men don't salute when in the field. I thought you might make an exception for an old General."

"With great respect, sir, no. The last thing I want to do is to mark you out to any Boer sniper as a worthwhile target."

"I see your point, but don't let the practice spread to the rest of the army. Bad for discipline, you know."

"Indeed, sir. How can I serve you this fine morning?"

Buller smiled. "Well, unless age has caught up with me, I can smell breakfast cooking. Do you have an extra plate?"

"Follow me, sir. We're down in the donga keeping out of sight."

"How did you know I was coming then?"

McGuire pointed to the left. "If you look carefully at that scrubby bush you'll see one of Sergeant Donnelly's men on watch. He gets his breakfast later than the rest, but we give him the biggest steak."

"Steak for breakfast? I was expecting fried bully beef."

"Not today, sir. Corporal Macklin brought down an antelope yesterday, bloody big thing it was. Samuel tells me it's called a kudu. So we are having kudu steak and eggs for breakfast. All except Samuel, he's having bully beef. He just loves the damn stuff. Can't get enough of it."

"And what's happening over there?"

"That's one we've learned from our Boer friends. Those three are cutting up the kudu meat into strips and then we dry it in the sun. They call it biltong. Very chewy, but it keeps for a long time and it's light enough to carry on the horses."

Buller sat down on the saddle that lay on the ground and McGuire sat on his. "So what are you doing out here? Apart from giving me an excuse for a quiet ride away from headquarters."

"It's a training day, sir. We're polishing up our marksmanship skills and practising fighting without weapons."

Buller took the metal plate that was handed to him and, resting it on his knees, cut a slice of the dark meat. He put it into his mouth and chewed slowly. The smile crossed his face again as he swallowed.

"Ah, it's a long time since I've had kudu. Always tastes better out on the veldt, I find."

"I'd forgotten you served in the first Boer War, sir."

"That's right, and this time we are going to win. But tell me, I thought your men were all marksmen with a rifle already."

"All except Samuel, our African, sir. He's still learning, so this is mainly for him. Mind you, he has the keenest eyes I've ever seen. He can spot an enemy way before the rest of us."

"And the fighting without weapons?"

"Ah, now there Samuel is good value. We all have skills, but he has some exceptional Zulu moves that he is teaching us. So we all learn together."

"Don't you find it detracts from your authority as an officer to fight with your men?"

"The secret is never to let them beat me, sir. They've all thrown money into the hat and the first one that beats me gets the prize. It makes them all support each other."

Buller nodded thoughtfully as he carried on eating his breakfast. "I have a confession, Captain. This was not just an excuse for a ride. I have a job for you. It's dangerous, but it needs to be done and I think your marksmen are the ones to do it. Once we've finished this excellent breakfast you and I will talk it through."

The General handed his metal plate back to Private O'Riley and stood up. He dusted down his uniform trousers and waited for McGuire.

Together they walked along the sandy bottom of the donga until they were out of earshot of the men.

"You've never been to an Aldershot field training day, have you, McGuire?"

"No, sir. Never served in England. After training in Ireland I was sent to Egypt and I'd been there ever since until this came up."

"On the Aldershot heath our tactics work like a finely tuned machine. The artillery pound the enemy, then as they stop, the infantry march in solid column of fours to the attack. Once the enemy turns and runs, the cavalry swoop in and complete the rout. Then it's back to the mess for a stiff gin before dinner. It's worked beautifully for many years while we've been fighting native warriors. The trouble is the Boers have never been to Aldershot either and don't know their part. They duck down in their trenches and wait until the artillery has finished, then they pop up and rip holes in the infantry as they advance. If they have to retreat, they jump on their horses and ride, leaving us to pick up our dead."

McGuire waited without speaking.

"You told me when we spoke at my headquarters that our tactics were out of date and I agreed. Since then my staff and I have been working on the solution and I think we now have it."

Again McGuire waited in silence.

"Aren't you curious, Captain?"

"Very sir. I was just waiting for the other shoe to fall when you tell me where I come in."

Buller chuckled. "Other shoe; very good. Now then, here is how it works. The artillery will fire and progressively raise their barrels so the impact area moves forward onto the Boer positions. The gunners have christened it a creeping barrage. The infantry will move up closely behind that barrage so that as the Boers pop out of their holes our men are almost on top of them. Then, it's in with the bayonet and chase the buggers back to Pretoria with the cavalry at their backs."

McGuire stroked his chin before speaking. "It sounds interesting sir, provided the gunners don't live up to their nickname and hit our infantry."

Buller smiled. "The 'drop shorts' will be very tightly controlled, I promise you. The risk to the infantry will be minimal and, if it all goes to plan, should save a lot of my men's lives."

"And my troop, sir?"

"Ah yes. I want your marksmen right at the front of the infantry. As the barrage passes the braver Boers will be the first to stick their heads up for a look round. I want you and your men there to show them that it's a bad idea."

"So we are to be snipers and take out their best?"

"That's the ticket. Make the rest of them keep their heads down for just a little longer so our infantry can get closer, before they come under fire."

"Damned risky, sir."

"True, but can you do it?"

"Being forward of the army was always our intended role, so we'll be there."

Chapter 35
Breakthrough

Four days later, the reconnaissance troop sat in the darkness at the foot of the kopje that the British had christened Hussar Hill. They were out to the east of Colenso and still south of the river. It seemed an unlikely route for the advance, but the troops as ever had confidence in Buller.

Swallowing his own nervousness, McGuire gathered his men around him. "I know I've said this all before, but I'm going to say it again so there are no mistakes. No talking and no smoking as we move into the final positions. Lie flat and stay down until you see me move. If you find a fold in the ground, get into it. It's going to get noisy when the artillery start the bombardment and we are going to be closer to it than is comfortable. As the bombardment moves forward, so do we. Keep a lookout for Boers appearing from their trenches and drop any one you see, without waiting for orders. The infantry are going to be about two hundred yards behind us and if the Boers open fire, in any numbers, so will they. If that happens get down and keep out of the crossfire. Any questions?"

"Just one, sir."

"Go on, Corporal Fine, what is it?"

"What are we having for breakfast? This biltong is making my teeth ache. It's like chewing an army boot."

The small joke relieved the tension and he heard the men chuckle a little in the darkness. "Right, we'll worry about that later. Let's move."

The men rose quietly from the ground and walked carefully towards the hill. Samuel hissed to show they were at the point he had been told to lead them to and the men sank down and lay flat. McGuire checked his watch in the faint moonlight. Only just in time. The shelling should start any second. He looked back over his shoulder to see the red flare arc into the sky and then the first gun barked.

The first shells whistled out of the night and the ground in front of them erupted in a roar of dust and stones. Then the drumming of the guns became constant as the batteries fired onto the ground they had identified earlier. McGuire felt his heart beating hard as the ground below him vibrated with the impacts. He risked a look up and saw that the barrage had started the planned creep forward. Once he was convinced that all the guns had raised their elevation, he rose to a crouch and started forward. He did not look round to check on his men. He was confident they would all follow him.

They stayed low and moved slowly, carrying their rifles at the trail. As it got lighter McGuire caught a glimpse of Samuel. His rifle was slung across his back now and the assegai was in his hands. He thought that was probably a good idea; the African was far more deadly with his spear than he was with a rifle.

225

The pounding continued and McGuire wondered if he would ever hear anything clearly again. The barrage continued to creep forward and then there was the first Boer. A bearded face under a slouch hat rose uncertainly out of a hidden hole in the ground. McGuire brought his rifle to the aim and fired a snap shot. The hat flew into the air followed by a gout of blood as the face disappeared from view.

There was another to his right and he swung the rifle, but saw the man go down as one of the troop fired. Another rose almost at his feet and he jumped to one side, swinging the rifle round as he went. The silver-bladed assegai flew past him and buried itself in the man's throat. The Boer clutched the spear with both hands and fell backwards as his lifeblood pulsed out of the wide gash. Samuel ran forward and grabbed the assegai. He had to put his foot on the man's face to hold him down as he pulled the weapon out again.

McGuire checked behind him and there were the infantry. They were moving forward confidently and he could see their bayonets catching the weak sunlight. He turned back and saw the line of Boers rise up together from their trench. As he flung himself to the ground he heard the volley from behind him and the trench was empty.

The infantry ran past him screaming their war cries and as he rose he saw the Boers scampering up out of their remaining trenches and running towards the back of the hill, where their horses

226

must be waiting. They stood and looked around to find his men rising from the ground and staring up the hill.

"To me, reconnaissance troop! Over here!"

The men looked at each other in silence as they walked over to him. "Anybody down? Patrol leaders, check your men."

The NCOs checked and from their smiles he knew they had made it through unscathed. The plan the artillery had developed had worked. He walked back down the hill to where the man he had shot lay in his trench. He felt only pity for the man as he looked down at his contorted body.

"Corporal Fine!"

"Yes, sir?"

"Let's get the men back to the horses and then you can sort out that breakfast you were worried about."

***

The Boer lines crumpled in the face of this new tactic. From Hussar Hill they took Cingolo, then Monte Cristo and on to the Hlangwe. There were casualties, but they were making progress and the reconnaissance troop led at each attack.

With the guns now dominating the plain beyond the river from the captured hilltops, the pontoon bridge was rebuilt and the Tugela was crossed once again. The Boers retreated, leaving lock, stock and barrel behind them. Ammunition, food and bibles had all been abandoned in their haste to leave.

From the top of Hlangwe McGuire watched the collection of the wounded through his field glasses. The Boers had agreed to a truce to allow the stretcher-bearers to come forward and pick up the men who had laid out in the sun, for three days in some cases. He could only imagine the suffering of wounded men in this heat with no water. As the stretcher-bearers did their work he could see officers chatting with Boers on the hilltops across the river.

He felt Donnelly walk up beside him. "The Dervishes would never have done that, eh, sir?"

McGuire lowered the binoculars. "No, I guess they would have slaughtered all our men by now. But then we were killing a lot more of them than we are the Boers."

Donnelly grunted. "What was it the Colonel called them on the ship? Peasant farmers? They're doing pretty well for farmers."

"They are indeed. Did you want me for something?"

"Yes, sir, messenger just arrived. The General wants to see you again."

"Probably wants us to earn our salt again. I just hope it's not another of those games of following the bombardment. My ears are still ringing from the last one."

He put the field glasses back into leather case that hung round his neck. "Do we know where the General is?"

"He's just over there, sir, behind that low ridge."

"I didn't hear his staff officers clatter up."

"No, sir, he rode up with just a couple of escorts. He's been watching across the valley, like you."

McGuire strode across the almost flat top of Hlangwe and found Buller sitting on a rock and scanning the hills on the other side of the river. He saw the General's great bull head turn as he watched him approach.

McGuire saluted. "Good morning, General."

"A salute in the field from McGuire? I am honoured. Not expecting snipers then?"

"No, sir. This hill has been well and truly cleared out, and it's a bit far even for Boers across the river."

"True enough. Now then, I need you and your troop again. Are they fit to ride?"

"They're tired, but they can still function, sir."

"And what about their commander?"

"Also tired, but still capable, thank you, sir."

"Good. Right then, take a look over there." Buller pointed to the row of hills across the river. "We can take them the same way we have taken the hills over this side of the Tugela, but I will lose more men than I am happy with. Colonel Sandbach and his intelligence people have come up with an alternative."

McGuire looked across the river and the flat plain beyond it to the hills where the Boers waited. Any alternative would save the stretcher-bearers a lot of work.

"I want you and your troop to provide an escort for Colonel Sandbach. He is going to follow the gorge of the Tugela as it turns north. If the Boers are there and ready for you it could be, shall we say, difficult. Alternatively, if it is suitable for troops, they could move forward and be sheltered from the Boers."

"When do you want us to leave, sir?"

"Right now. Collect your troop and go and find Sandbach. He is down with my headquarters getting ready to go."

"Very well, sir. I'll be off."

"One thing, McGuire, I value my intelligence officer, so keep him alive, would you?"

McGuire grinned. "I'll do my very best, sir."

***

At this time of day the walls of the gorge threw shade onto the track that ran beside the river. Connolly rode beside Colonel Sandbach making notes for one of his maps as they went. Before and behind the pair rode the rest of the troop, their rifles in their hands and their eyes scanning around them in all directions.

The gorge led them to the base of the three hills that were their objectives: Hart's Hill, Railway Hill and Wynne Hill. From there the troops could burst from cover and make a coordinated assault on the Boer positions.

The Colonel called McGuire to him. "Well, Captain, reconnaissance is your speciality. What do you think?"

"Sir, I think you have found the key that the General has been looking for. Once we turn it we should unlock the road to Ladysmith. Samuel tells me that some of the Boers are already leaving the area, so I think they know they're in trouble."

"How does he know that?"

"He took a walk through the lines last night and had a word with some of the Africans the Boers are using as virtual slave labour."

"That's good to know. Now I think I've seen enough, so we can turn back. If your man can get his map to me as soon as possible I would appreciate it."

"You'll have it before dark, sir."

The attack was almost a let-down. The artillery pounded the Boer positions while the infantry moved along the gorge, invisible to the enemy. At the appointed time the shelling stopped and the infantry surged out of the river gorge. As the troops advanced in short sharp rushes, the Boers melted away after a short resistance.

On the 28th February 1900 McGuire stood among the wildly cheering soldiers and looked out across the veldt from one of the hilltops. He could see the Boers riding away, and beyond them, through the heat haze, he could see their objective. Ladysmith sat out on the plain; theirs for the taking.

Two squadrons of the Imperial Light Horse and Carbineers rode forward and brushed the Boer rear guard aside before cantering into the streets of the beleaguered town. The road to Ladysmith was

open and the rest of the army prepared to march
down it.

Chapter 36
Back To Kitchener

The reconnaissance troop rode slowly towards Ladysmith, off to one side of the road to keep out of the way of the infantry who marched along it. There was no singing or shouting, just weary men trudging through the heat to the town they had paid for in so much blood and pain. McGuire saw Buller riding through with his staff trailing behind them. The General was passing comments to the soldiers as he rode by. The men's heads came up as they felt the pride their General was giving them.

Buller looked across to where the troop was riding and called a rider forward. The man nodded and turned his horse before riding across to McGuire. He called the troop to a halt to wait for the messenger.

The young Lieutenant rode up and reined in his horse in a cloud of dust. McGuire could hear the troop behind him coughing and spitting the dust from their already parched mouths.

"Careful, Lieutenant, you wouldn't want to get dust on your shiny boots, now, would you?"

The officer looked at McGuire and was puzzled by what he saw. The badges of rank on his filthy and tattered uniform were almost invisible. In fact, the only thing that really marked him out as an officer was the Webley revolver on his waist belt. There was something about the eyes, though; a calm confidence that seemed to radiate from him.

The Lieutenant cleared his throat. "Ah, sorry ,sir, didn't mean to cause the dust cloud. However, General Buller's compliments and would you please come and find him in the headquarters at Ladysmith once all the fuss has died down?"

"I'll be there as soon as I find my men somewhere to sleep."

The messenger saluted, wheeled his horse and cantered back to the road to join the General's entourage. Donnelly and Parks rode up on either side of McGuire and the three of them watched the officer ride away.

"What do you think that's about, sir?" Parks asked.

"I think I know. Kitchener wants us to go across and join him with the main army. General Buller wanted to keep hold of us until he had Ladysmith in his hands. So my guess is that we are on our travels again."

McGuire took his men into the town away from the main streets. He knew that the relief force was to parade past the Ladysmith headquarters and General White was to take the salute. Somehow he felt uncomfortable at the thought of parading in triumph past the half-starved defenders. His men found a quiet spot to make camp and in minutes they had the fire started and the meal beginning to cook. He gave it a time for the parade to finish and then rode his horse towards the building where he had spoken with General White.

After tying his horse's reins to a tree, McGuire walked up the path to the white-painted bungalow and asked for General Buller. He sat in the shade and waited until the same young officer came and found him. The younger man led him around the house to a garden where Buller sat on one of the lawn chairs scattered there.

"You look tired again, McGuire. How are your men?"

"Settled down making their dinner, sir. They'll be glad of a rest."

Buller leaned back in the chair. "Sit down before you fall down, man. Now you recall that Kitchener wanted you to join him and I held you back until this was over? Well, obviously now it's over and, though I wish I could, I can't keep you any longer. Kitchener is getting impatient and I'm sure I will be getting an order from Lord Roberts soon if I don't comply."

"We'll be sad to leave your command, sir. It's been impressive to watch what you've managed without the proper number of men."

"Decent of you to say so, Captain, but I fear that is not how this campaign is being viewed in London. My friends there tell me that I am being set up as the villain of the piece. After all, someone has to be sacrificed so the politicians gather no blame."

"That doesn't seem fair, sir."

Buller chuckled. "Never become a General, young man. There is no fairness when you deal with politicians. None at all. But enough of that. I asked you to come here for two reasons. First to give you these orders. They instruct all transport

235

officers to give you priority to get you to Lord Roberts' headquarters, wherever that may be. He is on the move, taking the army forward towards Pretoria. Second, I want to thank you for your service with this part of the army. You and your men have been useful to me and please tell your men how much I appreciate their efforts."

McGuire stood and saluted. "Sir, it has been a privilege to serve you and, no matter what London thinks, the men here know what you did and admire you."

"Kind of you to say so, McGuire. Now, before you dash off, Kitchener has sent me another telegram that concerns you. He demands that you move at best speed, which is typical of the man; less typical is that he wants you to arrive with him wearing the rank badges of a Major. Congratulations on your promotion, Major McGuire."

"Thank you, sir, though where I will find any new rank badges in the middle of a war I have no idea."

"Sadly, I do. Ride out to the hospital on the edge of town. There will be rank badges left there by the officers that succumbed to disease during the siege."

McGuire took the General's advice and rode through the town and out to the hospital that had been set up there. As he got closer he could see the rows of graves that told the story of the siege better than any journalist's fevered tales. As he reached the tents he dismounted and tied the reins of his horse to a post before walking on to find the administrator. The Captain he found in his tent was sitting at a folding table working on his ledgers.

He looked up. "Can I help you?"

"I hope so," McGuire said. "A little gruesome, I'm afraid, but I have just been promoted and the General suggested there might be some rank badges here from one of your causalities."

The harassed officer ran his fingers through his hair and stood up. "I need a break anyway. I'll show you. Walk with me."

Together they left the tent and walked across the compound. As they rounded the end of a large white tent McGuire was shocked to see a row of blankets on the ground. From beneath each one protruded a pair of feet. There must have been twenty of them.

The administrator stopped. "Sorry, I should have warned you, but we have become used to this, I'm afraid. The diseases of siege, it seems, do not stop as soon as the siege is lifted."

"I was just a bit surprised they have been left here and not buried."

"We bury them daily, Captain, or should I say Major. This is just the crop for today."

The officer walked on and McGuire followed him, skirting around the row of dead men. They came to an area where two orderlies were sorting uniforms. Those with blood or other fluids were thrown onto a pile, while cleaner ones were put into sacks.

"Jenkins! Can you sort this officer out with the rank badges for a Major?"

The older of the two men straightened up and arched his back to ease the stiffness. Without a word he walked across to a wooden box that stood against a tent wall. After a few seconds of rummaging he returned and handed a set of Major's crowns to McGuire.

"Congratulations, sir. I hope you wear them longer than their last owner."

***

At every stop, Sergeant Parks chased the men out of their carriage and down to the cattle wagon to water the horses. The movement orders they had been given had made them a priority to move and overworked transport officers had been helpful, if not particularly gracious. McGuire stood in the window of his compartment and watched as the train pulled in to the station at Bloemfontein. This was the first train to arrive from the south since the British had captured the town the day before and the army was everywhere.

McGuire left his men unloading the horses and went in search of anyone who could tell him where to find Kitchener. Having received directions, he watched as the last of the horses was saddled and then the troop rode together through the town. As they reached the headquarters building General Kitchener was riding in from the other direction and stopped to wait for them.

"McGuire. You've taken your own sweet time to get here."

"Yes, sir, it's been a difficult trip. We had to keep making way for ammunition trains going through and casualties being evacuated the other way."

Kitchener grunted. "Well, you're here now. Come inside and I'll tell you what I want from you. The Major's crowns look good on you, by the way. Colonel Wingate wanted me to promote you at Omdurman, but it rather fell through the cracks in all the excitement. Still better late than never, eh?"

McGuire smiled. "I seem to recall you were a little busy at Omdurman, sir. One or two more serious issues to deal with, I think."

Kitchener gave McGuire one of his rare smiles. "Indeed, it was a rather exciting time and I think you had quite a lot to do that day as well."

"A simpler war than this one, I think, sir."

"All wars have their own special problems and this one is no different. My problem is knowing where the Boers are. They range far and wide across this country, making it difficult to know where they are and in what strength. Our shortage of cavalry is not making that any easier, so I am going to use you initially as you are. The reconnaissance troop will be my eyes and ears, reporting directly to me. Later on I may have another task for you."

"Very good, sir. When do we start?"

Chapter 37
K of Chaos

"Good morning, sir, and how can I help you?"

"Good morning, Quartermaster. I'm hoping you can help me to re-equip my troop somewhat."

"That rather depends what you need, sir. With the supply transport problems I am a little at sixes and sevens."

"Transport problems? I thought the trains were running freely up to here?"

The Captain ran his hand over his bald head. "I'm surprised you haven't heard about it. The trains are fine now, but the wagons are all over the place since the reorganisation."

McGuire sat down across the desk from the Quartermaster. "You'll have to forgive me. I've only just arrived over here. I've been with Buller up to now."

"Ah, you might not know then. As soon as Lord Roberts and Lord Kitchener arrived they reorganised the transport system. The old system of each regiment having its own wagons and an officer responsible for them was swept away and all the wagons were concentrated under central control. Frankly, it's been something of a disaster. That's why the men have changed Kitchener's nickname, from K of K, to K of Chaos. Not very kind. It might have been a good idea if introduced gradually and not in the middle of a war."

McGuire leaned back in his chair. "So you are short of some things, I take it?"

"I'm short of an awful lot of things, and after the debacle at Paardeberg our Chief of Staff has damaged his reputation quite a bit."

"I'm not aware of Paardeberg either."

"Ah well, I wasn't actually there, so I would be repeating hearsay, but it seems quite a few men were killed for no good reason. However, that's by the by. Tell me what you need and I'll see what I can do."

"My men's uniforms are virtually in rags and their boots are pretty well worn out. As you can see, I'm in much the same state."

"How many men?"

"Including me, sixteen."

"Sixteen? With you being a Major I was expecting at least a company. Sixteen sets of kit I can do. And I see you are carrying the old Mark 1 Webley revolver. I can give you a more up-to-date one of those as well, while we are at it."

"Thank you for the offer, but a very special person made me promise to carry this weapon for her."

"I see. Well, bring your men in to the storehouse and we'll kit them out."

McGuire nodded his thanks and went back to the door. He called the troop and Donnelly led them into the storehouse where a row of long tables had been set up. The Quartermaster Captain bustled in and stopped when he saw Samuel.

"Major? You aren't expecting me to equip a Kaffir, are you?"

"I would appreciate you not using that term, Captain. Samuel is a member of the Zulu nation and is one of my soldiers. He gets the same equipment as the rest of the troop."

"I'm not at all sure about that, sir."

"Captain, this small troop reports directly to General Kitchener. If you would like to go and explain to him why we are unable to carry out his orders then please feel free."

"I can equip the rest of the men without a problem. It's just …"

"All or none, Captain, and a very uncomfortable interview with the General if you decline. Your choice."

***

An hour later the troop was sitting together under the shade of a wide tree down by the river. They had all bathed for the first time in days and were now cutting the badges off their old uniforms and sewing them on to the new ones. Samuel had been left in charge of the cooking while Fine did his sewing for him.

"I thought you were going to punch that Captain at one stage there, sir."

McGuire grinned at Donnelly. "No, Sergeant that's your speciality. I prefer blackmail when it works."

"Good job it worked. The lads are feeling good about the new kit. Better than walking around with our arses hanging out."

"Especially as we seem to be in a more civilised area now. Wouldn't want to scandalise the ladies now would we? How is Parks getting on with the horses?"

"He found himself a farrier and all the hooves have been checked. All the shoes have been repaired or replaced. Him and his lads have had them in the river to wash off any bugs and now they are quietly feeding in a spare barn he found. They'll be in good shape when it's time to move."

"Right then. Keep the men working. We'll camp here tonight and let them rest. I'll go and get our orders from the General and see if I can find out a bit more about what's been going on with this part of the army."

"Going on, sir?"

"Yes. The Quartermaster had a couple of odd things to tell me. I'll be back for dinner."

As he rode up to the headquarters building he saw an officer he knew from the regiment. The man was sitting in the shade of the veranda with his arm in a sling and the red tabs of a staff officer on his collar.

"O'Brian! Good to see you. I thought you'd been captured with the rest of the battalion?"

"Hello, McGuire. No, I was left behind in Ladysmith to try and recover the regimental baggage when the disaster happened. How about you? How did you get away?"

McGuire took the cane chair next to O'Brian. "The Colonel had sent me on a reconnaissance task to the south that day. So I missed the surrender too."

"I heard you were operating with Buller's army. I didn't know you'd come across to the main theatre."

"Kitchener wanted us back with him. He's got me reporting directly to him. In fact, I've come today to get my instructions."

O'Brian pointed to his injured arm. "Be careful of Kitchener. I owe him this."

McGuire raised an eyebrow. "How so? How did you get that?"

O'Brian looked around him. "Have you heard of Paardeburg?"

McGuire nodded. "Yesterday somebody mentioned it, but didn't want to tell me the details. Were you there?"

"Come for a walk with me. The General is in a conference right now, so you'll only be hanging around."

McGuire stood and followed O'Brian down the path that led to a bench at the end of a long garden. They sat in the shade of a tree and O'Brian sighed as he leaned back.

"I don't know what the hell was wrong with Kitchener at Paardeburg, but he cost a lot of lives for no good reason."

"That doesn't sound like him. He was careful with the men's lives in the Sudan."

"So I'd heard. Well, let me tell you the story and you can make your own mind up. In any case, you need to be careful of how he uses you. He seems to be impatient and that's dangerous."

"Fair enough. So what happened?"

"The Boer General Piet Cronje and his people had been defending Magersfontein for over two months. When our numbers built up enough we were going to attack, but he was too wise for that and one night he pulled his five thousand men, and a massive bullock cart train, out of there. He just walked them past Kelly-Kenny's 6th Division and nobody saw a thing. The infantry caught them up a day later. He abandoned about eighty of his wagons and kept on going. The troops needed food, so the wagons were a godsend. Then French and his cavalry got involved and Cronje called a halt on the banks of the Modder River. They dug in and made a warren of defensive trenches. I think that was a mistake, but it was fine by us, of course."

McGuire waited for the rest of the story and said nothing.

"Well, we surrounded the laager they had created and started to shell them. Of course, because of the trenches we didn't do them a lot of damage, but it must have been unpleasant in there. Especially as they had their women with them. They couldn't move above ground as the soldiers were all around and they were well within range of our rifles. De Wet and his Commando tried to relieve them, but we were in far too strong a position and he had to back away. All we needed

245

to do was to wait them out until they were forced to surrender. They had no real option.

O´Brian paused and looked up at the vulture circling above them. "We had learned our lessons about attacking Brother Boer when he was entrenched. He's damned useful with those bloody rifles. So Kelly-Kenny was content to sit back and shell Cronje into surrender. Then Kitchener arrived having no experience of dealing with entrenched Boers and their magazine rifles and not willing to listen. He insisted that Kelly-Kenny mount a major infantry assault. The men had to cross a wide expanse of totally flat, exposed river bank to get at the Boers, but Kitchener would not be denied. Some of the Boer wagons had been set on fire by the artillery. We could see it all develop; all we had to do was wait, but that was not good enough.

"The storm of rifle fire from the trenches started to slaughter the men as they went forward and they were driven to earth. Trapped out on a flat plain with virtually no cover under a blazing sun. Any man who rolled to one side to get at his water bottle was shot. It was a nightmare. Kitchener's answer was more attacks. He sent in the Mounted Infantry and they, too, failed with a lot of empty saddles, including their commander. Then Kitchener ordered a half battalion of the Cornwalls forward and they were cut down in just the same way. We got the wounded out of there at night, but Kitchener and Roberts had cut the number of ambulance wagons by three quarters so we had to move them in ordinary bullock carts with no suspension. Damned painful, I can tell you.

"I was hit at almost the end of the battle. I had been sent forward to discover the condition of the Boers. I know Roberts was considering a retreat away from there, but that is a huge secret. In any event, Cronje surrendered with more than four thousand men. The newspapers crowed about our great victory and nobody mentioned the men who had died for no good reason."

The two men sat in silence for a moment or two before McGuire spoke. "That doesn't sound like the Kitchener I know. He was the master of strategy in the Sudan."

"As I said, he's impatient and that's dangerous, but not for him of course. Plus, he does not understand that the Boers are so very different from the Dervishes of the Sudan. They stand and fight with swords and spears, while the Boers dig into the earth and use modern weapons. An awful lot of senior officers are having to learn a new kind of warfare out here."

"I've seen that for myself under Buller, but I didn't expect it of Kitchener."

"Remember what I told you. He's impatient. He wants to be the hero again."

Chapter 38
Sannah's Post

McGuire sat quietly waiting for Kitchener to finish giving instructions to one of his staff officers. As usual there was nothing in writing from the General. He looked at Kitchener's scarred face with its stern expression. The scar made him look even more ill-tempered, yet the piercing blue eyes were still bright and that face changed completely when he favoured McGuire with one of his rare smiles.

"Now, McGuire, how does it feel being back working for me?"

"It's a little like coming home, sir."

Kitchener chuckled. "Then home must have been damned hard work. I suspect I am going to be working you as hard as I did in the Sudan. Are your men up to it?"

"Yes, sir. We caught up with our sleep on the train to get here and the horses are rested as well. We just need to know what you want of us."

"Just like the Sudan, I need information. The Boer commandos are proving damnably elusive. I've got cavalry out trying to find them and now I want you out there as well. How many are you now?"

"Including me, there are sixteen of us, so I can give you four patrols."

Kitchener stood and walked to the large map on the wall. "Come and look at this." He waited until McGuire joined him and then started to point at different areas. "This is where the cavalry are looking, and here, and around here. I want you and your patrols to cover the areas in between them."

"And if we spot the Boers?"

"Then ride like the wind back here and tell me. The usual stuff, where are they, how many, do they have wagons with them and, most importantly, do they have artillery. It seems they are using our own field guns against us. Presumably the ones they took at Colenso. Any questions?"

"Just one, sir. You mentioned another task for us later on. May I know what that is?"

Kitchener nodded and sat down again. "You may. Your troop served me well in the Sudan, but this war is different. I have an idea for how to deal with the Boers once we have defeated their main army in the field."

"Surely once their field army is defeated, it's over?"

"I would like to think so, but I think the Boer is a different enemy and I suspect there will be more to do. So, once you have completed a couple of tasks for me, I will want you to use your troop as the nucleus of a Mounted Infantry company. You will no doubt choose the independent thinkers that don't fit with the rest of the army, as you did once before. You will be different to the other MI units as you will report directly to me and will be outside the normal chain of command."

"And where will I find these men, sir?"

"You can ask the battalions if they have any troublemakers they would like to be rid of and you can go down to Stellenbosch and see if any of those who have been sent down there are any good to you."

"Very good, sir. I'll be on my way then if there is nothing else?"

"On your way out collect a pile of the leaflets you will find there. They offer the Boers amnesty if they give up their arms and swear loyalty. It might be another way of undermining the commandos."

***

The Boer General Christiaan De Wet lay on the summit of the kopje looking through the field glasses he had taken off the body of a British officer. Beside him lay his brother, Piet, who was also his second-in-command.

"Are you clear on the plan, Piet?"

Piet took the binoculars and scanned the small British position below them around the waterworks at Sannah's Post. "And we are sure there are only two hundred of the khakis at the waterworks?"

"We are. One of the scouts crawled right up to them last night. With our fifteen hundred men they should pose no problem."

"And when we destroy the waterworks the British in Bloemfontein will have an even bigger problem with dysentery."

"That's right. The spies say that drinking contaminated water is causing them a major difficulty and men are dying from it. They may even have to retreat without clean water from here."

"Well then, brother, we attack at daybreak."

***

McGuire rode across the Modder river and on to the waterworks with Corporal Fine by his side. Behind them rode Samuel and Private O'Driscoll. The ride had been long and fruitless and the prospect of a night's rest before the ride back in Bloemfontein was appealing.

As they reined in and dismounted a Lieutenant strolled across. He saluted McGuire as he saw the rank badges. "Welcome to Sannah's Post, sir. Are you the advance party for General Broadwood's column?"

"No, we are a reconnaissance patrol sent out by General Kitchener. Are you expecting a column?"

"Any day now. General Broadwood has been carrying out a sweep of the area and said he would call in here on his way back to the army."

McGuire handed the reins of his horse to O'Driscoll. "Should I report in to your commanding officer?"

"No need, sir. He's catching up on his sleep. I'll show you where your men can set up their camp. I assume you will join us in the officers' tent this evening?"

McGuire removed his helmet and shook his head. "I'm afraid I would be poor company. We've been riding hard. All I want is to grab a meal and then sleep. We'll be on our way again just after dawn. So I'll stay with my patrol."

The Lieutenant raised an eyebrow, but said nothing about a Major bedding down with his men. "Very well, sir, if you follow me I'll show you a good place to camp. At least we can offer you clean water from the machinery here."

"And a can or two of bully beef, if you have it to spare. Samuel here just loves it, while we will be having an impala we shot on the way in."

"I'll send the beef over for you. I haven't tried impala. How does it taste?"

McGuire grinned. "Oh somewhere between kudu and sable. You should come over and try it with us."

"I don't think my CO would like to see me eating with private soldiers and a kaffir, sir."

"Samuel is not a kaffir. He's a Zulu and a private in my unit."

The Lieutenant looked surprised at the sharp tone in McGuire's voice. "Yes, sir. I'll send the bully beef."

McGuire woke just after midnight. He was disorientated for a moment and then realised he was hearing horses as the advance party of Broadwood's force arrived. From then until around half past three in the morning the rest of the force moved in. Two cavalry regiments and a brigade of mounted infantry with U and Q batteries of the

252

Royal Horse Artillery in support. Riding with them were civilian wagons driven by settlers fleeing from the Boers.

Still lying under his blanket, McGuire watched the exhausted men unsaddle their horses and then drop down beside the wagons. He was surprised to see that no sentries were set, but presumably Broadwood was confident that the Boers were nowhere nearby.

As the false dawn started to brighten the sky Fine shook McGuire awake and handed him a mug of steaming tea. "Horses are saddled, sir, and we're ready to go unless you want breakfast first?"

McGuire sat up and blew on the scalding brew. "No, we'll get moving while it's still cool. Better for the horses. We can eat biltong on the way."

Fine stepped back as McGuire threw off the thin blanket and stood up. "Anything going on?"

"No, sir. Quiet as a graveyard, apart from the snoring all round us. These lads look pretty worn out to me."

"Well, let's not disturb them as we go." He tossed the remains of his tea to the ground and walked with Corporal Fine to where the horses waited. "Sleep well, O'Driscoll? Samuel, you ready to go?"

"I'm ready, baas. That officer sent me four tins of bully beef last night, so I don't need breakfast this morning."

McGuire swung himself into the saddle and the others followed suit. He gently pulled the horse's head around and they walked away from the wagon lines with the men sleeping beside them.

"Patrols going out, sir." O'Driscoll said.

McGuire turned in the saddle to see three small mounted patrols riding out of the camp around the waterworks. At least there was somebody awake in that mass of exhausted troops.

They had been riding for no more than ten minutes when they heard rifle fire off to one side. McGuire reined in and raised his hand to stop the others. They sat in silence to listen while the horses cropped at the stubby grass around their feet.

"What do you think, sir?"

"Well, Corporal, I think we can't just ride away without reporting that to General Broadwood. It may be nothing to worry about, but he can make that decision."

McGuire sighed and turned his horse back the way they had just come. "Right, with me, and keep your eyes open for any problems."

The patrol rode at a canter back to the camp they had just left. As they reached it McGuire signalled for his men to wait while he rode up to where he knew he would find the General. Reaching the tent, he dismounted and saluted the bleary-eyed officer with the luxurious white moustache.

"Good morning, sir. Major McGuire reporting that I have just heard rifle fire over in that direction."

The General looked to where McGuire was pointing. "There doesn't seem to be anything there now, Major. Thank you for your report, but I don't think it is anything to be concerned about. Dismissed."

McGuire felt his mouth drop open as the General turned away. He rapidly snapped it closed and saluted before turning and remounting his horse. He rode carefully between the still sleeping soldiers until he reached his patrol.

"Nothing to worry about, apparently. Let's go. The other patrols should be back in Bloemfontein by now."

***

Christiaan De Wet stood on the kopje looking down at the British around the waterworks. His scouts had told him about the unexpected increase in the numbers of soldiers, but he believed he would still have the upper hand if every one of his burghers played his part.

From his vantage point he could see his brother and the majority of his force moving into position on the east bank. His own smaller contingent was moving west to assume a blocking position around the drift at the Korn Spruit. He could see that they were almost all in the ravines along both sides of the wagon road where it entered the drift. He smiled as he saw that the khakis below him had seen nothing and seemed to be unconcerned. He walked back off the kopje and mounted his horse before riding around to join his men by the drift. It was nearly time.

It was full daylight now and the men around the wagons were beginning to stir and struggle out from under their blankets. The mounted patrols had returned and the men started to light their cooking fires for breakfast. The barrage from the hidden Boer artillery was a total surprise and men fled in panic trying to find shelter from the screaming shrapnel. Officers could see that the fire was coming from the far side of the Modder, but the gun positions were invisible to them. They had no idea of the size of the force that was attacking them.

Now the burghers opened fire with their Mauser rifles, making it impossible for the British to stay on the open grassland around the waterworks. Broadwood assumed he was being attacked by the five-thousand-strong force commanded by General Olivier that he knew was somewhere in the region. He gave the command to withdraw to Bushman's Kop on the far side of the Korn Spruit and men ran to mount their horses and to get the wagons on the move to safety.

The wagons and a few carts arrived at the drift and began to struggle across in a panicked mass of shouting and screaming drivers. The few military escorts were unable to sort out the mess and rode through the river to wait for the confusion to subside. All around the Boers stood up from their hiding places and yelled "Hands Up!" The soldiers were rounded up and disarmed before being marched to a holding area under guard. Under the direction of the armed Boers the wagon drivers formed a single line and drove to where they were directed. They were all warned that if anyone tried to signal their predicament they would be shot out of hand.

Next came the disorganized soldiers on foot and on horseback. They streamed into the drift and once again the Boers appeared from their concealed positions and forced them to surrender. Both batteries of horse artillery had now been ordered by Broadwood to withdraw to the west. The guns were limbered up and drove towards Korn Spruit with U Battery leading. The intention was that they would cross the drift, then take up a position on the far ridge to provide covering fire for the rest of the force to withdraw.

U Battery, led by Major Taylor, started to cross the drift first. As Taylor reached the far bank with his teams in the river behind him De Wet appeared from nowhere and took him prisoner. Under the rifles of the rest of the Boers, the battery had no option but to comply. One gunner at the rear of the column spun around and rode hell for leather back to the following battery. He reined in alongside Major Phipps-Hornby, the Q Battery commander, shouting that they had all been taken prisoner.

Realising that he was about to suffer the same fate and that he was well within range of the Boer riflemen, Phipps-Hornby wheeled the battery around and rode for the cover of the railway buildings that gave Sannah's Post its name. The men rode hard, lying along their horses' necks to try and avoid the swarm of bullets that followed them. Their commander spotted a low ridge just in front of the buildings and there they unlimbered their guns and dragged them into position.

The rearmost gun crew and their horses were ripped into by the Boer rifle fire and stopped, abandoned, out on the plain. Two ammunition wagons overturned in the panicked retreat, but five guns made it to the firing position.

McGuire and his patrol watched the battery from the shelter of the stone wall just behind the gunners. Rifle rounds were striking the stone work and whining off into the distance. Around them dismounted cavalrymen cowered away from the hail of bullets.

The guns were brought into action by the sweating gunners and the battery opened fire. The flat trajectory of the guns made it difficult to hit the Boers in their hidden positions. The Boers, with their long range Mausers, had no such difficulties and the gunners began to fall. By ten o'clock in the morning thirty-eight of the fifty members of the battery were down and Phipps-Hornby knew it was hopeless to continue. He turned to face the wall behind him and called the men forward to help move the guns to safety.

Most of the men refused to move until McGuire drew his heavy Webley revolver and offered them the choice of danger or certain death at his hand. Men scrambled over the wall, led by

Corporal Fine, and McGuire followed up in the rear to prevent any shirking. The men pushed their flimsy helmets down tightly on their heads and leaned forward into the storm of fire as they moved.

Major Phipps-Hornby stood calmly amongst the mayhem directing the recovery and inspiring the men as the guns were manhandled by panting, swearing men. McGuire had hold of the spokes of a wheel and was heaving to make it turn when bright blood spattered across his hands. He spun round to see O'Driscoll clutching at his throat where a Mauser bullet had ploughed through the flesh. The young Irishman looked at McGuire with terror in his eyes before crumpling to the ground.

The guns were pulled back into cover and hitched to the gun limbers. The few remaining gunners and drivers mounted and drove the teams away to the south. They could do no more. In front of them the rest of Broadwood's command was fleeing towards Bloemfontein while De Wet and his Boers stood and watched them go.

McGuire waited until the sustained rifle fire from the Boers had ceased before he went back to where O'Driscoll lay in a pool of his life's blood. He bent and picked the younger man up and walked back with him to where the patrol's horses waited patiently. With the help of Samuel, he lifted the body of his soldier and laid him across his saddle.

"We could leave him here for the burial detail to deal with later, sir."

"No, Corporal, we can't. We'll take him with us and the troop can bury its own."

Chapter 39
Mafeking

"You look exhausted, McGuire. Are you fit for another job for me?" Kitchener asked.

"Not tired, sir. Just feeling a little low. I lost a man at Sannah's post and two more have gone through dysentery."

"How many does that leave you with?"

"Just twelve, plus me. This war is costing me dear. They were all good men."

"I heard you did well at Sannah's Post. Phipps-Hornby was complimentary about you when he told me about the action. Good to see that General Gordon's old Webley is still useful. However, I have a task that you might enjoy. It's away from the army and its diseases; out behind the enemy lines."

McGuire sat forward in the wicker chair and placed his whisky and soda down on the table. "Right, sir, what do you need from us?"

"You will be aware that Colonel Baden-Powell is under siege in Mafeking? He has been doing a remarkable job of keeping the Boers at bay, but I am concerned that despite his best efforts, morale may be slipping in the town."

"I see, sir, and how can I help?"

"In the near future our advance will start again, once Lord Roberts is convinced we are prepared. I need the people in Mafeking to hold out just a little while longer. So what I need from you is a gesture. I want you to get through the

Boers and into Mafeking. Let them know they are not forgotten and that we are coming."

"And once we've done that?"

Kitchener picked up his own whisky. "Stay there and stiffen the defence. Only thirteen of you, but make yourselves visible to the defenders. Encourage them. As I said, it's a gesture, but gestures are important in these situations."

McGuire looked down at the map spread on the table in front of him. "When would you like us to go, sir?"

"As soon as you are ready. Carry as much food with you as you can. No doubt they will be starting to run short."

McGuire saluted and left Kitchener in his room. He stepped out of the headquarters building, grateful for the cool breeze blowing across the open veldt. For a moment he stood looking up at the stars, their clarity reminding him of the way they looked when out in the deserts of Egypt. He walked along the path and untied his horse. Before he could mount he became aware that there was somebody there in the shadows.

"Who's there? Step forward."

The figure moved. "Major McGuire? Sorry to startle you. I've been waiting to speak to you. I'm Captain Howat, Westland Mounted Rifles."

"And how can I help you, Captain?"

"We're a militia unit from New Zealand. Just arrived here and one of the staff officers recommended we travel with you for a couple of days to get used to the way things are done around here."

"I see. Well, we're heading north very shortly on a task for General Kitchener. You can ride along for part of the way, if that would suit you?"

"It would indeed, sir."

McGuire nodded. "Good, then ride with me now and I'll show you where we are camped. You can bring your people across in the morning and then we'll go."

"Don't you bunk in the officers' quarters?"

"No, I stay alongside my men. That way I know what condition they are in. I eat the same food, I sleep in the same place. It lets me judge how far I can push them."

"Interesting. The rest of the army don't seem to do things that way."

McGuire chuckled. "We're not the rest of the army. That's why we get sent on interesting tasks."

***

As dawn broke the reconnaissance troop was already in the saddle waiting for the New Zealanders. After around twenty minutes McGuire saw Howat leading the horsemen through the mass of tents towards him.

As they arrived Howat saluted. "Sorry we're a little late, sir. It all looks different in the daylight."

"First lesson, Captain: once we are out of camp, no more saluting."

"Really? Why ever not?"

"Take a look at my men and then me. We all look very much the same. No shiny officers' badges, no Sam Browne belt and no sword. Those things got a lot of officers shot in the early days. Now officers try to blend in with the men to keep from making themselves a target. I have yet to convince the army that saluting in the field has the same effect, but no luck so far. So, no saluting, eh? It's a gift for a Boer marksman."

Howat looked around him slightly nervously. "I notice you still wear a pistol on your belt, though."

"It's a rather special pistol. It once belonged to General Gordon and I recovered it from his body down in Khartoum. Her Majesty told me I should keep it and carry it with honour. So I am rather obliged to keep it with me, even though the rifle is much more effective."

McGuire pulled his horse's head around and tapped with his heels to start it walking forward. Howat fell in alongside him and they rode towards the north. The reconnaissance troop rode behind McGuire and, after a slight hesitation, the militia joined them.

"I see you have the Lee Enfield rifle in your saddle boot. I heard they were being issued."

"We were one of the first units to get them to replace our old Lee Metfords. The troops have taken to calling them Emily."

"We're stuck with the old Martini Henry. No sign of us getting anything better any time soon."

"Wait until the next battle then go round and pick up any weapons you want. You'll find you have to bend the rules a little to be effective out here."

"And I see you have a kaffir riding with you. What's his role?"

"Captain, I know it's common in the army, but please don't call Samuel a kaffir. He is a Zulu and he is one of my soldiers, just like all the rest."

***

McGuire sat on the edge of the donga the troop was camped in, waiting for Donnelly and Samuel to return. He could smell the meat frying on the small fire below him and he felt the hunger rumble in his stomach. It had been a long time since breakfast and they had spent the day sneaking past Boer patrols with no chance to rest or eat. He heard the dry grass rustle as the two men slipped down beside him.

"Good job we're back in time for dinner. That smells good."

McGuire grinned at the big Sergeant. "It would have been out of character for you to miss a meal, so I was expecting you around now."

"Shall I tell you the news now, or do you want to eat first?"

"Tell me now. We'll be called when it's ready."

"Well, it's going to be difficult. The Boers have got positions all round as far as we could see. There are artillery emplacements in various places and there are patrols wandering the veldt. They seem to know what they are doing, unfortunately."

McGuire took the piece of grass he had been chewing out of his mouth and tossed it to one side. "So what's the answer? How do we get in?"

"Honestly, sir, I don't know. I think we need one of Connolly's maps and then we can see if there are any weak spots."

"That could take some time."

"Better that than being taken prisoner or worse. Plus, we can't risk the Boers getting their hands on Samuel, or he'd be in deep trouble."

McGuire pushed himself up. "Let's think about it some more. But for now we need to get down there before those gannets eat it all."

***

The men clustered around and looked down at the map Connolly had made. The routes of the patrols were all marked as well as all the static positions they had found in two days of careful reconnaissance. The Boers had planned well and the patrol routes and observation points were effective. Even though there was a large area to cover, their rifles could do just that and the flat ground was in their favour.

McGuire looked around his men searching for signs of nervousness. "Are you all clear on the plan?" There were nods from all of them. "Never mind, same as always, I'm going to run through it one more time." He smiled at the groans from the men.

"Never mind groaning, just listen in. We wear the Boer jackets and hats and ride as if we are a patrol or reinforcement arriving. We keep clear of the patrols as much as we can, but a slight wave to acknowledge our Boer comrades as we ride past should be fine. You can see the route we've chosen and with just a little luck the mounted patrols should be elsewhere if we have got the timing right. Now any questions?"

"Two, sir, if I may?"

"Yes, Peters, what are they?"

"Sir, if everything goes exactly to plan we ride up to the defences around Mafeking looking like Boers. Are we sure the defenders are not going to shoot us down?"

McGuire sighed to himself; he had explained this so many times. "No, we're not. It's a risk. As we get close we shed the Boer disguise, slap on our helmets and trust to luck. The defenders will have seen us coming and I hope they will realise we are something different to the patrols they are used to. Next?"

Peters looked at Samuel, sitting next to him. "It's Samuel, sir. The Boers don't have black fellas riding with them and if they see Samuel it could give the game away."

McGuire rocked back on his heels. He was so used to having Samuel in the troop he had forgotten that. "Now that is a good thought. Well done. Any ideas anyone?"

"I do, sir, if Samuel doesn't mind."

"Yes, Sergeant Parks?"

267

"Well sir, by the edge of the stream over there is a patch of pale earth. If we mix some up he could smear it on his face to look a bit paler. Sorry, Samuel."

Samuel gave Parks a beaming smile. "A bit of mud is better than a bullet or being whipped to death if they catch me, baas."

The troop waited while Parks helped Samuel smear the pale mud across his face. Up close it looked a mess, but from a distance maybe it would work. McGuire watched as Samuel came back to where the horses waited before he and the troop mounted. They had their dark Boer jackets and slouch hats on and rode off trying to look as casual as possible.

Once out of the donga there was no cover and they could be seen from all the Boer positions. They rode past an artillery gun pit and McGuire saw that the Long Tom was being prepared to fire. He raised a casual hand to the men, who stopped and watched them ride by. They rode on and McGuire could almost feel the eyes boring into his back, but the rifle shot didn't come.

They rode forward to where they knew there was a patrol route, but the Boers should be at the end of their track at this time. Damn! The Boers were early and riding towards them. The Boer leader raised a hand and yelled something. McGuire gave him a small wave, but carried on riding. The shout came again and when McGuire turned to look over his shoulder the Boers were spurring their horses forward and unslinging their rifles.

This was far sooner than he had hoped as he yelled to the troop. They broke into a gallop towards the British lines at Mafeking and the Boers followed. Rifle shots cracked past them, too close for comfort, and then McGuire saw a second patrol angling in from the left. He eased his horse's head a little to the right to avoid them, but that took him towards a group of rifle pits and he could see the Boers running to their position with their rifles in their hands.

The slouch hat flew off McGuire's head as he wrenched the revolver from its holster. As the men in the rifle pits came closer he fired and fired again. They ducked down into their holes in surprise and then they were past. But now the bullets flew thick and fast after them.

Ahead McGuire could see khaki uniforms running to man the defences and any second they, too, would open fire. He shrugged out of his jacket and let it fall to the ground behind him, then slapped the helmet on his head and sat more upright in the saddle so he could be seen.

From his right front came the boom of a field gun. The shell whistled past and exploded as it hit the ground in front of the first pursuing group. A second gun fired and the shell was aimed at the group to the left. Rifles opened up from the row of stone sangers in front of him, but the bullets flew wide; they were aiming at the Boers. Seconds later, they rode through between the sangers and behind

269

a raised ridge of piled earth. McGuire flung himself out of the saddle and ran to the top of the bank with his rifle in hand. The Boers were still in range and he took aim and fired. A man fell, but he couldn't tell if it was his shot or one from the British troops that had hit him. The rest of the troop were on the top of the bank now, laughing at their narrow escape and firing at their pursuers.

The Boers beat a hasty retreat and McGuire walked down the bank to where an officer was waiting for him. "Captain, I owe you a stiff drink if there is one to be had in Mafeking. The Boers were getting a little too close for comfort out there."

The Captain raised a weary salute to McGuire. "You're more than welcome, sir, but it was a good job you shed your coats. We weren't quite sure what was going on until then. By the way, sir, just who are you?"

"Major Michael McGuire, late of the Royal Irish Fusiliers, but now working directly for General Kitchener. He sent us here to reassure the garrison that the army is coming and you haven't been forgotten."

The Captain smiled. "That's good to know, sir, and I'm sure Colonel Baden-Powell will want to see you as soon as possible. I'll give you one of my men to guide you to him."

***

McGuire tied his horse to the low fence around Baden-Powell's sandbagged two-storey headquarters. As he walked up the path to the door a smartly uniformed Colonel with a well-trimmed moustache and a bald head emerged. McGuire stopped and saluted.

"So you are the reinforcements Kitchener has sent me, are you, Major?"

"Not really, sir. We are here to try and help you reassure the garrison and the civilians that help is on the way."

"And it's been a damned long time coming. However, would you like to see the message I received from the Boer commander today?"

"I would indeed, sir."

Baden-Powell reached into his breast pocket and pulled out a note that he then passed to McGuire.

'To Colonel Baden-Powell. I see in the Bulawayo Chronicle that your men in Mafeking play cricket on Sundays and give concerts and balls on Sunday evenings. In case you would allow my men to join in the same it would be very agreeable to me as here outside Mafeking there are seldom any of the fair sex and there can be no merriment without their being present. Wishing you a pleasant day, I remain your obliging friend. S. Eloff Commandant of Johannesburg Commando'

McGuire handed the paper back. "Cheeky devil."

"He is indeed, but somewhat more civilised than his predecessor, Cronje. He sent me a message castigating me for arming the blacks and demanding that I disarm them immediately.

Apparently he felt this was exclusively a white man's war."

"There are some among our own officers who feel the same way, sir."

"Well, I'm not one of them. The Africans are stuck in here with us and if the Boers launch an assault they deserve the chance to defend themselves. So now then, McGuire, we've held out for two hundred days so far. How much longer do I have to wait for the cavalry to ride over the hill to our rescue?"

"In truth, sir, I do not know. Lord Roberts is preparing the army and will move as soon as he is able, though he does have some serious issues, the lack of cavalry and the slowness of the support transport among them."

"And what about you? Are you and your men to ride back to the army?"

"No, sir, we are to stay here under your command until the relief arrives."

"Then I hope you don't mind short rations. Find your men a place to stay and then come back and tell me what you know of Lord Roberts' plans."

Chapter 40
Attack on the Stadt

"Tell me something, Major. Your men seem to be wearing a surprising number of trade badges. Why is that'"

McGuire put down his whisky and water. Soda had run out weeks ago, but Baden-Powell had hoarded a few bottles of whisky for special occasions. "When I first joined the regiment in Cairo there was no post for me so the Colonel created one. He asked me to form a reconnaissance unit to move ahead of the regiment in the desert, to scout ahead and prevent ambushes, for instance. The seven men I was given were the dross that nobody else wanted. I had to do something to make them feel special if they were to succeed. So all of them were trained in all of the skills we might need. It allowed me to use them in independent patrols later on. I also had the red diamond with an 'R' in it made by a tailor in the bazaar. It made them stand out from the rest of the regiment. After a while it became the mark of an elite unit."

"So you think your scouts feel special because of these badges?"

"Not just the badges, sir, but what they have had to do to win them."

"Interesting idea. However, now we need to discuss how to use you. Your men will be seen around the town by the people. No doubt they will be asked why they are here. Do they know what to say?"

"They do, sir. They've all been briefed that we are just the advance guard of the army. Here to help you hold out for just a little longer."

"As you Irish say, 'From your mouth to God's ears'. For now, though, I would like you to move your men close to the Stadt. That's the name that has been given to the area where the Africans live. Lots of close-packed huts with trenches for defence. The people who live there have rifles, or at least three hundred of them do. I would like you to improve their training and, if anything happens, to stiffen their resistance. Can you do that?"

"With pleasure, sir. Whatever you need."

"Good, now tell me what you know about Lord Roberts' intentions."

***

McGuire rejoined his men, sitting under the shade of a baobab tree. "Right then, what have you found out while I was speaking with the Colonel?"

Donnelly spoke first. "This is a very different siege to Ladysmith. They've been stuck in here for longer, but they are still full of fight. They have mounted a number of sorties against the Boers and given him some trouble. They think they had about six or seven thousand of them around the perimeter at one time, but they held them off."

"Sergeant Parks?"

"As you'd expect, they've been eating their horses, although they have managed to keep a few for raids on the Boers. They're on short rations and I don't know how they are stringing them out. I guess it's the rigid control from the Colonel."

"Corporal Fine?"

"I went with Corporal Connolly to have a look at the defences. Like the sangers we came through, they've got good defence positions all over. They've got lines of trenches dug and they look ready for an attack."

"And you wouldn't believe the artillery, sir," Connolly said. "They found an old bronze muzzle-loading cannon being used as a gatepost and they've brought it into use. It's dated 1770, but they can still fire a ten-pound cannon ball out of it. And then there's the one they're really proud of. They call it 'The Wolf' and it started life as a four-inch steel pipe. They mounted it on an old threshing machine and the railway foundry manufactured a breech. It can fire an eighteen-pound shell for four thousand yards."

"Samuel?"

"Things are not so good for the black man. There is starvation in the township and many die. Some of them have been used to dig the trenches the white men are so proud of. Others have been given old guns and shotguns to defend their part of town. Those ones get food, the rest none."

McGuire suppressed his surprise. "Well, the Colonel has asked us to camp down by the township. They call it the Stadt. We are to help with the defence there."

275

"We'll move over there now then, sir. I'll find us a decent place to set up shop." Donnelly said.

McGuire nodded. "All right. Samuel, you come with me. We are going to speak to some of your people down there in the Stadt."

"Baas, they are not my people. I am a Zulu, from a warrior tribe. These ones are of the Barralongs and Fingos. They grub in the earth for their meat."

"Nevertheless, come with me. It will be good for them to see you serving as a soldier of the Queen. You can tell them we will fight alongside them if trouble comes."

"Yes, baas, I can do that."

McGuire smiled at the Zulu. "At least you look normal now with all that muck off your face. You won't frighten the children while you are finding the head man for me."

***

McGuire was struggling to sleep under his thin blanket. He gave in and decided to do something useful. By the light of a flickering candle he started his weekly letter to Emma. '*12th May, Mafeking. Dearest Emma, The troop and I are sleeping in tents now. Much better than being under the stars when the rain comes, but not so good for imagining you looking up at the same stars ...*'

There was a flickering to the light. He took a moment to realise that it was coming from the walls of his tent. The light was outside. He checked his watch. Quarter to four was too early for the dawn. Putting the letter to one side, he stood and walked to open the flaps of the tent. There was a fire in the Stadt. One of the roofs of the huts was blazing fiercely. Then another caught fire and another. He could hear the yells and screams from the Barralongs as they ran to safety. Then another fire burst into life. This one was quite a way from the first few; that seemed strange.

Silhouetted against the fire he could see people running, then behind them came more. These ones had slouch hats and rifles in their hands. Boers! He spun round and grabbed his rifle before running to the next tent. Parks and Fine were just coming out of it as he reached them.

"Stand to. Chase the men out. The Boers are attacking. Hurry!"

McGuire was pleased by the reaction time of his men. In less than a minute they were all outside the tents with their weapons at the ready. He paused to see where the Boers had got to and saw that they were heading across the flat plain towards the main town. His place was with the Africans, so he led his men into the Stadt.

The Barralongs who were armed had been taken by surprise. They had withdrawn from the attack to organise themselves and were now in a line that straddled the Boer escape route and also blocked any possible Boer reinforcements from entering that way. From the main garrison McGuire could hear the sound of bugle calls, so the fires had been seen there as well.

The light from the spreading fire worked better for the defenders. McGuire could see that the attackers had split up into different parties with one group moving into an area of limestone boulders that had been used as a cattle kraal. The Barralongs saw it, too, and they raced forward to the attack. McGuire and his men were hard-pressed to keep up with them.

The flood of bullets from the yelling Africans swept over the stone kraal from all directions. The Boers were unable to rise up and return fire. In a very few moments white flags were being waved from behind the stones and the Barralongs rushed forward to take their revenge. McGuire and his men managed to stop them and to take the Boers prisoner. It was a close-run thing and there could have been a massacre.

With the Boers disarmed and sitting on the ground with their hands tied, under the watchful eyes of the Barralongs, McGuire climbed to the top of a large boulder and scanned with his binoculars towards the garrison. In the light from the burning township he could see men running to take up positions around the old police barracks.

"Sergeant Parks! Your patrol and Samuel stay here and make sure the Barralongs don't get carried away. They've got good reason to take their revenge, but I want the same number of Boers here when I get back."

"I'll see to it, sir. What are you going to be doing?"

"It looks as if this fight has moved to those police barracks, so I'm going to take the rest of the troop and see if we can lend a hand."

McGuire and his men ran across the flat veldt between the kraal and the main town. As they arrived they saw Colonel Baden-Powell standing alone and watching the troops who were firing into the barracks.

"Can we help, sir?"

Baden-Powell turned slowly and looked at the group of panting men. "You seem to have been running, Major. Always good to take exercise."

McGuire smiled. "Indeed, sir. We've taken a bunch of the attackers prisoner around the stone kraal. The Barralongs have them, with five of my men keeping an eye on them."

"Good work, McGuire. Well, as you can see, our visitors have barricaded themselves inside the barracks and are now surrounded. With the men firing into the building I doubt they are having a good time in there."

"Do you have a plan to get them out?"

"Not really. They have no way out of there without being slaughtered and in a little while I'll remind them of that and invite them to surrender. In the meantime, I'll let them stew in their own juices."

"Very well, sir. Then with your permission we will wait here in case you need us."

Three hours later, the surrounding soldiers heard a voice they recognised as Colonel Hore shouting, "Cease fire! Cease fire!" and then a white flag appeared through the doorway.

Commandant Eloff had realised his situation was desperate and had surrendered to the men he had taken prisoner and held in a storeroom within the police barracks. Later that morning Eloff with a French and a German officer under his command were entertained to breakfast at Dixon's Hotel by Colonel Baden-Powell and Winston Churchill's aunt, Lady Sarah Wilson. McGuire sat at the foot of the table and marvelled at the English idea of good manners.

Less than a week later the first part of the relief column arrived and the besieging Boers mounted their horses and melted away.

Chapter 41
Back to the Army

The troop crested a rise and reined in, marvelling at the sight before them. They had seen the huge dust cloud as they approached and now, across the veldt, they could see what was causing it.

Donnelly gave a low whistle. "God Almighty, would you look at that. That must be what the Israelites looked like crossing the desert."

"Except the Israelites weren't dragging field guns with them," McGuire said.

In front of them, they could see the bulk of the army under Field Marshal Lord Roberts marching northwards. The thousands of infantry and cavalry were accompanied by masses of slow-moving ox carts with the African drivers yelling and cracking whips across their animals' backs. Then came the field guns of the Royal Horse Artillery, almost a hundred of them.

Corporal Fine shook his head. "How the hell can the Boers stand up to that? Surely now we're on the move the war is almost over?"

McGuire raised his binoculars and stared at the massive column. "I truly hope you're right. A return home would be damned welcome about now. Right then, let's go and join the advance."

The troop kicked their heels to get their horses moving again and then trotted across the plain towards the advancing army. Parks was the first to spot the command flags flying from one of the carts and McGuire led them towards it. The troop hung back to one side of the column as their commander rode alongside the wagons to ask for General Kitchener.

The staff officer stood up in the back of the wagon, clinging on to the canvas cover and pointed off to the left. "See the horseman up on that ridge? That's Kitchener. He rides out at least twice a day on his own. I think he likes to breathe clean air without all this damned dust."

Thanking the officer, McGuire eased his horse between the carts and marching troops, then once clear he set off at a trot towards the General. As he got closer Kitchener saw him coming and started to walk his horse towards him.

"Good morning, sir. Reporting back from Mafeking. That column is quite a sight for sore eyes."

"Glad to have you back, McGuire. All your men fit?"

"No injuries, sir, thankfully, though we did have a little excitement in Mafeking. And I have a personal letter for you from Colonel Baden-Powell."

Kitchener took the letter that McGuire held out and ripped the envelope open. He sat silently on the horse to read it before he looked up again.

"It seems the good Colonel appreciated the gesture of sending your men through the lines. It helped with morale. He speaks rather highly of you and your troop of scouts, as he calls them. Speaking of which, I am holding to my intention of having you raise an independent company, but now is not the time. We need you and your roughnecks out in front of the column. There are a number of rivers that cross our path to Johannesburg and Pretoria and I suspect the Boers will try and stop us there. I want your men way out in front of the column to reconnoitre just what they are doing."

"Very good, sir. With your permission, we'll top up our rations and be on our way. We left all that we had in Mafeking. I think the men will appreciate being out of that dust cloud at least."

Kitchener looked out across the plain at the moving host. "At least you should have no trouble finding us when you need to report back."

Having found the quartermaster's ox carts the troop loaded themselves with three days' rations and then rode away in front of the trudging column. Away to their left they could see a troop of cavalry swinging out in a flanking movement to attempt to come at any Boer emplacement from the side. Somewhere over to the right there was another, though this one was invisible from where they were.

They rode in a loose line until they were at least a day's march in front of the column and saw the stunted trees along the banks of the first river. Ahead of them they heard the thud of explosives and saw a cloud of grey smoke rising. Beyond the smoke they could see a small group of horsemen riding away. As they reached the river they found the bridge down and the current swirling around the wreckage.

The troop split in two with each half riding along the river banks to find a drift that could be used by the army. Once they had it they crossed and returned to the area of the bridge. The Boers had dug a system of trenches that dominated the river crossing. There was nothing there but a mass of hoofprints that they had left as they faded away.

McGuire sent one of his men back to the column with a despatch describing what they had found and instructions on how to find the drift. The rider would lead a company of Royal Engineers back to have them improve the drift before the column arrived.

The troop continued north. Wary now, they expected to run into Boer ambush parties at any moment. Pushing on, they reached the next river crossing and again they saw the smoke rise from the destroyed bridge. Culverts were blown, anything to slow the army, yet again the defensive trenches that had been made with such care were empty. The only sight they had of the Boers was the backs of the demolition parties as they rode to catch their companions.

The story repeated itself at each river crossing. With the huge army coming straight at them and cavalry swooping in from either flank, the Boers pulled back as soon as they saw the first British uniforms appear. As they crossed the Vaal some forty miles from Johannesburg McGuire called a halt. His exhausted men needed a rest before they pushed on and it would be at least two days before the army arrived. Parks brought down a buck and they had their first fresh meat in days. As they settled for the night the sentry heard hoofbeats approaching and the men scattered to take up defensive positions.

A lone rider emerged from the night and McGuire recognised the hat with the large feather in the brim. "Churchill, you're going to get yourself killed doing this one day."

The reporter, his face- flushed, gripped McGuire's hand. "Owe it to my readers, old chap. I can't tell them tales of adventure stuck in that huge mass of transport. So I thought I'd come and see what the eyes of the army were doing out here."

"Just getting ready to bed down for the night. Anyway, we'd better let you eat what's left of our dinner. Sergeant Parks, can you get someone to look after Mr Churchill's horse?"

As they woke in the morning, the men were swearing and grumbling as usual at the hoar frost that once again covered their thin blankets. They warmed themselves round the fire and sipped the tea that helped to wash down the hardtack ration biscuits. As the sun rose higher it warmed their bones and they felt the life come back as they saddled the horses. Once mounted, they followed the dirt road to the north with Corporal Fine and his patrol taking their turn in the lead.

McGuire heard the burst of rifle fire from in front of them and then Fine and his men galloped back, with one man hunched over his saddle and blood soaking his jacket. Fine reined in alongside

McGuire as others helped the wounded man down and began to staunch the bleeding.

"There's a ridge up ahead, sir. Got a white farmhouse perched on it. The Boers seem to have decided to make a stand at last."

"Could you see the defences?"

"Trenches, as usual, and all I could see was riflemen. No sign of those damned pom-pom guns. I'm guessing their horses are on the other side of the ridge."

"Any idea of numbers?"

"Too many for us to take on, sir, and there's no cover worth a light on the hillside."

"Very well, a job for the column then. If I write the report, will you take it back, Churchill? Find whoever is commanding the advance guard and tell him what we've got here."

The advance troops marched up rapidly once the message had been received and the infantry were deployed in a wide line ready to advance while the cavalry was to sweep in from left and right as usual. Churchill had come back with the troops and stood with McGuire watching the infantry deploy ready to assault the ridge and farmhouse they now knew was called Doornkop. It was famous as the place where the men of the Jameson Raid had been forced to surrender.

"What the hell?"

McGuire spun round to see what had alarmed Churchill. He struggled to believe what was happening. Without waiting for the cavalry to outflank the enemy, the infantry was advancing up the bare hill. With their glittering bayonets fixed they made a brave sight, but a foolish one.

The Boers waited until the soldiers were well within range and then opened rapid fire. Khaki-clad figures started to fall all along the line. The advance never faltered and the Highlanders marched upwards with their kilts swinging. The British returned fire as they went and the firing was now thick and fast with the roar of hundreds of rifles at once. The khaki figures started to appear on the skyline. A few at first, and then more and more. The firing died away. The hill had been taken and the surviving Boers were riding away as fast as their horses could carry them.

As dusk came on McGuire and Churchill wandered along the line of bodies that had been brought down from the ridge. They lay in a neat row with their feet protruding from under the blankets that covered them, while the men of their regiments dug the graves that would hold them.

"Is this what your readers want to read over their breakfasts?"

"They should, but my editor will no doubt change it to include just the brave charge. The cost will be left out of the report, so the armchair warriors can still wave their flags and boast."

The army had pushed on after the battle and was making camp for the night in the outskirts of Johannesburg. The men were using wooden pit props, intended for the mines, to make their bivouac fires.

Chapter 42
On to Pretoria.

The reconnaissance troop rode through the camps by the roadside and on towards Johannesburg. They rode through quiet streets that were almost deserted. As they reached the main square they came upon the tail end of the Boer defenders pulling the last of their big guns out of the town. McGuire held up his hand and they stood their horses quietly in a side street, until the Boer army had left. The Boer flag still flew from the flagpole in the centre of the square and McGuire resisted the temptation to pull it down as a souvenir. They split up and rode along a number of streets before returning to the square.

"Anything to report?" McGuire asked as they all joined up again.

The men all shook their heads. For some reason it felt right to be quiet in this town. They rode back towards the army and McGuire found Kitchener to report what he had found.

The next morning the army marched into the town behind the drums and bugles of the Guards Brigade. They marched into the main square, followed by three companies of infantry. The Boer vierkleur was pulled down from the flagpole and the Union Jack that Lord Roberts' wife had sewn was hoisted in its place. Doctor Krause, the chief officer of the municipality, stood on the saluting dais next to Lord Roberts and took the salute with the Field Marshal as the troops marched by.

McGuire and the troop did not see the ceremony. They were away to the north following the retreating Boers and watching them stream into Pretoria. They came to the first of the major forts that had been built to defend the town and were now standing with their gates open. Three men went inside and found it deserted, with marks on the ground where the heavy guns had been dragged out.

McGuire stood with his two Sergeants on top of the fort and scanned the town through his binoculars. In every direction he could see Boers streaming away in ones and twos or in small groups. They were going home.

The army delayed in Johannesburg dealing with a spurious offer of peace talks. In fact, this offer was intended to buy time for the Boers who had stayed loyal to remove weapons and, more importantly, the national gold reserves from Pretoria. It worked and when the army moved north again the gold was already gone.

The reconnaissance troop waited by the side of the road. They could see the army marching towards them preceded by a single rider. As the rider brought his horse to a stop McGuire saw that it was Churchill.

"Churchill, what the devil are you doing here this time? More excitement for your readers?"

"Not this time, my friend. This is where the Boers held me prisoner before I escaped and the people I was locked up with are still there. If the Boers are running I want to be the one who throws the gates open. Ride with me and we'll do something special today."

McGuire was tempted. "So tell me, were the Irish Fusiliers locked up with you?"

Churchill nodded. "Their officers were. Where the men have been held, I don't know, but we can find out. So are you coming?"

"To hell with it, yes we are."

Churchill looked surprised. "All of you? I thought only you and I would go."

"No, the troop will go. Mount up! We're going to find Colonel Murphy."

The men scrambled to their feet and threw themselves into the saddle. McGuire saw that they were all grinning like schoolboys. To a man, they drew their rifles out of the saddle boots and waited for the word to move.

"After you, Mister Churchill. This is your mad scheme."

Churchill smiled and turned his horse towards the town. McGuire fell in beside him and raised his hand. His hand came down and pointed forward and the troop moved off in column of twos. As they neared the edge of the town they broke into a trot. People on the pavements by the side of the road watched them go by open-mouthed. Nobody tried to stop them and they saw no sign of any resistance.

As Churchill saw the State Model School ahead of him he took his hat off and waved it in the air with a loud cheer. Men in khaki uniforms wandering around the yard stopped and turned towards the advancing troop. Churchill spurred his horse into a canter and the troop followed suit. As they reached the now unguarded gates Churchill flung himself off the horse, shot the lock with his Mauser pistol, and pushed the gates open. In moments he was surrounded by cheering officers slapping his back and calling his name.

McGuire sat his horse and looked across the crowd for a familiar face. Then he saw the tall erect figure walking calmly towards him with excited officers making way for him as he walked. McGuire dismounted and saluted.

"Good morning, Colonel. I hope I find you well?"

"You do, McGuire, you do indeed. I didn't expect it to be you who came to release us and I am damnably glad to see you." He looked at the rank badges on McGuire's jacket. "A Major? How did that happen with the regiment locked up in here?"

"That was General Kitchener's doing, sir. I'm sure he will want to confirm the promotion with you, though."

"Knowing Kitchener, I doubt that very much. Congratulations, anyway. Now I'd like to say hello to the troop, if you don't mind?"

McGuire looked at the grinning members of the troop. They were dirty, they were tired and he was proud of every last one of them.

"Sir, the men will be delighted to see you again. When they knew we were coming for you I could hardly hold them back."

The silken flag made by Lord Roberts' wife flew over Pretoria the next day and the Field Marshal waited for the surrender of the Boer army he had been expecting. It did not come and on the 11th of June the battle of Diamond Hill was fought. The British lost one hundred and eighty men. The Boers retreated again, but the fight had put new heart into them and inspired their people to continue to resist.

Chapter 43
The Company

"Right then, McGuire, it's time for you to build me my company."

McGuire watched Kitchener across the wide, paper-strewn desk he had commandeered. "Very good, sir. Can you tell me what you are expecting me to produce?"

"Simple. I want a larger version of your reconnaissance troop. Fast-moving, flexible and highly trained. You will answer directly to me."

"I see, sir, and what is our task to be?"

"Lord Roberts has declared the war to be virtually won. The Boer main armies are defeated and their towns are taken. The Field Marshal is therefore going home, leaving me in command. I feel he may have been a little previous in his declaration of victory. The Boer commandos are still in the field and show no sign of giving up. I suspect we have quite a way to go yet before this country is pacified. Your job is to find, capture or kill as many of the still-active Boers as possible."

"And my remit, sir? What authority do I have?"

"Recruit suitable men from wherever you find them. Train them your way. Equip them as you wish and make them effective and soon. I want you back in the field as quickly as possible. You will have a letter of authority from me that will instruct quartermasters and others to supply what you need. Will that suffice?"

McGuire smiled. "Almost as good as a licence to print money, sir. I understand that many of the men that nobody wants get sent to work at the main base camp in Stellenbosch. I'll start looking for my misfits there."

Kitchener nodded. "A good place to start. They should also have any equipment you need. Expect some resistance. There are a lot of disgruntled people there who will resent what you are doing, I'm sure. Anything else?"

"Just one thing, sir. Do I have authority to promote my soldiers?"

"You can't have them shot without my authority. Other than that, do whatever is necessary to give me an effective tool that I can use."

McGuire stood up and saluted. "I will be back with my company as soon as possible, sir."

"One thing, what are you going to call yourselves?"

"I'd thought about that and with your permission I thought the 1st Independent Reconnaissance Company had a nice ring to it."

"So it does. Now go and make it happen."

As he walked to the door of the headquarters, a harassed staff officer ran after him and handed him his travel orders and his letter of authority signed by Kitchener. McGuire read them both as he walked down the pathway to where his horse waited. He got to the third document and smiled. It was a copy of the letter to London instructing the War Office to have his promotion published in the

London Gazette. Once that was done, he would be confirmed in his new rank and would no longer be just an acting Major but a substantive one.

The troop packed up their camp in less than an hour and rode with McGuire down to the train station. The authority letters secured them places for the men and horses on the first available train. No cattle cars for the men this time; the transport system seemed to be starting to settle down.

Once into the massive camp at Stellenbosch, McGuire waited until accommodation had been found for the troop before he went to find a bed in the officers' mess. He would have preferred to stay with his men as he did when in the field, but in a major camp it would be unacceptable. Having thrown his kit on the bed in the small private room, he walked back into the anteroom and looked around him. All around the large room were comfortable chairs and most of them were filled by officers who seemed to have nothing better to do than to read newspapers or play cards.

He walked to the mess manager's office and took paper and pen from the desk. He sat down and composed a notice calling for volunteers to join his company. Once satisfied with it, he walked to the mess notice board and pinned it up, right in the centre where it could not be missed.

Having started the ball rolling, McGuire walked through the depot towards the troop. He passed compounds filled with horses. Hundreds of horses. Farriers were working on fitting horseshoes and veterinarians were examining the animals for defects. He passed the open-fronted sheds where saddles were being made and repaired. At least there was some useful activity in this place.

Reaching the troop, he called them around him and had them sit down on the crates and boxes that were scattered about. "Right now, all of you listen. I'm going to tell you why we are here. Back in Egypt when I joined the regiment I was told to create a reconnaissance unit to go out in front of the battalion when it was on the move. I was given the worst bunch of misfits in the regiment, the men nobody wanted as they didn't fit the army mould. They were just the right people for the unconventional job we had to do. As we went to take back the Sudan we expanded to make the troop and went looking for more people of the same type: independent thinkers, men who could work away from the rigid structure of the army, and that was you lot. I think you've worked out pretty well."

He looked around at the men, who were now smiling. They enjoyed their unconventional reputation and the red diamond badges on their arm gave them a bit of a swagger.

"Well now, General Kitchener wants us to expand again. We are to make a company that will answer to him alone. Your job is to find me the misfits we need. You recall that we did not keep all the people who tried to join us in Egypt? Well, it's going to be the same here. If they can't come up to the same standard as you then we won't take them. Once we have the volunteers, you are going to be the ones training them. Any questions?"

Sergeant Parks raised his hand. "Yes, sir. Are there any limits on who we take? Some of these people are going to be criminals."

"Good point. Minor infractions like a little light stealing I can live with. Serious crimes like murder or outright mutiny are too much, but that kind will probably be locked up. Anything else?"

He waited, but there were no more questions and the men were about to stand up. "Before you all leave there are a few changes I want to make. Sergeant Donnelly, you are now the Company Sergeant Major. Sergeant Parks you are now a Colour Sergeant. Corporals Fine and Connolly I want to see Sergeant's stripes on your arms by this evening. There will be other promotions when I see what sort of men you all bring me. Now go hunting."

The men split up and started to walk off into the base camp, while Parks and Donnelly walked across to McGuire. "Sir, are you sure about this? I'm not sure about being the CSM."

"And I feel the same about being a Colour Sergeant, sir."

McGuire had expected something like this. "Listen, you two, I need people I can trust with my life and that's you two. Donnelly, as CSM you will be in charge of discipline and I know nobody who can get respect and obedience faster than you. Parks, we are going to have to look after over a hundred horses and train the men to ride them and care for them. Who better than you for that job?"

"A hundred?"

"That's right – the 1st Independent Reconnaissance Company is going to be one hundred strong. We have to find the men, train them and get back in the fight as soon as possible. Now go and get your new rank badges from the quartermaster and then join the hunt for the men we need."

Leaving the men to the task he had given them, McGuire took a slow walk back to the mess. As he walked in he saw two officers reading his notice. He walked closer to hear what was being said.

"What the devil is a Reconnaissance Company and who is this Major McGuire anyway?"

"That would be me, gentlemen. And the company is a Mounted Infantry company as it says on my notice. Are you looking for gainful employment or are you happy idling your days here?"

The Captain looked McGuire up and down, noticing the rough state of his uniform. "I have quite enough employment here, thank you, sir."

The Lieutenant paused until the Captain had stalked away back into the anteroom before he spoke. "I'm interested, sir. It's driving me batty being stuck here doing nothing while men are dying out on the veldt."

"Then why are you here? Why not with your regiment?"

The Lieutenant looked down at his shoes and then back up at McGuire "I disobeyed a direct order from my company commander, sir."

"What order was that?"

"He ordered me to burn down a Boer farmhouse, sir. The father was away with De Wet's commando and there were just women and children there. I declined."

"Why would he order that?"

"Instructions from Lord Roberts. He has issued orders that any farmhouse where the men are away fighting or if they are providing support to the commandos is to be burnt to the ground."

"And you refused to do it?"

"That's correct, sir."

"What about now? Would you burn it if ordered today?"

The young man looked over McGuire's shoulder for a moment as he thought. "No, sir, I wouldn't. The thought of leaving those women and children homeless out on the veldt is too awful."

McGuire smiled. "You might suit me rather well, Lieutenant. Can you ride and shoot?"

"Of course, sir. I am a gentleman."

"Oh well, never mind. I can turn even a gentleman into a soldier with a bit of effort. Your name?"

"Lieutenant Dawson, sir."

"Very well, Dawson, if you want the job I'll give you a try. If you make the grade, you'll be

299

back in the field in no time with the best bunch of roughnecks you have ever served with."

McGuire was happy to have found his first potential officer. He was far less happy when he turned away from the board and saw the officer walking along the corridor towards him. Very smartly uniformed with highly polished leather riding boots, the man strode along confidently slapping his boots with his riding crop. He slowed as he approached McGuire and his mouth dropped open just a little.

"Good God! McGuire, the Dublin guttersnipe. You haven't been cashiered yet then? What is the army coming to, keeping scum like you on the books?"

"Storr-Lessing. I might know you'd be found in a rear area while your regiment is fighting. Abandoned any positions lately?"

Storr-Lessing snorted. "Mind your manners, McGuire. You're speaking to a Major now."

McGuire smiled sweetly at the officer, who had abandoned a key position during the Sudan campaign. "And so are you, so I think my manners are just fine, thank you."

"God above! A bloody ex-ranker a Major? That's ridiculous!"

Storr-Lessing slapped his boot with his crop once more and walked past McGuire without another word. McGuire shook his head slowly. How the devil had that man managed to stay in the army after his behaviour in the Sudan? Probably something to do with having a General for a parent, he thought.

He was about to walk to his room when a voice called to him. "Major! A word, if you please."

The red-faced Colonel walking towards him seemed put out about something. "Yes, sir?"

"Major, I have seen you in the mess twice now and it really will not do. I realise you have just joined us from the field army, but you really must do something about the condition of your uniform. I can't have officers looking like that in my mess."

McGuire realised he was a long way from the fighting army now. "Yes, of course, sir. I'm having all my men re-equipped shortly and I will deal with my uniform as well. Sorry, sir."

"Humph! Well see that you do. There are standards to maintain. You might take a leaf out of the book of that officer you were speaking to. He's always smart, but then one expects that of the Grenadier Guards."

"Indeed, sir, I will do what I can."

As the red-faced Colonel stalked away full of his own importance McGuire heard another voice. "You the one put that notice up, Major?"

Leaning against a wall was a tall thin Captain with a small smile on his face.

"That's me."

"I heard you being put straight by the Colonel. Anybody who irritates that fat fool can't be all bad. So where do I sign?"

"Who are you?"

"Captain James. Dublin Fusiliers."

"And what sin did you commit to get sent to this place?"

"Oh, I told my Colonel he was a bloody fool and was going to get his men killed. I probably shouldn't have done it in front of the men in question, though."

"When was this?"

"When we were marching into the loop of the Tugela river in close-order formation. The Boers used us for target practice all that bloody day."

"I watched that happen. I'd say you were right about your Colonel."

James nodded. "I'm damned sure I was. So what about it? Can you get me out of here?"

"You want to go back to the field army after a nice cushy posting here?"

"Have you been in that anteroom and seen all those idle swine sitting around doing nothing? I'll go out of my mind if I have to listen to them telling everyone how they would win the war in two weeks if only they were listened to. Bloody armchair warriors, the lot of them."

McGuire smiled. "We start training tomorrow. If you make the grade I'll have you out of here in short order. You may live to regret it, though. A man can get used to all this comfort and safety."

Chapter 44
Training Again

"Good morning, Sergeant Major. How did we do with finding our volunteers?"

CSM Donnelly saluted smartly and indicated the ranks of men drawn up on the parade square. "One hundred and eighty-two volunteers, sir. There's a lot of men sick to death of being in this bloody place."

"The troop did well. Where are they?"

"Drawn up behind the rear rank of volunteers, sir."

"Good. Let's make a start on weeding out the sick, lame and lazy, shall we?"

McGuire marched with Donnelly across the square to where the volunteers waited. "Good morning, men. I'm glad to see so many of you still have some fire in your bellies. Let me explain what we are going to do here. This is going to be an independent mounted infantry company answering to the Commander in Chief directly. Judging by our previous experience with General Kitchener, we will be worked hard and we can expect to be sent where there is considerable risk. If any of you thought this was going to be a soft option, please feel free to fall out now."

"You heard the Major. If any of you are going to shy away when the bullets start flying, leave now. It will save me the trouble of shooting you myself," Donnelly said.

There was a pause and McGuire was pleased to see that not a man moved. That was a good start. He saw Donnelly nod towards the left and looked over to see his two officer volunteers strolling towards him. As they reached him they both raised a salute.

"Good morning, sir. Is there anything you'd like us to do?"

"Yes, Captain, I'd like you to be on parade on time and certainly before I arrive. Can you do that, do you think?"

"Certainly, sir."

"Good. And the next time you are late for anything you can take yourself back to one of those comfortable armchairs and read the newspaper. This unit works together in all things and that includes its officers. Unless you would prefer to leave now?"

James stood a little straighter and the colour drained from Dawson's face. "Yes, sir, my apologies."

"And mine, sir."

"Accepted, now fall in with the men."

"With the men, sir? But we're officers."

"Not in this company. Not until I say so. Now fall in."

The two startled officers marched across and fell in with the men. McGuire returned to the front of the parade. "Now then, we are going to start weeding you out. I only need one hundred men and I already have twelve, so a lot of you will be sent back to your units. Colour Sergeant Parks, double march around the square, if you please. Reconnaissance Troop spread out and if you see any man who is incapable of keeping up, weed him out."

The original troop members spread themselves around the square and watched as Parks ordered the volunteers to turn to the right and then to double march around the edge of the parade square. Almost immediately Donnelly spotted men who were limping and dragged them out of the squad. They were sent to stand at the side of the square with Sergeant Fine.

After three circuits of the huge square Fine had twenty men standing in a line and McGuire called a halt. The remainder stood back in their ranks, panting but unmoving.

McGuire walked across to Fine. "Good morning, Sergeant. The new stripes suit you."

"Thank you, sir, they do feel good."

"Right, men. Thank you for volunteering. It takes nerve to volunteer to serve in this company, so there is no shame involved in being sent back to your units. Sergeant Fine, march them away."

"What's next, sir?"

"We need to see if they can shoot, Sergeant Major. March them to the armoury, draw weapons and ammunition. Fifty rounds a man should do it. Then out to the ranges and we'll see how much training they are going to need to come up to our standard."

After a day on the range with targets being moved progressively further away, more men had

305

been weeded out: the gun shy, who closed their eyes as they fired, the incompetent who could not hit a target even at short range, and the dangerous ones whose weapon-handling skills were abysmal.

The remainder were paraded on the square before being taken away for weapons cleaning. "Men there is one more test before we start training in earnest. Tomorrow we will see if you are capable of learning to fight effectively without weapons. Wear your worst uniforms because, I promise, you will be landing in the dirt, time and again."

McGuire walked back towards the officers' mess, pleased with the way the first day had gone. The two officer volunteers caught up with him and fell in beside him as he walked.

"A question if I may, sir?"

"Of course, Captain."

"While the men are engaged in this war without weapons what would you like us to do?"

McGuire stopped and sighed. "You still haven't got it yet, have you? You have to be as capable as the lowest private soldier and they have to see that you are capable. They have to trust you and not just for the rank on your jacket."

"You expect us to fight each other in front of the men?"

"No, Captain, I expect you to fight one of the members of my original troop. Then, when we begin to train you in this skill, you will be practising with any man I choose. Don't worry, I won't let them kill you."

Chapter 45
The War Continues

Far to the north of Stellenbosch, Kitchener sat alone in the compartment of the train taking him back to the headquarters. The report in his hand made dismal reading. At Roodewal railway station a battalion of the 4th Derbyshires had been attacked by De Wet. Despite being a recently raised militia unit they should have done better against De Wet's eighty men. Admittedly, the Boers had a field gun with them, but eighty men beating a battalion was humiliating. The quantity of supplies that the Boers had ridden away with and the prisoners taken were a severe blow to British prestige. Kitchener sighed and turned to the next report. On the same night there had been another attack on the nearby railway ridge by Froneman, one of De Wet's deputies. Kitchener looked through the window as the dark veldt rolled past him. He had to find a solution to these hit-and-run attacks.

Kitchener started, alert as the train lurched and he heard the scream of hard braking from the locomotive. There was light from the front of the train that had no business being there. Then he saw the figures riding out of the night. Their slouch hats and beards marked them out as Boers. An ambush. He grabbed his despatch case and rapidly stuffed the official papers inside it, then left his compartment and ran down the passage way to the goods wagon that was being towed directly behind his carriage.

There were shots now as the soldiers in the front carriages were subdued. Kitchener reached the rear of the carriage and climbed across the coupling to the goods wagon. He leaned precariously around and pulled the locking pins that allowed the side ramp to crash down. Wasting no time, he jumped to the ground then ran up the ramp. Inside was his favourite horse already saddled for his arrival, and he quickly mounted. He rode down the ramp, then spurred the thoroughbred animal into a gallop away from the train. He was seen and pursued by a couple of Mauser bullets, but one escaping man was not worth chasing when there was a train to loot.

A little over two weeks later the Boer army was trapped in the basin of the Brandwater River. Around nine thousand Boers were hemmed in by steep mountains and sixteen thousand British troops. Once the British were in position the Boers would have no choice but to surrender or face annihilation. There was no easy way out for the Afrikaners.

The Boers made the decision to form four columns and to force an escape through any unguarded passes. Only one of the columns made it, through a pass where the British had been slow moving in. The column led by De Wet and with President Steyn riding along escaped, but behind them four thousand Boers with more than four thousand sheep and six thousand horses were forced to surrender. It was a massive blow to the

Boer cause, but the most dangerous and effective of the Boer commanders was still on the loose.

In the days that followed, many Boers who had made an escape individually lost heart and rode in to surrender to the British. The commandos under De Wet and De La Rey began making a nuisance of themselves south and west of Pretoria with lightning raids on railways and other lines of communication targets. The war had entered the new phase that Kitchener had predicted.

***

McGuire and his company continued training until he was satisfied that he had melded the one hundred men of the Independent Reconnaissance Company into an effective fighting unit. His two officers had got over their prejudice about training alongside the men and had become accepted and trusted leaders. The men themselves were confident and walked around the barracks with the swagger of men who know they are part of something special.

On the day before they were due to leave and rejoin the army McGuire paraded the company on the main square. Every man had been issued with a new uniform and equipment, often over the objections of the quartermaster's staff. The last remaining issue to deal with was the variety of unit identification flashes being worn on the helmets of the men, who had come from a variety of regiments and corps.

At the end of each of the silent and immobile ranks of men stood a Sergeant with a cardboard box. "Men, as of today you are the 1st Independent Reconnaissance Company. We are not part of any regiment until the war is over. We report directly to the chief of staff and will operate under his orders. To reflect that the identifying flashes on your helmets have to come off. Sergeant Major, if you please."

"Company! Remove headdress! Now remove the identification flash. Sergeants!"

At the word of command the Sergeants moved along the ranks issuing new identification flashes. These were red with a yellow embroidered letter 'R'. With the colour flashes fitted to the helmets McGuire nodded. The company was ready.

As McGuire and his two officers left the square, Donnelly marched the company off to their accommodation to complete final preparations to move out. The officers removed their helmets as they entered the mess and hung them on the hooks along the corridor wall.

"What's this, McGuire? More fancy dress for your toy soldiers?"

McGuire sighed and turned round to see the sneering face of Storr-Lessing. "Don't worry, we're leaving in the morning, so we won't disturb your quiet life here."

"Interesting. Well, we may meet out on the veldt. I have been called back to the regiment to take over my own company of MI. At least I will be with Grenadiers, a proper regiment, not just a bunch of misfits and reprobates."

McGuire said nothing as Storr-Lessing turned on his heel and stalked away, slapping his boot with his riding crop as usual.

"You don't expect a hero to be so unpleasant," said Lieutenant Dawson quietly.

McGuire glanced at him. "Hero? That one?"

"Oh yes. Didn't you know he gave quite distinguished service during the Sudan campaign? I overheard him telling some new arrivals in the mass a couple of nights ago. I'm surprised he didn't get a medal."

"Really?" McGuire said. "I'm surprised he wasn't shot."

"I don't understand, sir. Is there more to the story?"

"Considerably more, I suspect, but there aren't many people left who saw what actually happened."

"Do tell."

"Another time maybe. For now we need to eat and get ready to leave first thing in the morning. Then we'll see how reprobates and misfits perform."

***

As the train rattled through the night, taking the Reconnaissance Company back to the war, De Wet lay on his belly looking out at the sentry's fire burning by the drift. Every crossing point now seemed to have a small garrison of troops waiting

311

for him. He could probably force his way across, though he would lose men that he could not replace and the British would then know where he was.

He heard the quiet hoofbeats as his brother returned from a scouting task and walked back to where the horses stood patiently in the donga. "What did you find, Piet?"

"There are more shallows around two miles that way. The banks are steep but the horses should make it with care. If we had wagons it would be a different story."

"Good, well done. Louis, go and rouse the men. Piet will lead us to the crossing point."

The silver sliver of the new moon gave them enough light to ride, though not enough for the British sentries to see them. Piet had been right, the banks were steep and they had to dismount to guide the horses down to the waterside. The water was turbulent as it boiled around the rocks and pushed at the horses. Even for horsemen like the Boers it was a challenge, but they met it and crossed undetected. Now they were south of the river while the enemy was still searching for them to the north.

De Wet gave his men two hours to sleep and recover before they rode towards their next target. The rail lines that brought the supplies the British needed were guarded, although, even with the thousands of men, there were places to be found where they could rip up the rails and cause delays. Maybe they would be lucky and an inattentive train driver would derail his locomotive and cause serious problems.

Chapter 46
Chasing Ghosts

McGuire left his company unloading the train under the supervision of the two officers while he rode to the headquarters building to report in to Kitchener. There was the usual confusion with staff officers bustling around carrying papers and doing their best to look important. He found one of Kitchener's clerks and told him he was there. The man promised to tell the General as soon as possible and McGuire went to find a shady tree to sit under while he waited.

A two-hour doze was welcome after the long train journey and McGuire was surprised when he felt the touch on his shoulder. He looked up to find a young officer standing over him. The man waited until McGuire had climbed to his feet before he spoke.

"The General can see you now, sir. May I suggest you might like to brush yourself down before you see him?"

McGuire smiled at the eager young officer. "You may suggest all you like, but for now, lead on. I'm sure the General is in his usual hurry."

"Ah, you know him then, sir. Come this way, please."

McGuire was ushered into Kitchener's office to find the usual chaos with papers scattered over every flat surface. "Good to see you, McGuire. Have you brought me my company?"

"I have indeed, sir. They are getting their horses and equipment off the train. In fact, they have probably done that by now, so we are at your command."

"Are they going to be as effective as your troop was?"

"I think so, sir. We weeded out many who were not quite good enough, so I'm happy with what is left."

Kitchener gave McGuire one of the rare smiles that transformed his scarred face. "I take it they are the same sort of ruffians and ne'er-do-wells that your original troop was made up of?"

McGuire returned the smile. "They are, sir. All the sort of men that the army really does not know what to do with."

"Good. Now to start with I'm going to give you a wide brief. Hunt down Boers. Capture them, kill them, disrupt their operations – just find them and fight them."

"Fair enough, sir. Isn't the rest of the mounted infantry doing the same job?"

"They are. They are making wide sweeps across the veldt and trying to trap the Boers. I want you to act somewhat differently. Track them, follow them to where they are hiding and ambush them the way they ambush us. I want you to be more Boer than the Boers."

"That sounds like fun, sir. When do we start?"

"As soon as you have your horses saddled. Get out there and track these damned people down.

We have offered them amnesty if they surrender and swear loyalty and that is working to some extent. You are looking for the hard core commandos."

"Very good, sir. Any other instructions?"

"Yes. We have also adopted a new policy. If you find a farm that has been supporting the commandos with food and shelter, then burn it to the ground."

McGuire was shocked. He had heard rumours of soldiers burning farms, but had dismissed it as just wild talk in the mess at Stellenbosch.

"May I speak freely, sir?"

"Of course. What is it?"

"Sir, you may not know my history. When I was a very young man in Ireland my father was the manager of an estate. He died and we were thrown out of the house to make way for the new manager. We had nothing. We slept in ditches until we got to Dublin and then found a hovel to shelter in. I remember my mother and sister were devastated by the way we were treated."

"Unfortunate, but I don't see the relevance."

"Sir, with huge respect, I simply cannot obey that order. I cannot do to Boer families, women and children, what was done to me and mine."

"Are you refusing an order?"

McGuire swallowed. Refusing a command was a serious matter. "Sir, I will chase the Boers from here to the gates of hell, but I beg you not to ask me to burn farms and make civilians homeless out on the veldt."

"And if I insist?"

"With regret, sir, I will resign my commission."

"Resign? In the middle of a war? You will be branded a coward and made a pariah to the rest of the army. Are you serious?"

McGuire nodded sadly. "I'm afraid I am, sir."

Kitchener sat back in his chair. There was no hint of a smile on his face now. He grunted and stood up before walking to the window and staring out.

He turned back and regarded McGuire bleakly. "It's lucky for you that I know your quality and that I know you well. You are excused from burning farms. However, you will not interfere with any unit that is carrying out my orders, is that clear?"

"Very clear, sir, and thank you."

"Now get out and find me some damned Boers before I change my mind."

McGuire rode back to the station through the throngs of ox carts and moving troops. As he approached he could see his company had found a quiet area on the far side of the station and the horses were being watered under the supervision of Colour Sergeant Parks. He dismounted as he reached them and handed the reins to one of the new privates. Then he went in search of the Sergeant Major and the two officers.

Away from the men, the four of them sat in the shade of a tumbledown railway hut. "We have

317

our orders. We are to track and attack Boer raiding parties."

"Where do we start, sir?" Donnelly asked.

"We find the site of the latest attack and then we follow their tracks. We will put a small tracking party out in front, with the rest of the company following at a distance. Hopefully, that way we can find them before they see us coming. The tracking party can use the Boer disguises we have."

Lieutenant Dawson looked uncomfortable. "Is that right, sir? Dressing in the uniforms of the enemy seems wrong somehow."

"Two things. One, the Boers do not wear uniform, so if we are wearing a rough wool jacket and a slouch hat we are not in enemy uniform. Two, the term *'ruse de guerre'* has been in use since the Napoleonic wars. As long as we are in British uniform during any attack I see no problem. Satisfied?"

"Yes, sir. Thank you, sir."

McGuire's starting point came a day later when the 13th Battalion of the Imperial Yeomanry became the latest embarrassment for the British at Lindley.

This battalion had become fashionable back at home and was populated by well-to-do men about town from both Ireland and England. It had been raised by Lord Donoughmore, who also insisted on paying the cost of passage to South Africa for his pet battalion. The only regular soldier was the commander, Lieutenant Colonel

Basil Spragge. They were sent to Lindley, but on reaching it they found that it was back in Boer hands. Instead of making a fighting retreat, the Colonel decided to take up a position on a kopje and wait to be rescued. When the rescue column of three Yeomanry battalions arrived they found the kopje scattered with the British dead, many of them killed by the field guns Piet De Wet had employed. Five hundred and thirty men had surrendered and been marched north into captivity.

The Reconnaissance Company rode out to the scene of the battle, which was now marked by rows of graves, and began to analyse the tracks they found. The Yeomanry horses had covered over any sign of the Boers until Samuel found the marks left by the wheels of the field guns. The hunt was on.

Chapter 47
First Blood

Samuel was down on one knee examining the dusty ground; he rubbed the horse dung between his fingers, then stood up. Sergeant Fine had been watching the Zulu and wondering what it was he could see in the tiny marks.

"Sergeant, they have split up here. The ones dragging the wheels have gone that way and the riders with no wheels have turned away to the north."

"Wheels? So the two guns are moving on. We need to tell the Major so he can decide which group to follow."

Fine brought the heliograph equipment out of the carrier behind his saddle and set it up. He knew which of the small kopjes McGuire and the rest of the men were resting behind and aimed the lens in that direction. He lined the mirror up with the sun and then flashed his message across the veldt. There was no reply, but he had not expected one. He knew there would be a watcher to receive the message and that a reply would pinpoint their position for any watching Boers.

Samuel and Fine led their horses into the shade of a couple of scrubby mopani trees and waited. After around twenty minutes they could see two riders coming towards them. Despite the Boer slouch hats and dark jackets, they knew they were from the company and as they came closer they could see that it was McGuire and Connolly.

The two riders slowed and stopped before dismounting and walking the animals into the shade.

McGuire and Connolly squatted down. "Well, what can you tell me about Brother Boer?"

"Right, sir. Well, according to Samuel, they have split up, the main party turning north, but a smaller party with the guns carrying on in much the same direction as before."

"Are you sure about that?"

"Samuel hasn't been wrong yet, sir."

"That's true. Do we know how far ahead they are?"

Samuel gave McGuire his broad smile. "Maybe three hours, baas. The dung is starting to dry."

"That trick with the dung is disgusting. I hope you aren't going to cook with those hands?" He looked at the watch that he pulled from the pocket of his tunic. "We should be able to catch up with them a little after nightfall if nothing goes wrong."

"Which group are we going to follow, sir?"

"The small group with the field guns."

"What about the group with the prisoners?"

McGuire grinned. "The rest of the army is looking for them by now. So if we can recover those guns we can do the Boers a good bit of damage."

"You think they're the British guns that the Boers captured?"

"I do. I was shown an intelligence report last week that said the Boers are just about out of

321

ammunition for the guns they started the war with. Now their artillery is made up of captured British guns and shells. So now, Sergeant Connolly, use the heliograph to call the company forward. Sergeant Fine, you and Samuel follow the party with the guns. Don't get too close. I want to reach them after they have settled down for the night."

***

The horses were left about a mile from the encampment that Samuel and Fine had found and now Samuel was leading half the company forward, to one side of the wide donga. Fine was leading the other half of the company in a wide arc, to reach the far side of the donga. McGuire kept close to the silent Zulu as they advanced. As Samuel stopped he whispered in McGuire's ear and pointed to the edge of the gulley they could just see. The glow of a watch fire was outlining the edge of the donga before them.

McGuire gave the signal and the men spread out to left and right. They dropped to the ground and crawled the last few yards to the edge of the deep gulley, then waited. Below them the Boers were wrapped in their blankets and spread around the two guns. The horses were picketed in lines off to one side. It took McGuire a couple of moments to spot the sentry. He was sitting by the fire and, by the smell that drifted upwards, he was brewing coffee in his metal can.

Across the donga McGuire strained to see any of his men. Then he saw the white handkerchief that Captain James showed as the prearranged signal. McGuire smiled to himself. Now it was their turn after so many Boer ambushes had embarrassed the army in the last six months. He raised his rifle and took careful aim. The single shot echoed in the night, followed by the sentry swearing loudly as the hot coffee from the punctured can splattered across his legs.

There was a flurry of movement as the Boers struggled out of their sleep and their blankets. McGuire stood up and called out to the startled enemy.

"Do not go for your weapons, gentlemen! I have no wish to kill you, but any man who raises a rifle will be shot. You have soldiers all round you and there is no way out. Just stand still and raise your hands."

Down in the donga the Boers froze and looked around them. They could see nobody except the lone figure standing on the lip of the gulleys above them. Two men on the far side made their decision and dived for their rifles. Their dash was met by the fire of at least a dozen rifles and both men dropped. An older man standing close to the fire pulled a dirty white rag from his pocket and held it up.

"We surrender. Do not shoot."

McGuire stood very still and watched the Boers for a moment or two. "Let me remind you that your people have used the white flag before and then opened fire when British troops came forward. So unless you want to have wholesale slaughter all of you should stand very still."

The man with the white flags spoke in Afrikaans to his men and then looked back up at McGuire. "I have told them not to move, English."

"Very well. Sergeant Major Donnelly, detail ten men to advance and collect the weapons. Remainder, stay where you are and keep our friends covered."

The ten men rose from their hiding places and followed their commander down into the donga. They quickly moved around, picking up the mixture of Mauser and Lee Enfield rifles and stacking them by the field guns. McGuire walked to the man who still held up the white rag.

"Are you in charge of this group?"

"Yes, I am Field Cornet Van Der Merwe. What happens to us now?"

"Once your men are disarmed, we will all mount up and ride to my army where you will be taken into custody as prisoners of war."

"And then?"

"And then a decision will be made about where you are sent. Some of you may be sent to St Helena or one of the other prison camps. If you swear not to take up arms again, some of you may be allowed to return to your farms. Not my decision."

One of the Corporals walked across to McGuire. "All weapons collected, sir."

"Good. Get the teams hitched up to the guns and then stand by to watch our prisoners."

The Corporal turned and walked quickly back to where the rest of his detail waited. McGuire watched them collect the horses and start to take them to the guns. He spun round as the sharp crack of a rifle rang across the donga. The Boer who had moved was now standing stock still.

"Field Cornet, if you don't want to lose any more men then you had better tell them to do exactly what they are told and nothing more. Do you understand?"

"I will tell them."

"Good. Now shortly I am going to tell you to saddle up and then mount. Any man that attempts to ride out of here before I give the order will be shot. Then, once we are on the move, if any of your people attempt to ride away, you should know that every one of my men is a marksman and your people will not make it."

Van Der Merwe nodded briefly. "I will tell them all of that, but some of them are young and may not listen."

"Then the next one to try will be a lesson to the rest."

"You are a hard man, Major."

"I learned my trade in the deserts of the Sudan and only a hard man survives up there."

Chapter 48
Smoke on the Veldt

The prisoners rode behind the two field guns with McGuire's men to either side of them. The rifles held across the saddle horns of the British troops were not lost on the Boers and they made no attempt to ride away across the open veldt. McGuire rode at the front of the column with Van Der Merwe alongside him. The Boer seemed almost happy to have been captured.

"Have you seen the smoke in front of us, Major?"

"I have. We are going to pass that way so we can see what is causing it in a short while."

"I fear that I know already. There is a farm there and we stopped for water from their pond as we came through this way."

McGuire said nothing, but he, too, feared that the Boer was right. They crested a slight rise and there, in front of them, they could see the farmhouse and the few small buildings burning fiercely. Without a word the two men broke into a trot towards the farm. As they came closer they could see women and children standing to one side staring at their home being consumed by the flames. In the distance McGuire saw the dust of the column that had started the fire riding away.

As they reined in Van Der Merwe turned in his saddle. "Is this how the mighty British Empire wages war? Burning farms and leaving women and children out on the veldt at the mercy of the kaffirs?"

McGuire looked around at the sticks of furniture that had been dragged or thrown out of the house. Children's clothes were blown across the dry ground by the wind. The women stood and looked at him. Their silence cut through the Irishman. He remembered how devastated his mother had been, all those years ago.

The column rode up behind them and stopped at the command of Captain James. The two officers rode forward and came to a halt beside their commander.

"Who would do this?" Dawson asked.

"Our people," McGuire said. "They have orders from the top to burn any farm giving aid to the commandos. The idea is to force the Boer army to surrender for lack of supplies."

"Yes, but these are civilians. What are they supposed to do now?"

"I don't know, Lieutenant, I really don't. However, these ones we can help. Make room on the gun carriages for the children and let the women ride the spare horses. We will take them with us into town. Mister Van Der Merwe, will you explain that to the ladies, please?"

McGuire sat on his horse and watched his men help the Boer women to pack up their pathetic bundles and carried them to the gun carriages where they found room to stow them. Crying children were picked up and carried with amazing gentleness by these rough men. They were put on horses or on the gun limbers and given small comforts by the troops, who had virtually nothing themselves. He spotted the oldest of the women being helped onto the seat of the first gun limber and rode slowly across to speak to her. She turned her face away and refused to acknowledge his presence. McGuire sighed, but could not find a reason to blame her.

The column moved off and left the smouldering ruins of what had been a family's life behind them. That evening they made camp and McGuire had Donnelly set double sentries in case the Boers attempted to escape. The prisoners seemed to have been depressed by the farm burning and sat in a wide circle around the stricken family. McGuire's men apparently felt the same and made sure the children and women were served their evening meal first. Even CSM Donnelly was affected. He sought out McGuire once the sentries were detailed and in position.

"Begging your pardon, sir, but can I have a word?"

"That's very formal from you after all we've been through together. What's the problem?"

Donnelly paused. "It's that burnt-out farm, sir. Seeing those women and children just abandoned, like. The men don't like it, sir. Not one little bit."

"And?"

"And if we get ordered to do it, sir, I think there might be trouble. Sorry to say it, sir, but I thought you should know."

McGuire raised a hand and patted the big rough man from Belfast on the shoulder. "Thank you for telling me. I feel the same way. In fact, I have a promise from Kitchener that this unit will never be ordered to do it. You can let the men know that I'm proud of the way they behaved this afternoon. They may be the men the army doesn't want, but they have the right kind of compassion."

Donnelly smiled. "I'll let them know, on the quiet, like."

"Thank you and I want the column moving at dawn, so have the sentries wake us early."

***

With the dawn rushing across the veldt, the column started off on its slow way back to the army. Behind them were more columns of smoke, rising into a clear blue sky. McGuire reined in and watched them as the company rode past him. He wondered how the Boers would ever forgive them for this, even when the war was over.

By the afternoon they had reached the main army encampments and rode slowly along the road through the lines of white bell tents. Men came out and stood by the road as they realised that the Reconnaissance Company had done something exceptional. As they reached the headquarters building Kitchener came out and stood on the covered veranda. He walked down the path to where McGuire waited for him.

McGuire dismounted and saluted the General. "Sir, beg to report the capture of sixty-five prisoners and the recovery of two guns."

"Excellent work, Major." He turned and called forward an artillery Captain. "Take a look at the guns, Thomson, and tell me who they belong to."

The Captain went forward and read the identification plates on the two field guns before coming back to Kitchener. "They belong to 'U' Battery RHA, sir. They must be the ones lost at Sannah's Post."

Kitchener nodded. "Thank you, Captain. Now McGuire, who the devil are all these civilians you have riding on my guns?"

"Their farm had been burned to the ground when we came upon them, sir. I couldn't just leave them out on the veldt with nothing."

The General stroked his luxurious moustache. "Yes, I thought it must be something like that. Luckily for you, we have developed a solution to that problem. We have established a number of camps where displaced Boer civilians like these can be concentrated, to be looked after until the commandos surrender."

"Very good, sir, and what should I do with them now?"

Kitchener pointed towards the railway station buildings. "Take the civilians there and hand them over to the transport officer. He will arrange to move them to a camp. Take the prisoners to the Provost Marshal and then deliver the guns to the artillery park at the end of this road. Then I want you to come back and see me. I want to know how your hunt went in more detail."

With the tasks complete and his men settled, McGuire reported back to headquarters. This time he was expected and there was no waiting around before he was ushered into Kitchener's chaotic office.

"Well, Major, tell me how it all went."

"As planned, sir, we tracked the Boers who had been at Lindley. They split up with the main body turning north and the smaller party with the guns carrying on to the west. I decided the loss of the guns would hurt the Boers more than the recovery of the prisoners and followed the smaller party. We ambushed them in the dark and, as you saw, we took them prisoner and recovered the guns."

"Any casualties?"

"Two Boers went for their rifles and were killed. After that there was no resistance. From talking to the prisoners on the way in I got the impression that they have lost a lot of their fire. With the exception of a few of their leaders, the Boers are losing heart for the fight."

Kitchener steepled his fingers in front of his face as he rested his elbows on the desk. "You may be right, although the commandos are still active and are still doing us damage."

"May I ask, sir, are you sure about burning the farms? It seems to me that this policy will only cause bitterness and strengthen the Boers' resolve."

Kitchener sighed. "Major, this is a new kind of war. The enemy has been defeated and his army scattered. He should have surrendered, but the commandos are still active and fighting a guerrilla campaign against us. They hate us already, so my policy will not change that much. However, if the Boers cannot find food, water and shelter at these farms, it will force them eventually to capitulate. What we are doing is hateful, but I must force the Boers to come in and surrender."

"I see, sir. And if it doesn't work?"

"On its own it may not work, but now that I am Commander in Chief, with Lord Roberts' departure for England, I have another plan to run in parallel with it."

"Are we part of that other plan, sir?"

"You are, McGuire. I am going to build fences across the veldt to corral these people into smaller and smaller areas. There will be armed blockhouses to defend the fences. You and others like you will harry the Boers and make their lives miserable. Once they finally realise there is no way to drive us out they must surely surrender."

Chapter 49
Disgrace

McGuire rode at the head of the company towards the railway halt where there had been yet another attack. Once there, he planned to adopt the same tactics and follow the tracks until he could ambush the Boers. He had three scouts riding ahead of the company and two to each side to ensure they were not surprised by any Boer commando that might see them.

As he rode on he could see one of the advance scouts riding back towards him at the canter. The man wheeled his horse and came up alongside McGuire in a cloud of dust. The man took a second to control his horse, then rode close to him.

"Corporal Taylor's compliments, sir, and he wishes to report that there is a farm ahead with a mounted infantry company about to burn it. They found a lot of tracks and they are sure they have been supplying the Boers."

McGuire sat up and looked forward. "I don't see anything."

"The ground drops away into a shallow valley. They've got a dam across a small spruit where we can water the horses and there's even a grove of trees for a bit of shade if we want to rest up."

"Sounds like a good place for us to camp for the night." He turned in his saddle. "Sergeant Major, order the trot, if you will."

Donnelly raised his voice and gave the command. The company perked up and the horses broke into a trot towards the water they could smell on the breeze. As they came to the edge of the shallow valley McGuire looked around. The farm wasn't burning yet, although personal possessions littered the ground in front of the modest white house. To the right was a small group of women and children. The oldest of the women was screaming and pointing almost hysterically.

McGuire rode closer until he came to a Lieutenant sitting on a wooden stock fence. "That lady seems particularly upset, Lieutenant. What is she screaming about so loudly?"

The Lieutenant jumped down off the fence when he saw McGuire's rank badges and saluted. "You know how it is with these Boer women, sir. Probably banging on about her bible or some such."

Sergeant Fine rode up with one of the younger volunteers alongside him. "Something you should hear, sir."

"Go on."

"You know Davies here speaks Dutch?"

McGuire nodded. "I do. What's going on, Davies?"

"It's the older lady, sir. She's screaming about her daughter. She says she's been dragged off to those trees by one of the British."

McGuire spun back to the Lieutenant. "Is that true? What the hell is going on?"

"Oh, it's just the Major having his bit of fun, sir. He always likes to interrogate the pretty ones personally."

McGuire stared at the young officer in disbelief. "Are you bloody serious?"

The young officer said nothing, but just shrugged. McGuire spurred his horse and galloped towards the stand of trees beyond the glistening pool of water. As he rode into the copse the sound of his hoofbeats faded away on the sandy soil. He broke through into a clearing and reined in his horse, horrified at what he saw.

A young blonde woman was being held down by a soldier with her clothing wrenched to one side. The man was scrabbling at the front of his trousers, but was finding it awkward with just one hand free. McGuire flung his leg over the saddle and dropped to the ground. As he reached the struggling couple he aimed a kick that caught the man in the ribs and lifted him off the woman to roll in the dirt.

The attacker looked at McGuire in a fury. "How dare you? Get away from here. I'll deal with you later!"

McGuire could not believe his eyes. "Storr-Lessing? God above, this is a new low, even for you."

"The Dublin guttersnipe. Well, this is a bonus."

Storr-Lessing drew the Webley revolver from its leather holster and swung it up to point at

McGuire. "Now I can deal with you before I finish with this trollop."

Storr-Lessing smiled as he thumbed back the hammer and took aim, then froze as he heard the metallic sound of a rifle being cocked. McGuire looked towards the sound to find Sergeant Fine sitting on his horse with the Lee Enfield held very steadily pointing at Storr-Lessing.

"Just say the word, sir, and I'll rid the world of this creature once and for all."

"What do you say, Storr-Lessing? Shall we end it here or would you like to drop that pistol to the ground?"

McGuire saw the bead of sweat roll down his enemy's face and then he dropped the pistol and raised his hands. Picking the revolver up, McGuire let the hammer go forward slowly to make the weapon safe again. He looked into the eyes of the coward who had tried to kill him three times now and then swung the heavy Webley in a short arc. The pistol caught Storr-Lessing across the side of his head and ripped a piece of his ear out. The blood ran freely as he hit the ground and lay still.

"Did you see that, Sergeant?"

"I did indeed, sir. The officer tripped over his own feet as he lunged at you and struck his head on that stone there. I think his trousers being half down must have caused it."

"Thank you, Sergeant."

McGuire walked over to the young woman, who lay sobbing on the dusty ground. There was blood at the corner of her mouth where she had been struck. He held out his hand and waited. She looked at him fearfully, then saw something in his blue eyes and reached up to take his hand. He pulled her to her feet and slipped off his jacket before wrapping it around her shoulders to cover her torn dress.

"Sergeant Fine, would you go and bring me two of our biggest and ugliest troopers to arrest that officer. They will need some rope to bind his hands."

Fine wheeled his horse and rode back to the company as McGuire escorted the woman back towards the farmhouse. On the way he took the reins of the horse and led it behind them. As they walked out of the trees the screams of the older woman became louder and she broke free of the soldiers who were holding her back and ran across the flat ground to her daughter.

The two women hugged and sobbed while McGuire stood back. As they stood there Fine and two of the larger men from the company rode past them and into the trees. The two women started to walk back to the farm buildings and McGuire followed on, careful not to intrude on them in their almost hysterical condition.

Captain James and Lieutenant Dawson rode across to rein in beside McGuire. "What the devil has been going on, sir?"

"We'll find that out in a moment. Would you two go and find the Lieutenant I was speaking to and bring him here? If he declines, do feel free to wrap a rifle around his head, won't you?"

McGuire stopped where he was, well clear of the troops who were now milling around the farm in some confusion. His two officers returned with the Lieutenant between them.

"Right, Lieutenant, let's see if you are going to court martial as well as your commander. How the hell can a company of Grenadier Guards act this way?"

"We aren't Grenadiers, sir. This is a militia company. Major Storr-Lessing was in command of a Guards company, but then he came to us."

"And you knew bloody well what he was doing while you stood idly by. You should be ashamed. How the devil can you command these men and condone that behaviour?"

"Sir, he's a Major. I'm just a Lieutenant. What could I do?"

"Dear Lord, you are an officer and, supposedly, a gentleman. How could you not report him, at the very least? You will be required to give evidence at his court martial and I suggest you start working on your own excuses. Now get your men together and get the hell out of here."

"Very good, sir. I'll burn the farm before we go."

"You damn well will not! After what has happened here today you want to burn their farm as well? Get on your horse and leave before I have you shot right here."

McGuire and his officers watched the militia Lieutenant scurry away towards his own men and then they walked towards the farmhouse.

338

"Are you going to tell us what happened in the trees, sir?" James asked.

"Something I never dreamed I would see. A British army officer attempting to rape a young Boer woman while his company stood by and let it happen."

James stopped. "Dear God. Are you serious?"

"Hardly a thing for me to make jokes about, wouldn't you say?"

"No, of course not, sir. What are you going to do with him?"

"When he recovers consciousness he will find that he is under close arrest. I am going to send him back to headquarters and have him handed over to the Provost Marshal. Lieutenant Dawson here will escort him with a detail of men to guard the prisoner. I will write a detailed report for you to take with you and, come to think of it, I want a report from that Lieutenant before he leaves here. Captain, will you go and stop him leaving. I want his full written report of what went on here today and what he has seen in the past. Stand over him while he writes it and bring it to me. Then he can go."

"What would you like me to do, sir?"

"You, Lieutenant Dawson, will form a detail of the men and help this family pick up their possessions and put them back in the house. Be gentle with them. They've had a bad time. Oh and send the Sergeant Major and Private Davies to me as well, please."

McGuire sat down with his back against a low wall and opened his despatch case. He drew out the blank report form and started to write. He stopped as a shadow fell across him and he looked up to find Donnelly and Davies standing there.

"That was quick. Now, Sergeant Major, I take it you are aware of what is going on?"

"Yes, sir. Sergeant Fine told me what happened. The men are furious. They want to shoot the bastard now. Pardon my language."

McGuire smiled slightly. "Indeed. Well, sadly we have to do this legally. He is going to be taken in for court martial. Now, Davies, I need you to persuade the ladies involved to write down what happened here today. Can you do that?"

"Not sure, sir. My Dutch isn't all that good, but I can try."

"Try hard. It's important, and would you also tell them how sorry we are for what happened or rather what nearly happened? Off you go."

McGuire paused as the Private left and walked towards the house. "Sit down, Sergeant Major. I need your advice."

Donnelly leaned his rifle against the wall and then sat down with a sigh. "Right, sir, what do you need?"

"Lieutenant Dawson is taking the prisoner back to the army. I need three of your best to go with him, to make sure this creature does not get away. Then I need a small detail of reliable men to stay here and guard this place. That will be for just a few days, to make sure that damned militia company does not come back to finish the job. We will pick them up on our way back."

"Consider it done, sir. Anything else?"

"Yes, get the men bedded down for the night. We will stay here and then leave at dawn tomorrow. We'll follow the tracks of the Boer commando that called in here and caused all this trouble in the first place."

"I'll get it set up, sir, and with your permission, I'll send a couple of men out to hunt. I saw some springbok on the way in here and they always taste good."

"Do that, and tell them to drop a couple of extra ones so we can give the meat to the ladies."

***

The hunt for the Boer commando was fruitless. Even with Samuel tracking, the trail was too old and they lost it as it climbed the shoulder of a rocky kopje. Disappointed, the company turned back and headed for army headquarters to wait for another Boer attack that they could track. The men who had been guarding the farmstead rejoined and the company rode into the main army encampment just before dusk.

McGuire sent his men to their bivouac area and rode up to the headquarters building. He left his horse by the water trough and went to find Kitchener. The rooms were strangely quiet, with only a few junior staff completing paperwork. He took himself to Kitchener's office door and knocked. The gruff voice ordered him to enter.

"McGuire, your timing is impeccable. I had just decided to award myself a brandy and soda and now you can join me. In fact, you can make them. All the bottles are in that cabinet."

McGuire did as he was bidden and made the two drinks before carrying them over to the chairs either side of the empty stone fireplace. He sat and sipped appreciatively. The dust in his throat needed to be washed out and this was perfect.

"Well, McGuire, what have you come to report? Any more guns recovered?"

"Not this time, sir. We lost the commando we were following, so no success this time."

"Never mind, you can make up for it next time. So what did you come to see me about?"

McGuire put down his glass. "I came to make sure my report about Major Storr-Lessing had reached you safely."

"Oh yes. Your young Lieutenant was most insistent that he had to place the reports in my hands. You seem to have put the fear of God into him."

"I did make it very clear to him that you should be the one to see the reports first, sir."

"Indeed. We can't have a distasteful scandal like this being discussed around the lines. One of those damned reporters might hear of it and then it would be all over the newspapers."

McGuire paused. "Surely that will happen at the court martial, sir? It can't be kept a secret then."

Kitchener sipped his brandy and looked into the fireplace before he spoke. "There won't be a court martial. Storr-Lessing is on his way to England already."

McGuire's mouth dropped open a little before he snapped it shut. "I beg your pardon, sir. I don't understand. Was my report not clear enough?"

"Your report was crystal clear and made uncomfortable reading. There should have been a trial, of course. However, I have to take the wider view."

"The wider view, sir?"

"Yes. You are aware that Storr-Lessing's father is a very distinguished General with a justly deserved reputation for courage? He has been elevated to the peerage and now sits in the House of Lords. His influence is extensive. It would do no good to have his name dragged through the mud by his son's trial. Additionally, I have to protect the reputation of the army. We have considerable support at home and I cannot risk that being lost if this incident becomes public."

"So a coward, an attempted murderer and now a rapist walks free? And all because of his father?"

Kitchener nodded sadly. "I would have preferred to have him cashiered in disgrace and then incarcerated for a long time. However, I have told you my reasons and you must accept them."

"Yes, sir."

"And now some good news for you. I have issued an instruction that the particular farmhouse involved is to be left alone. A letter from me has been sent to them to show to any army unit that visits them. Additionally, your promotion has been published in the *London Gazette*, so you are confirmed in rank."

"Thank you, sir. On behalf of the outraged ladies."

"Get off your high horse, young man. I have also done something else. A letter from me has gone to Horse Guards to be placed in Storr-Lessing's file. He will not be picking up any promotions, no matter what his father thinks. His regiment has also been informed, so I suspect he will be on detached and unpleasant duties from now on. That's the best I can do in the circumstances."

Chapter 50
Long Live The King

The three officers were sitting by their small camp fire discussing the plan for the next part of their patrol when Colour Sergeant Parks returned from collecting extra rations in Bloemfontein. He rode up to them and dismounted.

"Problems?" McGuire asked.

"No, sir, but some bad news, I'm afraid."

"Go on."

"Sir, while I was in the quartermaster's compound, daily orders were published. News has just come through from London. The Queen has died at Osborne House on the Isle of Wight. Her body is being taken to Windsor and she will be buried with Prince Albert."

McGuire, was stunned, he leaned back against his saddle and said nothing. He waved Parks away without a word. Lieutenant Dawson glanced across at Captain James before he spoke.

"Are you all right, sir?"

"Not really," McGuire said, shaking his head. "I owe that lady everything."

"You say that as though you've actually met Her Majesty."

McGuire paused, staring into the flickering flames. He roused himself and looked up.

"What? Oh yes, well I have, you see."

Dawson looked at James again. "Actually met the Queen, sir? Was that when you passed out of the Academy?"

"The Academy? No, I never went to Sandhurst. Mine was a field commission at the end of the Gordon Relief Expedition."

Captain James sat up and took notice. "I didn't know you were part of that."

"Oh yes," McGuire said. "I was part of that as a Private in the Grenadier Guards. That's when I first met that coward, Storr-Lessing."

James tossed another couple of small logs on to the fire. "Come on, sir. It's going to be a long night and you can't leave a story like that untold."

McGuire smiled sadly. "You feel the need of a bedtime story, Captain?"

James smiled. "Yes please, sir, and can you start it 'Once upon a time' like my nanny used to?"

McGuire chuckled. "Very well, just for you. 'Once upon a time' there was a young Irishman who joined the Grenadier Guards in Dublin Castle. As you can see, he was very handsome, so he was selected as one of the few to go on the Gordon Relief Expedition, to try and rescue General Gordon from Khartoum. It all went well until we reached a place called Abu Klea."

"I've heard of that," Dawson said. "Isn't that where the Dervishes came close to crumpling a British defensive square?"

McGuire nodded. "It is. The young Irishman with his friend and Lieutenant Storr-Lessing had been positioned on a hilltop to try and make sure there were no Dervishes about. As dawn broke we saw there were thousands of them all around the camp below us. Storr-Lessing lost his nerve and

346

ran, but the two signallers were naïve and stayed to warn the square with a heliograph. The column managed to form square just as the Dervishes came screaming out of a wadi to attack. It was bloody close, but the lines held – just."

"And then?"

McGuire poked the fire with his boot. "And then the Colonel decided that, to protect the honour of the regiment, the young Irishman had to be sent away so he wouldn't talk about what had really happened."

"Sent away?"

"Yes, I was attached to Major Kitchener, who was off in the blue gathering intelligence with a bunch of Bedouin tribesmen. He needed a heliograph operator to get a message in to General Gordon at Khartoum, through the Dervish siege. I was sent with two of the Bedouin to try and send the message, but we failed to get a reply. So we decided to go into the city to find the General and give him the message."

"Wait a minute, I've heard this story. There was a single British soldier who got into Khartoum before it fell. Was that you?"

McGuire nodded again. "It was, but not alone. I had two Bedouin tribesmen with me. Those two were the bravest men I ever knew. In any case, we were just too late. The final assault on the city happened when we were there and we got swept into the residence with the attacking Dervishes. We were wearing their jibbas, so they didn't recognise us. I watched Gordon die. His sword was taken, but they missed his Webley revolver that had fallen under his body. I recovered it and brought it back."

"When my Colonel was sent back to England to take the despatches to the Queen at the end of the expedition, I was sent with him to tell her of the death of Gordon and to give her a letter he had written to her and the revolver. She gave me back the pistol and told me to carry it with honour."

"So that's why you carry the early model Webley, instead of the more modern one?"

"It is. However, Her Majesty was more than generous. Lord Wolseley had given me a field commission as a subaltern, but Her Majesty gave me a commission as a full Lieutenant. She also gave me a letter to the Colonel of the Royal Irish Fusiliers, asking him to give me a place in his regiment and to give me permission to marry, although I was well under the required age of twenty-five at the time."

"How did you manage to meet up with a lady while you were tramping round the desert? Or was it a childhood sweetheart back in Ireland?"

"I met my future wife when she was being dragged behind a Dervish horseman in the desert just north of Khartoum. Her father had been ambushed and murdered and she had been taken prisoner. She was destined to be sold as a slave and worse."

Dawson paused and then spoke. "How did you persuade the horseman to let her go?"

McGuire smiled. "He and his two companions lost interest in her when they met Mr Martini Henry."

"You killed them?"

"I thought it was a good idea as they were charging at me waving long curved swords at the time."

James shook his head. "No wonder Kitchener thinks so much of you. I did wonder about that, with him being such a cold fish."

McGuire shook his head. "He's far from a cold fish. He feels things deeply, but he doesn't express them at all if he can help it. You go and ask the Bedouin; they have huge respect for him and that doesn't come easily."

Dawson tossed another log on the fire. "Do you think they will tell stories like that about this war, sir?"

McGuire looked up at the stars and then down at the flames again. "I think the wars in the Sudan were in simpler times. There doesn't seem to be much glory in this war." He sighed and reached for his blanket. "Well, you've had your bedtime story. I hope your nanny would approve, but I for one am going to get some sleep. It's going to be another long, boring day tomorrow."

Chapter 51
Crossing the Orange

The time had come to take the war to the Khakis. Up to now the fighting had been in the Boer republics. The British had burned farms and killed cattle, but to the south in the Cape Colony all was peaceful. Some of the Boers of Cape Colony had come north and fought alongside their kin, but most had stayed at home and tended the farms. Now Jan Smuts and his commando of two hundred and fifty men were ready to cross the Orange River and raise rebellion among the many Cape Boers who sympathised with the Boer cause. As soon as Commandant Wessels returned from his patrol they would try and force the crossing at the Kiba Drift.

Smuts stood in the darkness watching for a movement. Behind him, his men lay around small fires set into the bottom of a deep donga. He knew that the men and horses were exhausted, but they were the best. The ones who had sworn to fight to the bitter end. Once past the British guard encampment and into the wide lands beyond, they expected support from the farms in the shape of food, water and fodder for the horses.

The men were mostly in the tattered rags that had once been their clothing. Shirts that had not been washed in months had rotted off them. Jackets and trousers were torn and gaping. Many had no boots left. Their rifles, though, were clean. Most of them were Lee Metfords that had been captured from the British when ammunition for the Mausers ran out. Even so, they had little of the .303 ammunition left either. Some of the men had stripped their prisoners for their uniforms and were now almost indistinguishable from their enemies. He smiled as he remembered how they had laughed as the naked Khakis had stumbled back towards their lines. More humiliation for the British could only be a good thing.

There in the night he heard the hoofbeats and Wessels and his patrol emerged from the darkness. Wessels and one other rode up to Smuts and dismounted while the remainder rode down into the donga.

"Who have you brought to join us?"

Wessels ushered the man forward. "This is Jan van Rieman. He farms just south of the river. He tells me that every path and every drift are blocked by the Khakis. There is no way across, at least not without his help."

Van Rieman moved closer. Smuts could now see that the man had a hunchback. No wonder he had never ridden with the commandos. The man smiled at Smuts and shook his hand.

"The British come to my farm a lot. They water their horses in my dam and they buy fodder from me. I hear what they say. They know you are coming this way and there is a force coming down from the north, to trap you with the river at your back. All the drifts are guarded and they are ready for you."

"So what help can you give me?"

Van Rieman chuckled quietly. "Near my farm there is a place that can be crossed. It is dangerous, but it can be done. I found it when I was a boy and it is my secret. No wagons could cross there, but a good man on a horse should make it."

"Can we do it at night?"

"It has to be at night. The British at Kiba Drift would see you in the daytime."

Smuts looked down at the twisted man while making his decision. "Pass the word to up-saddle. We go now. Can we get fodder for the horses at your farm, Van Rieman?"

"There is not much, but what I have is yours."

"I cannot pay you, my friend."

"Did I ask for payment? This I do for Boer freedom. With my twisted spine, it is all I can do."

In minutes the men of the commando were in the saddle and ready to move. Most of them led a spare horse on a long rein. Horses had not been a problem, though food for them had been, with poor winter grazing and nowhere to find proper fodder. Van Rieman led the way with a long line of horsemen each following the back of the man in front just visible in the night.

The clouds cleared away and, even with just the starlight, Smuts could see the white foam of the tumbling river in the gorge below him. The banks were steep. Far too steep for any wagon, but Van Rieman dismounted and led his horse down the bank to an area where the river had scoured a flat beach. Smuts followed him. It was difficult, but the horse was sure-footed and they stood beside Van Rieman to watch the others try.

"We need to go across soon. The moon will rise from behind that kopje and show you to the sentry down at the drift."

Smuts looked again at the river. He could see no sign of any shallows where a man could ride a horse through.

"You are sure of this, my friend?"

Van Rieman grinned. "I will go first. If I drown then you will know I was wrong. Ride exactly where I ride. The shallows are narrow. Go slowly so the horses do not lose their footing."

With that, the hunchback swung himself into the saddle and urged his horse forward. He rode across, with the tumbling waters splashing and pushing against the flank of the horse all the way. As he reached the other side he turned and waved back to Smuts, then sat his horse where it was, to mark the end of the crossing place.

Before the moon rose, all of the commando was across and out of the river gorge. They rode to Van Rieman's farm and he gave them what fodder he had left in his bins. It was pitifully little for the number of horses. It did not matter; they were in the Cape Colony and the British did not know where.

The first part of their invasion had worked. Now Smuts was confident he could appeal to the Boers of the colony to rise and join the fight. Together they could throw the British out of the whole of South Africa. At every farm he could expect support and supplies for his weary men. Once he had begun the rising, De Wet and the men of the Transvaal would sweep down and raise a firestorm that would send the Khakis reeling.

The commando rode out into the Cape Colony. North of the Orange River they had become used to seeing burned farms. Small dams choked with dead animals. Slaughtered cattle rotting in the pens. Then everywhere there seemed to be columns of mounted British troops sweeping the veldt. Here the farms were neat, with people working unafraid in the fields. They stopped at these farms and were given food. Smuts had his first slice of bread and butter in over a year. The men had their weather-beaten faces wreathed in smiles as they tasted coffee for the first time in months. There was no clothing to be had, as the British were controlling distribution to stop it being sent to the commandos.

There were still dangers here in the south. As they rode close to the Native Reserve at Herschel on the borders of Basutoland they were attacked by Africans. They had been told by the British to defend their reserve and repel any invaders. This they did, but their spears and blunderbusses were no match for the Boer rifles. Still, the commando lost three men dead and seven wounded.

Two days later Smuts and three men set out to reconnoitre the area around Mordenaar's Poort. They ran into a British patrol. The three men were killed and Smuts narrowly escaped by running along a filthy ditch. He returned to the commando on foot, having had his horse shot from under him.

The troubles for the commando got worse as the weather turned from sun to icy rain and a virtual tempest of wind. The storm worsened as they moved south-west into the Stormberg mountains. Here they were told by a sympathetic farmer that General French and his cavalry were throwing a cordon around them. The farmer offered to lead them out through a pass the British had not yet blocked. The screaming wind now became their friend for a while, as it let them walk past a British encampment in the dark without being heard.

They laboured on through the mud and crossed the railway line. By the time they reached the shelter of an outlying farm fourteen men were missing. In the morning they woke to find that fifty or more of their precious horses had died in the night and lay in heaps where they had fallen. Smuts and his men knew this could not go on. The recruits they had expected from the Boers of the Cape Colony did not materialise. They were on their own, with more and more British cavalry searching for them. It was now impossible to live off the land and the commando was becoming desperate.

Smuts made his decision; they had to find a way out of the net that French had thrown around them. They struggled onwards to a gorge that led into the Elands River valley. There a farmer came out of his house to tell them that the Khakis were camped at the end of the gorge in a place called Elands River Poort.

Smuts sent one of his commanders, Reitz, forward with a group that called themselves the 'Dandy Fifth'. They trotted forward across a stream and into a stand of mimosa trees. Coming the other way they met a party of twenty British troopers riding towards them. The Dandy Fifth had been at war for more than two years and the troopers were relative newcomers to this country. There was no contest and the British were massacred.

The mist in the valley had worked in favour of the Boers and when the British had seen the khaki uniforms they had shouted, "Don't shoot! We are the 17th Lancers!" The Boers had replied, "And we are the Dandy Fifth" before opening a withering fire.

The commando moved forward to the encampment and once again the British sentries were confused by the khaki uniforms the Boers were wearing and allowed them to come closer. The Boers opened fire without warning and in the bloodbath that followed twenty-nine British soldiers were killed and forty-one wounded. Smuts lost one man killed and just six injured.

The Boers herded their prisoners together and then went to search for anything that might be of use to them. Having moved forward with virtually nothing left, they now found themselves in command of more than they could carry. They collected fresh horses, food, saddles, ammunition and medical supplies. When they had all that they could shift, the rest, including a field gun and wagons, were burned. The prisoners were left to fend for themselves and the Boers rode away.

The success was short-lived and Smuts was soon on the run from the vengeful troops that harried him. The foray of the commando into the Cape Colony to raise the Boers to rebellion and pave the way for the full invasion of the Transvaal army had failed. Further north, Botha had mounted a similar foray into Natal to disrupt the British supply lines. He, too, had some successes, but again the weight of numbers were just too much and the last hopes of a Boer military victory started to fade.

Chapter 52
Enforced Leave

Samuel and Sergeant Connolly stood by the side of the track as McGuire rode up with Captain James. "What have you got, Sergeant?"

"Not me, sir. Samuel, as usual, is playing out of his socks. The tracks are clear, or at least they are to him, and between us we've worked out there are about fifty Boers, maybe a few less."

"How far ahead, Samuel?"

"Well, baas, the dung beetles haven't found this yet, so not long. I think maybe one hour or two hour. No more."

"Can you tell where they are going?"

Samuel pointed. "That way, baas, is a flat place next to the river. They got a place down there where we won't see them till we right there. It's a good place for the night and it going to be dark in maybe one hour."

"You've been here before? Can we get close to them without being seen?"

Samuel stroked his ear. "Maybe, baas, and maybe not. If they have guards around they will see us coming in the moonlight. Maybe if we get there before the moon rises."

"Right, then. How far away is this place?"

Connolly held up a map. "According to this, sir, it's about a mile from here. If you look that way you can see there is mopani scrub between us and them, so there is some cover."

McGuire dropped down from his horse and waited until James joined him. He drew a rough plan in the dirt with his finger.

"We send one third of the men through the mopani on foot. You'll command that. Then we'll send a third out to each side on horseback. As soon as you start shooting we ride in and catch them in a pincer movement. With luck they will be too interested in you to notice us coming in, until it's too late."

The captain sat back on his heels. "Nice and simple, assuming they are there, of course."

"If the river bank is empty when you get there, fire three rounds in the air and we will use it as our camp for the night."

"When do you want to move in?"

"Assemble your men here and we will move as soon as it is full dark. You should be able to cover a mile well before the moon rises."

***

McGuire stood by his horse in the darkness stroking its muzzle to keep it calm and quiet. All around him he could hear the soft breathing of the rest of the horses in his detachment. The men murmured quietly to their mounts while they waited for the shots that would signal the start of the action. The tiny sliver of moon sent a silver light across the veldt as it peered from behind the highest kopje. Then the first shots crashed into the silent night. With no word of command, the company mounted up as one man. McGuire heard the rifles slide out of the leather boots attached to their saddles and then the sound of those weapons being cocked.

He paused for a moment to make sure all the men behind him were mounted and then yelled, "Forward!"

The river glinted to their right as they cantered towards the Boer laager. A gallop would have been too risky in the dark and they were close enough for it to make little difference. McGuire could see the rifle flashes from the Boers, who were firing at the initial attack now. It was working.

Then in front of him there was a burst of fire that was aimed his way. The Boers had been waiting. It was a trap. In the increasing light of the moon he could see the Boers spread out in front of him. They were down behind their saddles taking aim with those damned Lee Metfords they had captured. He heard men around him cry as out as they were hit. He fired his old heavy revolver and kept the attack moving. His horse jerked beneath him and then pitched forward. He was thrown over the animal's head and crashed to the ground in a burst of intense pain.

He had kept hold of his Webley, but he found he could not lift it with his right hand. He reached across with his other hand and took the weapon from himself. He raised it left-handed and looked for a target. Not ten feet from him a Boer appeared from behind his saddle and took aim at one of his men. McGuire fired and the man's head almost exploded in a mist of blood and bone as the heavy lead bullet smashed through his forehead.

To his front McGuire could see Lieutenant Dawson and his detachment arriving and opening fire. The Boers had not anticipated a three-pronged attack and were thrown into confusion by the sudden arrival of horsemen from behind them. Some jumped up and ran, others turned to fire at the new threat, but that exposed them to McGuire's men, who were now off their horses and providing effective rifle fire onto their enemies. In seconds it was over and the Boers were throwing down their weapons and raising their hands above their heads.

"Are you all right, sir?" It was Donnelly who appeared out of the confusion.

"No, Sergeant Major, I'm afraid I'm not. I seem to have broken something and my right arm isn't working. How is my horse?"

Donnelly looked behind his commander. "Dead, sir. Bloody great hole in her forehead. It was probably meant for you."

"Damn. Can you get someone to find me a spare?"

"That won't be a problem. A few of the lads are down."

McGuire closed his eyes. "Oh Christ. Help me up, will you?"

The pain from his arm and shoulder was intense as the big man helped him to his feet. He stood and surveyed the area around him. There were men lying in crumpled heaps, unmoving, and horses stood with their reins drooping.

"How many?"

"Still counting, sir. Lieutenant Dawson saved a lot with his attack. His lads were firing from the saddle as they came. Frightened the hell out of the Boers."

"Can you get Sergeant Fine to make me a sling of some kind.? He's good at that kind of thing."

Donnelly looked at his feet and then up again. "Sorry, sir, Fine's down. Took a round to the chest. I don't think he knew what hit him."

McGuire stood for a moment, stunned. "Oh dear God, another one of my originals gone. What about Connolly and Parks?"

"They made it, but Parks was winged in the leg. Just a flesh wound. It'll hurt like the devil, but he should keep the leg."

Captain James and Lieutenant Dawson walked up to him. "Thank you, Sergeant Major. Please tell me when you have the casualty count." He turned to his officers. "Nice work, gentlemen. Did you lose many men?"

"One dead and two wounded, sir," James said.

"And you, Lieutenant?"

Dawson smiled. "Not a one, sir. I was lucky."

"Lucky? Yes, but also damned effective. You frightened the life out of the Boers. Good work, both of you. Now get round and make sure the

Boers are searched. I don't want any nasty surprises."

"Are you hurt, sir?"

"Unfortunately, yes. I dismounted a little too enthusiastically."

The ride back with a broken arm and collar bone was painful, but the sight of empty saddles among his company hurt him more. The company had lost eight men killed, with seven wounded. The Boers had fared little better, with ten of their men buried by the riverside. They reached the army and McGuire made sure his wounded and the five injured Boers were being treated before he allowed the surgeons to look at his arm.

"You've been lucky, Major. Two clean breaks. One in the arm and one of your collar bones has gone too. The collar bone will be the most painful, as I can't splint that, but they will both heal if you rest them. You will be off any form of operations for a few weeks. The rest will do you good, anyhow. You're looking worn out."

"I can't rest. I have a company to look after. Can't you just strap me up?"

The surgeon sat down on the stool by the bed. "You don't remember me, do you?"

"Should I?"

"In the Sudan, you stuck that damned revolver against my head and swore you would kill me if I didn't treat an Arab boy who was under your command."

McGuire nodded. "Ah yes, I do remember that. My apologies, but that boy was important to me."

"I'm sure he was. Anyway, it would give me great pleasure to let you carry on riding with your company. The pain would be quite unpleasant. However, you would probably die of gangrene poisoning as the broken bones ripped your flesh, so I'm afraid I can't."

"You make your point well, Doctor."

The surgeon grinned. "I do, don't I? Anyway, you have a visitor."

The doctor stood up and walked to the entrance to the tent were he pulled the flap back. A tall figure ducked into the tent and McGuire was surprised to see Kitchener walking towards him.

"Good morning, sir."

"Been in the wars again, McGuire? The other side to your bullet wound from Omdurman, I take it?"

"Yes, sir. I felt I needed to even things up."

Kitchener sat down. "The sawbones tells me I can't use you in the field for some weeks with that injury. Is Captain James capable of commanding your company?"

"Highly capable, sir."

"Good, because I have a task for you while you are recovering and you are going to hate it."

Chapter 53
Miss Emily Hobhouse

McGuire stood on the platform at Bloemfontein and watched the train arrive in the customary clouds of steam. The doors opened and soldiers poured out of the carriages and immediately started to form up, with the Sergeants screaming to get them into their ranks. Officers descended from the first-class coaches more languidly and waited for their baggage to be unloaded for them. McGuire dared to hope the person he was waiting for had missed the train and he could go back to camp, but no, there she was. The only woman on the train was struggling to negotiate the steps down to the low platform with her full-length skirt catching on every obstruction.

He stepped forward and held up his left hand to help her down. "Miss Hobhouse, I assume?"

"That's right, and who, pray, are you?"

"Major Michael McGuire, Miss. I have been sent to help you during your visit."

She stopped on the platform and looked him up and down. Surreptitiously, he did the same to her. When he heard the name Miss Hobhouse he had imagined someone young and bubbly. A pleasant companion while he was recuperating. Maybe she would even be pretty? She was none of those things. She was obviously in her forties and had a distinctly sour expression on her chubby face. Her clothes were unfashionable and highly unsuitable for this country. In short, he decided, she was a frump.

"And what help do you imagine I will need?"

"Ma'am, this is not London. Transport is difficult at times and there are risks with the Boer commandos still on the loose. Accommodation is in short supply and many of the officers you will deal with are overworked and short-tempered. I will smooth your passage through all of this."

"So are you the son of somebody important to get an easy task like this while others fight?"

McGuire swallowed his irritation. "No, ma'am, I am a convalescing from an injury caused by falling off a horse. Colour Sergeant Parks, our carriage driver, was shot in the leg and was climbing the walls out of boredom. So he is delighted to have something useful to do, as am I, of course."

Miss Hobhouse allowed herself to be conducted to the carriage that waited behind the crowded platform and then McGuire went in search of her luggage. She sat in the vehicle looking around at the mass of soldiers moving hither and yon before she spoke to Parks.

"I hear you were wounded, is that correct?"

"It is, ma'am. A Boer bullet went through the fleshy part of my leg. Nothing too serious, but painful and I can't ride until it heals, the doctors say."

"Well, at least you have an honourable wound. Unlike the Major, who just fell off a horse. Drunk, I suppose?"

Parks chuckled. "Is that what he told you? Major McGuire fell off the horse when it was shot from under him in an engagement with the Boers. If the bullet had been three inches higher he would probably be dead."

"Oh dear. It seems I may have misjudged him."

Parks nodded. "Many people do, ma'am, but the ribbon of the Distinguished Service Order that he wears was not won for staff work."

"I see. Tell me, is it always so busy around the station?"

"No, ma'am. There are trains coming in bringing fresh troops to reinforce the army to allow us to deal with the remaining commandos."

"Why not just use the men you have here already?"

"Well, you see, ma'am, the Boers aren't fighting as they should. We defeated their armies and we took their towns. Their Presidents ran away and the governments of the two Boer states have been dispersed. They should have surrendered and we should have gone home. However, the Boer commandos are still roaming the veldt and attacking us."

"Is that why the farms are being burned and the women and children put in camps?"

"That's the way I understand it, ma'am. The veldt is huge, so we need to force the Boers to surrender by cutting off their food and support from the farms."

"How many farms have you burned?"

367

"Not a single one, ma'am. The Major won't do it. Says it's inhuman."

"And so I have misjudged him again, it seems."

"Here he comes with your luggage now. I think we will take you to the bungalow where a room has been put aside for you. Then you and the Major can decide what you want to see first."

***

"My God, what is that stench, Colonel?"

"Ah, that would be the latrines, Miss Hobhouse."

"Show me."

The Colonel shook his head. "I don't think you really want to see them now, do you, my good lady?"

Miss Hobhouse drew herself up and looked the tall Colonel in the eye. "You may command this camp, Colonel, but I have a letter from my uncle Lord Hobhouse that grants me free passage to see whatever I want. Now show me the latrines."

McGuire smiled to himself. He was beginning to like this tubby little woman. Whatever else she was, she was mightily determined. They had been in the camp outside Bloemfontein for only around half an hour and the Commandant was already looking uncomfortable.

Reluctantly, the Colonel led them to an area screened by sheets of hessian mounted on wooden poles. The stink announced that they had arrived.

Miss Hobhouse walked through the opening without ceremony and recoiled in horror at the smell of the overflowing buckets mounted beneath the rudimentary toilet seats. The huge mass of flies made breathing difficult.

"Colonel! Come in here!"

"I don't think that's necessary, Miss Hobhouse."

Emily reappeared from behind the hessian screens. "Don't you, Colonel? Don't you really? Have you ever looked at the latrines under your command? Have you seen what you are subjecting these people to? You should be ashamed."

McGuire took a look over the hessian and gagged slightly. The stench was almost visible and the overflowing buckets made using these facilities a recipe for disease. He turned away to see Miss Hobhouse stomping away towards the nearest tents. He saw her stop to speak to the old Boer lady who sat on the ground by the tent flaps and he hurried to catch her up. The old lady nodded and pulled back the tent flap behind her. Miss Hobhouse was inside for three or four minutes and then came out.

Her face was flushed with anger as she confronted the Colonel again. "There is a family of twelve people in that tent. Not only do they have to endure the smell of the latrines they are much too close to, they don't have a mattress or a bed between them. There are two sick children in there lying on the ground with nothing but an army blanket. Where are the supplies, Colonel?"

"Miss Hobhouse, you have to understand that is all I have to give them."

The small woman seemed to expand with rage. "Ridiculous! This war is costing the tax payer a fortune. It must be buying something. Put in a demand for supplies."

The Colonel shrugged and spread his hands. McGuire sympathised with the difficulties, but he had seen the massive stocks being built up in the army depot at Stellenbosch. Miss Hobhouse wasn't finished; she was away down the lane between the row of white bell tents. Then she stopped and turned to wait for them.

"I haven't see a water tap all the time we have been here. Where are they? I know there is fresh water in Bloemfontein. I have a tap in my room. Where are your water taps, Colonel?"

She didn't wait for the same old answer and set off down the road again. She stopped a woman carrying a covered pail of food and asked to inspect it. The weary woman took off the lid and showed her what was inside.

"Well, at least you give people enough food. That should make an adequate lunch."

The woman shook her head and touched her arm as she whispered something. Miss Hobhouse spun round in a fury.

"This is the ration for eight people for a day? That cannot be true, can it?"

The Colonel nodded almost sadly. "That is the ration that has been decreed for them and I can only distribute what I get issued."

"Major McGuire, we are leaving. Please would you bring the carriage to the gate. Colonel, I am going to inspect other camps and then I will be back. I expect you to have made improvements or you will be named in my report to my uncle and his friends in Parliament."

As she stomped off again the Colonel turned to McGuire. "Is there anything you can do to keep that bloody woman away from here?"

"I don't think so, sir. She has powerful friends and she seems to be a force of nature."

***

Days later the Colonel was waiting at the gate of the camp when the carriage pulled up. He helped Miss Hobhouse down and they waited until McGuire had joined them.

"Well, Colonel, I promised I would be back. Have you made any progress?"

"As you suggested, ma'am, I put in urgent requisitions for everything you recommended. I even asked for better rations and more staff for cleaning the camp. I asked the water company to supply me with pipes and taps for running water and a number of stand pipes. I have been turned down by everyone. The quartermaster's staff informed me that I have been issued with the full entitlement and the water company turned me down flat."

"Thank you, Colonel, at least you tried and I have to say that now I have been to the other camps you are not the worst. Come, Major McGuire, I have a train to catch."

Parks and McGuire watched the train pull out and slowly gather speed to the south. They walked back to the carriage. Parks' limp was now almost imperceptible and McGuire had removed the sling he had worn for weeks.

"Do you think she'll really write that report, sir?"

"I'm sure of it. She showed me the draft yesterday. She doesn't pull any punches either. If she really does have friends in Parliament there is going to be an almighty row."

"Begging your pardon, sir, but won't that be a good thing?"

"Yes, I think it might. The number of people dying in these camps is frightening. Way more than we or the Boer commandos are losing."

"Should you tell Lord Kitchener, sir?"

"I have already, but he assured me that I am exaggerating. Let's see if the amazing Miss Hobhouse can do better, eh?"

Chapter 54
Back on the Veldt

The Reconnaissance Company rode out from Bloemfontein on their next sweep to try and find the Boers commandos. McGuire was back at the head of the column with Captain James riding beside him. The welcome from the troops for him and Parks had been gratifying and he was pleased to see the men in such good spirits.

"You seem to have looked after the company rather well while I was recuperating."

"Thank you, sir. Not really difficult I have to say. They are as fine a group of men as I have ever served with. Remarkable when you consider what they were before they joined the company."

McGuire nodded. "I've found before that if you select men with an independent mind set and then treat them with respect they respond remarkably well. Conventional army discipline doesn't work for some men."

"I wonder what happens when all this is over and they get sent back to their normal units."

"That's a problem we will not have to deal with ourselves. What will you do when you have to go back to your regiment?"

James sighed. "I've been thinking about that for a while. The freedom of this company out on the veldt is intoxicating after the stuffy formality of a regiment in barracks. I'm not sure I can go back to that."

"Never mind, let's enjoy this while we may. I think Parks and I deserve a treat for being back on proper duty. Can you send out a hunting party and we'll have Samuel cook up one of his famous game stews tonight when we reach the blockhouse."

James smiled. "I'll go with them myself, if you don't mind, sir? I need some target practice. In fact I'd better go now; the blockhouse is just coming into view."

As the Captain wheeled away and called selected men out of the column to go on the hunt, McGuire lifted his field glasses and surveyed the round, squat structure in front of him. He had heard about Kitchener's new plan to contain and trap the remaining Boers, but this was the first of the blockhouses he had seen. The small forts were to be constructed across the country, with wire fences between them to slow the Boers and cause them to move elsewhere. Each blockhouse was to be manned by eight to twelve men armed with rifles. Many of these men were to be locally recruited Africans.

As he got closer McGuire could see that the walls of the circular structure had been loopholed to give secure firing positions for the small garrison. The roof was made of corrugated iron to keep the sun off and to protect from the savage rain storms which swept across the veldt in winter.

Once they reached the blockhouse, McGuire could see the next one in the chain. They were built within long rifle range of each other, so they

374

could provide support in the case of attack, or crossfire if the Boers were attempting to cut the wire fence that was strung between them.

As he dismounted in the shade of the blockhouse he was greeted by an expansive salute from a broadly smiling African Corporal. "Nice to see you, baas. I hope you got our rations?"

"Hello, Corporal. Yes, I've got a packhorse carrying two sacks of bully beef tins."

"Only one packhorse, baas? We get hungry out here."

"Nice try, Corporal. You get one load and the rest are for the other blockhouses along this stretch of wire. I've sent a party out hunting, so with a little luck we should have fresh meat tonight. You and your men are very welcome to join us."

"That's good timing, baas. We just finished brewing up some drums of beer. Your men should enjoy that, I'm thinking."

"Thank you, Corporal, it's a dusty road out here. Any sign of the Boers recently?"

The Corporal nodded. "Yes, baas, we saw a small party yesterday. They came and had a look at us, but never got in rifle range."

"Do you see them often?"

"No, baas, they stay away from us as much as they can."

The hunting party brought in two sable antelopes and Samuel had them butchered and boiling within the hour. As the smell of his cooking drifted around the blockhouse the Reconnaissance Company rolled out their blankets and prepared for the night. The eight men of the small garrison rolled out the drums of native beer and the men passed their tin mugs forward to be filled up.

"How's the arm after a day of riding, sir?"

"Just fine, Sergeant Major. I haven't had chance to talk to you. How have the men been while I have been away?"

Donnelly squatted down and passed a mug of the warm beer to McGuire. "They've been good, sir. We lost two in an attack near one of the drifts, but we got the Boers who did it. They were wearing British uniforms, so when we captured them they were shot straight away."

McGuire nodded. "I'd heard about Kitchener issuing that order. He reissued it after the 17th Lancers were ambushed down in Cape Colony. Apparently the Smuts commando walked right up to them in uniform and then opened fire. They killed twenty-nine men, six of them officers, and wounded forty-one."

Donnelly shook his head sadly. "It's turned into a dirty war, right enough. The days when you could treat the enemy decently have gone now, for sure."

McGuire nodded and nursed his beer. "The best thing we can do is to finish this as soon as possible and get home."

"How are things for you at home, sir? Have you heard from your wife?"

"Yes, I got a letter last week. She's upset about the loss of Sergeant Fine. You know he was working as her warehouse manager before he joined up again? And she's also not happy that my son wants to join the army. General Wingate has promised to sponsor him to the Royal Military Academy when he's old enough. Emma is hoping he fails the entrance examination."

"That doesn't seem likely, sir. From what I recall of him, he's a bright lad. He'd make a good officer."

"I think he would," McGuire agreed, "but I'm not sure I would want him in a war like this one. Anyway, enough of moaning, it looks like Samuel is starting to dish up. Let the garrison go first, will you? Being stuck out here they probably need a decent meal."

Once Donnelly had set the sentries for the night the company settled down and the usual snoring from the weary men filled the air. McGuire came awake at the first touch on his shoulder.

"Who is it?"

"Sergeant Connolly, sir. Keep quiet. We've got some friends arriving."

"Friends?"

"The Boers who were scouting around have come back. It's not a big party and they are sneaking between the blockhouses now. I think they are going to try and cut the wire to get through."

"Wake the men."

"Yes, sir, already being done. The Corporal has got the men in the blockhouse on standby for your orders."

McGuire threw back his blanket and walked around the blockhouse with Connolly. As they came to the front of the small building the Sergeant hissed quietly and pointed into the darkness. In the feeble light from the stars he could see indistinct shapes moving towards the wire. The snicker of a horse was the only noise. McGuire tapped the Sergeant on the arm and they drew back behind the blockhouse.

"Officers and NCOs to me," McGuire whispered.

"We're all here, sir," Donnelly said. "Sergeant Connolly anticipated what you'd need."

"Well done, Connolly. Right, let's keep this simple. The Boers are moving to the fence. No doubt they will cut the wire and go through if we let them. So I want you to split the men up into groups and then spread out rapidly and silently between here and the next blockhouse. Don't fire until I do and then pour it into them. Connolly, take charge of the blockhouse here and don't let them fire until we do. All clear what you are doing? Good, now move off, and for Christ's sake, no noise."

The company moved rapidly and silently with no words of command that could be heard more than a few feet away. McGuire stopped as he reached what he judged to be the mid-point between the blockhouses. He waited and tried to see whether the men were in position. In the end he decided to gamble that they were. Even if the spread was not quite perfect, it would do.

He raised his rifle and cocked it as quietly as he was able. He waited until he could pick out a dim shape in front of him and aimed at it. He squeezed the trigger slowly and carefully. The rifle bucked against his shoulder and sent a stab of pain through his recently healed collarbone. All around him the rifles roared and their muzzle flashes lit the night. McGuire slung the rifle over his shoulder and drew his revolver. He stared ahead and then fired again and again at the thickest mass of the enemy that the flickering flashes showed him.

There were screams in front of him from men and horses as the .303 rounds ploughed into flesh, both human and animal. He heard the voices of the Boers calling out for mercy. To be allowed to surrender.

"Cease fire! Cease fire!"

The firing died away around him and the panting men stared to move. "Stay down and stay ready. Lieutenant Dawson, forward with me."

The young Lieutenant trotted across to McGuire's side and they walked forward together, to accept the surrender of the Boers they had spared.

"That went well, sir. I don't think they got off more than one or two shots and they didn't hit any of ours."

"Sadly, I think we hit some of their horses. We may have to shoot them."

"That's always sad, but it ha …"

The rifle cracked from in front of them and the bullet ripped into Dawson's throat. He dropped to the ground, grabbing at his neck and gargling on his own blood.

McGuire dropped next to him. "Fire! All of you fire! Slaughter the bastards!"

He stayed low as the rounds cracked above him, hearing the screams as the Boers were hit. He heard their cries for mercy again and they yelled that they surrendered. This time he gave no quarter and did not order the ceasefire until all sounds from the Boers had died away.

"Right, cease fire!"

He heard the order being repeated along the line, but gave it a few seconds before he moved. He spun round to check on Dawson. The starlight reflected off the dead eyes that would never see the sky again. He swore under his breath and then stood.

"Captain James, Sergeant Major Donnelly, bring six men forward, each of you."

He waited until they reached him and then they all walked forward with weapons at the ready. As they reached the Boers they could see horses struggling to rise and then McGuire heard moaning from one of the fallen men. He walked across and looked down. The man was badly injured with blood oozing from at least three bullet holes; the British uniform he wore was almost unrecognisable. The blood looked black in the dim light.

"Captain James, to me, please, and you, too, Sergeant Major."

The two men reached him and looked down at the moaning Boer. "Tell me what you see there. Is that or is it not British army uniform?"

"It is, sir," James said.

"Sergeant Major?"

"Yes, sir, he's wearing our uniform. He's even still got the rank badges on it."

"Thank you. Now confirm our orders are to shoot any Boer found wearing British uniform."

"Yes, sir, but I didn't think you would follow that order."

"You were wrong. Go and take a look at Dawson, lying in the dirt with his throat ripped out by one of these bastards, after they had surrendered."

He lifted the heavy Webley revolver and aimed carefully between the wounded man's eyes. The big pistol bucked in his hand as he executed the Boer lying at his feet.

"Now go and check the rest. If any are still alive and in our uniform, shoot them. Then put the horses out of their misery."

Chapter 55
Appeasing the Enemy

"Ah, Major McGuire, I have a new task for you, and rather a distasteful one, I'm afraid."

McGuire smiled at Kitchener. "Miss Hobhouse isn't back, I hope?"

"No, she's made quite enough trouble already. There has been an incident of prisoners apparently being murdered by Imperial troops. I need you to go and arrest the men involved and then bring them back here for court martial."

"Were the prisoners caught wearing our uniforms, sir?"

Kitchener stood up from behind the cluttered desk. "That is not the point, Major. Your job is to go and arrest them, not to prejudge the outcome of a court martial. Captain Lewis is outside with the details for you, including an arrest order that I have signed. Now listen, the unit these men command has a reputation for being unruly, so take your whole company and brook no arguments from anyone. Is that clear?"

McGuire saluted. "As clear as day, sir. I'll bring them in."

On his way out he picked up the written orders for arresting four officers of the Bushveldt Carbineers, a mounted infantry unit that had been raised from mostly Australian volunteers. He mounted up and rode back towards the company bivouac; as he rode he read through the charge sheets. If this was all true these officers were in a world of trouble.

It took two days to ride out to Fort Edward where the company of Bushveldt Carbineers were stationed. McGuire halted the Reconnaissance Company outside the gates, then rode in with Captain James and Sergeant Major Donnelly. A thin-faced Lieutenant came out of one of the low buildings to meet them.

He saluted McGuire. "Good morning, sir. How can we help you today?"

McGuire returned the salute and dismounted. "I'm looking for a Lieutenant Morant and three other officers."

"Harry is away on a couple of days' leave at the moment, sir. He's due back tomorrow morning. Who are the other officers you want to speak to?"

McGuire consulted his list. "Handcock, Witton and Picton. All Lieutenants, according to this."

"I see, sir. Well, Lieutenants Handcock and Witton are in our small mess and I'm Picton. May I know what this is about?"

"Sergeant Major, take this officer's sidearm. You, Lieutenant, are under arrest for murder. Please don't be difficult and make me put you in irons."

Donnelly removed the pistol from the leather holster on Picton's belt and stepped back. The young man looked stunned.

"I don't understand."

"You will. Now lead on to your mess and we'll get this over with."

The startled officer led the way with McGuire and James close behind him. Donnelly walked in the rear, keeping a weather eye on the rest of the barracks. They came to a door with the words 'Officers' Mess' painted on it and went in.

There were three men inside. A Captain and two Lieutenants. The Captain stood up.

"I say, you really should remove your headgear as you come into a mess, sir. We have to maintain proper standards, even out here."

"Sit down, Captain. Good morning, gentlemen. I am Major McGuire of the Independent Reconnaissance Company acting on the direct orders of Lord Kitchener. Lieutenants Handcock and Witton, I'm afraid you and young Picton here are under arrest."

The Captain's mouth dropped open. "What? You can't just come into my post and arrest my officers."

McGuire said nothing, but handed him the arrest orders bearing Kitchener's signature. The man was dumbstruck and looked at McGuire and then at his officers.

"Murder? You can't be serious? The names on here are Boers. We're fighting a war against them, for God's sake. This is ridiculous."

Captain James walked to the short wooden rack on the wall and turned to face the irate post commander. "Which of these belts is yours, sir?"

"The left-hand one, but why?"

384

"Because I am taking possession of these officers' weapons, since they are now under close arrest."

McGuire removed his helmet. "These three officers will be confined to their quarters and I will have to put a guard on their doors. We will wait here for the return of Lieutenant Morant."

"Breaker? You're arresting him as well?"

"If by 'Breaker' you mean Lieutenant Harry Morant, then yes, I am. Now I suggest you inform your men about all this and keep them calm. Your command has an interesting reputation and I am not averse to arresting any man who gives us any trouble, Captain.

"Sergeant Major, would you go and collect six men to guard these officers. Now, gentlemen, I see no reason to be uncivilised about this, so you may of course have your lunch before being confined. Captain James and I would be delighted to join you. It's quite a while since we managed to have a meal at a proper table."

***

"Good morning, sir. Sentry reports a rider coming in."

"Thank you, Sergeant Major. Just the one rider?"

Donnelly nodded. "Just the one and he's in no rush, so I guess it's not a despatch rider."

McGuire stood up and collected his pistol belt from the hook on the wall. He strapped the belt around him and unclipped the holster flap.

Donnelly noticed the gesture and looked his commander in the eye.

"Expecting trouble from Lieutenant Morant, sir?"

McGuire picked up his helmet and put it on. "Not really, but I'm not going to be taken by surprise either. Let the Lieutenant come through the gate and then you and two or three men move in behind him. I don't want to have to chase him halfway across Natal."

The two men walked back outside. Donnelly strode across the open area to the gate and disappeared through it to where the company were camped. In the meantime McGuire positioned himself at the front of the officers' mess and sat down in one of the scruffy wicker chairs.

As Morant rode in through the gate McGuire watched him. There was no sign that he had been warned about his impending arrest. He dismounted and handed the horse's reins to an African stable boy, who trotted across to him. Morant walked up the steps towards the door of the mess. He stopped and saluted as McGuire stood up.

"Lieutenant Harry Morant?"

"That's right. Do I know you, sir?"

"Major McGuire of the Independent Reconnaissance Company."

Morant smiled. "Oh yes, I've heard of you. A very effective company at catching up with the Boers, I hear."

McGuire nodded. "And now we've caught up with you. Lieutenant Morant, you are under arrest for murder of prisoners of war."

Morant's mouth dropped open for a second or two. "You can't be serious? Any prisoner who was shot was in accordance with orders."

Donnelly stepped up behind the startled officer and rested a hand on his shoulder. "I'll just be taking your pistol now, sir."

Morant stood stock still, staring at McGuire while the flap of his holster was unclipped and the revolver removed. Donnelly stepped back with the weapon in his hand and waited.

McGuire waved towards the door of the mess. "You've had a long ride, Lieutenant. Come inside and get some breakfast. We'll be leaving for Pietersburg in about an hour.

Chapter 56
Drudgery

"Have we heard anything about how the court martial is going, sir?"

"No, Sergeant Major, no word at all through official channels, unless you have heard any gossip?"

Donnelly spat the dust from his mouth and leaned back against his saddle. "Nothing firm, but I know a lot of the lads are unhappy about it."

"Ours?"

"Not just ours. That column we rode with last week as well. The way people see it is, we're fighting these bloody people with one hand tied behind our backs, while they run rings round us. Now it seems we get dragged into court for doing what needs doing."

"What I was told last time we were in Bloemfontein is that Morant and his people went too far. There was even a priest killed who was going to raise a report on them."

"A priest? They killed a priest?"

McGuire shook his head "I don't know that for sure. He threatened to report them and a day later he was found face down in a ditch. As far as I know there are no witnesses."

"The way I heard it," Donnelly said, "they had a company commander, Captain Hunt, who was killed. When they got back to him the body had been mutilated badly. They even say he might still have been alive when it happened. He was friends with Morant and that's why the Lieutenant went a bit crazy."

McGuire paused, thinking back to the attack between the blockhouses. "There, but for the grace of God, go any of us."

"True enough, sir. Time to saddle up now?"

McGuire stood up and dusted himself down. "Yes, the men have had a decent night's sleep. Let's get these prisoners back to the Provost and see if we can pick up some decent rations, unless the Boers have derailed another supply train."

Captain James walked across to his commander while the horses were being saddled. "The men are done in, sir."

"I can see that. I'm weary, too. These constant sweeps across the veldt are wearing them down. A good stiff fight might help to relieve the sheer boredom of it all."

James looked around at the wide expanse of the African plain, dotted with blockhouses. "Have you heard how much longer this might go on? I thought Kitchener might have said something when you reported to him."

McGuire shook his head sadly. "Nothing specific. One of his staff officers told me that he is getting tired and frustrated with the pressure from London to bring it all to a close. Then when the Boers made a peace offer, London refused to let him make any concessions."

"So we carry on grinding at the Boers and wearing them down?"

"We do. Field intelligence has calculated there are about ten thousand Boers still under arms, but scattered in small groups now. The bigger commandos can't get enough food to stay together."

"So the blockhouses and the big sweeps across the country are working?"

"It seems so, but too damned slowly. Right, it looks like the horses are ready. Let's take our prisoners in."

Half a day later the company arrived at the gates of the stockade. Their twelve dispirited and exhausted Boer prisoners seemed almost relieved to be going into captivity. At least there they would be given food on a regular basis and have tents to shelter in from the savage winter storms. McGuire sent the men back to their bivouac area and rode through the bustle of the garrison to the headquarters where he had been summoned to see Kitchener again.

The General's eyes were half hooded with fatigue as he looked up from his desk. He waved a hand towards the two chairs set either side of the fireplace. As McGuire sat down and Kitchener took the other chair and an orderly brought in the now customary two glasses of brandy and soda.

"How many prisoners this time, McGuire?"

McGuire revelled in the coolness of the brandy as it ran down his dusty throat. "Just twelve this time, sir. Not very exciting, I'm afraid."

"Every little helps, but that's not why I asked you to come here. I have some good news for you and then some not so good."

"Do I get to choose which order they come in, sir?"

Kitchener shook his head. "No, not really. Firstly, your troop and then company have been very valuable in this war. At the end of our campaign in the Sudan you were awarded the Distinguished Service Order on my recommendation for all you did there. Now you have a bar to that DSO. It was published in the *London Gazette* three weeks ago and the notification has just arrived."

"That's very good of you, sir. And the bad news?"

"Not yet. You recommended three of your men for awards. Sergeant Major Donnelly and Colour Sergeant Parks and Sergeant Connolly have all been awarded the Meritorious Service Medal for gallantry."

McGuire smiled broadly. "Thank you, sir. They all deserve it. I'm only sorry Sergeant Fine did not live to be awarded one as well."

Kitchener gave a small shrug of agreement. "Now then, you may not have realised out on the veldt, but the war is coming to an end. The Boer peace delegation will be meeting me tomorrow and the preliminary work by the staff has been fruitful. I am under instructions from London to start to reduce our forces in South Africa. The cost to the Treasury has been excessive, apparently. You and your troop have been here since the beginning, so I intend to send you home to Egypt after one more task."

"But we are now a company, sir."

"So you are. Your company is to be disbanded and the men sent back to their respective regiments. The changes you have made in them through your training should make them welcome when they get back."

"When should the disbandment start, sir?"

"Today. Let them rest tonight and then start moving them out tomorrow. The troop will stay here for a few more days then, once a rather distasteful task is completed, you will be shipped back to Egypt. The Royal Irish Fusiliers are going as well, so you will be back in your own regiment."

"I see, sir, and the distasteful task?"

"The court martial of the Bushveldt Carbineers officers has concluded. They have been found guilty and two of them have been sentenced to death. I am awaiting the final confirmation of sentence from London. Once I have signed the death warrants I want you and your troop to provide the firing squad."

McGuire felt the blood drain from his face; he put down his glass. "May I ask why us, sir?"

"Very simple really. All your men are skilled marksmen and I want this to be as clean as possible. No muck-ups."

Chapter 57
Scapegoats of Empire

"Message for you, sir."

McGuire turned around and held out his hand for Sergeant Connolly to pass it over. He opened the paper and read it twice before he looked up at the waiting Sergeant.

"Any reply, sir?"

"No, Sergeant, this is a notice that the death sentence for Morant and Handcock has been confirmed. I am instructed to tell them."

"Oh hell, so we really have to go through with it?"

"I'm afraid so. Will you let the Sergeant Major know and ask him to inform the troop, please."

Connolly saluted, then paused. "What about you, sir?"

"Me? Oh I've got to find a way to break the news without being bloody brutal about it. I'll come and speak to the troop later."

He watched Connolly walk away and then looked across at the row of low farm buildings that had been converted into a military prison. He could see the sentry pacing around the square and envied him his simple duty. As he walked towards the building he heard the sounds of sawing and hammering coming from the carpenter's workshop.

He reached the cell door and called the guard Corporal over to unlock it for him to go in. As he stepped inside the dimly lit room he could see all four of the Carbineers officers sitting in their shirt sleeves, playing cards.

"Good timing, Major," Morant said, looking up from his cards. "These card sharps have cleaned me out of matchsticks."

McGuire sat down on a box against the rough wall. He took the paper from his pocket.

"I guess we know what that is, Major. We've been listening to the carpenter all morning. All we really need to know is how many coffins is he making?"

After a pause when the others studiously looked at their cards, McGuire spoke. "Just two. The prison terms for Witton and Picton are confirmed and you will be taken back to England to serve your sentences."

"And so it's a wooden box for me and Handcock then?"

McGuire nodded. "I'm afraid so."

"When?"

"Tomorrow morning at dawn."

"Will you be there, Major?"

McGuire nodded again. "Unfortunately, yes. My troop is detailed to provide the firing squad and I am the only officer."

Morant sat back against the stone wall. "Well, that's some comfort at least."

"How is that a comfort?" McGuire asked.

"Not for you, of course, but I've seen that all your men are wearing marksmen's badges, so it should be quick. And having the party commanded by someone who understands why we did what we did is a good thing as well."

"Not sure I understand you, Morant."

Morant chuckled. "I spoke with your men after we were arrested by you. They told me about your Lieutenant Dawson being killed after the bastards had surrendered. You had his blood all down your uniform when you shot the wounded Boer. You understand well enough. We had to do it after what they did to Captain Hunt."

McGuire stood up to leave. "Is there anything I can get you?"

"What for?"

"To make this evening a little more pleasant maybe?"

Handcock turned around from the card table. "Can we stay in the same cell tonight? Be good to have someone to talk to instead of lying on a cot staring at the ceiling."

McGuire banged on the door for the sentry to open up for him. "I'll arrange that and see if I can get you a decent meal as well."

***

The morning dawned cold and clear as the two men were brought out of their cell. The other two had left while it was still dark, to be taken to the railway station to start their journey to a prison in England. Morant and Handcock, wearing trousers and shirts, were lined up with the escort party under McGuire's command.

"Would you like to speak to a priest?" McGuire asked.

Morant shook his head. "No thanks. I'm a pagan."

Handcock looked at him. "What's a pagan?"

"One who doesn't believe in an almighty all-seeing deity."

"Me too, then. I'm a pagan."

McGuire had to smile at their defiance. "All right, Sergeant, march them up to the ridge."

The small party marched up the slope to the top of the low ridge where two rough chairs had been positioned. McGuire did not speak, but pointed to the chairs and the condemned men sat down facing back towards the low-roofed prison below them.

The firing squad, made up from the eight surviving men of McGuire's Reconnaissance Troop, marched into place, halted and turned to the left to face the men in the chairs. Sergeant Major Donnelly walked behind Morant and Handcock.

"I've got the blindfolds if you gentlemen would like them?"

Morant shook his head. "Take those damned things away."

Donnelly slipped the two cloths back in his pocket and came around in front of the two men. From another pocket he drew out two small pieces of red cloth and proceeded to pin them to their shirts above the heart.

As he finished he whispered, "I'm sorry about this, gents. We know you didn't deserve it."

"Don't worry, Sergeant Major. We are the scapegoats of the Empire. Killing us will make the peace process go more smoothly and the politicians can say they fought a clean war."

"Doesn't make it right though, sir."

Morant reached into his pocket and pulled out a silver cigarette case. "No, it doesn't, Sergeant Major, but here, take this so you don't forget us."

Donnelly stood upright and looked down at the case. He slipped it into a breast pocket and turned away to walk back down to the riflemen. As he prepared to give the order to aim he heard Morant shout.

"Shoot straight, you bastards! Don't make a mess of it!"

Chapter 58
Homeward Bound

The troop embarked at Durban for the voyage north across the Indian Ocean to Aden for coaling and then up the Red Sea to Suez. Once through the Suez Canal they would dock in Port Said and be loaded onto the train for Cairo. It would be long, hot and boring, but it was taking them where they wanted to be.

McGuire stood by the rail as the ship pulled away from the quay and headed for the open ocean. He looked long and hard at South Africa as it slowly receded into the heat haze. He knew he was a changed man and he knew he had a decision to make before he reached Egypt.

He felt the presence next to him and looked over his shoulder to find Donnelly standing there. "Hello, Sergeant Major. Are the men all settled?"

"They are, sir. Half of them are asleep already."

"Really? I thought they might be up on deck watching South Africa disappear behind us."

"I think we've all seen enough of South Africa to last a lifetime. We've swallowed enough of its dust as well."

"That's true, and we've left some good men buried in it too."

"Looking forward to being back in the noise and smells of Cairo, are you, sir?"

McGuire looked out to sea and nodded. "Mostly I'm looking forward to being back with my family. I need to spend some time with them, I think. What about you?"

"My engagement in the army is just about up, so I'm thinking about a small pub on the Falls Road in Belfast. The loot we picked up in the Sudan should be enough to set me up and let me find a good woman to share it with."

McGuire paused and let his hand fall from the rail. "I think my time in the army is nearly over as well. Kitchener is going to India as Commander in Chief. He offered me a post on his staff, but I declined. I think it's time for me to find out what it's like being a civilian."

"You, sir? I thought you'd stay in until they made you a General at least."

"I'd be a rotten General. I can't do the politics. Anyway, after this I think I've had enough of blood and killing. Let somebody else fight the next war. I've done my share. Now I'm due for a life of peace."

"I'll drink to that, sir."

"Good idea. Let's you and I go and find out where a man can get a long cold beer on this ship and you can tell me more about this pub of yours."

McGuire is finished with the army, after his experiences in the Boer War, but the army may not be finished with him and a most devastating war is coming.

The Road to Ladysmith – Factual Content

As with all my books, I like to give the reader a chapter on the actual facts I have used, to allow you to make a judgement on whether my story is credible. This book is no exception and so some of the facts about this remarkable campaign are laid out below.

The Royal Irish Fusiliers set sail from Alexandria, Egypt on the 25th September 1899. They arrived in Durban, South Africa, on the 12th October and were immediately taken up country. In the rush their baggage and much of their equipment was left behind. On the 13th October the battalion arrived in Ladysmith and took up outpost duty that same evening.

It is sadly true that the standard of leadership displayed by very senior officers of the British Army in the early part of the Boer War was painfully lacking. These men had learned their trade in the days of single shot rifles and most of their combat experience had been gained fighting in the colonial wars of the period against brave, but poorly armed natives. Many did not seem to have understood the power of modern rifles or the use of concealment instead of marching bravely up to the enemy. The Boers were looked down upon as a bunch of farmers, despite having won the first Boer war against the British. The value of these men armed with Mauser rifles and mounted on horseback was not appreciated, until a significant number of troops had been killed or wounded by these mere farmers.

Politicians back in London should also bear some of the blame for the debacle in the early months. They had delayed mobilisation of the Army and had withheld the funds needed to equip the troops properly for the conditions they would meet. In addition, the political control and oversight of the War Office was surprisingly poor and allowed ridiculous feuds between senior officers to damage the readiness of the army.

Many of the men sent to South Africa were reservists who had been called back to their regiments. Not all of these men were at the fitness standards required for campaigning and there was little or no time for training to increase their readiness.

It is true that Mohandes K Gandhi and many Indians from the Cape Colony served as stretcher-bearers during the war and displayed considerable courage, going forward under fire to collect the wounded. They were given the nickname of the body-snatchers and also gained huge respect from the soldiers they helped. In later life Gandhi became known as Mahatama (Great Soul) and led India to independence from colonial rule.

The battle of Talana Hill just outside the town of Dundee was a British victory, but a costly one. The walls and buildings at Smith's Farm did cause the British some difficulty and the Boers were dislodged after a small force moved around to outflank them. General Penn-Symons did go forward to inspire his men and was shot in the stomach, dying a day later from his wound. The movement of strong Boer forces towards them forced the British to retreat to the main garrison at Ladysmith and they had to leave their most badly wounded men to the mercy of the Boers. Luckily, the Boers were honourable and treated the wounded with respect and kindness. The march back from Dundee was difficult in the horrendous rain that Africa can bring. I have experienced such rain and it is impressive.

The Boers under General Kock did ride forward and take control of the railway station at Elandslaagte. They did cut the rail line and so cut off the exposed garrison at Dundee. The attack on them by the British took place much as I have described and the savage attack by the cavalry on the retreating commando also actually took place. General Kock was wounded and captured, dying of his wounds in the hospital at Ladysmith. The incident with the white flag did happen and it incensed the British, who had respected the flag of surrender. That incident and other, later, misuse of white flags by the Boers was to be the cause of some Boers having difficulty in surrendering as the British came to expect treachery.

The short sharp battle at Rietfontein, on the 24th October 1899, did allow the retreating column from Dundee to pass by and did prevent the two strong commandoes from linking up to attack it. But it was costly and demonstrated once again that the Boers, when entrenched and properly led, were a force to be reckoned with.

The action at Nicholson's Nek did take place and did result in the surrender of the Royal Irish Fusiliers and the Gloucestershire Regiment. The Commanding Officer did not authorise the white flag to be raised, but felt that once it had been raised he had to do the honourable thing and cease fire. The regiments were in a difficult position in any event, having lost their artillery support and their spare ammunition during the night when the pack mules all stampeded. They were surrounded and outnumbered and subjected to accurate rifle fire. Just after the loss of Nicholson's Nek the railway line south of Ladysmith was cut and the town surrounded by superior numbers of Boers. The trapped British forces settled in for a siege, confident that they would be rapidly relieved.

The main British force under the command of General Redvers Buller started to assemble for the relief of Ladysmith in Estcourt. Although Buller had been appointed to command the army in South Africa, his departure was delayed by the War Office in London which put him at a disadvantage as questionable decisions had been taken while he was still at sea. Politicians seldom, if ever, accept blame for their failings and so General Buller was chosen to be the sacrificial lamb for the setbacks of 'Black Week' while he was trying to relieve Ladysmith. In the opinion of people who were actually there, and served under the General, this was unfair. I tend to agree with them.

Queen Victoria took a keen interest in the army and their actions, so it is very possible that a General about to command forces in battle would be summoned to meet her. As readers of *No Road To Khartoum*, the first book in this trilogy, will recall, the Queen took a personal interest in McGuire and so would probably have mentioned him to Buller.

Winston Churchill, the future Prime Minister, arrived in Estcourt on November 6th 1899 as the correspondent of the *Morning Post* newspaper. He took part in an armoured train patrol soon after arriving at Estcourt. He also managed to secure a place on a second armoured train patrol under the command of Captain Haldane. The patrol did not go well and was ambushed by an effective Boer force. The attack happened much as I have described it in this book, taking Churchill's own first-hand account as my guide. Churchill and a number of others were captured and taken away as prisoners of war, although Churchill tried hard to protest that he should be released, as he was a civilian reporter. He managed to escape after a short internment and, despite the best efforts of the Boers, made it across the border into Mozambique, from where he took ship back to South Africa and rejoined the army. By pure chance he did knock on the door of the only Englishman for miles and he was helped by John Howard, the mine manager.

The action at Willow Grange was very poorly coordinated by the British and, from their point of view, inconclusive. Approximately 16 men were killed and around 60 were wounded. However, it did dissuade Joubert from continuing his advance and caused him to retire on Colenso. His plan to send a commando, of around a thousand men, into Natal to cause damage behind the British lines and to raise rebellion among the Boers living in Cape Colony was shelved.

Army headquarters did move up from Estcourt to Frere and the army concentrated there in preparation for the thrust to Ladysmith. The army grew rapidly to outnumber the Boers, but the lack of cavalry was a severe impediment to standard British tactics. The fast-moving and mobile commandos of the Boers were able to retreat, or to reinforce points under attack, with remarkable ease. In addition, the Boers had forced native labourers to build defensive trenches and emplacements ready for the British advance.

Buller's original plan was to throw the army across the Tugela at Potgieter's Drift. At the same time General White was to mount a thrust out of Ladysmith towards the south. The two forces were intended to link up and catch a significant part of the Boer force between them. They would then swing to the east and roll up the Boer lines by attacking them from the flank and rear. Just before this plan was executed Buller lost confidence that White would actually move and that would leave his force exposed and vulnerable. He therefore changed the plan from a crossing at Potgieter's Drift to a thrust towards Colenso.

It is true that the Boers strung barbed wire across the drifts below the water and that it caused problems until it had been cleared away. The railway bridge towards Colenso had been dynamited, but the wagon bridge had been deliberately left intact to tempt the British into using it and entering a killing zone in front of the Boer forward emplacements.

Buller did intend to throw a force across the Tugela at Bridle Drift and it is true that this force was led astray by an African guide in the dark, leaving them exposed to accurate Boer rifle fire from their hidden emplacements. Buller saw what was happening and sent staff officers to try and stop the column, but the commander of the column declined to listen. As the firing started the native guide vanished and the column was left confused. The men did try to scatter and were driven back into columns. Once the troops were pinned down in the loop Buller sent forward reserve troops to help extricate them, but for most of the day the men were pinned down, not daring to move for fear of being shot by the riflemen they never saw.

The action of the artillery over to the right of the battle of Colenso was equally disastrous and once again Buller's specific orders were not obeyed. Buller tried personally to extricate the guns from their exposed position, but realised that the men were exhausted and any further attempts would cause even more unnecessary casualties. Lieutenant Freddy Roberts, the son of Field

Marshal Roberts, was killed in a courageous attempt to recover the guns.

Buller was in touch with General White, the commander of the Ladysmith garrison, by heliograph and by signals flashed onto clouds by searchlight. The condition of the trapped troops and their ability to cooperate in the relief of the town was a serious concern to General Buller. In fact, White had been dismayed by the position he had allowed himself to be trapped in and had shut himself in his headquarters. His mental state seems to have been questionable and resulted in inactivity from the garrison. Some active officers tried to encourage sorties against the surrounding Boers, but were refused permission for most of the time. Others succumbed to the lethargy of the siege and neglected to improve defences in some parts of the perimeter.

It is true that the Boers used African labourers to construct their trench positions and it is also true that these Africans were treated extremely badly. Any perceived slacking was dealt with by the sjambok whip. The British, in general, also looked down on the native population, but when labouring for the army they were paid and were fed decently. Later the British armed Africans and used them in auxiliary units. These units were effective, but any of the native soldiers captured by the Boers could expect to be shot out of hand.

Strange as it may seem, the shelling of Ladysmith, by the gun the British christened 'Long

Tom' was as desultory as I have described. The Boers would fire from their hilltop position and when the muzzle flash was seen bugles were blown. The long range gave the troops time to take cover and very little damage was done. The British naval guns would fire one or two shells in return, but the shortage of ammunition made a major return bombardment impossible. It is also true that the Boers, to a great extent, kept the Sabbath and did not fire into Ladysmith on Sundays.

It is also sadly true that General Sir George White became disillusioned during the siege of Ladysmith and sank into a form of lethargy. He refused permission for some rather obvious defensive measure to be taken. For instance, he refused to allow minefields to be laid in front of the British positions and refused to allow corrugated iron huts to be dismantled to provide reinforcement for bomb shelters. A number of sorties against the Boers were proposed to him and were refused permission. Eventually an attack on the Boer guns was authorised and was successful. On the same morning White sent out a cavalry patrol that was badly managed and twenty-four men died.

The statement about Samuel running alongside horses may sound far-fetched, but Zulu and Matabele tribesmen, among others, did have this kind of physical prowess at this time.

The major assault on Ladysmith did take place in a change from normal Boer tactics. It was beaten off, but at some cost in casualties due mainly to the poor state of the defences. The panic at the gun position did take place and was stopped by the determined actions of Lieutenant Digby-Jones as I described in my story. The coordination by senior officers was poor and the fact that the town was held was due mainly to the courage and initiative of junior officers and the determination of the soldiers.

It is true that the crossing of the Tugela at Trikhardts Drift by General Warren was painfully slow. This lack of urgency allowed the Boers to transfer their strength across to meet the British advance and where there had been six hundred or so defenders there were over seven thousand by the time the crossing was complete. General Buller became aware that the attack was going wrong, but he declined to relieve Warren from command, a decision he bitterly regretted, though this was not made public until much later.

The decision to mount an attack on Spion Kop was in itself logical. However, the execution of that attack and its coordination were abysmal. Command of the attack force was changed during the battle, but other senior officers were not informed. Reinforcements were slow to advance when requested. General Warren made no apparent attempt to take a grip on the situation. The lack of entrenching tools is, to my mind, inexplicable and caused the loss of a considerable number of the British troops who could find no proper cover on the stony hilltop. A reconnaissance of the approach did take place, but did not detect that there was a second peak on the hill so that the troops were exposed once the morning mist cleared. The white dog did join the attack force and was nearly killed to keep it quiet. A boy bugler was detailed to take it back down the hill and saved its life.

At the end of a day's fighting on Spion Kop both sides retreated and abandoned the hill. Both sides thought they had been beaten. Only the British were correct. 243 British soldiers had died on Spion Kop. Many more were wounded. The Boers had lost 335, but they were less able to absorb such a loss. Churchill met the British survivors coming down the hill after the withdrawal. Despite his experience in previous wars, he was horrified by the injuries he saw on the men being carried by the Indian stretcher-bearers. The shrapnel from the field guns and pom-poms had done horrendous damage to some of the men who had suffered in that inadequate trench.

The tactics of the Aldershot field days were much as I have described and had proved effective against native troops. Against a mobile, well-armed and entrenched enemy they were nearly useless. The creeping barrage by the artillery was developed under Buller and was used later during the First World War. It was used to great effect in the final sweep forward to relieve Ladysmith and the stunned Boers were obliged to retreat for the first time in the Western theatre of the war. The reconnaissance of the Tugela Gorge by Lieutenant Colonel Sandbach did take place and proved to be decisive in the final push to dislodge the Boers.

After the relief of Ladysmith the relieving force did march past General White and he took the salute. A number of the officers were uncomfortable with this kind of triumphalism and the defenders were less than enthusiastic in their welcome. The hospitals were overloaded and not well run. Senior medical officers had held back rations from the patients during the siege and there were suggestions that these rations had been sold in the town. As was common at this time, the number of deaths from disease exceeded those from enemy action. The number of nurses in the hospitals was completely inadequate and this was a lesson that was learned in time for the First World War.

It is true that mistakes were made at the battle of Paardeburg and a number of lives were lost following Kitchener's orders. Senior officers objected to his proposals, but were overridden. Why he was impatient is not known and why the tactical mastery he had shown in the Sudan was lacking is equally a mystery. In any event, this, and his ill-advised reorganisation of the army's transport system, damaged his reputation with the army and his previous nickname 'K of K' (Kitchener of Khartoum) became 'K of Chaos'.

Sannah's Post was the name given to a way station on the uncompleted railway line and the waterworks that supplied Bloemfontein was nearby. The British were having serious difficulties caused by men being forced to drink contaminated water on the march to that town.

This was, in part, another consequence of the mess that had been made of the transport system. De Wet's plan to damage or destroy the waterworks could well have forced Lord Roberts to retire from the town. The large haul of booty in the form of captured supply wagons and prisoners seems to have distracted De Wet and so, despite it being a major defeat, it had little effect on the advance of the main British army. The actions of Q Battery RHA resulted in the award of four Victoria Crosses for extreme bravery. Broadwood was exonerated in public for his failings, but in private he was severely reprimanded by his superiors. In my story McGuire uses his revolver to get men moving to save the guns. This was actually done by Major Phipps-Hornby, the 'Q' Battery commander.

The Westland Mounted Rifles was one of the militia units sent by New Zealand to support the British during the Boer war. Other units came from Canada and Australia, among others, and all proved to be effective at the asymmetric type of warfare that the campaign became once the set piece battles were over.

The defence of Mafeking was a remarkable military achievement and Baden-Powell became a national hero. At one time the siege was holding down a fifth of the Boer army with men and equipment that could have been much more valuable elsewhere. History has rather glossed over the extremely poor treatment of the Africans who were trapped inside Mafeking. Those who did not work were forbidden to have rations and were encouraged to leave the town. Many did so and, if captured, were whipped or sometimes shot by the Boers. The infant mortality rate among these Africans was extremely high compared to the whites as a result of this starvation. The note I have included from Commandant Eloff to Colonel Baden-Powell is a direct quote and was actually sent. It is also true that the Boer Commandant Cronje demanded that Baden-Powell disarm the Africans within Mafeking on the grounds that this was a white man's war. The assault through the Barralong Township did take place and the armed Africans acquitted themselves extremely well. They took a number of prisoners and prevented any reinforcements reaching Commandant Eloff. The attack cost the Boers around 60 killed and wounded, with 108 being taken prisoner. The garrison lost 12 dead and 8 wounded; most of those were Africans.

The advance of the army north from Bloemfontein to Johannesburg and Pretoria did take place as a massive column. At each river crossing the Boers had prepared defences and at each they were forced to retreat as the British cavalry outflanked them. When the army reached Doornkop the same tactic was intended, but for some reason the infantry commander did not wait for the cavalry and carried out an assault up a bare hillside into the Boer's rifle fire. Around one hundred men were lost for no discernible reason. Winston Churchill was present at the action and reported on it for the *Morning Post*. He had moved across to the eastern theatre of operations once Ladysmith had been relieved.

Johannesburg was taken without a shot being fired as the Boers retreated to the north. Pretoria was much the same and British troops watched the last train full of armed Boers pull out of the main station. It is true that Churchill went into Pretoria ahead of the main army and rode up to the camp he had been imprisoned in to demand its surrender. He was greeted with considerable jubilation by the British officers confined there. Field Marshal Roberts did expect the surrender he had been promised in the peace overtures that the Boers made to delay him and his delay because of this allowed the Boers to escape with the gold reserves from the national bank.

Stellenbosch was the site of the main army base camp during the Boer War. Officers and men who were not wanted at the front for various reasons were commonly sent here to get them out of the way. Hundreds of thousands of horses were shipped through here as remounts to replace the alarming number of horses that died during field service.

Kitchener was on a train that was ambushed by one of De Wet's raiding party and was the only one to escape by riding into the night. The Boers had no idea who he was or there might well have been a pursuit.

The action at Brandwater basin should have seen the end of the Boers as an army. Once again it was fumbled and one of the most effective commanders escaped with his commando through an unguarded pass. De Wet had advocated 'hit and run' tactics for some time and now was his chance. The lightly loaded and fast-riding Boers were ideally suited to this form of warfare. Although they did have considerable difficulty obtaining supplies. This led to them ambushing British troops and stripping them of everything, including their clothes, before setting them free to walk back to the army.

Farm burning was an official army policy. The intention was to stop the Boers being able to find food and water at the isolated farms. Initially the women and children were just left behind. Later they were picked up and taken to camps where they could all be concentrated in one area to be looked after. This was the first use of Concentration Camps in war and it was a disaster. The camps when set up had inadequate hygiene facilities, food was poor and the medical staff provided were under strength and of generally poor quality. The number of women and children who died in these camps from the diseases caused by poor sanitation and food was a major scandal. The reaction of the army authorities, including Kitchener, was initially denial and later inadequate action. These camps left a legacy of bitterness that soured relations with the Afrikaner population of South Africa for many years.

Miss Emily Hobhouse was a very real person. Aged forty-one at the time of her visit to the concentration camps, she was an unlikely force for good. She spent much of her early years looking after her parson father in Cornwall. She was frumpy and overweight. She was also intelligent and determined. She was horrified by the conditions she found in the camps and raised the issues with the relevant authorities on the spot. Their response was apathetic and ineffective, despite some good intentions. Emily did not let it rest. On her return to London she issued a detailed report of the appalling conditions and briefed any Member of Parliament she could corner. This resulted in a commission of ladies being sent to carry out a more formal inspection. They were expected to issue a whitewash report since they were carefully chosen from the establishment. In fact, the report they produced reinforced that of Miss Hobhouse and made some stinging criticisms and recommendations. These recommendations did result in improvements to the camps, but by then hundreds, if not thousands, of Boer women and children had died because of the conditions in the camps. The figures for deaths in the camps were hidden until halfway through 1901. Those figures caused shock in Parliament and the country – in May, 550, June, 782 and July, 1675.

I have told the tale of an attempted rape by a British officer. Would he really have been sent back to England and avoided a court martial? Sadly, I believe he would. In 1902, Captain James Robertson, commander of A Squadron of the Bushveldt Carbineers, was accused of sexual assault. He was given the option of resigning and leaving South Africa or a court martial. He chose to resign. Whether he was actually guilty was never tested, but a potential scandal for the British army was avoided. The influence of having a very senior establishment figure as a father would have influenced the decision in my fictional attack, in those days.

Boers did capture British troops and strip them of their uniforms. In some cases this was because their own clothes had dropped to pieces and they had no access to any other replacements. However, they also used the uniforms to get close to British positions and then attacked them, the attack on the 17th Lancers being an example that incensed the high command. Kitchener issued orders that any Boer found in British uniform was to be shot out of hand and this order was repeated by a number of senior officers. By this stage of the war any chivalry had died away.

Lieutenants Morant, Handcock, Witton and Picton of the Bushveldt Carbineers were arrested and charged with the murder of prisoners of war. At their courts martial they claimed that they were obeying a shoot on sight order that had come down from Kitchener himself. Kitchener denied that any such order had ever been given. The conduct of the trial has raised questions, particularly in Australia where there have been attempts to gain a pardon or a retrial for the four men. Such attempts have been unsuccessful up to the time of writing, but there is a belief that the men were deliberately sacrificed to appease the Boers and help with peace negotiations. Morant and Handcock were sentenced to death and shot by firing squad. It is reported that Breaker Morant's last words were, "Shoot straight, you bastards! Don't make a mess of it!"

The Distinguished Service Order (DSO) is a military decoration of the United Kingdom, and formerly of the Empire, awarded for meritorious or distinguished service by officers of the armed forces during wartime, usually in actual combat. The bar for an additional award is plain gold with an Imperial Crown in the centre. The back of the bar is engraved with the year of the award. The Meritorious Service Medal (MSM) is a medal for distinguished service, or for gallantry, usually by non-commissioned officers of the British armed forces.

Queen Victoria died on the 22nd of January 1901 after a series of strokes over the few days beforehand. She had been on the throne for 64 years and was the longest reigning British monarch until she was surpassed by Queen Elizabeth II. Throughout her life she had had taken a keen interest in both the Army and the Navy and commonly corresponded with officers. This made her popular with the troops. She died at Osborne House on the Isle of Wight, but was taken to be interred with her husband, Prince Albert, at the Frogmore Mausoleum in Windsor Great Park. She had left instructions that she was to be given a military funeral as the daughter of a soldier and the head of the army.

Weapons and Equipment

The Maxim gun was a more advanced machine gun that had replaced the Nordenfelt in British service by the time of the re-conquest of the Sudan in 1898. The mechanism of the Maxim gun employed one of the earliest recoil-operated firing systems in history. The idea is that the energy from recoil acting on the breech block is used to eject each spent cartridge and insert the next one, instead of a hand-operated mechanism. It was found to be particularly effective at the battle of Omdurman and was used throughout the Boer war.

The Webley Revolver was, in various marks, a standard issue service pistol for the armed forces of the United Kingdom, and the British Empire and Commonwealth, from 1887 until 1963. Firing large .455 Webley cartridges, Webley service revolvers are among the most powerful top-break revolvers ever produced. The W.G. or Webley-Government models produced from 1885 through to the early 1900s were the most popular of the commercial top-break revolvers and many were the private purchase choice of British military officers and target shooters in the period.

The Lee Metford rifle was the first magazine rifle issued to British troops. With an eight-round magazine it was designed to be fired and loaded by hand as the Martini Henry had been. The magazine was used as a reserve for close quarter battle. Since the magazine was slow to load, this method ensured that a steady fire could be maintained. This was also the first rifle used by the British army which used smokeless ammunition. The absence of dense clouds of white smoke allowed the soldiers to fire far more accurately.

The Lee Enfield was the replacement for the Lee Metford and was in the process of a full issue as the Boer war started. It is a bolt-action, magazine-fed repeating rifle that served as the main firearm used by the military forces of the British Empire and Commonwealth during the first half of the 20th century. It was the British Army's standard rifle from its official adoption in 1895 until 1957. The original version was the MLE or Magazine Lee Enfield, and was commonly known as the 'Emily' by the troops.

The Mauser Model 1893 is a bolt-action rifle commonly referred to as the 'Spanish Mauser', though the model was adopted by other countries in other calibres, most notably the Ottoman Empire. The M93 introduced a short staggered-column box magazine as standard, holding five smokeless 7×57mm Mauser rounds. The accuracy of the German-manufactured 7×57mm Model 1893 and 1895 Mausers in the hands of Boer marksmen during the Boer War made a big impression on the British.

The 155 mm Creusot 'Long Tom' was a French siege gun (artillery piece) manufactured by Schneider et Cie in Le Creusot, France and used by the Boers in the Second Boer War as field guns. Four guns, along with 4,000 common shells, 4,000 shrapnel shells and 800 case shot were purchased by the Transvaal in 1897. During the war the guns were deployed as field guns and siege guns at Vaal Krantz, Ladysmith, Mafeking, Kimberley and Bergendal. During the early stages of the war these guns gave the Boers an advantage as they had longer range than any British guns that were deployed in South Africa at the time. However, after all their ammunition had been expended, the guns were destroyed one by one, to prevent them from falling into British hands.

The Ordnance BL 15 pounder, otherwise known as the 15 pounder 7 cwt, was the British Army's field gun in the Second Boer War. While the gun could fire a shell up to approximately 5800-5900 yards, the No. 56 time and percussion fuse in use in 1899 could only be set for a maximum timed range of 4100 yards because it only burned for 13 seconds. The shrapnel shells in use were usually time-set to burst in the air above and in front of the enemy. Hence the gunners had to get within approximately 4200 yards of the enemy to fire on them. The fuse could be set to explode on contact (percussion) up to the maximum range, but shrapnel exploding on contact was of little use. This was rectified later in the war by the No. 57 'blue fuse' which could be time set up to 5800-5900 yards

The QF 1 pounder, universally known as the pom-pom due to the sound of its discharge, was a

37 mm British autocannon, the first of its type in the world. The British government initially rejected the gun, but other countries bought it, including the South African Republic (Transvaal) government. In the Second Boer War, the British found themselves being fired on with appreciable success by the Boers with their 37 mm Maxim-Nordenfelt versions using ammunition made in Germany. In response, Vickers-Maxim of Britain shipped 50 guns out to the British Army in South Africa, with the first three arriving in time for the Battle of Paardeberg in February 1900. These early versions were mounted on typical field gun type carriages.

The Field Service Helmet worn by the British army at the time of this story is commonly mocked, yet it was in fact a good piece of design for the hot climates the troops were operating in. Made of cork, sometimes referred to as 'pith', the official designation in British service was 'The Wolseley pattern cork helmet'. It had a peak to shade the eyes and a further peak at the rear to protect the back of the neck. It could be soaked in water overnight and would cool the wearer as the water evaporated during the day. It did not protect the wearer from bullets or shrapnel and was not designed to do so. Originally worn with a regimental badge at the front, this had been removed by the time of the Boer war and identifying colour patches were worn, usually on the sides of the helmet. Some units removed the plumes from their dress uniforms and used these as identifying features on the helmet.

The Sam Browne belt was made of leather with a strap over the shoulder to support an officer's sword. Officer casualties were excessively high at the start of the Boer war and it was found that Boer marksmen were picking out officers due to these distinctive belts. For field officers their use virtually stopped as they adopted web equipment to blend in with the rest of the men. These belts are still in use today for British officers and senior Warrant Officers when wearing service dress uniforms.

In researching the actual history for this book I have drawn on a number of sources. Some of these are listed below so that you can follow up if you find the subject interesting.

Kitchener by John Pollock. A detailed biography of this remarkable soldier.

The Boer War A History by Denis Judd and Keith Surridge.

Our Regiments in South Africa by John Stirling. A listing of all the British regiments that took part and a brief resume of the actions they took part in.

Private Tucker's Boer War Diary by Pamela Todd and David Fordham. Based on the diaries of a Private soldier in the Rifle Brigade who soldiered throughout the war. Considerably different from other books that concern themselves with the actions of generals and politicians.

The Boer War by Thomas Pakenham. A very detailed look at the causes and actions of the war. The author takes a more balanced view of the 'blame game' that took place due to the intense rivalries in the British High Command. In particular, he treats Redvers Buller fairly, which is more than the politicians and the War Office did at the time.

The Boer War by Winston Churchill. Made up of despatches and letters he wrote at the time and sent back to the *Morning Post* in London.

Butchered To Make A Dutchman's Holiday
Poem by Harry 'Breaker' Harbord Morant

In prison cell I sadly sit,
A dammed crestfallen chappie,
And own to you I feel a bit—
A little bit—unhappy.

It really ain't the place nor time
To reel off rhyming diction;
But yet we'll write a final rhyme
While waiting crucifixion.

No matter what end they decide
Quick-lime? or boiling oil? sir
We'll do our best when crucified
To finish off in style, sir !

But we bequeath a parting tip
For sound advice of such men
Who come across in transport ship
To polish off the Dutchmen.

If you encounter any Boers
You really must not loot 'em,
And, if you wish to leave these shores,
For pity's sake, don't shoot 'em.

And if you'd earn a D.S.O.,
Why every British sinner
Should know the proper way to go
Is: Ask the Boer to dinner.

Let's toss a bumper down our throat
Before we pass to heaven,
And toast: "The trim-set petticoat
We leave behind in Devon."

Although probably not completely acceptable today, Rudyard Kipling expressed the respect that British troops gained for their enemies in South Africa in the poem below. The Boers had been underestimated and they taught the British Army a salutary lesson. They were defeated eventually, but proved that even a modern well-trained army needs to be careful when opposing people with modern rifles and considerable courage.

Piet
(Regular of the Line)

I DO not love my Empire's foes,
  Nor call 'em angels; still,
What is the sense of 'atin' those
  'Oom you are paid to kill?
So, barrin' all that foreign lot
  Which only joined for spite,
Myself, I'd just as soon as not
  Respect the man I fight.
    Ah there, Piet!—'is trousies to 'is knees,
    'Is coat-tails lyin' level in the bullet-sprinkled breeze;
    'E does not lose 'is rifle an' 'e does not lose 'is seat,
    I've known a lot o' people ride a dam' sight worse than Piet.

    I've 'eard 'im cryin' from the ground
  Like Abel's blood of old,
An' skirmished out to look, an' found

428

The beggar nearly cold.
I've waited on till 'e was dead
   (Which couldn't 'elp 'im much),
But many grateful things 'e's said
   To me for doin' such.

     Ah there, Piet! whose time 'as come to die,
     'Is carcase past rebellion, but 'is eyes inquirin'
why.

     Though dressed in stolen uniform with badge
o' rank complete,
     I've known a lot o' fellers go a dam' sight
worse than Piet.

     An' when there wasn't aught to do
   But camp and cattle-guards,
I've fought with 'im the 'ole day through
   At fifteen 'undred yards;
Long afternoons o' lyin' still,
   An' 'earin' as you lay
The bullets swish from 'ill to 'ill
   Like scythes among the 'ay.

     Ah there, Piet! – be'ind 'is stony kop.
     With 'is Boer bread an' biltong, an' 'is flask
of awful Dop;
     'Is Mauser for amusement an' 'is pony for
retreat,
     I've known a lot o' fellers shoot a dam' sight
worse than Piet.

     He's shoved 'is rifle 'neath my nose
   Before I'd time to think,
An' borrowed all my Sunday clo'es
   An' sent me 'ome in pink;
An' I 'ave crept (Lord, 'ow I've crept!)

On 'ands an' knees I've gone,
And spoored and floored and caught and kept
    An' sent him to Ceylon!
        Ah there, Piet!—you've sold me many a pup,
        When week on week alternate it was you an'
me "'ands up!"
        But though I never made *you* walk man-naked
in the 'eat,
        I've known a lot of fellows stalk a dam' sight
worse than Piet.

        From Plewman's to Marabastad,
    From Ookiep to De Aar,
Me an' my trusty friend 'ave 'ad,
    As you might say, a war;
But seein' what both parties done
    Before 'e owned defeat,
I ain't more proud of 'avin' won,
    Than I am pleased with Piet.

        Ah there, Piet!—picked up be'ind the drive!
        The wonder wasn't 'ow 'e fought, but 'ow 'e
kep' alive,
        With nothin' in 'is belly, on 'is back, or to 'is
feet—
        I've known a lot o' men behave a dam' sight
worse than Piet.

        No more I'll 'ear 'is rifle crack
    Along the block'ouse fence—
The beggar's on the peaceful tack,
    Regardless of expense;
For countin' what 'e eats an' draws,
    An' gifts an' loans as well,
'E's gettin' 'alf the Earth, because

'E didn't give us 'Ell!

Ah there, Piet! with your brand-new English plough,

Your gratis tents an' cattle, an' your most ungrateful frow,

You've made the British taxpayer rebuild your country seat—

I've known some pet battalions charge a dam' sight less than Piet.

The Project Gutenberg eBook of Barrack-Room Ballads, by Rudyard Kipling

If you are kind enough to read any of my books, an honest review on Amazon.com would be hugely appreciated.

For more information please visit **www.nigelseedauthor.com**

Photograph "Courtesy of Grupo Bernabé" of Pontevedra.

Nigel Seed

Born in Morecambe, England, into a military family, Nigel Seed grew up hearing his father's tales of adventure during the Second World War which kindled his interest in military history and storytelling. He received a patchy education, as he and his family followed service postings from one base to another. Perhaps this and the need to constantly change schools contributed to his odd ability to link unconnected facts and events to weave his stories.

Nigel later joined the Army, serving with the Royal Electrical and Mechanical Engineers in many parts of the world. Upon leaving he joined the Ministry of Defence during which time he formed strong links with overseas armed forces, including the USAF, and cooperated with them, particularly in support of the AWACS aircraft.

He is married and lives in Spain; half way up a mountain with views across orange groves to the Mediterranean. The warmer weather helps him to cope with frostbite injuries he sustained in Canada, when taking part in the rescue effort for a downed helicopter on a frozen lake.

His books are inspired by places he has been to and true events he has either experienced or heard about on his travels. He makes a point of including family jokes and stories in his books to raise a secret smile or two. Family dogs make appearances in some of his stories.

Nigel's hobbies include sailing and when sailing in the Baltic he first heard the legend of the hidden U-Boat base that formed the basis of his first book (V4 Vengeance) some thirty eight years later.

The Other Books by this author

Drummer's Call

Revenge of a Lone Wolf

Simon Drummer is on loan to a bio-warfare protection unit in the USA when the terror they fear becomes real. A brilliant Arabic bio-chemist is driven to bring an end to the suffering of his countrymen. He believes that the regime that oppresses them could not exist without the support of the US government and the weapons they furnish. He needs to bring the truth to the American people in a way that will grab their attention. So begins his journey to bring brutal death and understanding to the USA. And now Simon must help to find him and stop him.

The Jim Wilson Series

V4 – Vengeance

Hitler's Last Vengeance Weapons Are Going To War

Major Jim Wilson, late of the Royal Engineers, has been obliged to leave the rapidly shrinking British Army. He needs a job but they are thin on the ground even for a highly capable Army Officer. Then he is offered the chance to go to Northern Germany to search for the last great secret of World War 2, a hidden U Boat base. Once he unravels the mystery he is asked to help to spirit two submarines away from under the noses of the German government, to be the central exhibits in a Russian museum. But then the betrayal begins and a seventy year old horror unfolds.

Golden Eights

The Search For Churchill's Lost Gold Begins Again

In 1940, with the British army in disarray after the evacuation from Dunkirk, invasion seemed a very real possibility. As a precaution, the Government decided to protect the national gold reserves by sending most of the bullion to Canada on fast ships that ran the gauntlet of the U boat fleets. But a lot of gold bars and other treasures were hidden in England. In the fog of war, this treasure was lost. Now, finally, a clue has emerged that might lead to the hiding place. The Government needs the gold back if the country is not to plunge into a huge financial crisis. Major Jim Wilson has been tasked to find it. He and his small team start the search, unaware that there is a traitor watching their every move and intent on acquiring the gold, at any cost.

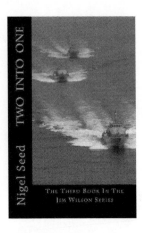

Two Into One

A Prime Minister Acting Strangely and World Peace in the Balance

Following his return from Washington the Prime Minister's behaviour has changed. Based on his previous relationship with the PM, Major Jim Wilson is called in to investigate. What he finds is shocking and threatens the peace of the world. But now he must find a way to put things right and there is very little time to do it. His small team sets out on a dangerous quest that takes them from the hills of Cumbria to the Cayman Islands and Dubai, but others are watching and playing for high stakes.

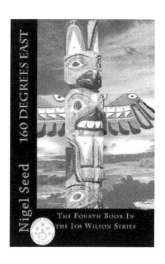

160 Degrees East

A fight for survival and the need to right a terrible wrong.

Major Jim Wilson and his two men are summoned at short notice to Downing Street. The US Government has a problem and they have asked for help from Wilson and his small team. Reluctantly Jim agrees, but he is unaware of the deceit and betrayal awaiting him from people he thought of as friends. From the wild hills of Wales to the frozen shores of Russia and on to the mountains of British Columbia Jim and his men have to fight to survive, to complete their mission and to right a terrible wrong.

One More Time

*A Nuclear Disaster Threatened By Criminals Must
Be Prevented At All Costs*

Jim and Ivan have retired from the Army and are making their way in civilian life when they are summoned back to the military by the new Prime Minister. Control of two hidden nuclear weapons has failed and they have been lost. Jim must find them before havoc is wreaked upon the world by whoever now controls them. It is soon apparent the problem is far bigger than originally envisaged, and there is a race against time to stop further weapons falling into the hands of an unscrupulous arms dealer and his beautiful daughter. The search moves from Zimbabwe to Belize and on to Norway and Spain, becoming ever more urgent and dangerous as the trail is followed.

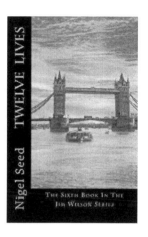

Twelve Lives

A Threat to Millions But This Time It's Personal

During a highly classified mission for the British Government, Jim Wilson and his two companions make a dangerous enemy. A contract has been put on their lives and on those of their families. Jim moves the intended victims to safety and sets about trying to have the contract cancelled. However, his efforts to save his family uncover a horrendous plot to mount a nuclear terror attack on the United States and the race is on to save millions of lives.

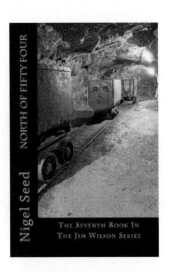

North of Fifty Four

A Crime Must Be Committed To Prevent A War

Jim Wilson is forced to work for a Chinese criminal gang or his wife and child will be murdered. While he is away in the north of Canada, his wife manages to contact Ivan and Geordie for help. The two friends set out to save all three of them, but then the threat to many more people emerges and things become important enough to involve governments in committing a serious crime to prevent a new war in the Middle East.

Short Stories

Backpack 19

Nigel Seed

A Lost Backpack and a World of Possibilities

Backpack 19

A Lost Backpack and a World of Possibilities.

An anonymous backpack lying by the side of the road. Who picks it up and what do they find inside? There are many possibilities and lives may be changed for the better or worse. Here are just nineteen of those stories.

The Michael McGuire Trilogy

No Road to Khartoum

From the filthy back streets of Dublin to the deserts of the Sudan to fight and die for the British Empire.

Found guilty of stealing bread to feed his starving family, Michael McGuire is offered the "Queen's Hard Bargain", go to prison or join the Army. He chooses the Army and, after training in Dublin Castle, his life is changed forever as he is selected to join the 'Gordon Relief Expedition' that is being sent south of Egypt to Khartoum, in the Sudan.

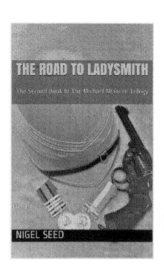

The Road to Ladysmith

Only just recovered from his wounds Captain McGuire must now sail south to the confusion and error of the Boer War.

After his return from the war in the Sudan, McGuire had expected to spend time recovering with his family. It was not to be, and his regiment is called urgently to South Africa to counter the threat from the Boers. Disparaged as mere farmers the Boers were to administer a savage lesson to the British Army.

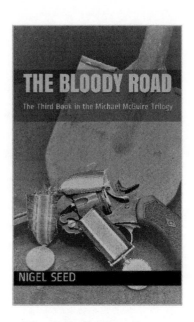

The Bloody Road

Michael McGuire has left the army, but as the First World War breaks out his country calls him again.

At the start of the war the British expand their army rapidly, but there is a shortage of experienced officers and McGuire is needed. He is sent to Gallipoli in command of an Australian battalion that suffers badly in that debacle. He stays with them when their bloody road takes them to the mud and carnage of the western front.

If you have enjoyed this book a review on Amazon.com would be very welcome.

Please visit my website at
www.nigelseedauthor.com

for information about upcoming books.

Printed in Poland
by Amazon Fulfillment
Poland Sp. z o.o., Wrocław

54400271R00251

THE BRINI BOY

Three years ago Jane retired from a long career directing and writing for theatre and opera, to become a full time writer of fiction. Her recent work includes three novels which make up a family saga - *Parallel Lines, Triangles in Squares*, and *Full Circle* - all these books are available from Amazon in paperback and kindle.

Details of Jane's other work can be found on her website www.janemcculloch.com

She has four children, ten grandchildren and is now based in London.

THE BRINI BOY

JANE McCULLOCH

For Fran – who has always fought for Justice

Although a work of fiction this novel is based on real people and actual events. The case of Sacco and Vanzetti has been very well documented. I have changed some locations and the structure of the Brini family, because it has no bearing on this story, which is seen entirely through the eyes of one child, Beltrando Brini.

Transcripts from the Sacco and Vanzetti Trials have been used and I have incorporated letters and interviews.

CHAPTER ONE
AUGUST 27TH 1927. JUSTICE CRUCIFIED.

The great storm had so darkened the sky that although it wasn't yet ten in the morning it seemed to Trando Brini it was almost as black as night. He stood at the hotel window and peered into the gloom, trying hard to make out the contours of Boston Common amidst the swirling clouds. The Frog Pond was just about visible, and the Bandstand, but he couldn't see much further. There was another flash of lightning and he stepped back a little. It had been alarming enough watching the flashes of lightning right across the skyline, but it was that last crack of thunder that had brought him to his feet, indeed it was so loud he reckoned it must have been right overheard. A shiver ran through him. He'd always had a dislike of thunder storms. 'The gods are angry' his father used to say, 'they're at war in the heavens'. Probably not the most comforting thing he could have said to a frightened child thought Trando, although today the Gods had every right to be angry. After the events of the last few days a sense of impotent anger hung over them all. 'Justice Crucified' had been embroidered on his armband and he reflected that the words were horribly apt.

Fifteen minutes passed. He remained by the window watching the progress of the storm as if held by some strange compulsion. At last the rumbles began to fade into the distance moving out over the ocean, the lightning stopped and the skies lightened to a leaden grey. But the storm wasn't finished. Now the rain started, not a gentle rain but heavy drops falling with great force and beating noisily against the window pane. It should have been a relief after the stifling heat of recent days. But it wasn't. Not today.

He glanced across the Common to Tremont Street which

he could now see more clearly. In a short while the sidewalks would be lined with thousands of people waiting for the funeral procession to begin. Surely the rain wouldn't deter them? He thought not, though it did seem relentless and small rivulets of water were already beginning to flow down Beacon Hill. This weather had settled in and it looked as if it could go on for many hours, even days.

Giving up his watch he walked over to the bed where his jacket was laid out, along with the embroidered red and black armband. He put them on, dragging with some difficulty the tight armband over his jacket sleeve. After this he seemed uncertain what to do next. The thought crossed his mind to join the others but he quickly decided it was too early and returned to sit at his desk feeling restless and unsettled. It couldn't be much longer now and then this awful waiting would be over. He tried not to think about it. Instead the sound of the rain brought back a memory of his childhood, a time when a storm like this had gone on for days. How old had he been, eleven, twelve? He clearly remembered that the skies like today had been an unbroken grey and the little Italian community in Plymouth had become fearful because the rain just didn't stop. To them it seemed like an omen signifying some sort of catastrophe. His mother, with one or two of her more devout friends, had rushed to Father O'Connor to make their overdue confessions before the anticipated disaster overtook them, but just as they were threatened with major flooding, the skies had quite suddenly cleared and the only remaining evidence of the whole event was the heavily sodden ground in his father's vegetable garden and the huge puddles in the road. Thinking of those puddles made him smile. There had been one glorious day when he had spent his time jumping into the deepest ones he could find, until Bart had quite rightly reprimanded him for getting himself so wet and muddy.

Oh God…must he remember?

He sighed. Strange to think that those were the last carefree days of his childhood before all the terrible events had overtaken him. Now here he was, eight years later, in yet another rainstorm, with the final moments of the tragedy about to unfold.

A knock on his door made him jump and someone gave a shout,

"Trando, it's time to go. We're all leaving now."

Thank God for that he thought, no more time for looking back. Taking his raincoat from the hook behind the door he went down the stairs to the lobby to join the others.

JUNE 1919

The small boy looked down at the muddy water as it oozed slowly over the edges of his galoshes. It felt cool and sticky, spreading over his toes and creeping up his leg. He smiled. Not a triumphant smile but a smile of pure pleasure and anticipation. The days of rain had at last stopped but had left these great puddles for him to jump into all the way from his school to his home. Right now, in front of him, was the largest puddle of them all. It looked really deep, deep as a rock pool, much more enticing than the sea, which was always there and didn't appear and disappear like these mysterious circles of dark water. He paused for a moment, then standing back he took a short run. Hop, skip and one huge...

"Trando!"

A voice behind him brought him to an abrupt halt and he spun round almost losing his balance. A man was hurrying towards him. He immediately recognized him. It was Bart Vanzetti. You couldn't mistake him for anyone else, not with his thin, sallow face, his long, drooping moustaches and large, deep set eyes. Many would have found him odd looking, but not Trando. He often thought that Bart Vanzetti looked more like a dog than a man, a sort of sad hound, but this only increased the affection he had for him and his eyes lit up as Bart drew level with him.

"Hi Bart" he said cheerfully, ignoring the stern look on the man's face.

Vanzetti was panting, the hurrying had left him out of breath and his words came out in short gasps, making his Italian accent seem even more pronounced.

"Trando Brini, what do you think you do? You make yourself all dirty and muddy. Why do you give your poor mother more work when she has so much? She is working, working, all day long and now she has the small baby. Do you not think of that?"

Trando looked down at his muddy legs and galoshes. He thought Bart was making a bit of a fuss. If anyone needed a wash it was him because he always smelled of fish, but nobody seemed to mind that and anyway it was only his socks that would need washing the rest of the mud would come off with a good scrub. He didn't think his mother would mind and it had been fun. Bart was still looking stern.

Trando sighed. "Sorry Bart, I didn't think of that. I will say sorry to Mama for causing her extra work."

A glimmer of a smile lightened the man's face. The boy did indeed look contrite. They started walking together towards the house on Suosso Lane, now taking care to avoid any further puddles.

Trando walked in silence for a moment and then said, "This will please you Bart. I have learned a new piece of music, out of the book of Italian songs you gave me. I think you will like it."

They turned the corner into a lane with a row of neat two-storey houses of unpainted shingles on one side and communal gardens on the other, with a pathway beyond the gardens that led past the church and the cemetery to the sea and the miles of sand dunes. This was where Trando often played with his friends and he often thought how lucky he was to have the ocean so near his home.

They walked on towards his house which was halfway down the lane right opposite the area his father used for growing vegetables.

Bart now put his arm round the shoulder of the boy. "Will you play to me tonight?"

Trando nodded and Bart went on," You must know Trando, one of the great pleasures of my life since coming to lodge at your house is to hear you play your violin. It is such a great talent you have, such a very great talent. You must always treasure it. That talent is not a gift given to many."

Trando shrugged, embarrassed by the passion in the man's voice. Bart was such a strange man. Most of the time he showed no outward feelings at all and then he would suddenly make these emotional statements which made him squirm a bit. He was very different to all the other men in his life; his father, his uncles, his father's friends. They were all from Italy as well but they talked loudly and some of them swore a lot. Bart was not like them at all. He always spoke quietly and almost never raised his voice.

Bart now stopped suddenly, a look of concentration on his face. "How long is it I have been lodging with you? Two years? Three years? It was when I came back from Mexico, yes?"

Trando thought for a moment. "It must be at least two years because I had only just bought my violin when you first came to stay with us."

This made Bart laugh. "That is right! You had been picking blueberries all summer to earn enough money to buy it and I thought to myself 'who is this strange boy with the blue hands'?"

They both laughed then.

Trando looked down at the bag Vanzetti always carried and noticed it was bulging. "What's in the bag Bart?" he asked, although he already knew the answer.

"It is a big and beautiful fish. I bring it for your Mother. She knows she must come to Bartolomeo Vanzetti if she wants the best fish in all of Massachusetts."

Trando looked at him and solemnly remarked, "You seem to love only two things in your life Bart, your fish and Italy."

The man frowned and it seemed as if he were about to say something else, but they had reached the front door so instead he just nodded. Trando removed his galoshes, washed the mud off his legs and ran up the stairs to his room. Having put on some clean socks he opened his violin case and was about to take out the violin when he heard raised voices coming from the kitchen. He crept out onto the landing, crouched down by the banisters and listened. Some words he could just about catch; 'anarchist' was mentioned several times and 'bomb'. He strained to hear more but the voices became quieter.

Later he wrote in his diary:

June 2nd 1919

I didn't much like today. Mama was cross when she found the muddy galoshes and socks and Papa and Bart shouted at each other over tea. Well, mainly Papa because Bart never gets angry, he just looks sad. Papa says that someone tried to kill the Attorney General in Washington. But the bomb went off too early and the killer was blown into little bits. Ugh! Imagine that. It's horrible. Little bits of him spread all over the sidewalk. They think it was an Italian immigrant who did it because he was an anarchist whatever that is. But Papa is angry because he says it will put all Italians under suspicion. He says the police will arrest us and send us all back to Italy. And then he told Bart he shouldn't go to any more of his meetings and that's when they argued. Bart told Papa he shouldn't worry because we are a good Catholic family but Papa said that made no difference as we are still Italian and he wanted no suspicion brought on our family. I could hear Bart getting upset and I don't want him upset. He is the best person in the world. I know I shouldn't write this but he is kinder to me than Papa, who often shouts at me for no reason and he doesn't like my violin playing and says it screeches. Mama is kind but she is always busy and now with the baby she is always tired. Bart is very generous too. Last year at Halloween we all had jack-o-lanterns. The others had theirs lighted but mine didn't have a candle in it. Bart asked me why I didn't get a candle and I told him I didn't have any money. So he gave me the two cents to buy one.

He stopped for a moment and then added,

I don't ever want to be grown up. I am going to be 13 soon and Bart says that is almost grown up.

He paused again before writing,

I wish I could stop thinking about the man blown to bits all over the sidewalk.

Trando put down his pen and shook his hand, aching from the exertion of so much writing. He closed the book and put it in his special box under the bed, carefully closing the lid. As he stood up he could hear music coming from Bart's room and he smiled. It was always the same piece he played, over and over again. It was Caruso, who Bart said was the best singer in the world. And sometimes Bart would join in. He had a strong powerful voice, but coming from such a small dapper man, it always made Trando laugh.

Leaving his room he crept along the corridor. His parents were in the front room and he could hear them talking so he knew it was safe to knock on Bart's door. It opened at once and Bart said, as he always did each evening,

"Trando, how nice you come to visit me!"

This made the boy smile every time.

Bart's room was sparsely furnished, with only a wooden truckle bed, a table and a small chest for his clothes, with a peg behind the door for him to hang his best suit. There was one photograph on the chest, a faded sepia image of an old lady, which Trando always took to be Bart's mother although he never asked in case it made his friend sad. He knew how much he missed Italy, especially his mother. On the table, in pride of place, there stood an old phonogram with quite a few recordings lying beside it, although the only one he'd ever heard Bart play was this man called Caruso singing. Opposite the bed were some shelves with several books, most of which were copies of a larger red book.

On this particular evening, instead of sitting down, Trando walked over to the bookcase and took down one of the large red books. It was very heavy and he had to put it on the table.

"Bart, I have been meaning to ask you. How come you have so many copies of this book?"

Vanzetti smiled. "It is my Bible, 'Faccia a Faccia col Nemico', 'Face to Face with the Enemy'. I get many copies and give them to all my friends."

Trando looked down at it. "Can I have a copy Bart?" A frown crossed Bart's face. He hesitated and looked worried. "I am your friend," Trando persisted.

The frown vanished and Bart's face broke into a smile. "Of course you are my great friend Trando, but this book is for my Italian friends."

Trando felt indignant. "I am Italian Bart. Beltrando Brini.

You can't get more Italian than that."

At this Bart laughed. "But you are now an all American boy and go to a good American school. Believe me, you are a real American boy now Trando and that is a good thing. You speak proper American."

Trando thought about this for a minute. "But you are teaching me to speak Italian Bart, so it would be good practice for me to read this book as well."

Again the man hesitated. He looked down at his hands still covered in some flaky fish scales which he now brushed off. When he looked up he could see that the boy was waiting for his answer and he sighed.

"I know you work hard at your Italian Trando and the speaking makes good progress. But you are not yet good enough for this book."

Trando was not to be put off. "Please Bart. I know it would help me to learn." Bart still hesitated. Trando looked at him. "Is it because it's about anarchists?" No reply was given to this so Trando continued, "I don't understand about those anarchists Bart. They seem to kill people. And why did Papa get angry about your meetings? Is it because you are an anarchist Bart? Is that why you go to the meetings? Do you plot to kill people?"

Bart stood up, walked to the window and looked out. When he turned back he spoke in one of his passionate outbursts, not loud but full of feeling.

"All my life Trando, all my life I fight for justice. I want justice for my fellow man, justice for the workers. But Bartolomeo Vanzetti does not fight with bombs and guns. He fights with words, always with words..." He broke off and Trando asked,

"Is that why you went on strike at the factory?"

"Yes, Yes." Bart was animated now, excited and started to gesticulate with his arms. "You must understand this Trando. I fight for a better life for the workers."

Trando looked puzzled. "But you lost your job Bart. Papa said they took away your job for organizing the strike so what good did it do?"

Bart shrugged. "Yes they took away that job, so now I am a fish peddler and I like my work. I am a happy man in this work. But my fight for the workers goes on. There is still so much injustice and hardship Trando. That is why I go to the meetings every Friday evening."

"Where do you have the meetings Bart?"

Bart looked at him for a moment as if deciding whether to tell him, and then said, "In an old hall between the church and the garage not far from here. It is a good to place to spend time with my comrades and discuss ways to make our lives better."

Trando thought about this and then looked down at the red book, "Is that what is written in this red book?"

Bart took the book and put it back on the shelf. He said quietly, "I said to your parents I would not talk to you of such things."

"But you are not a bad man," Trando burst out. "You don't want to harm people?"

Bart smiled. "I swear on my blessed mother's grave Trando, I am not a bad man and I hurt no-one."

The boy hesitated and now continued a little nervously. "But you do have a gun Bart. I have seen it."

Bart sounded indignant. "Sure I do, but I never use it. It is a big joke gun, a rusty old thing. I respect all life and all persons Trando. I don't like to kill or harm anything, not even the rabbits that eat all your Papa's vegetables."

They both laughed at this but Trando persisted. "Then why do you keep the gun Bart? Why do you have it, if you don't use it?"

Bart frowned again but answered patiently enough, "Because my young friend, these are dangerous times. It is safer if I am known to carry a gun, even if I never use it."

With this Trando seemed satisfied, but he once again turned back to the bookcase. "Can I have a copy of the book Bart, the one that is your Bible?" He looked pleadingly at him. "It will be good practice for my Italian."

Bart hesitated again then sighed. "I know you will not give up my friend, so I give you a copy. It is just to teach you Italian you understand? You will need a dictionary too. I give you that as well."

*

Triumphantly Trando carried the red book and the dictionary carefully back to his room and put them under the bed in the box with his diary. It was where he kept all his things that were secret and of importance. He now lay on the bed thinking. He would read the red book and then when he was grown up he could help Bart with his fight for the workers. It might have to wait until after he had got into a big orchestra and worked with the famous conductor he had seen when Papa had taken him to a concert last year. Or perhaps he could do both at the same time? Although it was certain his father would want him to help in the vegetable garden. He knew that although his father worked in a factory they badly needed the extra money they made from the sale of his vegetables. Wouldn't it be difficult for him to do all these things at the same time? He sighed. Perhaps it would all seem easier after he was thirteen and nearly an adult. In the distance he could hear his sister crying and his mother singing an Italian lullaby. She always sang in Italian and when alone, or when they didn't want him to hear something, his parents talked to each other in Italian because he'd heard them. Trando smiled to himself. He would work hard at his Italian and then they wouldn't be able to keep anything from him. Whatever Bart said he would remain definitely both Italian and American.

*

Over the next few months Trando made great progress with the red book. Each evening he would give an hour to working at it with the help of the dictionary. He would then go to Bart's room for his Italian lesson. It pleased him that Bart seemed so impressed with his work and with how fast his Italian was improving. Then, at the end of each lesson he would play his violin and would always finish with the same tune "Old Black

Joe" and every time he played it, Bart's eyes would fill with tears. One day Trando said, "Perhaps I should play something else Bart, if this tune makes you so sad?"

Bart shook his head. "I am sad and happy at the same time." He looked at the boy. "Do you know the words to that song Trando? They have a very good sentiment, but it is the music that accompanies that sentiment that I find so beautiful and you play it like an angel.

I never get tired of it. Never."

*

So it was that the summer of 1919 passed happily and peacefully in the house in Suosso Lane in Plymouth, Massachusetts. If his parents were worried about the amount of time Trando spent with their lodger, they never mentioned it. He was a contented, happy boy doing well at school and in spite of his father's comments about the noise his violin made everyone else who heard him play praised him highly and thought him very talented. Even his teacher thought him something of a prodigy. Certainly in those long, hot summer days nobody could have had any idea of the clouds gathering on the horizon, or the terrible events that were about to close in on them and change all their lives forever.

CHAPTER 2

Trando limped slowly and painfully towards the fence and leant against it, his breath coming out in a mixture of gasps and sobs. Gingerly he put his hand up to his nose which was dribbling blood and he could feel his right eye closing up. This was no good; he must get home quickly and get to his room without being seen. Think Trando, think of somewhere to hide, somewhere dark, maybe under the bed or in a cupboard. He knew it was vital that he gave himself time to get his story straight before facing his parents. The blood was still trickling from his nose and he took out a handkerchief and dabbed it gently, wincing slightly at every touch. He felt a sense of panic as the bleeding just wouldn't stop. Dab, dab. He closed his eyes...

"Trando? What in heaven has happened to you?" His father was looking at him, not with anger, but concern. The boy was in a terrible state, he could see he had a bruised eye and a bleeding nose. Never before had he seen Trando in such a bad way. "Come, take my arm. We will sit down on the bench in the gardens and you can tell me why you are in this state and why you have a fight." He looked at the boy again and seeing his distress tried to give him words of comfort. "Fighting is not such a bad thing Trando," he paused and added, "as long as the other boy came off worse," and here he gave one of his bellowing laughs.

Trando glanced at his father and was surprised to see he was looking at him quite kindly. This made him want to cry all the more, especially as he knew the explanation he was about to give would make his father angry.

They walked slowly to the gardens and sat down on the bench. Both were quiet for a moment then his father said, "So you tell me what happened yes? Who gave you the black eye and the bleeding nose?"

Trando began slowly, "It happened because of something at school this afternoon. I was in class and we were being asked about things that were of interest to us." He paused, uncertain how to go on.

His father said encouragingly, "So you talked about your violin yes?"

Trando shook his head and his words came out in a rush. "No, I told them about the Italian book Bart had lent me which was about fairness for the workers and how we had to make conditions better for the Italian people who are working here..."

His voice trailed away as he saw his father's expression change and now he sounded angry and stern. His father was a big man, broad shouldered and strong. Although he had never physically hurt Trando, when he was angry he could be very frightening and this was certainly one of those times. He started to shout.

"You told them that? You told your teacher that? You told him that you wanted to make conditions better for the Italian workers?" Trando nodded nervous now and his father went on with his voice mounting to a crescendo, "That was a very stupid thing to do Trando. Stupid!"

Trando could feel the throbbing in his eye. He didn't want to continue but knew he needed to finish his explanation, so he said a little defensively, "The teacher didn't seem to mind one bit. He just said it was very interesting and after that the class ended." He paused to see if his father was going to say something but when he didn't Trando went on, "It was afterwards, when we were walking home that suddenly about six boys set on me. They punched me and knocked me to the ground and they were shouting at me, 'Friend of the Anarchists' 'Red Dago' 'Trando Brini Dago Bastard!'." His voice faltered and he clenched his fists at the memory. "I tried to fight back Papa but there were too many of them." His father nodded but his expression was grim. Trando went on, "A girl shouted at them to stop and they ran off and then this girl came over and gave me this handkerchief for my nose and helped me to my feet. I'd never seen her before. She said her name was Ella."

At this Vincenzo Brini gave a short laugh. "That's my boy, he gets in a fight and then he gets the girl. You're a Brini all right!" Trando thought it very odd that this should have pleased his father but he was hurting so much he said nothing and was just relieved when his father stood up and said, "Come, let's get you home and clean you up."

As they reached the door of their house he turned and took the boy's shoulder in both his hands. "You must give that book back to Bart and never mention such things again in school, do you understand? It will only bring trouble, big trouble to all of us. Promise me that Trando."

Trando nodded. He felt miserable. He had let his father down and now he had betrayed Bart. He knew instinctively that in some way this fight would have serious consequences and in this he was right. It took less than an hour for his worst fears to be confirmed.

He crawled into his listening position on the landing and heard the angry voices coming from the kitchen below. The angriest was his father and he was shouting at Bart.

Trando went back to his room, quickly unpacked the red book from his school case and put it in his box for safe-keeping. He then lay on his bed waiting for Bart to go to his room.

After a while he heard footsteps coming up the stairs and first Bart's door was opened and then firmly shut. He listened out for the familiar sounds, but tonight there was no Caruso being played. Instead the house was eerily quiet. Even his sister wasn't having her usual evening cry. He looked out of the window and could see his father working in the vegetable garden opposite. The coast was therefore clear, so he tiptoed along the landing and knocked on Bart's door.

It was opened but there was none of the usual greeting. Instead Bart said in a weary voice, "Ah Trando, that is good, you have come to help me pack."

Trando felt a rising panic. "Help you pack? Why? You are leaving us?"

Bart nodded.

"But why Bart, why?" Trando started to cry. "It is my fault, I am so sorry Bart, I know it is all my fault. I don't want you to go. Please don't leave. I will talk to Papa. I will go and see him now and explain."

Suddenly the boy was in the arms of the man sobbing as if his heart would break. Bart gently stroked the boy's hair until the sobs died down. He then sat him on the bed and spoke quietly but firmly, "It is really best I go Trando. Please believe me, it is not your fault. I have things I have to do for my comrades and this is not good for you or your family. I can find new lodgings close by here not far from your house. I will still be able to see you." He looked at the boy, sitting hunched and sad, with his black eye and bruised face. "It will be a better arrangement for everyone and you can still help me with my fish round and visit me with your violin and play to me. It will not be so often, that is all."

Trando calmer now thought about this. "Will you still teach me Italian?"

Bart hesitated. "Of course I will, but you had better return to me that red book. We don't want any more trouble."

Looking back on it Trando was never quite sure why he lied to Bart that night. Somehow, deep down, he knew he wanted to keep hold of the book, so he said quickly, "The teacher has it at school. I'm very sorry Bart. I will try and get it back for you."

Bart shook his head. "No, leave it. It is best the matter is now kept closed." He opened up a shabby old suitcase. "Come Trando, you can help me pack." He gave a wry smile. "It won't take long, I have very few things."

Trando opened a drawer and took out a couple of shirts. "Can I come and visit you tomorrow? I could bring my violin."

Bart hesitated then shook his head. "Not tomorrow Trando. I have to visit my good friend Nick Sacco and his wife Rosina."

Trando felt a stab of jealousy. He, Trando, was Bart's friend. He didn't want him to have other friends, especially if they could do him harm. He suspected this man was an acquaintance from the meetings.

"Is Nick Sacco an anarchist?" he asked.

Bart looked a little startled and for once sounded a little impatient. "What is it with all these questions Trando? Nick is like me. He is not an anarchist, but like me he wants justice for the workers." Here Bart smiled. "But unlike me, Nick is strong and brave like a lion. And he has a temper too. Ah what a temper! But it is all over very quick. You would really like him Trando and you would like his wife Rosina too. She is a lovely person. They are so proud of their little boy Dante, who you should know is named after the great Italian poet."

Trando thought for a moment. For some reason he wasn't so sure he would like Nick.

"Does Nick Sacco go to your meetings?"

Bart nodded. "Yes of course he does. We talk and discuss with our comrades how to make things better for the workers, like I told you. That is all. We just talk."

Trando burst out, "But the boys at school say all Italians are murderers and anarchists."

Bart's expression changed and he looked sad. "It is not true Trando. You must know in your heart that is not true. You should take no notice of them." He pushed down the lid of his suitcase and shut it. "Enough of this silly talk, come help me carry my things downstairs and I will go and fetch my fish cart to take them to the new place."

They reached the bottom of the stairs and he gave Trando a hug. "I will see you very soon, yes?"

The boy nodded but felt an overwhelming sadness as he watched his friend walked out of the door and disappear out of sight.

A week later Trando wrote in his diary:

November 28th 1919
Bart has moved to new lodgings and I miss him a lot. Now in the evenings instead of going to Bart's room I have to help Papa in the garden. He tries to make up for Bart going by teaching me things and telling me the Italian words for all the vegetables and I have to repeat

them after him; da cipollo for onions, ravenelli for radishes. bietola for beetroot and many more. I would prefer to learn my Italian from Bart's Red Book, but I have to keep that a secret. I am up to Chapter 7. I don't understand much but I am learning some very long new words. Sometimes I feel guilty I lied to Bart but I am glad I kept the book. Bart says there will be a lot for me to do helping him on his fish rounds in December on account of Italians always eating eels at Christmas. I just don't know why that is. Those eels can really squirm. UGH! But it will be nice to spend time with Bart again and I will earn a little money as well. I want to save enough to buy Mama a new shawl.

A few days later, as it was a Friday, Trando made the decision to attend one of Bart's meetings. He had been planning this for some time and already knew where to find the place because he had made a detour one day on his way back from school. The problem was that if he was to do this he would have to lie to his parents and tell them he was visiting a friend for the evening. He didn't like doing this but felt that in the circumstances it was important to find out for himself exactly what took place at these meetings and why they were so important to Bart. His parents offered no objection and a little guiltily he set out on the short walk to the hall. Deliberately arriving a few minutes late, he let himself into the back of the room, which to his relief was dark and dingy so he felt sure he wouldn't be seen.

There was quite a crowd at the top of the hall and they seemed to be a very noisy group. Trando hoped they were all Bart's loyal supporters, although he noticed there were two men at the back the other side from him but quite apart from the others, who didn't look so friendly and one of them was writing all the time in a notebook. He wondered who they were and if they were anarchists too.

The meeting seemed to be late in starting but at last Bart walked up the steps to the platform and banged on the table several times until the chatter died down and the room fell silent. Although Bart's voice was not loud, Trando thought he spoke with great authority and conviction.

"Comrades, I hope you have all seen and studied the pamphlet and had time to discuss it amongst yourselves." There was a murmur of assent and Bart continued, "I beg you to take the content of what is written very seriously." He paused and then spoke slowly and firmly, "Now is the time for you to listen very carefully to what I say, because it is of the greatest importance." He banged his fist on the table. "My friends I urge you at this time to take great care. The government spies are everywhere and they are watching every one of us. As you all know, since the May bombs many of our number have been deported back to Italy including Galleani our leader. More comrades will be sent back, but this must not stop us, the fight must go on." He again banged his fist on the table. "That means the strikes must continue..."

Someone shouted an interruption, "What good are the strikes Bart? They break the strikes and then we lose our jobs."

Another voice from the back shouted "Where is your job at the factory now Bart?" There was some laughter at this and more shouts and Bart banged on the table again.

"So, I lost my job. But I have kept my honour and self-respect. Now I work for myself. I am a fish peddler and I can still continue our fight. This is what we all have to do. We must not give up comrades. Our fight has to go on." He paused. "I am only here tonight to give you a warning. The word is out, Dago Reds are bad. I tell you there are spies everywhere. Galleani tells me that they have even planted spies right here in the middle of our Boston Group..."

A murmur went around the room at this and in the gloom Trando could see that the faces of the men looked grave and anxious.

Bart finished with a flourish, "Comrades, you have been warned. Read the pamphlet and I beg you, be on your guard at all times." His fist went into the air as he shouted, "Viva L'anarchista!"

And the comrades, some also with raised fists, shouted back waving their pamphlets, "Viva L'anarchista!".

The two men at the back left immediately and as this seemed to be the end of the meeting Trando also quickly let himself out of the hall, before they all dispersed.

He ran all the way home, calling out to his parents that he was back and then went up to his room. For a while he lay on his bed thinking over what he had just seen and heard, but decided he was too tired to write anything in his diary that night.

CHAPTER 3

It had been snowing for days, but at last just before Christmas it stopped and on Christmas Eve the sidewalks had little snow left, only a covering of grey watery slush remained.

Trando rose early and left the house at seven thirty sharp for his appointment with Bart. Today was the occasion on which they delivered the famous eels, because for some reason that Trando failed to understand, Italians always liked to have their eels for Christmas.

He reached the corner of Cherry Street and saw Bart in the process of loading the fish on to the cart. "Hi Bart!" he shouted and waved. Bart stood up and waved back, but at this precise moment Vincenzo Brini arrived on the scene.

"Trando," he shouted as he drew near, "what are you doing wearing those shoes in all this wet? Go back for your rubber shoes now this minute."

"But Papa," Trando protested, "I don't have time. Bart needs me here to help him now."

Bart said firmly, "Trando do as your Papa says, I can finish loading and will wait for you at the top of the hill. It won't take you long."

He watched as Vincenzo dragged the boy back down the street. Then he finished loading the fish and pulled the heavy cart to the top of the hill.

Half an hour later Trando was back, breathless and apologetic. "I'm sorry to take so long Bart. I couldn't find my rubber shoes anywhere."

Bart handed Trando a large basket and said with a smile, "It is no problem, we have plenty of time."

It was bitter cold. Trando could feel his fingers going numb and he struggled a little with his load "I wish we had a horse and cart," he grumbled.

Bart threw back his head and laughed at this. "So, you would like to sit up high on the cart like a grand gentleman eh?"

Trando laughed too. "No not like that but a cart would save me carrying this heavy basket."

Bart looked at him. "I think you are a little scared of all those wriggling eels, yes?"

"Me? Scared?" Trando was indignant. "Of course I'm not." After a moment's thought he added in a serious voice, "But I am like you, a lover of my fellow creatures and I do not like to think of these eels getting killed in such an unpleasant way."

Bart once again threw back his head and laughed, which was quite startling because Bart hardly ever laughed and not loudly like this and it was the second time that morning. "You are a funny kid," he said. "I think if they are not killed, you and I will be out of a job. Remember Trando the more deliveries we make, the lighter your load will be."

They were both out of breath now, but at last Bart stopped. "Here we are, this is the house for our first delivery."

*

So they walked on, the man and the boy; from Terrace Street to Magoni Lane, to Castle Street, then down Cherry Street again, finally ending up at Cherry Court. It was hard work but it passed pleasantly enough, although Trando was quite exhausted by the time they reached home and his hands were sore from carrying the baskets, but in spite of his tiredness he felt pleased because they had done so well. All the fish, including the eels had been sold and he had been rewarded generously for his hard work. At first he had protested that Bart was giving him too much but Bart wouldn't take any money back. Not for the first time Trando noticed that Bart had no interest in money, or indeed in making it. He always said that as long as he had enough to eat, somewhere to sleep and good friends, he was content.

That evening he had joined them for supper and Trando felt a huge feeling of contentment sweep over him. His diary entry later that night was short because he was so tired. It was to be the last happy entry he was to make for a very long time.

Christmas Eve 1919
Today was one of the best days ever. I helped Bart with his fish round and we sold everything, even all those wriggling eels. Later he came to our house and we had a great meal. Afterwards we opened a few presents. Bart had bought me some more violin music of Italian songs and Papa and Bart sang duets and Mama played the piano and everyone seemed happy. I think it is going to be the best Christmas ever and I am really looking forward to 1920 because then I will be thirteen.

A few days later this optimism was shattered by a terrible event, the outcome of which meant that Trando's happy childhood days were lost forever.

The day had started like any other ordinary day, certainly there was no indication of the ordeal that was about to affect them all. He was having his breakfast in the kitchen and watching his mother go through her usual morning ritual of trying to feed his sister, when his father came in and stood looking at them. Immediately Trando knew something was badly wrong. There was an expression on his face that he had never seen before. It was mainly a look of fear, but this was combined with what he recognised as anger.

He spoke directly to his mother and burst out, "Alfonsine, I have some terrible news." He then broke off as his mother stopped what she was doing and looked anxiously up at him.

"Bad news? What is this bad news?"

Vincenzo looked at her, "There's been a terrible raid, a hold-up, on the White Shoe Company Payroll truck at Bridgewater. It happened on Christmas Eve."

"At Bridgewater?" his mother gasped out and was obviously shocked, "But that must be only thirty miles from here. Was anyone hurt?"

His father shook his head, "No, I don't think so, but there was a lot of shooting. The truck was completely smashed up. The driver swerved and went into a telegraph pole. Whoever did it didn't manage to get the payroll, which they say must have been about thirty thousand dollars. They also say it was three men who did the hold-up and that they made a fast getaway in a black Hudson. The police have the number plate. Everyone's talking about it. There's a lot of anger among my customers. It's a terrible thing to happen. It's a stupid, terrible thing."

He slumped into a chair and put his head in his hands.

Trando watched the two of them as they both sat at the table shocked and silent. He asked "But who did this Papa?"

His father looked up and replied in a weary voice, "They don't know yet, but it will be us Italians who will get the blame," and he added bitterly, "Oh yes, the 'Red Dagos' will be blamed. We are all anarchists to them. Now they will start to round up people and there will be more arrests you see. They will arrest the low paid workers first and then ask for ten thousand dollars bail. I ask you? Who has money like that?" He made a despairing gesture with his hands.

Trando felt worried. This was all new to him. He had never seen his father like this before. He was a big man and strong and liked to laugh and sing. Sometimes he would shout and swear, but that was just his way. Now he spoke out of character, in a small despairing voice.

On impulse Trando went to him. "They won't arrest you Papa. You wouldn't do anything like that and anyway, you are always here with us."

His father pulled him on to his lap. "No Trando, they won't arrest me. But some of our friends in the Italian community will be in danger, so you see it's bad, very bad." He looked at Trando as if deciding whether to say more and Trando longed to ask him if Bart Vanzetti was in danger, but thought better of it. He got up and went back to his place to finish his breakfast while his parents talked on in low voices. His father mentioned names he'd never heard before; Boda, Coacci, Orciani, and he saw his mother look anxious as she whispered, "But those are friends of Bart." His father nodded and they both looked at Trando.

Then his father changed the subject and there was no more discussion about the raid after that.

*

A few weeks later when the raid was almost forgotten, Trando was in his room practising his violin, when he heard the front door bell ring. He went out onto the landing to see who it was and saw his mother open the door to Bart. He was just about to run down the stairs when he heard her say, "Bart whatever is it? You look terrible. Come on in and tell me what's happened." Then he saw that his mother had taken Bart to the front room, not the kitchen, and had firmly closed the door. Knowing he shouldn't, but desperate to know what was worrying Bart, Trando crept down the stairs and crouched by the door to listen. Bart's voice sounded different from usual and he kept apologising for bothering her. His mother seemed fearful as she said, "But Bart, what is it? Have you had bad news from home?"

There seemed to be a long silence after this and Trando pressed his ear closer to the door. Finally Bart said, almost in a whisper, "No, no, it is not from home. It is right here. The bad news is here." There was another pause and then he said in a stronger voice, "Two of my comrades have been arrested in New York."

Now his mother punctuated everything Bart said with cries of 'Oh sweet Jesus' or 'Oh my God' as he continued, "They are now in the Department of Justice and you know what that means Alfonsine. They will be beaten and tortured until they give up names. It means we are all in danger. All the comrades are in danger now," and he repeated, "we are all in terrible danger."

His mother began to sound desperate and it was almost as if she were shaking him. "Who did they arrest Bart? You tell me. Tell me! Give me their names."

There was another long silence until Bart finally answered, sounding calmer. "It wasn't anybody you know Alfonsine. It was two comrades called Elia and Salseda. They are printers. They printed everything for Galleani our leader before he was deported, all our journals and pamphlets. So they know everything and everyone. They know everything that happened at the meetings. The police raided the garage where all our papers were kept. You know what will happen now? They will torture them; torture them until they give up all the names of the comrades. So I tell you Rosina every one of the comrades is in great danger." He kept repeating this over and over again until finally he said, "I will not visit for a while Alfonsine. I am told there is a Pinkerton man on the case and we will all be followed. I do not want to bring trouble to your family. Will you tell Trando for me, explain to him if you can...?"

Trando did not listen further but returned to his room and lay on his bed thinking. If Bart was in danger he had to help him. But how could he do that? His best idea was that Bart should go back to Italy. He should return before these men were tortured into giving up names. Yes. That would be the answer and he would definitely suggest it to Bart next time he saw him.

He felt too miserable to write his diary. Maybe he should pray? He didn't often pray. In fact he hated Church and the long services his mother made him attend. But on this occasion he thought a prayer might help. He would ask God to make things better for Bart and his comrades, so no further harm would come to them.

*

But Trando's prayers were not to be answered. Events now took an even more drastic turn. On April 15th, 1920, there was a second payroll raid at South Bridgewater, not far from Plymouth and this time a gang of five bandits shot two men in the back and they both died. The whole country was plunged into outrage and uproar. Trando had to spend most of his time eavesdropping at doors in order to find out the latest situation because annoyingly the grown-ups had started to talk in low whispers and always kept the door shut. His parents became increasingly anxious and meal times were conducted mainly in silence.

Trando wrote down in his diary as much of the information he had managed to gather.

April 20th 1920
The news is very bad. Bart hasn't been here since he told Mama about the arrests in New York. Now there has been another raid and it is worse this time because two men have been shot dead. I heard Papa say that one man was called Berardelli and he was full of slugs, which I think must mean bullets, and the other man who was called Parmenter was shot in the back. The police found the getaway car which was a Buick, in the wood. They say five men were involved. Mama keeps saying the same names over and over again, Boda, Coacci, Orciani and now she has added Sacco. I am so frightened because I know Nick Sacco is a friend of Bart's and the others were probably at that meeting. I want to tell Bart to go back to Italy before he is arrested but I don't get to see him anymore. There is another awful thing which I haven't told anyone because everyone is so worried and anxious. They keep talking about the torture they use on Salsedo in New York and now I have nightmares about it. I wish none of this had happened.

He thought for a moment before finally adding,'

It seems hard to remember now that we were all so happy on Christmas Eve.

CHAPTER 4

The week that followed was a stressful and anxious one for everyone in the Brini household. Trando kept to himself and far out of the way of his parents who seemed to be irritated by the very slightest thing. Bart made another visit, but once again he was taken into the front room and the door firmly shut. Both his parents were with him this time and as soon as the door closed Trando tiptoed down the stairs to listen. At the start Bart talked in such quiet, low tones Trando couldn't understand what he was saying. His father on the other hand talked loudly and with urgency. He heard him say "I don't understand you Bart. Why put yourself in such danger? Why did you go to New York at a time like this? That was a mad thing for you to do, to take such a risk."

Bart now spoke louder and Trando heard him say quite clearly, "I had to do it Vincenzo. There was nobody else who could go. Boda and Sacco had already made plans to return to Italy. Coacci has a deportation order. Someone had to visit our new leader, Carlo Tresca, and in the end Bart Vanzetti was the only one left who could do it. We urgently needed to find out if Salseda has given up any names. You have to understand that this was desperate for me, because if he had told them names, if poor Salseda has talked, then Vanzetti is as good as dead!"

Trando had to stop himself from crying out at this. He stuffed his fist in his mouth and continued to listen with his ear right up against the door as his mother asked, "So did you see this Tresca man Bart?"

Bart now spoke more firmly, "I did indeed. He told me Salseda's wife says he has turned crazy with the torture. It is pretty certain he will talk soon because he won't be able to hold out much longer and then there will be more raids and more deportations. Tresca also told me I must get rid of all the evidence; that means all the papers, the propaganda and the literature." He paused before saying in an agitated voice, "And then there are the guns and ammunition. You see I am the only person who knows where they are all kept, so I have to take full responsibility for the Boston group and be sure to get rid of it all."

His father broke in with an interruption here, "No Bart! That is something you cannot do. It is far too risky. If you are caught with any of that stuff on you it will mean you will go to prison and for a very long time."

Bart sounded resigned. "I know this Vincenzo, but there really is nobody else so it is a risk I have to take. I have to be the leader now and take responsibility." He paused. "Carlo Tresca is starting a defence fund in case we are in need of lawyers..."

Trando longed to burst into the room and tell Bart he must go back to Italy, but he knew he would be in great trouble if he did that. He also knew he would need to listen at doors in the future and he didn't want to lose his ability to do that. So reluctantly he crept back to his room.

*

A little while later there was a knock on his door and Bart came into the room. He looked tired and somehow much older and his voice was sad, but he talked firmly enough, carefully keeping his emotions in check.

"Trando, I have come to say goodbye because I won't be seeing you for a little while,"...

Before he could say any more the boy rushed into his arms crying hysterically, "I don't want you to die Bart. You must give up being an anarchist, you must, please Bart. I don't want you to be arrested. I don't want you to die."

Bart held on to him for a moment and then gently pushed Trando back on to the bed and sat beside him. "Hey, hey, what is all this? Where do you get a stupid idea like that? Listen to me I do not lie to you because I love you like a son Trando. I do

34

not intend to die. I like life far too much and we still have lots of things to do, you and me. Yes?"

Trando nodded and tried his best to stop the panic that had been rising in him all afternoon. His sobs subsided as Bart said, "See? That is much better. No more worrying about Bart." He pulled the boy to his feet. "Now, dry your eyes and fetch your violin and play me my special tune, yes? You know the one I choose, it makes me sad and happy at the same time."

So Trando played and Bart cried and then he laughed and then he cried again.

They both felt a great deal better by the time he left but it was only after he'd gone that Trando realised he'd forgotten to tell Bart to save himself and go back to Italy.

*

Events moved swiftly after that. Trando wrote in his diary,

May 4th 1920

Today I heard some terrible news. Salseda, the man who was being tortured, threw himself out of the Department of Justice in New York onto the sidewalk below. He was 14 floors up so it must have been a horrible mess. I can't stop thinking about it and last night I had a bad nightmare and Mama had to come in because I was screaming so loudly. I don't like going to sleep now and I am really worried about Bart. I feel so angry with everyone and everything. Why does Bart have to be the leader and get rid of all the stuff? I hope he throws away that rusty old gun. If the police find it on him they won't mind if it is old and rusty. They will send him to prison. I haven't seen Bart since he came to my room. He won't visit us now. I know it. And I feel so bad I never told him to go back to Italy.

May 5th 1920

I don't want to write this in my diary but I feel I must, because today something awful happened. I behaved very badly, although it didn't seem like it at the time.

He thought for a moment before continuing,

*I was with some other boys and we were coming back home from school and playing with a ball when it got kicked into a vegetable garden, not Papa's garden, another one. I went to get the ball and I had to go some way into this garden to get it. A man came out of the house opposite and he was very angry and shouted at me for trampling on his vegetables. All the other boys were laughing so I shouted back at him, 'Makes me no never mind Mister' which is something I heard a girl once say to Bart on the fish round. I then ran off and joined the other boys who jumped about and clapped me on the back, leaving the man shaking his fist at me. The other boys then went off home, but when I turned round to go down our lane I saw that Bart was standing there, watching me. I knew at once he must have seen everything. He crossed the road and came over and shook me. It didn't hurt because Bart is not like that, but I knew he was angry. He said, 'You think that clever? Why do you behave like this Trando? To please the other boys? You think that clever? You should say sorry to the man for doing damage to his vegetables, not give him answer back. That is bad Trando, very bad." He let me go then and I know I must have looked ashamed because I was. Bart went on, 'I never want to see you act this way again. There is too much sorrow and unhappiness in this world already.' I think he took pity on me then because he said in a kinder voice, "I know how it is Trando. You try to be a big man in front of your friends. But you must always do what is right for **you** Trando, not right for other boys. Always. You understand?' I remember everything he said very clearly because somehow it seemed important. After that I must have nodded, or said yes or something, because then we walked home. At the door he wouldn't come in, he just gave me a hug and walked away. I am so sorry Bart saw me behave like that, especially when he has all his other troubles. I do miss him being in the house. I still work at my Italian but he hasn't given me a lesson in a long time.'*

Trando put his diary away in the box under the bed, wishing he could write something happy for a change. He made a silent vow to try his hardest to be well behaved and not cause his parents any bother and to be especially good to Bart the next time he saw him and perhaps offer him extra help with his fish rounds at weekends.

It was on the following day, when Trando returned from school, that his father called him into the kitchen. His mother was sitting at the table and he noticed at once that she looked pale and her eyes were red as if she'd been crying. His favourite cookies were on the table so he quickly realised there must be something badly wrong, because his mother only ever put these cookies out on Sundays or on special occasions. She now gave him one and his father told him to sit down and sat down beside him. He looked tired and worried as he took Trando's hand, which again was very unusual. He hesitated before he spoke.

"Trando, I want you to be brave and try and stay calm while you listen to what I am going to tell you..."

Trando felt a panic rising in him. This must be about Bart. It had to be about Bart. But somehow he forced himself not to interrupt and let his father continue.

"Trando, the police arrested Bart and Nick Sacco last night and they are being held in the police cells in Bridgewater." He paused, noting his son had lost colour in his cheeks, so he continued quickly, "We think they were also after some other men who were at Bart's meetings. Some of these men have disappeared and two of them called Orciani and Boda seem to have got away, maybe back to Italy..."

Trando could stay silent no longer and leapt to his feet. "But why Papa, why? What do the police say Bart has done? They must have the wrong man. Bart would never harm anyone. He is not an anarchist. He told me. How can they arrest him when he has done nothing wrong?"

Vincenzo shook his head sadly, "Trando, you have to understand, they found a lot of bad things on the two men, particularly on Bart. They found guns, ammunition and some printed leaflets about his comrades' war and about rights for the workers. In these difficult times that doesn't look good."

Alfonsine looked up at him and said, "But we all know Bart was only trying to get rid of all those things, to save his comrades. He'd told us he was going to do that."

Trando added, "He would never use a gun. He told me."

Alfonsine put her arms round the boy. "Trando you must

try and be brave for Bart. He wouldn't want you to worry. It is a big mistake and we all know they have the wrong man." She started to cry, "I know Bart never hurt anyone. You will see they have arrested the wrong man."

Trando was crying now too. "He will die like Salsedo I know it. They will torture him and he will die. He should have gone back to Italy. He would have been safe then. I meant to tell him, but I never got a chance. Now it is my fault he is in prison."

His parents exchanged glances and his mother tried to comfort him. "Don't cry Trando. Your Papa will find a clever lawyer to help Bart. He will soon be free and we will all be happy again, like we were at Christmas. Yes?" She wiped his tears away with her apron.

His father added. "You mustn't blame yourself son. Bart would never have left for Italy even if you had asked him. We'd already told him to go and he refused. He felt he had to look after his comrades. He would never have gone back to Italy until he knew all the comrades were safe."

Trando nodded. In his heart he knew that to be true. He now asked if he could go to his room and his mother nodded, but his real intention was to go to his place on the landing so he could hear his parents talking without him being there. He realised they had only spoken to him like that in order to break the news to him as gently as possible and he was grateful at their efforts to try and spare his feelings.

Reaching his place on the landing he saw with relief that the kitchen door was slightly open, so he could just about hear them and his instinct proved right, they now talked more freely. In hushed voices they spoke of a top prosecution lawyer who had been summoned by the police to prosecute Bart and Nick Sacco. His father said this man was a lawyer who had a reputation for always winning his cases. More worryingly he added that the country wouldn't worry which Italians were punished as long as somebody was, and everyone knew the raid was the work of Italian anarchists so they didn't mind who was arrested.

This seemed like the worst possible news. His mother added angrily that this big shot lawyer would be sure to make people think all Italians were anarchists and tell everyone they were all the same and his father agreed saying that the Americans would now be looking for capital charges of murder and would not be satisfied until they got it.

Trando could listen no more. He returned to his room, lay on his bed and stared at the ceiling. He knew he somehow had to find a way to help Bart but just couldn't figure out how he could possibly do that. It was all so bewildering. How had things gone so badly wrong for Bart in such a short time? He had no answers and it made him feel sad and helpless.

*

A few days later events took yet another twist, but at last, to Trando's relief, he was to be offered the opportunity he had longed for and that was a chance to help Bart in a way that nobody else could.

For his parents it turned out to be a nightmare which had only just begun.

CHAPTER 5

A few days after his parents had broken the news of Bart's arrest, Trando was having his breakfast when he was given strict instructions to hurry home after school. It was a strange request but his parents gave no reason for it and he knew better than to ask for one. The atmosphere in the house had now become extremely tense and to him it seemed everyone was cross all the time, tempers were frayed and even the baby cried more than usual.

As instructed, once the last bell had rung in the afternoon, Trando dutifully left school and ran all the way back to Suosso Lane without stopping even though he was carrying his heavy school bag as well as his violin case. The sun was beating down and he arrived at the house very hot and out of breath. His mother met him at the front door and quickly ushered him into the kitchen. She washed his face and hands and combed his hair with a parting in the middle which he hated and as soon as she wasn't looking he pushed it back to one side again.

His mother then spoke to him in a very serious voice, "We are going into the parlour Trando where there are two men who want to talk to you, and so you have to be on your best behaviour." Trando again wondered why she always called the front room 'the parlour' when they had company because to him otherwise it was just the front room. He also wondered why whoever it was he had to meet couldn't have seen him in the kitchen.

His mother now almost pushed him into the front room which as always was neat and clean with everything highly polished. Today there was not a speck of dust to be seen and the smell of polish was so strong he imagined his mother must have been at the cleaning all morning. All their best furniture was kept in this room including the piano. Now, in one of the two smart chairs, sat a thin man with spectacles wearing a smart pin striped suit. On the other was a man who looked older and was a good deal shorter. He was also in a suit but plain grey and he wore a bow tie. They both looked rather important.

The thin man stood up to greet Trando. He was extremely tall and towered over the boy.

His father said, "Trando I want you to meet Mr Vahey and Mr Graham. They are lawyers who are going to help Bart and they want to talk to you. They think you might be able to help him."

Trando solemnly shook hands with both men and they all sat down. There was a short silence and then his father started to speak rather fast.

"The thing is Trando, Mr Vahey and Mr Graham think you could give Bart an alibi. That will be very important for Bart, but it would also mean you would have to appear in Court."

Trando wasn't sure he understood this. "What is an alibi?" he asked.

The first man, Mr Vahey, said "Shall I try and explain Mr Brini? I need the boy to understand just exactly what it is we are asking of him." His father nodded gratefully and the man turned back towards Trando. "I would like to go through a few things with you. Would that be all right?"

Trando nodded and then said politely, "I'm sorry I don't think I know what an alibi is, but I would like to help Bart in any way I can."

Mr Vahey gave a thin smile, "Don't worry, that will become clear once you understand what we need from you." He put his hands together and looked directly at Trando. "Now, I know from your parents that you are a great friend of Bart Vanzetti and want to help him, which is excellent. Mr Graham and I also want to help him. However, first we are going to need a few facts from you." He picked up some papers from the low table in front of him. "Your friend Bart has been accused of a crime which took place on December 24th last year, I think you know that?"

41

Trando nodded, then added firmly, "But that can't be right because I was with him on that day."

Mr Vahey nodded. "Precisely, and that is what we call an alibi." Trando still looked puzzled so Mr Vahey explained further. "If a crime is committed and the person accused could not have done the crime because they were somewhere else, we then say they have an alibi."

Trando thought about this and it made a great deal of sense to him. He then burst out, "What I don't understand is, if they know Bart was with me, why don't they just let him go? He already has this alibi thing."

Mr Vahey looked serious. "That Trando will be for a jury to decide, which means you would have to tell your account of that day to a court and before a judge. The jury then have to decide if they think you are telling the truth."

Trando felt indignant. "Of course I will be telling the truth. I was with him that day helping him to sell fish. Mama, you can tell them I was with him can't you?"

His mother was looking nervous. "Yes Trando, but you must listen to Mr Vahey, he is a clever lawyer and he knows what is best for Bart."

Mr Vahey gave another of his thin smiles which looked to Trando as if he was a bit in pain and doing his best to be patient. "Believe me Trando, you are a very important witness. Some of the other witnesses only speak Italian and will need an interpreter and this can make things difficult for the Jury. But you speak like a proper American boy, so we want to make sure that what you say is very clear. Do you understand me so far?" Trando nodded. There was a long pause as Mr Vahey seemed unsure of how to proceed. Then he cleared his throat, "There is something else that it is very important for you to understand Trando." He wasn't smiling anymore and he spoke slowly, with great emphasis. "I want to make it absolutely clear. You don't have to do this. You don't have to go to court. Nobody is forcing you to undergo this cross-examination. It won't be an easy experience for you, or pleasant and I want you to think carefully about that."

Trando was thinking all this was rather a waste of time and he burst out once again, "Of course I want to do it. I don't mind what happens. I want to do it for Bart. He is my best friend."

Mr Vahey smiled thinly once again, but still he spoke in a serious and stern way. "I know you want to help Trando, but there is something else which you might find difficult to understand. Your friend Bart is well known for his," he paused, "his anarchist views. I think you know this. But you must also understand that these anarchist views are not popular with most Americans. Some terrible things have been done by these anarchists. You will have heard of them; bombings, shootings, robberies..."

Trando leapt to his feet his eyes blazing with anger, "But not Bart. Bart was not like that that. He swore to me he never hurt anyone. Everyone knows how gentle and kind he is. He does not even like to kill a spider, or, or, the rabbits in Papa's garden. He would never hurt anyone. Ever."

He was close to tears and his father went and put his hands on his son's shoulders saying, "Calm down Trando, calm down," and he pushed the boy gently back to his seat and gave a curt nod to the lawyer.

Mr Vahey spoke in milder tones, "We know that Trando, but you have to understand that to most Americans Bart Vanzetti is just another anarchist. And to most Americans, all anarchists are bad men." He hesitated again. Trando wondered not for the first time why it was all being made out to seem so difficult. It seemed plain enough to him. If he had to speak out to save Bart then that is what he would do.

Mr Vahey had taken off his glasses which made him look a good deal younger. "Trando, your parents tell me you are a gifted violinist with a promising future. You hope to play in an orchestra when you're older, is that right?"

"Sure." Mr Vahey seemed to be choosing his words very carefully. Trando noticed his father now leaned forward and was listening intently, so this was obviously something important.

"And I am sure you *will* play in an orchestra one day." The lawyer paused and then continued, "However, there is a possibility that if you take the action of defending an anarchist, you might, and I emphasise the word, *might,* be jeopardising your future as a musician."

Trando couldn't follow this at all and he must have looked puzzled because Mr Vahey said, "Let me try and explain. There is a possibility that you could become known as 'the Brini Boy who testified for an anarchist' and that might make people angry with you. Your action in this case could shadow you for the rest of your life." He put his glasses back on. "Your parents thought it important you should know this before we go any further."

Trando thought about this for a moment and looked at his parents. They said nothing but he could see they both looked worried. He turned back to the lawyer, "You say that I am the best witness Bart has?" Mr Vahey nodded. "And if I don't tell them Bart was with me that day he could be sent to prison?"

"That is correct."

Trando again looked at his parents. "Then I must do it, for Bart. When they understand that Bart is innocent, they won't hold it against me, I am sure of it." He turned back to the lawyers and said firmly, "I will testify and give Bart his alibi Mr Vahey."

The lawyer seemed satisfied with this. "Very well then, if you are quite sure, thank you Trando." He pointed to the other man, who up to that moment hadn't said a word. "Mr Graham here will now take you through the questions you are likely to be asked and explain what will happen to you during your day in Court."

He nodded at Mr Graham, who then began to speak with a rather strange accent. His mother told him later that Mr Graham was from South Carolina and that was the southern way of speaking. Trando rather liked it, because it was slower and less like a schoolmaster than Mr Vahey.

*

Some four hours later Trando was in bed, very tired but pleased with the way the day's events had gone. He wrote in his diary,

June 10th 1920

This was a tiring day but I think an important one. I am very pleased that I can now help Bart. I saw two lawyers who seemed quite kind and helpful and they want to help Bart too but they do make things complicated. They are worried that I will be frightened by this Mr Katzmann who they told me is appearing for the prosecution. I don't know why that is. I can only tell him the truth about what happened that day. Mama keeps saying I don't have to do it. I felt quite cross with her for going on and on about it when my mind is made up, but she does seem very worried. I told her lots of times I was all right with it. Bart would be set free. They had made a big mistake. Soon we would put all this behind us and be happy again like we were before all these horrible things started happening. I am almost looking forward to the day of the trial, which Mr Vahey says will be June 22nd.

He put his diary away under the bed and wondered what it would feel like, standing in the witness box, being sworn in and all the people in the court room watching him. But he was now thirteen and Bart was right, thirteen was almost grown up and defending Bart did seem quite a grown-up thing to be doing.

For the first time in a long while he fell asleep as soon as he climbed into bed.

CHAPTER 6
THE TRIALS - JUNE 22ND 1920

On the day of the trial Trando woke very early. His smartest clothes had been laid out at the foot of his bed the night before and he now regarded them thoughtfully. This was quite probably going to be the most important day of his life.

It was too early to get up yet and as he lay in bed he thought about Bart and all that the lawyers had told him, going over and over it in his mind. Then as the sun came up he decided he could now get dressed. As he did so he told himself that he wasn't exactly nervous although he did have a weird feeling in his stomach. He put this down to excitement and anticipation. After all, the sooner he could tell them all about Bart's alibi, the sooner Bart would be free.

He carefully tied the laces of his very polished shoes and went downstairs to the kitchen. They were all up early as well. A large plate of food was put in front of him but in spite of his mother's urging he found he wasn't hungry. Why did grown-ups always think that food was the answer to everything?

He could tell that his parents were nervous and nobody spoke much as they set out. It was only a short journey to the Plymouth Court House and they could easily have walked, but one of his father's friends had insisted on driving them in his large Buick. His father sat silent, in the front with his friend, while his mother was with him in the back. She was dressed all in black; even a black hat and Trando wondered why on earth she had done that. It wasn't a funeral they were going to. She had worn a brightly coloured flowered dress for the Johnston's wedding last year which would have been much more cheerful, and cooler too. It was a hot day and her face was already flushed with the heat. Suddenly he felt a little sorry for her. She looked so worried and fiddled with the purse in her lap the whole way, only speaking once to ask him if he was sure he wanted to do this and telling him it wasn't too late to back out now. Trando yet again told her he was fine and that he needed to do this for Bart. The rest of the journey passed in silence.

They finally arrived at the Plymouth Court-House and Trando thought it looked rather impressive. He stared at the large red brick building with its flight of steps leading up to a very grand colonial white portico. At the top of these stood Mr Graham, who must have been waiting for them because now he hastened down the steps to meet them florid and sweating, speaking in that strange southern accent.

"Well done Brini family. It sure is a relief to have you here so nice and early. I'm always pleased to have the witnesses arrive in good time." He put his hand on Trando's shoulder. "And how are you doing young man?"

Trando assured him he was feeling fine and wished people wouldn't keep asking him how he was doing. He thought to himself that Mr Graham was the one who seemed nervous as he kept hopping from one foot to the other in a rather strange way.

"Where is Bart?" he asked.

Mr Graham explained that Mr Vanzetti and Mr Sacco were already in the Court Room but that it would be a little while before the witnesses were called. He added that the Judge who was presiding was called Judge Webster Thayer. This meant nothing to Trando but from the low and ominous way Mr Graham said this it didn't sound as if this Judge was a good man for them. Would this make a difference? He glanced at his parents and could tell they didn't seem to know anything about this Judge Thayer either.

They all moved into the noisy corridor and were told to wait until Trando was called. Mr Graham then hurried back into the Court Room. After a few minutes his father said he would go on ahead to the Visitor's Gallery and told Alfonsine to join him as soon as Trando had been taken to the witness box. His mother looked pale and only spoke once after he'd left when she asked Trando if he wanted anything to eat, but he still didn't feel like eating, so shook his head.

At last a man came out and said in a solemn voice that he would conduct Trando into the Court Room. His mother clung to him, which he round a bit embarrassing and he wriggled trying to free himself. At last she let him go and to his relief went to join his father in the Gallery.

*

Trando's first thought as he walked into the Court Room was that it was very hot although there were great fans whirring overhead. He glanced up at the Gallery which was packed with people. He could clearly see his parents because they were sitting at the front beside a pretty lady with lots of dark curls who he thought might be Rosina Sacco, the wife of Bart's friend Nick. There were also some of his neighbours from Suosso Lane that he recognised and one or two of them gave him an encouraging wave. He was told to go up the two steps into the witness box and the man gave him a box to stand on so he could see properly.

It was then that he saw Bart, who was with Nick Sacco in the prisoner's box in the centre of the room. They were both handcuffed and neither of them looked very well. Bart had great dark rings round his eyes, but he managed a little smile when he saw Trando. Mr Graham and Mr Vahey were on one side of the prisoners, and a big florid man, who he took to be the great Mr Katzmann because he looked so important, was on the other. To the far side sat the Jury. He didn't want to look at them. Instead Trando looked straight ahead at Judge Webster Thayer and at once decided he didn't like him. The man had a fierce, hawk-like face and Trando had an instinctive feeling that this Judge would be neither sympathetic nor fair. In Trando's mind he had already become the enemy, along with Mr Katzmann, the police and the Pinkerton man.

Trando was sworn in and his cross examination began.

The following extracts are taken from the exact transcript of the trial.

GRAHAM	Your full name is what?
TRANDO	Beltrando Brini.
GRAHAM	They call you some other name for short?
TRANDO	Yes. Trando.
GRAHAM	How old are you?
TRANDO	I am thirteen years old. My birthday was on March 14th.
GRAHAM	You live with your mother and father in Suosso Lane?
TRANDO	Yes.
GRAHAM	How long have you lived in Plymouth?
TRANDO	Since I was born.

At this point Trando gave a sigh of relief. So far it was all just as the lawyers had said it would be and he felt almost relaxed. Now, with the boring details over, Mr Graham turned to the proper examination. This was also familiar territory and again Trando wasn't worried, although he was determined to get his facts straight, so he concentrated hard. Mr Graham had told him to keep his answers short and not to add anything.

GRAHAM	You know Mr Vanzetti?
TRANDO	Yes.
GRAHAM	Do you remember a few days before Christmas last year?
TRANDO	Yes I do.
GRAHAM	Do you remember 23rd December?
TRANDO	Yes I do.
GRAHAM	How do you remember that?
TRANDO	I remember it because Mr Vanzetti on that night came to our house.
GRAHAM	Did he talk to you?
TRANDO	Yes he did. About helping him.
GRAHAM	Helping him when?
TRANDO	The next day, the 24th December.
GRAHAM	And did you see him the next morning?
TRANDO	Yes I did. On Cork Street near Maxwell's Drug Store.
GRAHAM	And did you talk with anyone else after you had

49

	talked with Mr Vanzetti?
TRANDO	Yes. I talked with my father.
GRAHAM	What did you talk to your father about?
TRANDO	About wearing my rubber shoes. He wanted me to go back home for them.
GRAHAM	And did you go back home?
TRANDO	Yes. I put them on and then met Mr Vanzetti again at Cherry Street.
GRAHAM	Can you tell me what time that was?
TRANDO	About eight.
GRAHAM	How do you place that time?
TRANDO	Well, it was seven thirty when I walked back to the house to get my rubber shoes and it took me a short time to find them and on the way back I heard the Plymouth Cordage whistle blow so I knew it was eight o'clock. Usually that is when I eat my breakfast.

At this a ripple of laughter went around the Court Room. Trando was surprised as he didn't think he had said anything funny. He also noted that the Judge didn't look amused and neither did Mr Katzmann.

GRAHAM.	When you reached Mr Vanzetti what was he doing?
TRANDO	He was preparing fish in the wheelbarrow. He gave me a basket.
GRAHAM	Where did you deliver fish that morning?
TRANDO	Cherry Street, Cherry Place, Standish Avenue and Court Street.
GRAHAM	How long did you continue with Vanzetti delivering fish that day?
TRANDO	I left between one and two.
GRAHAM	And you were delivering fish all the time since you returned to Cherry Street?
TRANDO	Yes sir.
GRAHAM	Did you see Mr Vanzetti again that day, December 24th?
TRANDO	Yes. At my home, at about seven thirty in the

evening.

GRAHAM	And did he stay long?
TRANDO	I think quite late. I practised my violin and then went to bed.

He sneaked a quick look at Bart who was smiling, but Trando thought that even so he looked very sad. He was beginning to feel tired and wished he had eaten more breakfast. The next question startled him.

GRAHAM	Did you notice anything about Mr Vanzetti's moustache?

Trando thought about this for a moment.

TRANDO	It is a very long moustache I think. And in very good condition.

There was more laughter from the Gallery and this time Judge Thayer called for silence.

GRAHAM	Did you ever see Mr Vanzetti remove it, or trim it short?
TRANDO	No sir, never. He always has a long moustache.
GRAHAM	You're sure he never trimmed it in all the time you knew him?
TRANDO	Yes sir. I'm sure.
GRAHAM	Thank you Trando, that is all.

They adjourned for lunch after that. Trando sat outside in the sunshine with his mother. His father had decided to stay inside talking to various friends, but he also wanted to listen to what was being said about the morning's proceedings. Trando munched on the pie his mother had brought. He felt quite pleased with the way the morning had gone, especially when Mr Graham told him he had done so well. However, Mr Graham had added a warning that after lunch he would be cross-examined by Mr Katzmann and that would not be nearly so easy for him.

After a while his father came out and joined them. He was looking concerned and looked at his wife. "I think that Trando has the prosecution worried. I overheard the police and that Pinkerton man, who is called Hughes, saying that Mr Katzmann will somehow have to break Trando's evidence because he was so rock solid and I don't like the sound of that. My guess is they will start to use dirty tactics and things could get really rough for the boy."

His mother looked very alarmed at this and glanced across at him. "Couldn't we take him home now? They've heard what he has to say."

His father shook his head. "It doesn't work like that. Both sides have to be heard." He thought for a moment then added, "I tell you Alfonsine I don't like the look of that Judge either. My friends tell me he has a hatred of Italians and thinks we should all be deported."

Trando wanted to ask his father more about this but he'd moved away to have a smoke.

*

Shortly after that it was time to go back in. The noise in the corridor had now become deafening. Everyone seemed to be shouting and for the first time that day Trando began to feel decidedly nervous. What were these dirty tactics they were going to use? Would they torture him? Surely his parents wouldn't allow that to happen?

Mr Graham watching him seemed to sense a change in the boy's demeanour, so in a voice he hoped was reassuring he told him he wasn't to worry, that all he had to do was tell Mr Katzmann what he had already said that morning. Trando nodded and tried not to think about the churning feeling in his stomach. Then Mr Graham pointed out the Pinkerton man J.J. Hughes, who was talking to Stewart the police chief. He said grimly that this man, J. J. Hughes, had the reputation of being ruthless and that he usually got his man. This was why Trando's evidence was so important. Trando stared at Hughes. He did look extremely fierce with a set and grim expression. Yes, definitely a ruthless man he thought. It was going to be very important for him to get his answers right that afternoon. He felt hot and uncomfortable and could feel the sweat dripping down the back of his neck. He was about to ask his parents for a drink of water when something definitely odd happened. He noticed that their other lawyer Mr Vahey, had crossed over to Hughes and Stewart the policeman and they all started talking together. Although they looked serious, they also looked very friendly. Surely this shouldn't be happening? Mr Vahey was meant to be on their side and now there he was talking to the enemy. He turned to ask Mr Graham about it, but he had already gone back into Court. So he asked his father. His father said he didn't know why they were talking together, but he frowned and said that something wasn't quite right.

*

Once back in the witness box Trando looked at Mr Katzmann. He was a big built man, like those pictures he'd seen of someone in the military, with white hair, bushy eyebrows and a neat white moustache. He didn't look too frightening, not like the Pinkerton man anyway, and as his questioning started he seemed mild, even kind.

KATZMANN	How old did you say you were son?
TRANDO	Thirteen sir.
KATZMANN	Are you tired? Would you like to sit down?
TRANDO	No sir. Thank you sir.
KATZMANN	Have you a good memory?
TRANDO	I don't know as I have.
KATZMANN	Pretty good is it not?
TRANDO	I guess so.
KATZMANN	It is very good. So I want you to repeat the story, word for word that you told Mr Graham just now.
TRANDO	Without stopping?
KATZMANN	Yes without stopping.

Up in the gallery Vincenzo swore under his breath. Now he was beginning to understand those tactics. The bastards were out to prove that Trando had learned his evidence by heart. It was the only way they could get round it. His boy, who was telling the truth out there by recalling what had happened, was playing straight into their hands by repeating his evidence.

As Trando reached the bit about practising his violin, he looked across at Bart and smiled. At this Katzmann snapped at him. His voice and attitude had suddenly changed.

KATZMANN   Keep your eyes on me boy!

TRANDO   Yes sir.

He sounded aggressive and after Trando finished his account for the second time he fired his questions at him at great speed.

KATZMANN   So, this is just the same story isn't it?

TRANDO   Sure.

KATZMANN   How many times did you tell that story?

TRANDO   I told it to Mr Vahey.

KATZMANN   How many times did you tell it to Mr Vahey?

TRANDO   Twice.

KATZMANN   And you've told it here twice, that makes four times. How many other times?

TRANDO   I told it at home.

KATZMANN   How many times?

TRANDO   About two or three times.

KATZMANN   Wasn't it more than that?

TRANDO   I don't know. Perhaps.

Katzmann now shouted at him.

KATZMANN   How many more times? Tell me, how many more times? Maybe ten?

TRANDO   No!

KATZMANN   Maybe nine times?

TRANDO   Maybe five.

KATZMANN   Perhaps six, seven? Who did you tell it to?

TRANDO   My parents.

KATZMANN   Who else did you tell it to?

TRANDO   To Mr Vahey.

KATZMANN   You told it six times at home, twice to Mr Vahey and twice here. Did you tell it to your sister?

TRANDO   She was with my parents. She is not one years old, she would not have understood.

There was more laughter in the room which Katzmann stopped by raising his hand and so the ordeal went on between the small dark haired boy and the tall military gentleman.

KATZMANN   Tell me son, how long did it take you each time?

TRANDO   Sometimes I would leave some things out.

KATZMANN   And then your Papa would say "be sure to put that in."

The boy looked puzzled.

TRANDO   Sure.

KATZMANN   Did you ever learn anything to recite at school.

TRANDO   Yes sir.

KATZMANN   And the teacher would stand there and correct you, yes?

Trando nodded.

KATZMANN   And it was the same way with this was it not? If you left anything out your Papa would tell you and you would go back and put that part in, would you not? You learned it just like a piece at school did you not?

Trando was bewildered by this questioning and he wasn't sure what to do. He looked at Mr Graham, but he was turned away from him, whispering to Mr Vahey. He looked up at the Gallery and he could see that his mother was holding a hanky to her eyes and that his father was looking angry.

Katzmann wrapped out impatiently,

KATZMANN   Answer the question boy.

Trando answered with a whispered 'yes' and Mr Katzmann for the moment seemed satisfied with that. He changed the subject.

KATZMANN	Mr Vanzetti is a nice gentleman is he not?
TRANDO	Yes.
KATZMANN	It seemed a terrible thing to you that Mr Vanzetti was arrested did it not?
TRANDO	Yes sir.
KATZMANN	It made a deep impression on your mind yes? What date was that? What date was Mr Vanzetti arrested?
TRANDO	I could not say the date.
KATZMANN	So, you felt very sorry about the arrest and it made a deep impression on your mind, but you could not tell us the date.

Trando again felt bewildered. Katzmann turned towards the Jury as he said in mocking tones,

> It seems to me boy, you can tell me the things you are told to remember, but if you don't learn it, you don't remember.

He seemed pleased with himself and to Trando's alarm he saw that J.J. Hughes the Pinkerton man, who was sitting at the back, had a big grin on his face.

KATZMANN	Now how long was it after you heard that Mr Vanzetti was arrested that you told your story?
TRANDO	Shortly afterwards.
KATZMANN	Anybody ask you to tell it?
TRANDO	No, I told it myself. Some people were telling my mother saying, 'even the little boy brought my fish that day was with him.'
KATZMANN	You don't remember about this except that some people told you?
TRANDO	No, I remembered it.

The next question was fired at Trando like a pistol shot.

KATZMANN	What day of the week was the 24th December?
TRANDO	Thursday. No, Wednesday.
KATZMANN	Are you sure of that?

Trando was silent because he wasn't sure. Katzmann continued,

> Which day of the week was the 24th of November? I am not asking about December now, but November.

Trando was bewildered. How was he to know all the days of the calendar?

TRANDO   I don't know.

KATZMANN   You say the 24th of December was a Thursday?

He walked over and thrust a calendar under Trando's nose, stabbing with his finger at a day.

> Now do you want to change your mind?

TRANDO   Wednesday.

KATZMANN   So you were one day off. And if you were one day off on that, you were one day off all the way through. And that changes your whole testimony does it not? You said Thursday twice. You got it wrong twice.

TRANDO   Only the name of the day sir.

There was a murmur of approval in the room. Katzmann frowned.

KATZMANN   How many places did you go to with fish that morning?
                Was it as many as ten different places?

TRANDO   It maybe more. Maybe about twenty five.

KATZMANN   And how many times did you go back to load with fish?

TRANDO   Twice.

KATZMANN   How many packages did you get?

TRANDO   About ten.

KATZMANN   How many pounds of eels in each package?

TRANDO   At the most about three pounds.

KATZMANN   You don't want to tell this Jury that you could carry ten packages of eels do

	you? Twenty or thirty pounds of eels? A little boy like you? You could not carry that many could you?
TRANDO	Sure.
KATZMANN	You could not carry that basket all the way up the hill, weighing forty pounds?
TRANDO	As I walked up the hill the basket became less heavy. As I delivered more.

At this there was again much laughter in the Court. Trando noticed that Mr Katzmann was sweating and was now red in the face. He said, almost nastily,

KATZMANN	That wasn't part of your story was it boy? You didn't learn that by heart.
TRANDO	I didn't learn the other by heart.

A small cheer went around the court. Trando looked across the room and smiled. Katzmann immediately snapped at him again.

KATZMANN	What are you smiling at boy? Is it something funny that strikes you?
TRANDO	No sir.
KATZMANN	You say you delivered two baskets with this man?
TRANDO	The first time Bart gave me a basket and the other time he gave me two or three bundles in my hand and he said, 'Go up there and then come back and get some more.' Maybe I come back twenty times...
KATZMANN	But you said you went back twice. And now you say it maybe twenty times.

Graham got to his feet.

GRAHAM	Objection. The witness has made his answer very clear.
JUDGE THAYER	The witness must answer. Of course if the witness does not understand the question you have a right to say so.
KATZMANN	You understand me when I asked how many times you went back to load fish.

	You said twice. Now you say it might be twenty times.
TRANDO	No it might be twenty times I went back to the cart, but we only returned to re-load the fish twice.

Again a murmur of approval went round the courtroom. Trando looked towards Bart who was wiping his eyes. Katzmann once more barked at him,

KATZMANN	Keep your eyes on me boy. Now, you were not delivering fish for more than a couple of hours were you, altogether?
TRANDO	More than a couple of hours. It was more like four.
KATZMANN	And you got through between one and two. Was it nearer one o'clock or two?
TRANDO	I'm not positive.
KATZMANN	And yet you are positive you started out at eight o'clock. Are you sure it wasn't nine?
TRANDO	It was eight.
KATZMANN	Was it four hours between the time you started and when you finished?
TRANDO	Four hours or more.
KATZMANN	Can you tell us the time you left him then?
TRANDO	It was nearer to one than two.
KATZMANN	Was it one fifteen?
TRANDO	I don't know.
KATZMANN	Was it one twenty?
TRANDO	I don't know.
KATZMANN	Ten minutes past one.

Trando found himself shouting.

TRANDO	I don't know! I have no idea!

Katzmann shuffled some papers in front of him and then looked up at Trando. His voice once again changed.

KATZMANN	Your papa is a very good friend of Mr Vanzetti's is he not?

TRANDO	Yes, he is.
KATZMANN	Your papa went around, did he not, to collect funds for his defence?
TRANDO	I know he got some money. Yes.
KATZMANN	Did Vanzetti sometimes come to your house to talk to your papa?
TRANDO	Yes.
KATZMANN	When they were talking together. Did you hear them talking about our Government?

It was Vahey's turn to stand up.

VAHEY	I pray your Honor's judgement...
TRANDO	What do you mean by 'our Government'?
JUDGE THAYER	He may answer yes or no.
TRANDO	No.
KATZMANN	What society do your papa and Vanzetti belong to?

Vahey was again on his feet.

VAHEY	Objection.
JUDGE THAYER	Sustained. Re-phrase the question.
KATZMANN	Did your papa and Mr Vanzetti belong to any society or organisation?
TRANDO	No.
KATZMANN	Did you ever hear Mr Vanzetti making any speeches to the Italians?

Trando hesitated here but then shook his head.

	Did you ever hear Vanzetti talk about a man named Mike Boda?
TRANDO	No.

Katzmann gave a long look at Trando and then said,

KATZMANN	That is all.

And he sat down.

Trando felt his legs trembling. He was completely exhausted and it was with some relief when he was told there was to be a recess of fifteen minutes. He joined his parents outside and his father handed him a glass of water.

"Well done son. You did real good in there. I was proud of

you. I'm not sure I could have done it. I'd have lost my temper for sure." He turned to his wife, "Sweet Jesus! I could strangle that man with my bare hands. He twisted everything, made it out Trando had learned all that evidence by heart!"

To Trando's dismay his mother started to wail, "We should never have let Trando do it Vincenzo. He is too little. My poor boy, what he has been through. Three hours they made him stand there. For three hours!"

Trando put his arm round her. "It's all right mama really. I didn't mind. I just didn't understand some of the questions that's all. Mr Katzmann had me confused."

Mr Graham joined them. "It's almost over Trando. I have to ask you one or two more things and then you can go home. Are you ready?"

Trando nodded. He felt happier back on the stand with Mr Graham questioning him.

*

GRAHAM	Trando, did your mother, or your father, or anybody else, tell you anything to tell us here?
TRANDO	No.
GRAHAM	Did they tell you to change anything in the story you told them as to where you and Vanzetti were on December 24th?
TRANDO	No.
GRAHAM	Your mama knew you were out with Vanzetti the day before Christmas?
TRANDO	Yes.
GRAHAM	And your papa knew it because he told you to go back and get your rubber shoes?
TRANDO	Yes.
GRAHAM	Thank you. That is all.

With that Trando's ordeal was over.

He remembered very little of the journey home. It maybe

he slept most of the way. Once back at Suosso Lane he went straight upstairs to his room. His mother brought him a bowl of soup and an apple, but he was too tired to eat much. However, he did think it important to make a short entry in his diary. He thought for a moment and then wrote;

June 22nd 1920

I hope I managed to give Bart his alibi today. Some of the questions Mr Katzmann asked me didn't make any sense. I didn't like him at all. He wasn't a nice man and kept showing off to the Jury. I hated that but I hope the Jury understood that I really was with Bart delivering fish when the robbery took place. That is all that matters now. Mama gets so upset and Papa seems very angry about it all and doesn't trust any of them. He says all the Americans hate the Italians because of the bombs and killings. But they must be made to understand that Bart didn't do any of it. I hope that is the last of this and Bart can leave prison and come home. I haven't practised my violin for two days but I will have an extra-long practise tomorrow and play "Old Black Joe" even though Bart isn't here to listen to it.

CHAPTER SEVEN

Later that night Trando overheard a conversation between his parents that really gave him a shock. He'd woken up suddenly, switched on the light to see the time and then heard raised voices coming from the kitchen. Although his bedroom door was open he went out onto the landing to get a better listen and immediately noticed that his father sounded agitated,

"...I'm telling you Alfonsine, after what happened in Court today I'm worried that everything Bart told me when I visited him in prison, could well turn out be true."

His mother's voice was fearful. "What do you mean? You only told me it was a terrible place and that his cell was damp and cold and that he had angry red marks on his wrists from wearing the cuffs. What else happened during that visit that now makes you so worried?"

His father was obviously having a drink because there was a long pause before he gave his answer. "It was something he said after I told him that Trando would testify and give him an alibi. Bart didn't want him to do it. It brought tears to his eyes Alfonsine and he kept saying 'my brave boy, he shouldn't be put through this' but I insisted that Trando was his best chance..."

His mother sounded impatient. "Well Trando has given his evidence and Bart has his alibi, so what worries you now?"

There was another long pause before his father replied to this and Trando strained to hear what he said. "Bart didn't think the Jury would believe him and if they didn't believe Trando, who sounds like a real American boy, how would they believe any of the other witnesses, who were Italian? They would all be considered 'Dago Bastards' and that was that. Bart also didn't think they were interested in any alibis, only the fact that he and Nick were anarchists. He was convinced they would be found guilty because of what had been found on them when they were arrested. I tried to tell him they couldn't convict him for murder just because of a lot of anarchist literature. And then he reminded me…"

His father paused again and his mother almost shouted, "reminded you of what?'

"Of all the guns and ammunition they had on them at the time of the arrest."

Trando heard his mother gasp and she said "Sweet Jesus, I'd forgotten about that." Then she burst out almost angrily, "I just don't understand why Bart was carrying those weapons. He was never a violent man. How could he be so stupid?"

There was the sound of a chair being pushed back. Maybe his father was walking around. The door of the kitchen was slightly open but not enough for Trando to see inside. At last his father spoke again, "Bart was getting rid of the guns and ammunition for his comrades, along with all the literature. He and Nick had everything on them that day." He broke off and he also sounded angry, "I warned Bart before he went to New York that he was putting himself in danger, but he just shrugged and kept saying he had no choice, that his duty was to protect his comrades and that he was the only one left to do it. It only needed one more day and they would have been rid of the stuff."

At this point Trando thought he heard his mother say "Oh my God," and after a moment she added, "So what now?"

There was another long silence and then his father said, "We'll have to wait and see. Bart seems to have accepted his fate but he told me that his one regret was that Nick hadn't managed to get away to Italy, especially as Rosina was expecting another child."

His mother burst out, "What about American Justice? They heard Trando give Bart an alibi today. Was that all a waste of time? Was my poor boy put through that for nothing?"

"I don't know but I'm now worried Alfonsine." Trando could hear the agitation in his father's voice. "Bart could have been right. There was a lot of anger in the Court today and that Judge is certainly not friendly towards us. Someone is going to have to pay for the raids with those two murders and I don't think it matters to them who does. To them one Dago is much like another and Nick and Bart are the only two known anarchists left."

His mother sounded indignant and said again, "But today Trando gave Bart an alibi. That horrible man threw everything at him and it never stopped him from telling the truth."

"I agree," his father sounded tired, "but you saw the way that Katzmann threw the questions at him. He was implying Trando had learned his evidence by heart. The Jury may well believe that."

"Then they are stupid people. Stupid!"

Trando was just about to go back to his room when he heard his mother say, "Was Nick in the same cell when you saw Bart?"

"No, they had kept them separate. Bart told me Nick wasn't doing so well. He seemed to think he was terrified they would get the same fate as Salseda." He paused. "There was something else Bart told me. The other prisoners kept shouting all night, 'You're gonna fry you anarchist pigs'…"

At this point Trando decided he really didn't want to hear any more and went back to bed.

*

In view of his eavesdropping the previous night, Trando, over breakfast, desperately pleaded with his father to let him go back to the Court Room, but to no avail. His father firmly said no and didn't seem likely to change his mind. He told Trando impatiently, "You have to stay here and look after your mother. I will let you know what happens." Then, obviously seeing his disappointment he added, "I think Bart would find it hard to concentrate if you were there."

He didn't think that was true at all, but he could tell his father wasn't going to change his mind and as if to prove the point Vincenzo left for the Court House almost at once.

After he'd gone Trando spent a restless morning unable to settle to anything. His mother watched him anxiously and as soon as they'd finished their lunch she suggested he go over to the gardens to collect vegetables for their evening meal. She gave him a flask of lemonade and insisted he wore his sunhat because it was such a very hot day. Trando hated that hat and thought it made him look stupid, but his mother seemed so anxious he decided it was best not to argue, but as soon as he reached the garden where she couldn't see him he quickly removed it. Almost at once he could feel the sun beating down on his head but he didn't care. Walking over to the vegetable plot he smiled to himself. If his mother caught him without his hat he would just have to tell her that it was scratchy and didn't fit him properly. In any case, that was partly true because it did keep falling off every time he stooped down.

He worked hard for over an hour. It was hot and tiring work and after a while the constant bending down, combined with the afternoon heat, started to make him a bit dizzy. So he took a break and sat on the bench in the shade, thankful for the flask of lemonade he'd brought with him and which he now gulped down.

It was very peaceful. The only sound was the buzzing of bees and the occasional cry of a seagull straying in from the shore. His thoughts turned to the Court Room and he wondered how Bart was getting on with Katzmann's questions.

"Trando?" It was his mother's voice calling him from across the lane. "Are you managing all right? You can come back now if you're too hot."

Trando got up off the bench and shouted back, "I'm fine. I've nearly finished."

He picked up his basket and had just started to pull up a few more vegetables when he heard another voice call out his name. On looking up he saw it was a girl who he instantly recognised as Ella, the one who had rescued him that time when he was in the fight. He then remembered she had given him her handkerchief for his bloody nose and now felt guilty because although his mother had washed and ironed it, he'd never returned it to her. In fact it had been difficult to do so because he'd only ever caught the odd glimpse of Ella since that day and presumed she was in another building. Now he looked her up and down. She was a tall, skinny kid with very fair hair and a freckled face. Today she was wearing a pretty blue cotton dress and a large straw hat with a matching blue ribbon and he thought that maybe she had to wear a hat on account of all those freckles.

"Hello Trando Brini," she said cheerfully, "How are you? Do you want some help with those vegetables?" She pointed at the basket which was now over half full. Trando felt it was probably full enough for today, so he thanked her and said he had just about finished. He looked at her feeling shy and awkward.

"Would you like some lemonade?" he finally asked, "I have some in the flask by the bench. It's homemade. My mother makes it."

They sat side by side and she gulped down the remains of the drink. "Nice lemonade." She handed back the flask and said with a grin, "Sorry I seem to have finished it." She stretched out her long legs. "Phew, it's hot isn't it? You ought to wear a hat. You could get sunburn."

He shrugged. "I don't have fair skin like you." Then he added with a sheepish smile, "My mother gave me a hat to wear but I don't like it. Anyway it kept falling off when I was pulling up the vegetables."

She laughed and then said suddenly, "Why aren't you in Court today?"

Trando was startled.

"How come you know about that?"

Ella said scornfully, "Everybody knows about it. They're all talking about you taking the stand yesterday. My father is a lawyer and he said it was a very brave thing to do and I agree with him."

Trando shrugged. "I was only telling the truth, about what happened."

Ella swung her legs for a moment as she thought about this. "So what do you think will happen to those two men?"

He suddenly found he didn't know how to reply to this. Before yesterday in court he had felt certain they would let Bart go, but after what he had heard the previous night he wasn't so sure. Mr Katzmann was a clever man, even if he was a bully. He might make Bart tell everyone about the fight for the workers and then there was the fact that the Police had found him with guns and anarchist literature. That wouldn't look good. And then there was the Pinkerton man who apparently always got his man.

He turned to Ella, "I hope they will go free because they could not have done those crimes. But everyone seems to hate Italians because of some bad men who did wrong and violent things. But it wasn't them. At least, I know it wasn't Bart, because I was with him when the crime was committed. So I know he has an alibi."

Feeling he'd said rather too much he looked away, but to his surprise Ella spoke quite fiercely, "I don't know why they should hate Italians. should love to be Italian. All the Italian families at the school are so friendly, so happy and their parents are always nice to each other. Not like where I live." She broke off and then looked at him. "And I like your dark looks. I hate having fair skin, it means I'm always being told to be careful in the sun and then in the summer I get all these freckles! Ugh!"

Trando laughed. "I really like your freckles." And then he suddenly felt shy again. He wasn't used to talking to girls. All his friends at school seemed to be boys.

There was a moments silence and then Ella said, "Actually I have come to say goodbye. We are moving to New York next week. My father has a new job there, so I will be starting at another school in the Fall."

Trando was dismayed at this news and wanted to say how sorry he was that she was leaving because he felt he had just found a new friend, but he quickly covered up these feelings and asked, "Will you like it in New York? I've seen pictures of it and Bart went there a few weeks ago."

Ella thought for a minute. "I'm not sure I'll like it. It's huge, not like here. But my father says it will be a great new experience for me." For the first time that day he thought she didn't sound so confident, but then she shrugged as she said, "So I guess it will be." Smiling she added, "I will miss hearing you play your violin. You were great in the school concert, the best thing in it."

Suddenly she jumped up and held out her hand. He took it and they rather solemnly shook hands. At this moment Trando thought of the handkerchief and stammered out,

"I am sorry Ella, I never returned the handkerchief you gave me that day when I was in a fight. My mother washed and ironed it. I put it away in a drawer and then forgot about it." He grinned. "It's quite clean. She managed to get out all the bloodstains."

At this Ella laughed. "Don't worry, you keep it, I have lots. Goodbye Trando Brini and good luck. I hope your friend gets off."

And with that she was gone.

Trando watched her until she was out of sight and then walked slowly back with his basket of vegetables across the lane and into his house.

*

His father returned late from court that night, by which time Trando had already had his supper and gone to his room to do some violin practise. As soon as he heard the front door slam he opened his own door a little until he saw his father stride across the hall and into the kitchen. Trando went cautiously out onto the landing and was relieved to see that the kitchen door hadn't quite closed so he could see and hear what was going on. His father seemed very agitated and was marching up and down, banging his fist on the kitchen table at frequent intervals and shouting, "It's a farce Alfonsine, I tell you this whole trial is a farce!" He sat down and looked at his wife. "When my father came to this country he always told me it was for a better life and because of the American justice system they have here. But this is not justice. It is a frame-up. They tell lies, lies! All their witnesses tell lies."

Trando watched as his mother tried to calm him down giving him a bowl of the soup he'd had for his own supper made with all the vegetables he'd brought in from the garden that afternoon. It was usually his father's favourite soup, but now he didn't even seem to notice it as he continued to shout, "Take that Judge Thayer, it is obvious he hates all Italians because it must be clear even to him they have no evidence against Nick and Bart. And those witnesses they have called! Where in hell did they find them? They are all liars. One of them actually said that the man who did the shooting had a SMALL moustache. SMALL!" His father spat out the word. "And you heard what Trando told the court. He said clearly that Bart always had a long moustache. A LONG MOUSTACHE!" Again his father shouted, now waving his spoon about so that his mother told him to calm down or he would wake the baby.

All was quiet for a moment while his father finished his soup and his mother gave him another helping. When he spoke again it was in slightly calmer tones, although Trando could tell he was still angry.

"You won't believe it Alfonsine, there was one witness who said the bandit he saw ran like a foreigner. Ran like a foreigner! What did he mean by that? Do Italians run differently from Americans, or from Russians or a Swede? It's a farce I tell you. A farce!"

Trando craned forward to hear, as his mother asked if Bart and Nick Sacco had been questioned yet and his father shook his head. Then his voice became serious. "I had a long talk with the lawyers afterwards," and here he gave a short laugh, "I mean, after all, we did raise all that money to pay for them so they should realise they are working for us. I told them straight. I said I was worried with the way things were going. Do you know, that man Vahey looked really annoyed at this? He said it didn't help their case that Bart and Nick kept shouting out 'liar' at the witnesses, because the Judge and Jury didn't like these interruptions. Well, I said to him I agreed with Bart, those witnesses were all liars. And do you know? Vahey just shrugged as if that didn't worry him one little bit."

He finished his soup and pushed his bowl away. "And I'll tell you another thing that worries me Alfonsine. This trial is only for the December 24th crime. If they find Bart guilty for this one, then he will be tried for the other crime as well and that one is for a double murder and I'm not sure he has an alibi for that."

Trando could see that his mother looked very shocked by this and she sat down opposite his father. "But Caro, they cannot find Bart guilty after what Trando told them yesterday? Bart couldn't have been at the scene of the first crime. Not when he was out selling fish."

His father gave a short laugh that sounded more like a bark, "Well that is what I told the lawyers and Vahey just shrugged again and said there would be no case at all if Bart and Nick Sacco hadn't lied on that first night at the police station. He said they had already behaved like guilty men. They lied about the car, about the garage, about knowing Boda." He gave another of his barking laughs, "Apparently Nick Sacco even said he had been with a woman."

There was a pause and then his father burst out, "What else could they do? They were desperate and doing their best to protect those damned comrades. Bart had already told me it was vital he got rid of all the evidence. I warned him what would happen. I warned him." He paused again. "Then that other lawyer fellow, Graham, added that it wasn't just the lies that put them under suspicion, but what they were carrying on them when they were arrested. The fact they had guns and shotgun shells, a small arsenal. Bart had told Vahey they were going to sell the shells to make money for the Cause but that didn't help." His father was shaking his head. "You know, for a clever man, Bart could sometimes be so stupid. Stupid! Vahey had told him already that any mention of the Cause was the last thing the Judge would want to hear, given what Vahey called his 'Red Phobia'. He also said that the Jury wouldn't like it either because they were entirely made up of God-fearing, patriotic Americans. So any mention of the Cause would send Bart and Nick to the State Prison right away! But Bart just doesn't see it or understand the danger he is in. He is so obstinate. He just won't help himself."

His father pushed back his chair, lit a cigarette and sat thinking for a moment. "I'll tell you another thing. Something odd was said after that and it worried me all the way home." Trando now strained further to hear because his father's voice had lowered. "I was just about to leave, when Vahey suddenly announced that it was probably for the best that Vanzetti had agreed not to testify. He said it very casually but I noticed at once that Graham seemed greatly shocked by this. It was as if he didn't know anything about it and he immediately said that not letting Vanzetti give evidence would be a huge risk. But Vahey was real casual and insisted he had talked it over with Bart, and Bart had had agreed not to, happy to rely on the alibi given him by Trando." His father leant towards his mother and said slowly, "It was then that Graham asked Vahey if Bart had been made to realise that if a defendant failed to testify he was almost always found guilty."

His mother gasped, "Sweet Jesus, what did Mr Vahey say to that?"

"He just shrugged and said if Bart was allowed to mouth off about his religious and political views he'd be found guilty anyway, so he was damned if he did and damned if he didn't. Vahey even seemed to make a joke of it. He told Graham that in any case, the evidence that was likely to stick in the Jury's mind and what Katzmann would heavily lean on, was the guilty behaviour of Bart and Nick on the night of the arrest, added together with all those guns and shotgun shells. Their best and only way to prove Bart's innocence was to make sure Trando's alibi stuck in the minds of the Jury." He shook his head. "I tell you quite truthfully, I am now worried for Bart, really worried."

His mother was looking almost tearful. "Won't Trando's alibi be enough? He made it clear he was with Bart on the day of the robbery. Surely that will be enough?"

Trando waited anxiously for the reply, hoping it would be positive. Instead his father shrugged and said wearily. "I just don't know any more. I could see Mr Graham wasn't happy with this decision about Bart not being cross-examined and the witnesses they called today were a farce. Maybe it really does all rest on the boy's evidence." He put out his cigarette. "I'm not sure I trust that Mr Vahey. There's something about him that's just not right. I've thought that ever since Trando saw him talking to the police and that Pinkerton man. My suspicion is that he might have been doing some sort of a deal with them. After all, he knows this is an unpopular case he's defending. He might be thinking about his own career. If that is what is happening here we have already lost."

His mother said quickly, "You mustn't tell Trando any of this. The boy is worried enough as it is."

His father stood up, "I know he is, but even so, I think I should take him into court tomorrow." Alfonsine was about to object to this but to Trando's relief he stopped her. "It's only right that the boy should be there for the verdicts after all he did. I'm told they should be in by the afternoon if Bart isn't going to be called to the witness stand."

The kitchen door was then closed and although they went on talking, he couldn't make out what they were saying, so he returned to his room and pulling out his diary from under the bed he thought for a moment about what to say.

June 23rd 1920

Papa says the verdicts will be in tomorrow. I am very worried about it now as Papa doesn't seem to think that things have gone well for Bart today. They just HAVE to believe my account because everything now rests on that. I know it is a proper alibi because I only spoke the truth.

He thought for a moment and then added,

There was one good thing that happened today. I met Ella again. It is a pity she is now going to live in New York because I probably won't see her again so won't be able to have her as a friend. I would have liked her as a friend, especially as I now can't talk to Bart.

CHAPTER EIGHT

Trando sat on the bed, once again in his best clothes, now waiting to be collected for the journey to the Court House. His father had been called into work that morning, so Trando and his mother had an early lunch. The delay didn't matter because the verdicts weren't due until the afternoon anyway. He knew it was going to be a momentous day but during the morning he'd begun to feel increasingly worried about the verdict, mainly because of the conversation he'd overheard the night before. Desperately he kept reminding himself they couldn't possibly find Bart guilty as he'd been selling fish at the time of the crime, but this didn't stop the panic feelings he had inside.

He stared across at the window. There were two flies crawling up it side by side, on one of the panes. Trando watched fascinated and decided to make a silent bet on which fly would reach the top of the window first. At this moment they were level, but if the fly on the right beat the fly on the left, then it would mean that Bart would not be found guilty. He remained very still willing his fly to win, as the two flies moved slowly towards the top. They had only reached just over halfway when his father called out that they were leaving, so reluctantly he had to abandon his bet, grab his jacket and run down the stairs.

This time they didn't go by car but took the trolley bus.

As they approached the Plymouth Court-House they could see the huge crowds of people outside and some had cameras with them and Trando presumed that these must be the men from the press. They pushed their way with some difficulty up the steps and through the doors into the now familiar corridor. Here Trando was told to sit down on the bench while his parents went to the Gallery to make sure they had a seat at the front.

He glanced at the clock on the wall. It was just past two. People were standing around in small groups and everyone seemed to be talking excitedly so that the noise was deafening. Suddenly he caught sight of the Pinkerton man J.J. Hughes, talking to the policeman in charge of the case, who he now knew was called Chief Stewart. Keen to hear their conversation Trando made his way towards them, taking the greatest care not to be seen. He worked out that if he stood behind a group of people close to the men, he had a good view of them both but was still hidden.

J.J. Hughes looked at his watch and said he reckoned the jury had been out for about four hours. Stewart then asked what he thought about the verdict. At this Trando moved a few steps forward listening intently. To his horror he heard the Pinkerton man say that he was pretty optimistic they would get the verdict they wanted. His face wore a nasty smirk as he went on, "Their defence case was a mess. No-one could understand a word those Dagos were saying and as for those damned interpreters, they just drove the Jury crazy!"

Here Stewart interrupted, "But what about the boy? His evidence was rock solid. Even Katzmann couldn't shake him. Surely that must be our main worry."

Trando strained forward to hear but he had no difficulty as J. J. Hughes was speaking loudly now, full of confidence, "Yer I admit he was a problem and had us all worried at first, but Katzmann cleverly dealt with that by explaining the Brini boy had given his evidence after he had learned it by heart, parrot fashion. I think the Jury bought it, but Jesus I agree, that kid was good! He almost had me believing him." Here he gave a laugh. "Didn't you love the way he managed to cut the District Attorney down to size? There's not many can do that!"

Stewart was shaking his head, "What I still can't make out is why on earth Vanzetti didn't take the stand. It makes no sense at all. Surely he must know that it was a terrible risk to take? Who on earth was advising him?"

To Trando's horror Hughes gave another of his awful grins and tapped his finger to his nose. "That's simple. Vahey took advice and realised he just couldn't let the guy loose on the stand with the opportunity to spout out all his anarchistic rubbish. So weighing it up Vahey took it upon himself to persuade Vanzetti to see sense and refuse cross examination."

Stewart shot a surprised look at Hughes but the Pinkerton man had already started to move away saying, "Boy, I need a drink. Come on, I think we should have time."

Trando went dejectedly back to the bench and sat down. How could they think he had learned his evidence? It was a lie. And what was worse, Katzmann knew it was a lie, otherwise he wouldn't have had to use those dirty tricks. He idly wondered if his fly had reached the top of the pane first.

Looking up he saw his father coming towards him to take him to the Gallery and that had to mean that the Jury was back. He also noted that his father appeared anxious so he decided not to tell him what he'd just overheard.

On reaching their places Trando could see that the court was now absolutely packed, there was not a seat to be had and it was certainly noisier than on the first day. An air of anticipation was buzzing in the room. To his relief his parents had managed to get seats in the front row and his mother gave him her bag to sit on to enable him to see over the rail.

The lawyers returned to their places and the Jury filed back. Bart and Nick Sacco were brought in, still hand-cuffed to officers. They didn't look up, but stood waiting for the Judge to make his entrance. After a moment the side door opened and a hush fell over the room. Trando started to feel sick. His mother held his hand and squeezed it very tight. He didn't want her to, but felt it would be rude to remove it.

Judge Thayer addressed the Jury in dry, unemotional tones, "Gentlemen of the Jury, have you agreed upon your verdict?"

One man stepped forward and his father hissed in his ear, "That's the Foreman of the Jury."

The man said, "We have your Honor."

The Judge addressed him again, "How say you on the assault with intent to rob? Guilty or Not Guilty?"

There was a long pause. Trando could hardly breathe and he could feel his heart beating faster and faster.

"Guilty" the Foreman said and a gasp went up around the room.

The Judge asked him again, "And how say you on the three counts of assault with intent to murder? Guilty or Not Guilty?"

This time the answer was immediate. "Guilty."

Trando leapt to his feet shouting "No!" and then all pandemonium broke out. There was hysterical wailing from the women at the back of the gallery. Nick Sacco sank down on the chair as if he were about to faint. Bart Vanzetti remained upright and dignified, calling out in a strong voice, "Corraggio! Corraggio!" He turned, looked up and fixed his gaze on Trando, who was standing wide-eyed with horror. The hysteria increased and there were many shouts of, "They are innocent! They are innocent!"

Judge Thayer banged on the desk with his gavel. "Silence!" he barked. "Silence, or I will have the Court cleared."

The room instantly became hushed as Thayer turned and addressed the Jury in what seemed like a prepared speech.

"Gentlemen of the Jury, you may go to your homes with the feeling that you have responded, just as our brave soldiers responded, when they went across the seas to the call of their Country. Your duty is now done and I thank you all."

And without another word he left the Court Room.

Vanzetti stood impassive and calm until he and Sacco were led away. Trando wanted to cry just like his mother who wept silently beside him, but no tears would come. He felt an impotent fury at the utter injustice of it all.

Once outside they waited in the crowd while his father went to find the lawyers. Vahey was nowhere to be seen, but Graham came back with him. He looked quite distressed as he shook his head and said, "I am so sorry, so very sorry."

His father said angrily, "How could it go so wrong after what my boy said in that Court Room? You said he was the best witness you could have."

Graham shook his head. "I know you will find this hard to believe Mr Brini, but Katzmann made a very strong case for the prosecution this morning. He got the Jury to believe that Trando had learned his evidence by heart".

Trando was furious at this. "But I didn't. I only told the truth of what had actually happened."

Graham looked at him and his expression was one of genuine regret, "I know that Trando and you know that. Unfortunately the country is angry with the Italian anarchists who have committed these outrages and they don't want to believe in the innocence of our two men. The Jury was under great pressure as well. Both Katzmann and the judge made them feel it was their duty to bring in a guilty verdict. I personally believe it has been a grave miscarriage of justice, but there is little we can do now to put it right. They will be sentenced tomorrow. Believe me, I am truly sorry." He started to move away and then turned back and addressed Trando, "You should be proud of yourself Trando in spite of what has happened. You did really well in Court. I just regret there could not have been a better outcome for you."

*

Later that night Trando made a short entry in his diary.

This has been the worst day of my life. They didn't believe my evidence because that horrible Mr Katzmann said I had learned it. That is a lie. I just told them truthfully what had happened on that day. I thought I had given Bart an alibi but he has been found guilty and I KNOW he is innocent. How can I possibly help Bart now?

CHAPTER 9

Three weeks had passed since that awful day of the verdicts and the heavy atmosphere in the house in Suosso Lane did not lighten. For the most part their lives went back to normal but the strain was telling on them all. The only way to stop themselves from dwelling on the terrible recent events was to try and keep busy. Even so it was difficult to avoid the subject altogether. His father now spent a great deal of time going to meetings after he finished work, talking to other members of the Italian community and organising funds for the defence in the second trial. His mother often had neighbours round and the conversation was always of the Trial and how their men were innocent. Trando grew tired of hearing about it and spent most of his time alone in his room. Here he would lie on his bed and puzzle over why everything had suddenly gone so wrong. It was as if he was in a ship without an anchor. Always in the past, when he had been worried about things, he would immediately go to Bart and tell him. Now he was being tossed from one worrying thought to the next and there was nobody to advise him or help him understand.

The holidays arrived but he had no wish to see his friends who he didn't think would be interested in hearing about what had happened. If Ella had been around he would like to have seen her because he knew he could have talked to her about it, but she was now in New York. He hadn't even written in his diary since the day of the verdicts, mainly because there was nothing to report. Instead he spent long hours practising his violin and working away at his Italian with the red book and the dictionary. He was determined that Bart would be pleased with his progress when they next met.

*

One morning Trando found his mother once again polishing the furniture in the front room. She explained they were expecting a visit from a very important person called Carlo Tresca. He was the man Bart had visited in New York just before his arrest and this Carlo Tresca was now coming here to see them, to discuss what help could be given to Bart before the second trial. Trando kicked at the door and asked her miserably what good it would do to see anybody? It was all too late now. Bart had been sentenced to fifteen years in prison and there was nothing anyone could do about it.

Alfonsine looked at her son and for once didn't reprove him for kicking the door. She could see the affect this terrible situation was having on him and it worried her. He never played with his friends anymore but shut himself away in his room playing his violin for hours on end. Her son had changed and she felt helpless and unable to comfort him. Even his father had given up trying, but then his time was now taken up with other matters.

She put down her cloth and sat him down beside her on the window bench.

"Trando Caro, listen to me. You have to try and understand, things have now moved on. We only attended the first trial which was for the raid that took place on December 24th. Now Bart and Nick Sacco have to face a trial for the second crime where there were two murders done. This one is even more serious and they will need any help we can give them. That is why your father is busy trying to organise new lawyers because for this we will need more money."

Trando burst out, "I don't trust any lawyers. Mr Vahey wasn't on our side, I just know it. He played a dirty game and betrayed Bart.

His mother sighed, stood up and resumed her polishing. "We can only take the advice we are given Trando. Your father knows best. He will look for new lawyers, better lawyers. We will do everything we can to help Bart, you know that."

Trando nodded but his face had a set, angry expression. His mother sighed again and said, "Go and get your sister up from her rest and wheel her round the block. It will do you good to get out and you can buy a bottle of pop from the drugstore."

*

Carlo Tresca was due to arrive sometime during the afternoon on the following Saturday. The night before Trando heard his parents having yet another argument as to whether he should be allowed to sit in on the meeting. Once again his father over-ruled his mother's doubts by saying that as the boy was already involved he thought he had a right to join them, but only if he was made to understand that he was there to listen and not be allowed to say anything. When his father explained this to him he pretended he hadn't heard and nodded obediently, just grateful he was going to be allowed in on the meeting.

Just before noon a neighbour arrived and collected the baby, so that her cries wouldn't be a disturbance. After lunch the three of them sat nervously in the parlour waiting for the great man to arrive. They didn't have to wait long before a car drew up, but it wasn't one man who stepped out, but two. Vincenzo opened the door and led them into the parlour.

The first man was huge, quite the largest man Trando had ever seen. Seeing the expression on the boy's face the man laughed and bellowed out, "You think I am a big man yes? They don't call me the Bull for nothing!"

At this they all laughed and Trando saw his parents relax a little. "I am Carlo Tresca," he added in the booming voice which matched his great frame, "and this is my good friend Aldino Felicani who is also a good friend of Bart. We are pleased to be here and hope we can now be of help."

His father made the introductions, hands were shaken and they all sat down. Carlo Tresca looked across at Trando.

"I have heard a lot about you my boy. You testified for Bart in Court didn't you?" Trando nodded as Tresca said kindly, "Well, you did a great job kid. Believe me you could have done no more."

Trando could feel his face going red but was very grateful

for these kind words. Since the guilty verdict he had been lying awake at night wondering if it had somehow been his fault. Maybe if he hadn't got muddled with Mr Katzmann's questions the Jury would have been more ready to believe him. He had found it difficult to put these thoughts from his mind, but here was this man called the Bull who told him he couldn't have done more and the Bull seemed to him a man of great authority.

His father obviously thought the same and immediately addressed him.

"None of us in this community sir, can understand how this guilty verdict could have happened. Can you explain to us what went wrong with the trial? I mean the boy gave Bart a sound alibi."

Tresca turned to Felicani, "I think Aldino will be better able to answer you on that. He was there in the Court Room."

Aldino was as small and agile as Carlo Tresca was massive and ungainly. He put his hands together and thought for a moment. Clearing his throat he said in quiet precise tones, "I'm sorry to say this, but I have to tell you that those poor men didn't stand a chance. The whole Courtroom was against them. The defence was completely inadequate and quite frankly gave some very bad advice. Katzmann and Judge Thayer exploited the Red Dago and anarchist fear for all it was worth. Inevitably the result of all this meant that the Jury was only too ready to believe that Trando had learned his evidence by heart." He paused and then said with a wry smile, "Unfortunately the final blow was in not putting Vanzetti on the stand. That was fatal I'm certain." He paused again and then noticing that Vincenzo wanted to say something about that gave him no opportunity but continued more briskly, "However, that is all in the past. We now have to move on and concentrate on what best can be done for the next and far more serious trial. So, I am taking it upon myself to set up an official Defence Fund with a headquarters in Boston."

Trando was thinking that Aldino must realise that Vahey had done a bad job but presumably he didn't want to discuss it. Did he feel guilty about it? After all he had been Bart's friend.

Was he responsible for finding Vahey?

Vincenzo could contain himself no longer and burst out, "But fifteen years, it's unbelievable. Bart's an innocent man and he's been given fifteen years!"

Trando noticed at once that his mother seemed embarrassed by this outburst, but both visitors were nodding sympathetically and Tresca immediately said, "You are right Vincenzo of course. It was a terrible miscarriage of justice. But that is the reason we are here, to make sure we give you every help possible for the next trial."

Aldino Felicani added in his precise way, "And every help will be necessary I regret to say because," he drew in his breath, "it's the worst possible scenario for us. Judge Thayer is to preside in the next trial as well and Katzmann will again prosecute."

There was silence as this news sunk in.

Carlo Tresca was shaking his head, "It is damnably frustrating. Vanzetti only needed a couple days more, that is all. They'd have got rid of all the evidence by then and Sacco would have been on his way back to Italy. Now all the Italian comrades have fled and Sacco and Vanzetti are the only ones left in Massachusetts to take the full blame." He added drily, "I gather Boda slipped through the net and boarded a boat the day after the arrests."

Trando thought about this. Boda's name had kept coming up. Maybe he was one of the men who was really guilty of the crimes and now he had gone, leaving Bart to take the blame. He felt angry. What a coward that man was.

His mother stood up and offered to make tea for everyone. Trando knew he should have offered to help but was desperate not to miss anything so he stayed in his seat.

After she had left the room his father turned to Tresca and told him that their community would raise all the money they could. He then added that people had already given generously to pay for the lawyers in the first trial and now any spare money was hard to find, although they were doing their best.

Tresca nodded, seeming to understand. "Do not worry Vincenzo we realise that. It is why we will send all the finance we can from New York. We have already contacted the Workers Defence Union. They are going to organise a series of meetings in order to raise funds for you. I personally have also contacted the Civil Liberties Committee in Boston..."

Felicani interrupted with a wry smile and asked, "You can't mean those do-gooders? Don't tell me they are interested in our anarchists?"

"Well, surprisingly they are." Tresca replied. "They look on that trial as a miscarriage of justice and have taken our case on board. I'm please to tell you Aldino, that they have already sent five hundred dollars to the Defence Committee." He paused and then asked him "Do you know of a Mrs Elizabeth Glendower Evans?" Felicani said he only knew her by name. Tresca smiled. "Well you're about to get to know her pretty well. She's the widow of a Boston lawyer and is both rich and influential. For some reason she's taking a great interest in Bart and Nick's case. More importantly, she has put us in touch with Fred Moore!"

At this Felicani gave a start. "Do you mean the lawyer Fred Moore?"

Tresca smiled and said almost proudly, "Indeed I do."

Vincenzo asked, "Who is Fred Moore?"

Tresca gave Felicani a long look and said firmly, "He just happens to be the best radical lawyer in the country, added to which he has an international reputation. He will fight the cause of our guys the same way he did for the Lawrence Textile Strikers."

Trando saw that his father was impressed but he also noticed that Felicani was looking worried. "Is that really wise Carlo?" he asked. "Think of his reputation. He's a Bohemian, a womaniser, a drinker, and above all a Californian! That could really upset all those straight-laced Bostonians and more to the point, Judge Thayer!"

Tresca was about to reply to this but Alfonsine had entered with the tea things and all conversation came to a halt. Nothing more of any importance was said and the two men left soon afterwards.

*

84

Later that evening Trando wrote down the afternoon's events in his diary.

July 7th 1920

Today Papa let me sit in on a very important meeting about Bart's next trial. Two men had come down from New York to see us about it. One was called Carlo Tresca and he was nicknamed the Bull. I think he was the largest man I have ever seen and I was worried he would break Mama's best chair when he sat down. But luckily he didn't. He also had a black beard which made him look like a pirate. But I really liked him. The other man was, Aldino Felicani, who looks clever and apparently is a printer who knew Bart well. He and the Bull didn't agree on everything. Carlo Tresca told Papa they were getting in a new lawyer called Fred Moore who is very famous but who sounded a bit odd to me, although I am pleased we won't have Mr Vahey again. I don't think Aldino Felicani likes this Mr Moore much, in spite of him being famous. He finished by saying, "he may fight the cause Carlo, but can he WIN the case for us?" He almost shouted 'win' and that made me feel worried as he seemed a cleverer man than the Bull. After that we all had tea.'

He licked his pencil and then added,

'I think we had bad lawyers and I don't want to be a lawyer when I grow up. I think they are rather peculiar people and not always to be trusted.'

CHAPTER 10

It wasn't until some years later that Trando was to hear a full description of the headquarters of the Defence Committee in 5, Rollins Place, Boston. This was the large and expensive building that the new and flamboyant lawyer, Fred Moore, had chosen in order to run his operation. It soon gained the reputation of being a commune inhabited by poets, singers and actors, mixed in with the defence witnesses and a small army of helper volunteers.

Every morning Moore would arrive in his large and expensive limousine to make his way into the spacious offices that covered the entire ground floor. He would be followed into the building by his extremely large entourage, which it was noted always included several glamorous young women. Boston society observed all this and regarded it with some trepidation and a great deal of criticism. Fred Moore was rightly defined as a Bohemian in his behaviour, his looks, his way of dressing and in his companions. He had blonde hair which was worn long, right down to his shoulders and he always wore a broad-brimmed western hat. His presence was described as large in every way, which some admitted they found rather overwhelming. From the moment he arrived in the offices in the morning he made his presence felt, striding about and barking out orders in his distinctive Californian drawl.

The offices were always a hive of activity. There were at least five female stenographers, as well as Mr Moore's personal assistants, also female. The team of men, most of whom were Italians, worked long hours at trestle tables, piled high with books, files and papers and all this had to be paid for out of the defence committee fund which Aldino Felicani had started.

One of the more interesting members in the room was the

distinguished Bostonian lady mentioned by Tresca, who was called Mrs Elizabeth Glendower Evans. It was indeed Mrs Evans who later told Trando about these extraordinary times after she had become his greatest friend and ally. She gave him such a very graphic description it almost made him feel he'd been there. Her accounts always tended to be on the dramatic side. She told him that Moore's instructions were the same each day. On arrival every morning he would shout out, "We need to expand this case beyond Boston. This case is not just for the United States, but for the entire world. Appeals need to be sent out world-wide. International Unions must be informed that there is a frame-up in the offing!"

To those in the room it seemed that every day the case was becoming increasingly complicated. The prosecution were rumoured to be calling over fifty witnesses. Even the defence's witness numbers were mounting daily. The date of the trial had been set for May the following year so there was an enormous amount to be accomplished if the defence was to be ready in time. This was the pressure that Fred Moore daily put upon the hard-worked volunteers in that room.

*

While all this activity was in progress in Boston, the little house in Suosso Lane had almost returned to normal, although Bart was never far from their minds. Trando started school again, but never mentioned to his friends the subject of the impending trial. There was little he could do, but after some deliberation he decided to send a letter to Bart. He found it very difficult to write but just hoped it would give him some encouragement and let him know he was not forgotten.

January 2nd 1921
Dear Bart,
I hope you are not too lonely in prison. I miss you very much and am sorry I could not help you to get free. I am sending you a calendar which I made, which I hope you like. Papa says they have found a

famous lawyer who will save you and Mr Sacco. So I hope it won't be too long before we are selling fish again.

I am practising my violin like you said and on Saturday I am playing in a concert at the school and I will be performing your favourite, "Old Black Joe", and also a new piece, which I will play to you when they let me come and visit you. My sister Inez has now learned to walk and has to be watched all the time.

Mama and Papa are well and send their best wishes with mine, your true friend, Trando Brini.

He folded it carefully and asked his mother for an envelope. She promised to post it to Bart the next day.

A week later a letter arrived for Trando and he knew at once it must be from Bart. He ran up the stairs and into his room where he could read it in private. Bart's writing was not very legible and it took him some time to make out all the words.

January 10th 1921
Dear Trando,

I was so pleased to get your letter along with the calendar. Much obliged. And I am glad to hear all your good news. How I wish I could go to your concert and hear you play. But I tell you Trando, if I close my eyes, I CAN hear you play. I hear all my favourite music. And it brings me great joy in this dark and terrible place. So keep playing your violin Trando, and one day I will not have to close my eyes, but see and hear you for myself.

I send you love with best regards to your parents and your sister, Your true friend Bartolomeo Vanzetti.

Trando folded the letter and put it back carefully in the envelope before placing it in his box under the bed. That night he wrote in his diary,

January 17th 1921
Today I got a letter from Bart. I think he was pleased to hear from me and liked the calendar I sent him. I hope this new lawyer is not only famous but clever and they will find some witnesses to give Bart and Nick Sacco alibis.

I miss him and am beginning to find the red book too difficult

without his help. I wish he wasn't in prison. It is only four months now until the next trial. I hope they will then let him go free.

I often wonder how Ella is getting on in New York. I should like to go to New York one day. Perhaps I will when Bart gets out of prison. We could go together. I think he would like to meet Ella.

CHAPTER 11

In the three weeks before the second trial was due to take place, there was yet again a running battle in the Brini household as to whether Trando should be allowed to attend, or not. His mother was firmly against it saying he had been upset enough by the first trial but his father maintained that the boy was already involved and should be allowed to see it through. On and on it went, argument and counter-argument. His mother made a strong point in that it would mean Trando would miss school. His father countered this by saying he was a good scholar and would easily catch up. Trando would sit in his now familiar place on the landing outside his bedroom listening anxiously to the arguments and noted that they nearly always ended with his mother in tears.

"It is ruining my boy's life." she would wail, over and over again.

He was sorry that his mother should have become so upset on his behalf but he desperately hoped his father would win. His sense of panic increased as he heard his mother trying other reasons for him not to attend; 'it would make the boy ill, he would have no time for his violin practice and he would have to witness many unpleasant people saying horrible things about Bart'. Every point was argued out in heated discussion until in the end a compromise was reached. Trando would be allowed to attend the first two days. Then, when school had finished and if the trial was still running, he could go back to the Court until it was over. His father agreed to this, saying that the trial could possibly go on for weeks. He reasoned that at least if Trando went for a couple of days when it began, he would be able to see Bart again and that would be of some comfort to the boy.

Trando wondered, not for the first time, why grown-ups had

90

to make everything so difficult but he was relieved to be told of the compromise they had eventually hammered out.

*

On the morning of May 31st 1921, he was once again in his best clothes ready to set out for the Court House. This second trial was not in Bridgewater, but in Dedham in Norfolk County, which necessitated a longer journey.

The Dedham building was an even more imposing one than the Bridgewater Court House, with its high white central dome and windows shaped like portholes. When he first saw the building Trando thought it looked a bit like the picture of an ocean liner Bart had once shown him. He later learned from Mrs Evans that it was Greek revival in architecture and was exactly one hundred years old. It was situated on the main street but to each side there were lawns with large trees providing shade for those sitting in the hot summer sun. Trando and his parents arrived in good time and stood outside observing all that was going on. Already large crowds of people had gathered on either side of the street and were now spilling out on the lawns outside the Courthouse. This was no surprise to Trando as he had been told many times that Bart's case had become famous not only in the Boston area but throughout the country and even abroad.

Just after they arrived, a grand limousine drew up and the excitement of the crowd greatly increased. A tall man with long fair hair under his broad brimmed hat stepped out and waved to the crowds. Trando immediately knew that this had to be the famous lawyer, Fred Moore. One or two people clapped and there was the odd cheer, as Moore strode purposefully into the Court House, followed by a group of people all carrying heavy boxes and files.

The noise died down again and it was after this that Trando witnessed a scene that was to be etched forever on his mind. In the distance he caught sight of Bart and Nick Sacco, in grey prison uniforms and hand-cuffed, being marched in the middle of the street, flagged by two prison officers. The crowd on either side of the road fell completely silent as they watched the slow progress of the two prisoners. As they drew nearer Trando desperately wanted Bart to look round so he could wave to him, but both he and Nick stared straight ahead.

His father turned to him and said, "They have been brought down from the county jail" adding with a shake of his head, "it sure is a long walk if they have to do that four times a day." He looked at his wife, "We'd better go in Alfonsine. There is going to be a crowd in there. It's just as well we have been given passes."

With some difficulty they made their way inside, not into a corridor as with the Plymouth building, but into a large lobby which was heaving with people all pushing and talking excitedly. Nobody was being allowed into the Court Room yet, so they had to stand in line by the doorway that led into the public area.

Trando looked around and suddenly caught sight of the Pinkerton man Hughes, talking to the police chief Stewart. They were standing on the other side of the lobby. Listening to their conversations had now become something of a habit with him, so giving the excuse to his mother that he wanted to have a drink from the water fountain, he crossed over to where he could hear them talking. As he reached within earshot he distinctly heard the name Fred Moore mentioned. Stewart was saying, "... you know I watched Moore swearing in the Jury and he was like a madman, jumping up and down with constant objections and interruptions. He insisted on challenging every juror! Old Judge Thayer got mighty riled I can tell you..."

Hughes interrupted him with a chuckle, "I tell you Chief, that's just what I like to hear. It is great news for our side. The more the old judge is riled by that Californian the more likely we are to get a conviction," and he added scornfully, "That Fred Moore is just a showman. I've seen it all before. The Bostonians won't like him one little bit. I'm of the opinion that the defence has made a bad misjudgement getting him." He was quiet for a moment seemingly lost in thought and then he added, "Of course less good is the fact that Moore has the McArney brothers alongside him. Those two are damned good defence lawyers."

Stewart nodded, "I agree but Katzmann has Harold Williams. He's a good guy too and has given us plenty of convictions."

Hughes snorted, "Yer but take it from me, he won't get a look in. Katzmann will hold the floor on this one, you can bet your bottom dollar on that!"

He moved to wave at someone and Trando had to duck so as not to be seen. Hughes continued "How are the prisoners behaving themselves?"

This brought a shrug from the police chief. "I've no real complaints. Both continue to maintain their innocence, so there's no surprise there. My God that Sacco is a hothead but I don't pay much attention to him. Vanzetti on the other hand is different. He's a powerful guy and clever too. When I drove him to the Plymouth trial we were on quite friendly terms. Sometimes he'd even sing Italian songs. Then came the day I had to testify against him in Court." He paused and looked directly at Hughes. "The next time he saw me, he raised his hands and although he was handcuffed, he shook them at me. He's not spoken to me since." He paused again and gave a shudder. "That man has terrible eyes. It's like fire when he looks at you. I'm sure glad I don't have to drive him anymore. He is..."

At this moment Trando heard someone calling his name. He darted back to join his mother who said crossly, "Trando, what took you so long? I thought we had lost you. We need to get into the Court Room now. Your father has gone on ahead."

*

The upstairs gallery in the Dedham Court Room was reserved for members of the press, so this time those who had passes were on the ground floor. The public areas were packed with people and once again it was stiflingly hot. Trando looked around him. Bart and Nick were no longer handcuffed but were in a great iron cage in the centre of the room where they sat, staring straight ahead. He longed to call out but knew he shouldn't, so he studied the room instead. On one side of the cage were the defence lawyers, Moore and the McArney brothers that Hughes had just mentioned. He was glad the brothers had such a good reputation. They looked rather alike and he wondered if they were twins. It was evident they might need them if Moore was going to upset the judge. Then Trando caught sight of Katzmann again, white-haired and florid, sitting the other side of the cage. Feelings of hatred swept over him. He blamed Katzmann for the fact that they were here now, Katzmann and of course that Judge Thayer. Next to Katzmann was a man who he presumed must be Williams, the assistant District Attorney.

Suddenly the side door opened with a loud bang making him jump. Judge Thayer swept in and a hush fell over the room. Trando thought him even thinner and more shrunken than he remembered from the first trial. His skin was the colour of parchment, in stark contrast to his black silk robe. He looked like some terrible old wizard from one of those fairy stories.

"Court" shouted the Bailiff, so loudly it again made Trando jump. "Hear ye! Hear ye! All persons having anything to do before the Honourable, the Justices of the Superior Court, now sitting within and for the County of Norfolk, draw near and give your attention, and you shall be heard! God save the Commonwealth of Massachusetts!"

And with that the morning's proceedings began.

Trando noticed what he thought was a very distinguished-looking, grey haired lady sitting in the front row near Rosina Sacco. She sat very upright and had a notebook and pencil in her hand in which she seemed to be making a lot of notes. He wondered if this could be the important lady called Mrs Elizabeth Glendower Evans who Carlo Tresca had mentioned.

Williams rose to make the opening statement for the prosecution, setting out exactly what they hoped to prove. He had a rather monotonous voice which, combined with the heat in the room, made it difficult for Trando to concentrate.

He began by addressing the Jury, "Members of the Jury, this crime was committed by five men, two of whom we believe stand here before you. It is the contention of the Commonwealth that during this hold-up, use was made of a stolen Buick car. On the morning of the murder this car was taken from the Coacci house and was driven to South Braintree; there they picked up Vanzetti at East Braintree station. The man who drove that car, was familiar with the roads leading to and from the location of the shooting..."

Trando's attention began to wander. He looked across at the Jury, all of whom were men, and they seemed to be listening intently to Williams. Was it possible they had made their minds up already? Trando now looked at Bart and Nick Sacco. They were listening intently as well.

On and on the voices droned.

When Williams at last finished, one of the McArney brothers stood up and made the opening statement for the defence. This was shorter and more precise, but it had been a long morning and it was with some relief for Trando when they broke for lunch. With his parents he walked out into the bright sunshine.

His father looked at him and smiled, "I think you found that a bit boring didn't you son?" Trando smiled back. "Yes, I did a bit. I guess it will be more interesting when the witnesses are being questioned."

They sat in the shade and his mother unpacked their picnic lunch. Vincenzo suddenly laughed, "They tell me all the important people go to lunch at the Dedham Inn a few blocks from here. I'd love to be a fly on the wall in that place. I guess the prosecution and defence lawyers sit either side of the room, with Judge Thayer in the middle keeping the peace!" And he laughed again obviously greatly amused by this idea.

Trando thought about this and then asked, "Where will Bart eat?"

"Oh, they've been marched back to the jail poor bloody bastards." Alfonsine shot her husband a reproving look for his use of bad language in front of Trando but he took no notice. "Whether they get lunch or not I have no idea, but even if they do, the food is terrible in those prisons. Bart's already lost a lot of weight."

His mother murmured, "Poor, dear Bart," and looked near to tears again.

Trando had been searching for Hughes and Stewart among the crowd but they were nowhere to be seen, so he presumed they might be up at the Dedham Inn with Katzmann. "Can I walk around for a bit?" he asked.

"Good idea," his father said, "it might be a long afternoon." He gave a laugh. "These lawyer guys sure do like to hear the sound of their own voices."

"Don't be long," his mother called after him, "and don't get lost!"

Trando wandered off still hoping he might find Hughes and Stewart. He crossed over to the lawn the other side of the driveway and it was then that he noticed the lady he'd presumed was Mrs Evans sitting on a bench under a tree, still writing entries in her notebook. She looked up as he came closer and smiled.

"Goodness me, I do believe you must be the youngest person here. I noticed you in the Court Room."

Trando smiled back. "Yes ma'am. I think I probably am the youngest."

She held out her hand, "I'm Elizabeth Evans and I'm very pleased to meet you."

So he'd been right. He shook hands and said shyly, "I'm Beltrando Brini, although they usually call me Trando."

Mrs Evans immediately became interested and for a moment made a study of him. Then she patted the bench and he sat down beside her. "So, you are the famous Brini boy. I read the evidence you gave at the last trial."

Trando felt a little embarrassed. He hung his head and said sadly, "It didn't do much good Ma'am. The jury didn't believe me. They thought I had learned it by heart." He looked up and added hotly, "But I hadn't. Every word I said was true. "

She patted his knee. "Of course it was Trando. It was only that dreadful man Katzmann twisting everything you said, which led to such a dreadful miscarriage of justice. It is precisely why I am here. I am very much hoping that a wrong can now be put right." Trando felt encouraged by this as she went on, "You see Trando, my late husband was a brilliant lawyer who fought for justice all his life. He would have been horrified by that Bridgewater trial." She looked at him and asked, "Are you going to be here every day?"

Trando shook his head. "No ma'am. I want to be here but my mother didn't really want me to come at all. Luckily my father thought I should see Bart again, because Bart is my great friend and because I was a witness before. They will let me return tomorrow for one more day, when the witnesses start. After that I will go back to school. I am hoping to return when the holidays begin."

Mrs Evans spoke grimly, "I am very interested to see and hear all those witnesses that the prosecution have managed to dredge up."

Trando suddenly felt he had found a friend and ally, so he ventured to say, "I think I can be useful too."

Mrs Evans looked surprised, "Useful my dear boy? In what way can you be useful?"

Trando spoke quickly, "Well you see, I get to hear things. I listen in on conversations between the Pinkerton man Hughes and the policeman Stewart. They seem to know everything that is going on with the other side." He stopped, feeling a little guilty about his behaviour but Mrs Evans threw back her head and laughed.

"Why, that is wonderful Trando. You can be of real help to our cause. You can be our own special spy!"

"Except that after tomorrow I won't be able to." Trando pointed out.

"Don't worry," she said cheerfully, "I will do it instead. It's wonderful idea, quite wonderful, although I won't be able to make myself quite as inconspicuous as you." She looked up and pointed towards the road. "Look those poor men are returning. We had better return to the Court Room. I will see you again Trando Brini."

*

The afternoon turned out to be very similar to the morning.

On the journey home Trando was tempted to tell his parents of his lunchtime encounter with Mrs Evans, but then decided to keep it as his secret for the moment and just write an account of it in his diary,

May 31st 1921

Today was the first day of the second trial and to be quite truthful I found it a bit boring. But I was very pleased to see Bart again, although he didn't see me. Tomorrow I will try to get nearer to him and wave. He is very thin and looks ill. Papa tells me they have nasty food in the prison. Perhaps Mama could make him some cookies, although the guards might not let him have them.

I met a very interesting lady at lunch time and she is definitely on our side. She must be quite rich because she looked smart and grand and wore a fur collar even though it was a hot day. It seems she was married to a lawyer who believed in justice. I think she lives in Boston. She is going to be at the Trial every day. I told her about being a spy and she thought that was a great idea. I hope I can overhear some more conversation from Hughes and Stewart tomorrow. It is my last chance until school ends and I do have one worry. I know Mrs Evans wants to help and I didn't want to be rude but I think she would be noticed if she went near to them. I wish Papa would let me go to the Trial every day, but I know he won't. He has promised to tell me everything that is happening but it's not the same.

I hope Bart is all right. He and Mr Sacco look very tired and unhappy and Rosina Sacco cries all the time. Everyone is worried.

I wish none of this had happened.

98

CHAPTER 12

Trando woke up very early the next day and was immediately aware that his head was both painful and throbbing. He tried to sit up but this only made him feel worse. There was a strange sensation in his arms and hands and he realized he was very hot. A sense of panic overtook him. 'I can't be ill today, I just can't. I have to get to Court.' He lay back and waited for his mother to come to his room and immediately she confirmed his worst fears. After feeling his forehead she declared firmly that he had a fever and would be going nowhere until that had broken. Their friend Dr Freddi visited him later that day and reassured him that it was nothing serious, he would just need a few days in bed. Even so, it was nearly a week before Trando was well enough to return for the promised second day in Court. Reluctantly his mother declared at breakfast he was recovered enough to go and Trando thought a little guiltily that she was probably growing tired of the endless arguments. She told him she wasn't going to accompany them that day because of having to organise a fund-raising tea-party for the afternoon. Funds continually had to be found to pay for the lawyers and this was a desperate struggle, although Trando could see that everyone in the Italian community was doing all they could. Fund-raising events seemed to have taken over their lives.

He helped his mother prepare the food until his father arrived back from work. It was difficult not to show his impatience but he knew there had been a delay in setting out because his father had been called to attend to some business first thing. Because of this they didn't reach the Court Room until halfway through the mid-morning session and it was with some difficulty that they finally persuaded the man at the door to allow them to creep in and sit at the back.

Once in their seats Trando's attention was immediately drawn to the witness box where a large, blonde lady in a very low cut dress and wearing a very bright lipstick, was now being cross-examined by Katzmann. The lawyer was smiling at her and spoke in a patient way, almost as if he were talking to a child. He's much nicer to her than he was to me Trando thought and his feelings of anger towards the man increased.

"Now Miss Andrews..." she interrupted him at once.

"Oh please sir, won't you call me Lola?" and she gave him a smile, fluttering her eyelashes. Trando watched fascinated.

Katzmann started again. "Well then, Lola. Tell us in your own words what happened that day." He gave her an encouraging nod and she began, hesitantly at first, as if trying to remember what she had obviously been told to say, so the words came slowly.

"I was walking down Pearl Street towards the Slater and Pearl factory and there was this car parked..." she hesitated, took a big breath and continued, "...with a pale man in the driver's seat of a touring car, and there was this DARK man under the car. As the DARK man came out from under the car I asked him for directions. And he told me the way that would lead me to the factory office." She finished with a flourish and a look of triumph.

Katzmann leaned forward, "And do you see this dark man in the courtroom now?"

Lola Andrews, without a look and with no hesitation, raised a bare, fleshy arm and pointed at Nick Sacco.

"Yes sir, I do sir. Yes sir, it was that man there."

Nick leapt to his feet and shouted loudly, "I am the man? No! Do you mean me? You lie! Take a good look!"

Judge Thayer hit the desk with his gavel and rapped out, "The prisoner will be silent!"

Katzmann looked contented enough and sat down. Moore stood up.

Trando made his first proper study of the famous Fred Moore. He had only seen him with his hat on, but now it had been removed he saw he had great dark bushy eyebrows which in contrast to his fair hair gave his face a very fierce expression. He decided he was definitely a match for Mr Katzmann and felt relieved. Both men were very intimidating. It was going to be a real battle in the Court Room. He leant forward as Fred Moore started his cross examination in his Californian drawl.

"Miss Andrews, isn't it true that in January you were shown a selection of photographs, including one of Nicola Sacco and you maintained then that he was *not* the man you had talked with in South Braintree?"

Lola looked uncomfortable and said sulkily, "I don't recall no such thing."

Moore barked back at her, "It is on record in the stenographer's report." Her eyes widened as Moore continued, "And isn't it true that in February, Chief Stewart took you down to Dedham jail where you were shown Mr Sacco through the cell grating?" Lola was visibly beginning to crumble as Moore continued relentlessly, "And isn't it true that your companion of that day, Mrs Campbell, said that the *only* person on the street you talked to was a *fair* haired man dressed in khaki, who was *not* under an automobile?"

There was a ripple of laughter in the room. Moore held up his hand for silence. "Miss Andrews, are you *still* telling us that the man you talked to was a *dark* man?"

Before she could answer Judge Thayer intervened and said caustically, "I thought we had been through all this before."

Moore turned to the Judge and said politely, "I am merely trying to show your Honour, that much of the testimony of this witness is one of hopeless confusion."

The Judge said irritably, "That is an unfair criticism of any witness. You will kindly refrain from taking up a subject that has already been exhausted."

Moore gave an ironic bow and Lola Andrews looked gratefully at the Judge and gave him one of her simpering smiles. However, as she turned back she could see that the cross-examination was about to start again and she knew could expect no mercy from Mr Moore. So she decided to faint, which she did in dramatic fashion adding several gasps and sighs as she fell to the floor. There was immediate uproar in the room. It took several minutes for the ushers to remove Lola Andrews who was making the most of her moment in the limelight and by this time Judge Thayer had lost all patience and declared they would take an early lunch. His irritation was further increased by a momentary thunder storm and there was considerable delay while a car had to be found to take him up to the Dedham Inn.

Trando sat on a bench in the lobby with his father and ate some of their packed lunch, but he wasn't feeling very hungry. They discussed the morning's events and Trando felt pleased by the way that his father treated him more like an adult when his mother wasn't around. They both agreed that Lola Andrews had been a hopeless witness but Trando said that it had really been very funny and they both laughed. His father added, "If they go on like this they will have no case against Bart and Nick at all and they will have to find them innocent."

This sounded encouraging and Trando felt pleased with the way things were going,

"Can I walk around for a bit Papa?"

His father nodded and looked pleased, because in all honesty he wanted to have a wander himself. He had made some good friends during these first days of the trial and looked forward to hearing what they had made of the performance from Miss Lola Andrews.

Trando dodged in and out of the groups of people in the crowded lobby hoping to find Mrs Evans, to explain to her that he had been ill. He had seen her in Court writing away as usual, but now there was no sign of her. Instead he caught sight of Stewart and Hughes with another man, and from their expressions they weren't too happy. Maybe they were annoyed because they hadn't been able to go for lunch at the Dedham Inn with all that rain? Trando took up his usual stance, out of sight but within earshot. He listened to Chief Stewart saying, "The fact is JJ, your witnesses aren't holding up too good. Moore is driving them hard and even if that antagonises the Judge, it is still not great for us.

Hughes nodded grimly, "I'm afraid you're in the right there. I guess I under-estimated Moore's cross-examining powers." He paused. "On the other hand the Jury don't like his bullying tactics either." He suddenly sounded angry as he said, "Jesus! You'd think out of all those witnesses we rounded up we'd have been sure to get something to stick? God knows, we've paid them enough!"

"You're right." Stewart sounded grim, but then added more cheerfully, "I am pretty sure the Sacco and Vanzetti alibis are going to be very shaky, added to which the defence only have Italian witnesses and they will have to use those damned interpreters again, which will be irritating for the jury." He gave a laugh which sounded more like a bark. "In any case, Katzmann will make much of the fact that Dagoes always stand together."

The Pinkerton man sounded impatient. "Even so Mike, I need something positive if we are to get convictions." He turned to the other man standing with them who up to that point had remained silent. "Captain Proctor, you are the ballistics expert. Can you give us a definite on it being Sacco's colt that fired the fatal shot?"

To his great surprise Trando saw Captain Proctor shake his head. "I'm afraid I can't do that sir. You're not going to like me saying this, but I am not at all sure you have the right men."

Trando couldn't believe what he was hearing and gave an involuntary gasp. This was going to be great news to tell Mrs Evans, if he ever found her again.

Captain Proctor continued, "You see, in my opinion this hold-up was a real professional job and Sacco and Vanzetti are just not your professional guys."

Hughes looked shaken by this and sounded annoyed. He almost snapped, "That will be for a jury to decide." He glanced angrily at the man, "I want to understand you correctly Proctor, so let me get this clear. Are you saying that under cross-examination you couldn't say that Bullet 111 was fired from Sacco's colt?"

Proctor paused before replying, "In all conscience the best I could do is to say that the bullet is *consistent* with being fired by that pistol."

Hughes considered this and his voice became calmer. "Right, well, we just have to hope the defence don't pick up on that. In any case they still have to explain away the arsenal their boys were carrying when arrested." He looked at his watch, "We'd better report back to Katzmann and Williams before the afternoon session starts."

They moved away and Trando, excited about all this latest information once again looked round for Mrs Evans, but still unable to find her he returned to the bench to wait for his father.

The afternoon's session started with a strange and even comical incident. The thunder storm having passed, the humid atmosphere in the court room had yet again become stifling and everyone was beginning to feel discomfort with the heat, so Moore decided to remove his jacket and shoes just as the bailiff shouted 'Court!'

Everyone stood as Judge Thayer entered and then sat down waiting for proceedings to begin. However at this moment the Judge now noticed the state of Moore's appearance and snapped angrily, "For God's sake. Have you no sense of decorum sir? This is a Courtroom. Proper dress will be maintained at all times!"

For a moment it looked as if Moore would say something, but in the end he just shrugged his shoulders and with a rather bad grace put his jacket back on.

After that there were no more dramas. A series of prosecution witnesses were called and proved as inadequate as Lola Andrews had been. Katzmann took them through their shaky evidence only to have it blown away each time by Moore. Trando glanced round and was pleased to see the Pinkerton man was looking increasingly annoyed.

The last witness of the day was cross-examined about a cap, which was produced as evidence because it had been picked up at the scene of the crime. Katzmann now tried to prove that this cap belonged to Sacco. Nick Sacco had a very large head and it was obvious to everyone in the room that the cap that was shown could never have fitted him. A witness was called, who was the son of Sacco's employer. Katzmann asked him if the cap that was being shown to him belonged to Sacco. The poor man looked embarrassed and hung his head. Trando could tell that this man knew what Katzmann needed him to say and he didn't want to displease the Judge, but he eventually stammered out, he couldn't possibly remember the details of all the caps that were worn by the workers in the factory, so he couldn't say for sure if it belonged to Sacco. Moore then stood up and asked him in a severe voice to answer yes or no as to whether it was Sacco's cap or not, to which the young man replied, "No. I couldn't say right down in my heart that the cap belonged to Mr Sacco."

The Judge interrupted, "Do you mean it is alike in appearance to the one worn by Mr Sacco?"

The young man looked relieved. "In colour only," he replied.

Moore rose to his feet and said with an element of sarcasm, "I am most grateful to your Honour for allowing that to be made clear to the Jury."

At this there was a titter of laughter around the room, the Judge glowered and the poor man was allowed to step down.

*

After that proceedings for the day came to the end. Trando was convinced that it was all a ridiculous waste of time, it was quite obvious there was no case against Nick and Bart and he felt cheerful with the way things had gone. Not one of the witnesses he had seen had been able to identify either Nick or Bart being at the scene of the crime. He went outside and waited while his father went off and spoke to a group of his friends.

"So *there* you are Beltrando Brini! I wondered where you had disappeared to." He turned round and saw it was Mrs Evans. Trando quickly explained to her about getting ill and not being able to get to court. "Well," she said with a smile, "you haven't missed much. The whole trial is turning into a complete farce. I'm afraid it's another complete travesty of justice." And here she lowered her voice, "I must tell you Trando, I have taken a leaf out of your book and done a bit of spying myself! Today, at lunchtime, I went to the Dedham Inn, mainly because it was raining so hard I couldn't stay outside. I'm pleased to report it was a very good move. Judge Thayer and the lawyers were sitting at one table and quite near them, on another table, were several reporters. Suddenly the Judge threw down his napkin and walked over to the press table. He was obviously extremely angry because he actually shouted at them!"

And then, to Trando's astonishment, Mrs Evans imitated Judge Thayer's voice.

"I would like to know if you men of the press have ever witnessed so many leaflets that have been spread about, saying that people cannot get a fair trial in the State of Massachusetts? Have you ever seen the like of it before? Sibley, you're the oldest. What do you think? "

"What did Sibley think?" Trando asked fascinated by this account, especially as it was so graphically given.

Mrs Evans chuckled. "I know old Sibley. He is a devious fellow, but on this occasion this deviousness worked well for him. He looked at the Judge and said very calmly but emphasising every word, 'I can honestly say your Honour, that I have never seen anything like it before in my life.' Well of course this made all his companions laugh and that only made Judge Thayer even angrier and off he went again." She put on the Judge's voice once more, "'Well, I am telling you here and now, that I will personally see to it that the defendants *do* get a fair trial. So I think I am entitled to have *that* statement reported in the Boston papers. Do I make myself clear?' He was just moving away when he shouted to the entire place, 'I also want to make it clear to you men that I will have no long-haired anarchist from California running my court!'" Mrs Evans chuckled. "I'm afraid that was greeted with even more laughter from the reporters." Then she sighed, "But of course this does have a more serious side. The consequence of all this is that Mr Moore and Mr Thayer are now sworn enemies and it may not help Vanzetti and Sacco in the long run, although I have to admit that Moore has done a good job so far in demolishing their witnesses. I do so hope that now the McArney brothers can be given a greater role in future proceedings. They are good lawyers and will calm things down when Moore gets overheated!"

Trando felt very privileged that a great lady like Mrs Evans should take him into her confidence in this way and he was about to tell her about his own spying of the morning when he saw his father returning, so he quickly said, "I'm afraid I won't be able to attend Court again now, not until the school holidays begin, but I hope to see you after that."

She looked at him and smiled. "I think this Trial has a few more weeks to run, so I look forward to seeing you again soon Trando Brini. Meanwhile, I will try and remember everything of importance that has happened so I can report to you next time we meet."

With that she walked briskly away across the lobby. His father watched her as she swept majestically through the main doors that were being held open for her.

"Who was that lady you were talking to Trando?" To which he replied evasively, "Oh just someone who wanted to talk about the Trial."

On the way home he remembered that he hadn't told Mrs Evans about the bullets and made a mental note to tell her the next time he saw her.

CHAPTER 13

Trando reluctantly went back to school the next day. He informed his classmates only that he had been unwell and didn't mention the trial at all. It just seemed simpler than inviting the questioning he knew would inevitably follow. The summer holidays were only a couple of weeks away and it was his hope that once school was over his father would let him go back to Court.

A few days later he was up in his room practising his violin, when he heard the doorbell ring and looking out of the window he saw it was Rosina Sacco. He heard his mother greeting Rosina and then they both went into the kitchen. Trando returned to his practising. There was nothing very strange in this visit because his mother had become good friends with Nick's wife from their days in the court room together and Rosina would frequently come over at the weekends when there were no trial proceedings.

He had only just resumed his practice when there another ring on the doorbell. This time it was the two McArney brothers on the doorstep and it was his father who answered the door. They went into the front room and his father called out, "They're here Alfonsine. You can come and join us."

Something important was definitely happening. This had to be a meeting of some kind and Trando immediately took up his usual position on the landing. Unfortunately the parlour door had been firmly shut, so yet again he was forced to go down the stairs in order to be able to hear what was being said. With his ear right up against the door he heard his father thanking the lawyers for coming over at such short notice and then Rosina started talking. It actually sounded to Trando more like a long wail, because she seemed terribly upset and angry and she was obviously addressing the lawyers.

"You must understand, I ask Vincenzo to call you here because I want you to get rid of this Mr Moore. He is no good. I don't believe in him. Nobody believes in him. I want a proper lawyer for Nick and Bart, not this," here she paused, until she finally spat out the word, "showman!"

It was one of the McArney brothers who replied to this and he sounded most apologetic, "We do understand the problem Mrs Sacco. Your husband has said the same thing to us in even stronger words."

Trando wondered what Bart thought of Mr Moore as well and whether he had also spoken to the McArney brothers.

The lawyer continued, "I think you should know that during the swearing in of the Jury, we were already worried because we could see that Mr Moore was antagonising the Judge, which is never a good thing to do, especially with Judge Thayer. I even offered to forego my first payment in order to persuade Moore to retire. But he wouldn't and I am afraid it is now too late. We just have to try for damage limitation." He paused, "In all fairness, he has had some success in exposing the inadequacies of the prosecution witnesses."

The other brother added, "He *has* worked extremely hard on getting publicity Mrs Sacco. This trial is now famous world-wide."

Rosina Sacco burst out, "We do not need fame sir. We need justice. We cannot get that while this Mr Moore fights with everybody. He makes the Judge angry, the Jury angry. All the time he is," she paused, "how do you say it, over-turned?"

"Over-ruled."

"Yes that is it. He is over-ruled, all the time. And he spends the money the Defence Committee find for him on his big expensive house and his fast cars and his women and his grand eating. That money comes from poor Italians, who give all their savings to help Nick and Bart. Not to spend on this greedy man. Nick says to me, get rid of him. Nick says Mr Moore is only in it for the money and the fame of his own person." Her voice was getting more and more shrill as she cried out, "I say get rid of him. If he stays, I know Nick and Bart will go to the electric chair."

With this Rosina Sacco broke into loud sobs and everyone started talking at once.

Trando had heard enough. He went back into his room and took out the diary from under his bed, sat at his desk and started to write,

June 28th 1921

The news is so terrible I can hardly bear to write it. It seems Aldino Felicani was right. The famous lawyer Fred Moore turns out to be no good for Bart and Nick as he has made both the judge and jury angry. In fact he is making things worse and everyone thinks he is bad for us and Rosina Sacco thinks it will end up with them being sent to the electric chair. My hand is shaking while I am writing down such awful things. How could it all have gone so horribly wrong? When I was in court Mr Moore was doing very well with their witnesses, showing them to be liars. Now, it seems they don't mind about the witnesses being liars or which Italians are punished, as long as someone is. I MUST try and persuade Papa to let me go back to Court. Perhaps I can ask Mrs Evans to do something because she is rich and influential. I really need to see how Bart is.

He sat back and thought for a moment and then added,

Today I won a prize at school and was praised for my playing in the concert, but I don't really mind about these things. None of it matters if I can't tell Bart about them. I am not allowed to write to him, not while the trial is going on.

I will offer to help Papa in the gardens tomorrow and ask if I can go back to the Trial next week.

*

Vincenzo was both surprised and pleased to have Trando's offer of help the next day. The boy worked hard and in two hours they had picked all the vegetables they needed, a job that usually took him the whole morning.

As they sat on a bench in the shade, drinking the cool

lemonade, Trando said, "Papa, would it be possible for me to go back to the Trial next week? It is holidays now, so I wouldn't be missing any school. "

His father thought about this for what seemed a long time.

Trando watched him and wondered whether he should say more to persuade him. He was now fourteen and over the last year he knew he had changed. Maybe it was because of everything that had happened, but he no longer felt like a boy, more like a man. How could he say that to him? He also realised his father would be thinking about the effect his request would have on his mother. He knew only too well that she was worried and had made it very clear that she wanted Trando to stay away from the Trial. How could he persuade his father otherwise? And there was another thing. He was sure it would be good for his father to have some male company. All the women, that is the wives and mothers, became so emotional whenever the subject was being discussed he could tell that his father and his men friends now tried to avoid it altogether. It would be different with him. He could show his father that he could think things out, coolly and sensibly, and if he felt emotional, he wouldn't show it. It was important he should know he could talk to him about the trial, man to man. Trando suddenly felt impatient. Didn't his father realise it would mean everything to him to be able to get back to the court and see Bart again?

He gave a loud sigh which made his father look across at him.

"I'll ask your mother," he said at last. "I know Bart will be taking the stand next week, so that would be the best time for you to go in."

Trando thanked him and tried not to show his relief too much. He felt sure his mother could be persuaded because he had observed that his father usually had his own way in the end. Staring out across the allotment he noticed that the rows of vegetables almost shimmered in the hot sunlight. A few birds darted about. There wasn't a cloud in the sky and not a breath of wind. The tree under which they were sitting didn't move a leaf. All was calm and peaceful. Here he was, sitting with his father, who was treating him like a grown-up and they had just done a good morning's work together. Life felt good.

Yet, in another place, Bart was sitting in a dark prison cell, with the threat of the electric chair hanging over him. Not for the first time Trando thought that it was all very hard to understand. His mother was convinced that everything that happened in your life was down to fate, she was sure that you had no control over it because your life was ordained for you from birth. Of course she was also a devout Catholic and believed that God looked after us and would always take care of things. Trando was not so sure about any of that, especially now, because if that were true Bart would not be in this terrible situation. It made no sense at all to him. Bart was a good man, a peaceable man who wouldn't harm a soul, and yet there he was, wrongly accused and on trial for his life. What was God doing about that? He certainly didn't seem to be on the side of justice.

Trando had often thought, as he sat through the long services in church, that you could pray to be a better person, but there really didn't seem much point in asking God to intervene for you when things went wrong. In his experience God took absolutely no notice. No, he was convinced there had to be a way of seizing back control yourself and fighting to put things right on your own. Sitting in the peace of the garden he found himself making a solemn vow. He would not give up on Bart whatever happened. Not ever.

*

Over the next few days he did his best to be patient and took great care not to mention the Trial. He was also careful to keep to himself, although he did offer to help whenever he saw an opportunity. At last his patience and efforts were rewarded and he received the news he had been waiting for. His father came up to his room and informed him that he could go to Court the following day because it was very likely that Bart would be in the witness box.

Trando found sleep difficult that night and tossed and turned in his bed wondering what the day would bring. Sometimes he lay on his back and stared at the moon, not sure whether he felt nervous, or excited, or both at the same time. His fervent hope was that Bart would remain calm and not become angry when Katzmann questioned him. He also thought about the added worry of the apparent erratic behaviour of Fred Moore and this worried him. Maybe the McArney brothers would now take over some of the work.

*

At his request they arrived early the next day in order to get a good place in the Court Room, so they were already sitting when Mrs Evans made her entrance. She went straight to her seat at the front without looking round, which left Trando hoping he could find her during the recess for lunch.

The day's proceedings started with a good deal of boring preliminaries and clarifications. Then one of the McArney brothers stood up.

"That's Jerry McArney," his father whispered, "I think his brother is called Thomas. Jerry is the taller one."

Jerry McArney turned to the cage where the prisoners were sitting.

"Will the defendant Vanzetti be brought forward?"

An immediate murmur went round the room. A deputy unlocked the metal door of the cage and Bart stepped out, with a deputy on either side. He was led to the witness box and raised his hand in oath before the clerk. One deputy then put handcuffs on him again and they returned to their seats. Trando thought miserably how old and ill Bart looked.

The usual questions were asked about the prisoner's name and age. Trando took the opportunity to study Bart more carefully. He had lost that fiery look of nervous energy that had been so noticeable in the past and he now just looked frail, although it was some relief to Trando that his demeanour remained dignified and calm.

Jerry McArney said, "Mr Vanzetti, I want to turn to the

evening of May 5th, 1920. Can you tell me in your own words what happened that evening?"

Every pair of eyes in the room were staring at Vanzetti, with his long, drooping moustache and eyes so dark they were almost black; 'blackberry dark' one newspaper had called them. There was complete silence as Vanzetti began to speak, in a slow but clear voice.

"On the evening of May 5th I went with Nick Sacco to collect a car from Johnson's house. Orciani with Boda had gone on ahead. I had stayed behind to write a speech for the Sunday meeting."

At the mention of the meeting Trando glanced quickly across the room and saw Hughes and Stewart exchange meaningful glances. He wished Bart wouldn't talk about those meetings.

Vanzetti continued, "But when we got to Johnson's house, we were told that the car was not yet ready."

"For what purpose did you need the car?" McArney asked.

"We needed it to collect material like books and newspapers. Five or six of my friends had plenty of literature. We needed to get rid of it."

"Why did you need to get rid of it?"

Trando frowned and then started praying silently, 'Watch yourself Bart, be careful of what you say.' He felt an impatience surge in him. Surely Bart must realise it was not a good idea to tell the Jury about all the anarchist material? His worries increased as Bart went on,

"It was radical and socialist literature for our Cause. They had sent policeman to search the houses of these people who were my friends, because they are active in the radical, socialist and labour movement. They know that if they have literature on them, they will be put in jail or be deported." His voice became stronger now. "We all saw what happened to poor Salseda in New York. The papers say that he jumped, but we know better. We are all frightened now. All radicals and socialists are frightened now."

Katzmann was on his feet and almost shouted, "Objection!"

Inevitably Judge Thayer agreed.

Jerry McArney changed his line of questioning and the rest of the morning was taken up with trying to establish Vanzetti's alibi. He was of course selling fish, but this time there was no Trando to support the evidence, only some Italian witnesses who needed an interpreter.

As they walked out into the sunlight Trando was relieved that his father seemed happy enough to leave him once again to his own devices, so he started his usual wander around and was surprised to see Hughes and Stewart, not at lunch, but talking together in a corner of the grounds. The thought crossed his mind that they might no longer wish to go to the Dedham Inn after the Judge's outburst at the reporters.

Positioning himself again within earshot he could tell at once that they seemed very satisfied with the way proceedings had gone that morning. Hughes was talking in an animated and excited manner, waving his arms around.

"No you're wrong Mike. I do believe we've got the bastard. Don't you see? All that radical garbage has to come out now and Katzmann will go for the jugular! Think of what he is telling us? Men of peace carrying guns? Just wait until the Jury hears about that!"

Stewart seemed pre-occupied by something else.

"What bugs me is that Orciani isn't in there as well. I'm damned certain he was the guy who fired the fatal shot. I reckon he must have picked the gun off Berardelli's dead body and given it to Sacco and Vanzetti to get rid of. For my money Orciani is the cleverest of the lot. He made sure he rigged himself up with a bloody good alibi and believe me it was rock solid. We can't touch him."

Hughes said nothing in reply to that. Instead he muttered something Trando couldn't quite hear about Vanzetti's alibi. Then he gave a great guffaw and finished by saying, "However, peddling fish didn't do him much good last time in spite of that kid!"

Trando was so angry at this he had to use all his self-control to stop himself flying at Hughes with both fists and telling him yet again that he had been telling the truth.

"What about Sacco's alibi?" Hughes asked.

"That's definitely weak," Stewart replied with a grin. "He says he was in Boston getting a passport but nobody will be able to identify him. Thousands get in line for passports every day."

"Good." Hughes seemed pleased about this. He was silent for a moment. "But quite frankly, in the end it won't be the alibis that matter, or the witnesses, or the fact that they were conscientious objectors and dodged the draft. No I'm telling you, it will be their guilty behaviour on the day of the arrest, plus of course that arsenal they were carrying. They can't explain that away, however hard they may try."

The two men started to move across the lawn and Trando heard Hughes say, "You notice they have given Fred Moore a rest. Thank the good Lord for that! He was giving us all a headache."

*

Trando sat in the shade and took out the packed lunch his mother had made for him. As he ate he thought about what he had just heard. Those names, Orciani and Boda, they just kept coming up. He'd also heard the name Coacci mentioned as well. Suppose it was these men who had been involved in the raid. If they knew that Bart was on trial for something he hadn't done, why were they letting him take the blame? He thought angrily that these so-called comrades were cowards. They knew Bart would do anything to protect them so they had taken advantage of him. Then his thoughts turned to Nick Sacco, Bart's greatest friend. It was quite possible Nick *had* been involved as well. After all he was known as a hothead and Bart had described him as 'brave as a lion'. So he was probably quite capable of taking part in a raid and Bart might even know that. But he would also know that if his own innocence was proved, it might land Nick in deeper trouble, so he would stick by him whatever happened.

He sighed. Carlo Tresca had been right. If only it had been two days later, all might have been well as by then Bart would have got rid of all the stuff. As it was he had tried to protect his comrades and been caught with all the incriminating material, not to mention those guns. The only thing in the whole mess that Trando knew with absolute certainty was that Bart was completely innocent. He hadn't taken part in either raid or committed the murders.

He threw the remains of his lunch to some expectant birds and looked around to see if he could spot Mrs Evans, but once again she was nowhere to be seen.

*

It was halfway through the afternoon before Katzmann rose to his feet for his cross examination of Bart and from the outset his voice held a distinct note of contempt.

"Mr Vanzetti, I want to take you back to May 1917. Do I understand that you left Plymouth at that time in order to dodge the draft?"

"Yes sir."

Trando noticed that Bart looked and sounded more nervous and that immediately worried him because he knew that when Bart was nervous he lost his good use of English and sounded more Italian.

"So," Katzmann sneered, "you didn't want to be a soldier and fight in the war."

Vanzetti looked at him straight in the eyes. "If I refused to go to the war, I didn't refuse because I don't like this country. I would have refused even if I had been in Italy. It was because of conscientious objection."

Katzmann was having none of this. "So you won't fight for this country but you like to live and work in this country?"

"I always work very hard," Bart protested adding, "I always live very humbly."

Katzmann now thundered at him, "Mr Vanzetti, are you the man that on May 9th was going to address a public meeting containing men who had fought in that war? Men who had fought for their country? Are you that man?"

"Yes sir," came the reply. "I am that man. Not the man you want me to be. But I am that man."

Many in the room were shaking their heads in disbelief at this line of questioning about the war. It made no sense. It had nothing to do with the raids or the murders.

The interrogation went on for another two hours. Vanzetti wasn't a beaten man, but by the end of the afternoon he was in a state of complete exhaustion and his answers were coming in whispers. On one or two occasions the McArney's tried to intervene but every time they were over-ruled by the Judge and in the end they gave up.

*

Trando and his father went home in silence. As they reached the door his father said, "Are you sure you want to go back on Monday? It will be Nick Sacco's turn and I can't see him getting any easier treatment. It might be upsetting for you."

Trando assured his father he was fine with it, explaining he needed to see it through now. His father nodded, as if he understood. After a moment Trando asked him if he had ever known Boda, Coacci or Orciani. Vincenzo looked surprised at this.

"No I never knew any of them, but I did hear Bart mention their names on several occasions. They weren't from this part of Plymouth but I think they must have gone to the same meetings as Bart." He looked at his son. "Why do you ask?"

Trando shrugged and said casually, "I just keep hearing their names come up in connection with the raid, that's all."

His father looked as if he were about to question him further about this, but instead went into the kitchen to talk to his wife.

*

After the evening meal his father went out for a drink with his friends. Trando helped his mother with the dishes and was about to go upstairs for violin practice when his mother said,

"Sit down for a minute Trando."

He sat down opposite her at the table and noticed how tired and sad she looked. Her dark hair, usually so neat and shiny, now seemed untidy and he could see there were a few strands of grey. Also her face was pale and there were dark rings round her eyes and when she spoke her voice had a tearful edge.

"I cannot lie to you Trando. Your father says it doesn't look so good for Bart." She looked at him pleadingly. "I worry about you going back."

Trando looked at her and spoke gently, but firmly. He agreed that it was not looking good, but he tried to make her understand that he wanted to see it through to the end and hoped she would let him. To his relief his mother seemed to accept this, smiling through her tears and perhaps too exhausted to argue. Trando told her sadly that if only they had believed his evidence at the first trial, none of this would be happening. Now they would never believe that Bart was selling fish on the day of the second raid either.

"They think all Italians stick together," his mother said, with a mixture of anger and scorn in her voice. "They think we lie to get Bart off. But we don't. Now they won't listen and there is nothing we can do anymore. It's all up to those lawyers." She paused. "But that Mr Moore, he has become a joke. I feel such despair Trando. And that Mr Katzmann is a terrible man, terrible to you, terrible to Bart and he will be terrible to Nick next week."

She started to cry. Trando moved round the table and put his arm around her. "Mama, shush, please don't cry." But he had no words of real comfort for her because everything she had said was true.

He stayed with her until her sobs died down and the evening light began to fade.

CHAPTER 14

"Do you say you love your country?" Katzmann fired the question at Nick Sacco.

"Yes sir,"

"Did you love this country in the month of May 1917?" Nick hesitated, so Katzmann added, "Do you understand the question?" Nick nodded.

"Then will you please answer it."

"I cannot answer in one word."

Katzmann came back at him again. "You can't tell this Jury whether you loved this country or not?"

Moore rose to his feet, "I object to that."

The judge ignored him.

Nick said, "I could explain that yes, if you gave me a chance." Katzmann turned to the Jury speaking slowly for maximum affect.

"I ask you again. Did you love the United States of America in May 1917? Do you know whether you did or not?"

Nick repeated, "I cannot answer in one word."

Moore again rose to his feet. "I object your Honour."

Judge Thayer asked him on what grounds.

Moore said, "I object to the repetition of this question without giving the man an opportunity to explain his attitude."

Now Judge Thayer looked annoyed as he told Moore, "This is not the usual method that prevails in a court of law. Where the question can be categorically answered by yes or no it should be answered. The explanation comes later. You may proceed."

"Did you love this country in the last week of May 1917?" repeated Katzmann.

Nick shuffled uneasily in the box. "That is pretty hard for me to say in one word Mr Katzmann."

"There are two words you can use Mr Sacco, yes or no. Which one is it?"

"Yes."

"And in order to show your love for this United States of America when she was about to call upon you to become a soldier, you ran away to Mexico."

This time Thomas McArney rose to his feet but before he could say anything Judge Thayer intervened. He looked at Katzmann and said in mild tones, "He did not say he had 'run away' to Mexico."

Katzmann gave a brief nod to the Judge and re-phrased the question. "Did you go to Mexico to avoid being a soldier for this country that you loved? Yes or no?"

"Yes."

"And did you still love America when you returned?"

Nick hesitated before saying "I should say so, yes."

"Is that your way of showing love for your country? Don't you think going away from your country is a wrong thing to do when she needs you?"

Trando looked across at Bart in the iron cage, who was shaking his head sadly.

Nick chose his words carefully, "I don't believe in war."

Katzmann said in mock surprise, "You don't believe in war?"

"No sir."

Katzmann renewed his attack. "Do you think it is a brave thing to do what you did?

Nick looked puzzled, so Katzmann asked, "Would it be a brave thing to run away from your wife when she needed you?"

At this Nick shouted out, "No! No! No! That is different."

*

On and on it went, with no let-up in the relentless repetitive questioning. By the end of the afternoon Nick Sacco was completely worn down and Katzmann finally let him step down, content with his day's work.

Before they left for home, Trando stood with his father and a group of his friends in the lobby. The general feeling was one of shock and bewilderment at the way the day had gone. One said, "My God. It's a bloody shambles. Katzmann is getting away with everything. It's just terrible."

Another added, "That Judge is biased and in my opinion Moore has completely lost the plot. Why doesn't he prove that there is no evidence?" There was a nod of agreement at this. "I have kept a record," he went on, "thirty two witnesses have said Bart was not the man at the raid. Thirty two!"

Vincenzo agreed, "My boy made it very clear at the first trial that Bart always had a long moustache, while the man at the crime scene had been identified with a short moustache. This was completely ignored. The Jury forgets these things unless reminded of them, and in any case, they seem to think all Italians look alike."

The first man said angrily, "Those lawyers! Half the time our guys can't understand what they are saying, with those long, technical words they use." There was a murmur of agreement on this as he went on "But you can be damn sure that when Katzmann addresses the Jury he'll make certain they understand every point he makes. Our case is a shambles I tell you. I have sat in this court room for six weeks. I started out convinced our men would be found innocent. Now I have very little hope left."

Vincenzo shook his head. "No my friend, we have to keep hoping. All that nonsense Katzmann brought up about Mexico and draft dodging is not important. There is just no evidence to prove that Bart and Nick were in South Braintree that day. They have got the wrong men. That is what our lawyers now have to make clear."

A few nodded, but it was probable that everyone was thinking the same thing. Nick and Bart had been proved to be Italian anarchists and worst of all they were Italian anarchists who carried guns. This was the evidence that was going to be uppermost in the minds of the Jury. It didn't matter if they were the gang who were at the scene of the crime because it was obvious to them all that somebody had to pay for what had happened. Weren't the newspapers reminding the citizens of America daily of the 'Dago threat'? The members of the Jury would be only too aware of it. America wanted justice for those killed and they didn't mind which Italian anarchist paid for it as long as somebody did.

The dispirited group broke up after that, with no further discussion.

*

On the way home Vincenzo told Trando that tomorrow was going to be the most important day of the trial, as both sides would be giving their closing speeches. He added that he hoped one of the McArney's would be making the final argument for the defence, rather than Fred Moore. Trando didn't say anything in answer to this, but privately thought that a man like Moore would be unlikely to give up his last moment in the spotlight and hand over the speech to one of the other lawyers.

His father suddenly said, "Do you remember that lady you were talking to the other day?" Trando looked startled and nodded. "Well, I found out that her name is Mrs Evans." Trando tactfully didn't mention he already knew that and his father continued, "It turns out she is loaded with money. We had a problem last week when the funds for the defence ran out and then your Mrs Evans sent us a large sum which should be enough to see us through. It seems she has taken a great interest in the case and feels Bart and Nick aren't getting a fair trial. What do you make of that?"

Trando thought about it, "I'm sure glad she is on our side. That was very generous of her, although I expect she can afford it. She does have a chauffeur and a large car."

His father roared with laughter. "A chauffeur and a large car don't necessarily mean she has the money needed to support our cause. Lucky for us she did though. At least we now don't have the added worry about paying the lawyers."

*

The next day Trando placed himself on the sidewalk, jumping up and down and frantically waving, hoping it would attract Bart's attention desperate for him to turn round and see him. But Bart still stared straight ahead, marching in the heat, all the way down the street and into the Court House for this, the penultimate day of the trial. Tomorrow, thought Trando, I will call out. I have to make Bart realise that I have been here supporting him.

Back in the Court House his father asked, "Did he see you?" Trando shook his head and his father put a comforting arm around his shoulders. He knew how much it meant to the boy.

*

The morning was taken up with the final argument for the defence and it was soon evident that Moore was fulfilling all their worst fears. As his father and friends met in the lobby for the lunch break, the overwhelming mood was one of gloom.

His father was the first to speak, "I don't know about you guys but I guess that was a pretty bad morning for us. Instead of making a clear case for the defence, Moore just rambled on making no sense at all, his arguments were all over the place…"

Someone interrupted, "It was the last chance he had to prove that Bart and Nick were innocent. That was all he had to do."

There were nods of agreement and then a small, fat man who Trando hadn't seen before said angrily, "Where were the alibis? All that nonsense about draft dodging and going to Mexico made no sense at all. He should have been talking about the actual crime and lack of evidence. That man Moore just likes the sound of his own voice. He talked for three hours and none of what he said will have helped Nick and Bart. It was obvious that the Jury were bored and had lost interest. They've probably made up their minds already. Our boys don't stand a chance."

"We've been paying that guy Moore thousands of dollars for his services," another man said, "and for what?"

The fat man gave a grim laugh, "You're right. Who needs enemies when you have the likes of Moore and that Judge?"

There was a gloomy silence and then his father spoke again, "If only the McArney brothers had been allowed to speak it would have been far better. They would have made their points clearly and quickly, instead of all those long speeches about nothing that Moore gave. I mean, why didn't he point out that nobody had recognised either man at the scene of the crime? That was really important."

"Or the fact that none of the payroll has been found? Where is all that money? Bart and Nick don't have it." another man said, "That definitely should have been mentioned."

The angry man burst out again, "My God! Can you imagine what Katzmann will do this afternoon? Moore has handed the floor over to him and he sure is going to make the most of it."

Trando didn't wait to hear anymore but took himself off outside. A sense of panic had started to set in. Surely the Jury wouldn't find Bart guilty when there was so much to prove his innocence? He sat hunched and alone while a deep despair crept over him.

For the afternoon session a great many people were forced to stand at the back as every seat was taken and as usual there was a great deal of noise and excitement which steadily built until Judge Thayer entered and took his seat. Then Katzmann rose to his feet to begin his final argument for the prosecution. He stood, imposing and stern, waiting for complete silence. The noise died away and a hush fell over the room. The tension was palpable. Almost immediately Katzmann launched into a full attack, which Trando couldn't help noticing was in stark contrast to the ramblings of the Californian. This was exactly what the patriotic Americans in the room had been waiting to hear. This man was for them a lover of his country, noble minded, upright and above all a fighter for Justice.

As the afternoon progressed, the small Italian community saw their hopes fade. Katzmann knew exactly what his audience and above all the Jury wanted from him and he gave it to them in full measure.

"I want to remind members of the Jury," he said in solemn tones, "that when arrested, these two men had arsenals upon them." He repeated the word 'arsenals' with great force. "Vanzetti had a loaded 30-calibre revolver and this, ladies and gentlemen, was the man who ran away to Mexico because he did not want to shoot a fellow human involved in warfare!" Trando looked round the room and saw many people nodding their heads in agreement and obvious approval.

Katzmann continued, "This peace loving man had on him a loaded 38-calibre revolver, any one of the cartridges instantly death-dealing. This tender hearted man, who loved this country and who went down to Mexico because he did not believe in shooting a fellow human being – this was the man who, when he went to pick up a decrepit old automobile, was carrying a 38-calibre loaded gun!"

He paused to give his words full effect.

Trando knew with a sinking feeling in his stomach, that the Pinkerton man had been right. It was the arsenal Bart and Nick were carrying on them at the time of the arrest that was going to have the maximum impact on the Jury.

Katzmann now turned to Sacco. "And his friend and associate, Nicola Sacco, another lover of peace, another lover of his adopted country, who so abhorred bloodshed that he went down to Mexico," Katzmann paused again for full effect, "this man had with him," he empathised every word, "this lover of peace had with him, thirty-two death-dealing automatic cartridges, ready for action, and twenty-two more of them in his pocket! These two men, gentlemen of the Jury, had ammunition enough to kill thirty seven men if each shot took effect."

The damage was done. Every Italian heart sank. How could anyone believe their men were innocent now? Trando looked across at Mrs Evans. She was still writing everything down in the note-book on her lap, but her expression was stony-faced.

Katzmann continued his tirade for another two hours, by which time he was red-faced and dripping with perspiration. He finished with a final flourish and rallying call, "Gentlemen of the Jury, I ask you to do your duty. Do it like men. Stand together you men of Norfolk!"

This brought a cheer from some in the room. The Judge

rapped on his desk with his gavel and with that he brought the afternoon's proceedings to an end. All that was left now was his own charge to the Jury the following day and then their deliberations until they had reached a verdict. The moment had arrived. The trial was finally drawing to a close. Everyone involved was exhausted, both partakers and watchers. Now there was nothing more that could be done. After the Judge's summing up, there would be that terrible wait while the Jury made up their minds and then it would all be over. The fate of these two men was in their hands. Trando knew this only too well and the hopes and the beliefs he'd held onto at the start of the proceedings were now draining from him.

CHAPTER 15
JULY 14TH 1921 - THE VERDICTS

After seven long weeks of evidence and testimony that amounted to over three thousand pages, the last day of the Trial had finally arrived. Trando thought Mrs Evans had seemed resigned at their last meeting. She'd said with a shrug that the defence and prosecution lawyers had done their work and on July 14th 1921, it would be up to Judge Thayer to deliver his summing up, but she had added with some bitterness in her voice, that this same Judge Thayer was a man known to all for his hatred of the Italian anarchist and he had shown himself to be thoroughly biased throughout the proceedings.

This had also been the opinion of the Italian community as well and there was little hope left. Their belief in the American justice system was fast being questioned and consequently there was a great deal of anger and frustration being felt.

The Brini family sat gloomily at the breakfast table anticipating the day ahead. Nobody spoke and Trando was relieved when at last they left for the Court House.

*

As usual the two prisoners were marched from the jail, down the main street, flanked by officers on either side. Today Trando stood on the sidewalk, facing the Court House. He had dodged in out of the crowd desperately trying to get himself to this strategic position because he was determined to at last attract Bart's attention. It was his final chance.

As the small procession drew level with him he shouted, "Bart! Bart!" as loudly as he could, hoping it would reach above the noise of the crowd. Vanzetti stopped, looked around and then caught sight of Trando. His usual expressionless face broke into a smile and the boy smiled back and waved. Then one of the officers gave Bart a rough push and the men were moved on.

*

Once again the Court room was packed. On his way through the lobby, Trando overheard Hughes saying loudly that he hoped Judge Thayer would finish his summing up by lunch time so they could get a result by the end of the day, adding with some satisfaction that he presumed the Jury wouldn't take long as Katzmann had done a good job. Here he gave a laugh saying that it was high time for it all to end as his wife had almost forgotten he existed as he'd been away for so long. Stewart joined in the laughter. They seemed depressingly confident and Trando moved away not wanting to hear more.

His mother was with them today as she felt the need to support Rosina. He joined his parents and sat down, not telling them what Hughes had just said, but saying that he had finally managed to see Bart who now knew they were here. As if to prove the point, as Bart went into the iron cage he looked around the room searching for a sight of them. Vincenzo waved and once again Bart smiled.

Then Judge Thayer entered and everyone stood.

During the previous seven weeks, Judge Thayer's interventions had been in dry, unemotional tones. Today all this changed. Today he was full of passion. To everyone's surprise he completely ignored the usual practice of guiding the Jury through all the technicalities and legal explanations of the evidence. Nor did he advise them on what they were to decide and what they were not. No, today his charge to the Jury was on higher matters and given in a lofty style. His voice almost cracked with emotion.

"Gentlemen of the Jury, the Commonwealth of Massachusetts has called upon you to render a most important service. Although you knew that this service would be arduous, painful and tiresome, yet you, like true soldiers, have responded to that call in the spirit of supreme American loyalty." He paused to give especial weight to his next utterance, "Gentlemen, there is no better word in the English language than 'loyalty'…"

Judge Webster Thayer was to continue in this vein for the best part of two hours. When he did refer to the facts of the case, his statements were often misleading. He quite wrongly gave an account of Proctor's evidence on the bullet in the gun used in the raid, informing the Jury that it was Sacco's pistol that had definitely fired the bullet that had killed Bertarelli. That statement alone was enough to seal Sacco's fate. Trando felt his anger building. It was untrue and unjust and Thayer was getting away with it just because he was the Judge.

Finally he came to the evidence of materials found on Sacco and Vanzetti at the time of their arrest. This was the most damning of all.

"If a person is willing to use a deadly weapon such as a revolver upon an arresting officer in order to gain his liberty, then would you not naturally expect it would be the quality of the crime of which such a person would be consciously guilty?"

This was an ambiguous statement to say the least and the McArney brothers were frowning and one was shaking his head but Trando could see that the Judge's point went home. Thayer somehow managed not to mention a single alibi witness in his two hour speech, but dealt in great detail with the testimony of the arresting officers. The realisation came to Trando yet again that this whole Trial had hinged, not on Bart and Nick's innocence of the crime of which they had been charged, but on the anarchist material and weapons which had been found on them at the time of the arrest. If only they had managed to get rid of the stuff, there would have been no case. Now it appeared they needed a miracle.

*

At last it was over. The Jury were sent to an upper room to deliberate on their verdict and Judge Thayer retired to his chambers. Everyone else, including the lawyers, the reporters and the general crowd, moved outside to find as much shade as they could from the scorching summer sun.

"How long do you think it will take the Jury to decide?" Trando asked his father.

Vincenzo shrugged. "I'm told it can take anything up to three days. A quick decision would not be good for us. It would mean they had made up their minds quickly and not thought about the real evidence," and he added with some bitterness, "not that they were given much chance of that."

*

The afternoon wore on and it was dusk before the word went round that the Jury was back. The tension in the Court Room was palpable. Half the town of Dedham was packed inside. The prisoners were now not sitting but standing in their cage; Nick very pale and Bart looking tense and anxious.

Judge Thayer entered and immediately addressed the Clerk in brisk tones, "You will please take the verdict."

Clerk Worthington turned to the Jury who all stood, "Gentlemen of the Jury, have you agreed upon your verdict?"

The Foreman replied, "We have."

The clerk said, "Hold up your right hand Mr Foreman. Look upon Nicola Sacco. Prisoner look upon the Foreman. What say you Mr Foreman, is the prisoner at the bar, guilty or not guilty?"

The Foreman replied in a strong voice, "Guilty."

There was a gasp from the spectators as Worthington asked, "Guilty of murder?"

"Guilty of murder."

The Clerk then asked, "In the first degree?"

The Foreman repeated "In the first degree."

In spite of murmuring in the room the Clerk continued.

"What say you Mr Foreman; is Bartolomeo Vanzetti guilty or not guilty of murder."

"Guilty."

"In the first degree upon each indictment?"

For the last time the Foreman spoke, "In the first degree".

Clerk Worthington addressed the Jury in a loud, clear voice.

"Hearken to your verdicts as the Court has recorded them. You, gentlemen, upon your oath, say that Nicola Sacco and Bartolomeo Vanzetti is each guilty of murder in the first degree upon each indictment. So say you Mr Foreman? So say you all gentlemen?"

The Jury said, "We do, we do."

Judge Thayer stood. "I can add nothing to what I said this morning gentlemen, except to express to you gratitude for the Service you have rendered. The Court will now adjourn." There was silence as he left for the last time and then the place erupted in complete uproar. Vanzetti raised his fist in the air and shouted, "Sono innocente! Sono innocente!" He looked across at Trando who was standing white-faced, frozen in horror and disbelief. He gave him a little nod and a smile of encouragement before turning back to give his attention to Nick. Rosina had thrown herself against the iron cage, hysterical with grief and sobbing loudly, crying out over and over again, "Oh Nick. What am I going to do. I have got two children. They kill my man! They kill my man!"

Her hat had fallen off and her long hair tumbled in a cascade down her back. Nick put

his arm through the bar of the cage and stroked her head, murmuring words of comfort, until Jerry McArney moved across, disengaged her hands and gently led her away still sobbing. Shortly after this the prisoners were taken from the room.

Trando looked around. Moore was tidying up his papers looking stunned and shaken. Katzmann had gone to talk to Hughes and Stewart, who were both looking suitably pleased. Thomas McArney moved across to the Assistant District Attorney Williams and said drily,

"Congratulations on your victory." To Trando's great surprise Williams seemed distressed and there were tears running down his face. He looked at McArney and blurted out, "For God's sake don't congratulate me. This is the saddest thing that ever happened to me in my life." And with that he rushed out of the room.

Mrs Evans closed her notebook, stood up and before Trando could join her she moved over to speak to Thomas McArney.

"You and I both know, do we not, Mr McArney, that these men are innocent? If they are now to be punished by death it will be a legal crime. So the fight goes on. We none of us must rest until these innocent men are set free."

She then turned and looked at Trando who was standing behind her. "Do not give up Trando Brini. Remember. The fight goes on."

*

Later, in his room that night, Trando took out his violin and standing by the window, he played "Old Black Joe" and his eyes at once filled with tears. What was the point of playing that piece again? Bart would never hear it.

Putting the violin away he sat on the bed and thought about all that had happened in the months since that Christmas Eve of 1919. Downstairs he could hear his parents talking in low voices and he thought it sounded as if his mother was crying. He knew she would be especially upset for Rosina Sacco whose plight was the worst of all of them. She had two children to support and take care of on her own, and one of them was a very small baby. Bart would expect them to help her as much as they could, but no amount of comforting would take away those guilty verdicts. It was going to be terrible for everyone.

Trando sat on feeling numb with the shock of it all. All the hope and confidence he'd had at the beginning of the trial had gradually evaporated over those long weeks. Miserably he thought that if only Bart hadn't been an anarchist, none of this would have happened.

He took out his diary from under the bed and wrote,

July 14th 1921 Bastille Day in France.
Today has been the saddest in my life. Bart was found guilty of murder

133

by the Jury and I know for certain he is innocent. He is the kindest and most caring person I ever met. I do not understand why it has gone so wrong. Mrs Evans seemed to think the fight goes on and I take comfort from that. She is a woman of great influence and will tell us what can be done. I hope I meet her again so that she can let me know how I can help Bart.'

He closed his diary, wondering if it was worth writing in it any more. Staring out of the window he thought sadly that after today his life would never be the same again.

He put the diary back in the box and climbed back onto the bed.

Suddenly the tears so long held back, came to him. He sobbed now until his pillow was wet with them. Then, at last, with exhaustion overwhelming him, he fell into a restless sleep, full of disturbing dreams and frightening images.

CHAPTER 16
SIX YEARS LATER

Everyone who met him agreed that Beltrando Brini had grown up into a very fine young man. At the age of nearly twenty his achievements were impressive and his parents were rightly proud of him. For two years he had been a member of the Musicians Union and at the early age of nineteen had been offered the post of conductor of the Plymouth Youth Orchestra, the youngest conductor that had ever been appointed. His virtuosity on the violin was considered outstanding and he was confidently expected to gain a position in one of the major orchestras, following the completion of his studies at Harvard, where he was due to go the following year. So to the outsider it seemed that Trando Brini had the world at his feet.

There was a different picture for the friends and family who were closest to him. They were well aware that a dark shadow hung over the young man. Trando's moods would quickly change from elation to despair. He was a man driven by one obsession. Ever since the guilty verdict had been given to Bart Vanzetti for a murder Trando knew he had not committed, the injustice of it was never far from his thoughts. He particularly carried this burden, because he was the one person who knew with certainty that the verdict was false. It was an indisputable fact that he had been with Bart selling fish on the day of the raid. It was a rock-solid alibi to which he had testified in court but to his bewilderment and fury his testimony had not been believed. Even if this had destroyed his faith in American justice he had not given up. Trando was still determined to prove Bart's innocence no matter how long it took.

Bart and Nick Sacco had now been in prison for six years.

Appeal after appeal had been launched and then turned down. This meant that the threat of the electric chair still hung over them. The fight to prove Bart's innocence had become the sole aim of Trando's life, to the exclusion of almost everything else. He had been in constant touch with the Defence Committee in Boston and now that he was old enough, he was determined to take action himself and join the cause.

Over the last few years his mother had begun to watch him anxiously. He overheard her moan, "Why doesn't he get himself a nice girl? He is such a good-looking boy, he could have his pick of any of the girls around here." His father had given a shrug of his shoulders and then it seemed he pretended to agree with his wife. These days his father would do anything for a quiet life, although Trando hoped that even if his mother couldn't, his father realised that he would avoid any distractions until some resolution had been made over the fate of Bart.

*

On this bitter cold January day in 1927, Trando put down his baton and thanked the young members of the orchestra. It had been a good last rehearsal for their 'Twelfth Night' concert which was due to take place the following day. He had worked hard on what was to prove his last programme for a very long while. The concert included a selection of Christmas music and some popular classics, many of which Trando had himself arranged.

The last few weeks had been something of a struggle, especially working with the string section. To his great relief, the young musicians were at last playing well, or at least to the best of their ability and had turned their squeaks into a pleasurable sound. Just as well as the concert was sold out. Until today's rehearsal he had been apprehensive about the whole event. Now it seemed they were ready to perform and as he left the rehearsal room he felt more confident and was almost looking forward to it.

Outside the hall he was met by an icy blast of cold air. The sidewalk was covered in a grey slush and it reminded him of that Christmas Eve in 1919, when he and Bart had been on the fish round together selling eels to the Italian community.

So much had happened since that fateful day six years ago.

As he set off for home Trando's thoughts turned, as they so often did, to the terrible moment of the verdicts in 1921, when both men had been found guilty of murder. The great Mrs Evans had assured him that the Defence Committee which had been set up soon afterwards by Aldino Felicani, would not give up the fight for justice and indeed they never had. Trando had diligently recorded every moment of their struggle.

He turned into Suosso Lane and thought grimly to himself that right now he had another fight on his hands and this time regrettably it was to be one with his parents. The moment had come to inform them of his plan to leave home and move to Boston. It was a vital move he knew had to make, but he dreaded confronting them with this news knowing how much it might upset them, particularly his mother. Whatever protest they made nothing was going to deter him. Mrs Evans, with whom he had kept in constant touch, had informed him that Bart had been moved from Dedham Jail to Charleston State Prison in Boston so it had become necessary for the Defence Committee to set up their headquarters in a small hotel on Beacon Hill on Boston Common. She also told him that a final appeal was being prepared and that they urgently needed all the help they could get, including his. He was more than willing to do anything he could to help the cause but told Mrs Evans it was going to be impossible for him to make the daily return journey from Plymouth up to Boston. The remarkable lady quickly found a solution to this problem, not only offering him a small room in the Defence Committee hotel but also paying all his expenses in return for his work with the Committee. To this generous offer he had readily agreed but was now left with the difficult task of telling his parents of this decision. After careful consideration, he decided it would be unwise to tell them of his plans until after the concert the following day. He didn't want to spoil their enjoyment of that. Once the concert was over it didn't matter what they said, his mind was made up. It was inevitable there would be upset and arguments and inwardly he sighed at the thought of the battle ahead.

*

Letting himself in through the front door he heard his sister Inez practising the piano in the front room. He stopped to listen and smiled. She was only eight years old but had made great progress since starting lessons two years ago. Her playing was already as good as his, although he reflected that his piano playing had been mainly self-taught because he had chosen violin lessons instead.

"Is that you Trando?" His mother called out from the kitchen. "We won't be having the evening meal for another two hours. Your father is getting home late."

Trando assured her this was not a problem because he had some work to do and he climbed the stairs to his room. It had changed little over the years except for the addition of a large desk. This had been a present from his father on his fifteenth birthday and now he wondered how he had ever managed without it. The drawers on either side were crammed full and the top was covered in a disorganised pile of pens, papers and manuscripts. Above the desk on the wall, was a board where he pinned up anything to do with Bart's case and which he felt was of importance. This consisted mainly of the newspaper cuttings he'd acquired, along with some pictures referring back to the Dedham Trial. He had also collected and kept the many reports on the motions for a new trial that had been made since 1921.

He took off his coat, scarf and gloves and flung them on the chair. His mother had often reproved him for his untidiness, but he was thankful that when she cleaned his room she knew better than to disturb anything on his desk. Nor did she touch the box under the bed, which he now pulled out.

He removed the largest of the three notebooks and lay on the bed reading it through. These books contained his written account of everything that had occurred since 1921 in the Sacco and Vanzetti case. If he was to be of any help in Boston it was vital he was familiar with all the major events that had happened over the last six years. So he inwardly congratulated himself on being so conscientious in keeping track of everything he had seen or heard. This would now prove invaluable.

He started to look over what he had written and was at once reminded of the roller-coaster of emotions he had experienced over these years, with every twist and turn that had taken place in the desperate fight to save Bart and Nick from the electric chair. There had been so many moments of hope, all of which had so quickly turned to despair.

Some years back he had overheard his mother tell one of her friends that he was a very highly strung boy and how having to give evidence had really affected him. This made him smile. The events of those two years had of course had some affect, but he would have been in a far worse state if he had not been allowed to give his evidence. It was certainly true that for several months after the guilty verdict he'd had nightmares which mainly consisted of vivid images of what he supposed to be the electric chair, but he didn't think that made him particularly neurotic. Or indeed that he was now. He had been far less emotional than either his mother or Rosina Sacco, who would set about wailing if the subject of the two men was even mentioned. No, he was just determined to fight Bart's cause in any way he could, and if going up to Boston meant he could help, then that is what he would do, no matter how much his parents might object.

He started to leaf through the pages, finding them crammed with various snippets of information. But there was no order in what he had set down and to his dismay he found his writing was not always legible and events and reports were jumbled up together. This made understanding the relevant facts quite difficult. Feeling frustrated he left the bed and took the notebook over to his desk. Taking out a clean sheet of paper and picking up a pen he wrote,

THE MAIN EVENTS OF IMPORTANCE - SINCE 1921

1923. Hearings were held by Judge Thayer for five motions, demanding a new trial.

The first motion was started by a report that the foreman

of the Jury, one Mr Ripley, had been overheard by several persons during the trial saying, "Damn them, they ought to hang anyway!" This seemed to prove he was definitely biased. Second motion. Defence Attorney Fred Moore presented affidavits and testimony by three prosecution witnesses to the effect that they had been coerced into identifying Sacco at the scene.

Trando put down his pen. He was surprised that only three witnesses had been found. There had been so many who had obviously been coerced into giving false evidence. For one thing there had been all that nonsense over the size of Bart's moustache, and the cap that was far too small for Nick and he couldn't possible have owned.

He went back to his notes and wrote again,

However, when these witnesses were confronted by Katzmann they denied being subjected to any coercion!

No surprise there!

Another witness, Lola Andrews,

Trando smiled at his recollection of that particular lady,

had told the authorities that she had signed an affidavit stating she had wrongly identified Sacco and Vanzetti, but then signed a counter-affidavit the following day.

Third and most importantly of all, a motion was submitted that involved the forensic ballistic evidence that had been given by Captain William Proctor who, although he had died soon after the trial, had given an affidavit in which he stated that he could <u>not</u> say Bullet 111 was fired by Sacco's 32 Colt pistol.

That seemed to be something of vital importance but once again it had been ignored.

There were another two motions set down.

At the conclusion of the hearings, Thayer denied all motions for a new trial on October 1st 1924.

Trando thought back to that time remembering how the McAnarney's had been extremely hopeful, even optimistic, particularly on the re-examination of the Captain Proctor evidence. Once again all their hopes were dashed. Mrs Evans had been particularly worried by these latest developments because of the toll it had taken on the two men. Bart had reacted to the news very badly indeed and it was at this time that Nick Sacco had gone on a hunger strike. His mental state had been deteriorating for months. Bart at least could occupy the long hours in his cell with reading and writing letters. Nick was a man of action and spending all but two hours of each day locked up was driving him insane. At first his refusal of food was greeted with indifference by the prison authorities. Apparently their attitude was, if the Dago wanted to kill himself so be it. However after thirty one days when he was near to death they were finally ordered to intervene, fearful of the publicity he was getting. Rosina was in the papers almost daily with reports of her husband's state and was gaining a great deal of sympathy. So the decision was made to remove Nick to the Boston Psychopathic Hospital, where he was brutally force fed. This saved his life but proved to be such an unbearable experience that he finally gave up the hunger strike and after a few weeks of recovery he was well enough to be given outdoor work which suited him far better. The doctors in the hospital were more sympathetic than the prison warders and they would listen to him. They then refused to certify Nick as fit to return to prison unless his regime was changed. So after he went back to Dedham, the hours in his cell were reduced and he was given the task of basket weaving, which at least occupied him during the day. It was a minor triumph, but the main problem of proving their innocence still remained.

All these events had been reported to the Brini family in graphic detail by a tearful Rosina Sacco. Trando tried not to think of the indignities and hardships that the two men had suffered and once more focused his mind on his notes. He wrote again,

November 1925. The Madeiros confession.

This was the most astonishing turn of events and had given the Defence Committee and all the friends and family of the two men definite grounds for optimism.

An ex-convict, Celestino Madeiros, awaiting trial for murder, confessed to committing the Braintree crimes and absolved Sacco and Vanzetti of any participation. He had added that the two men

were not professionals and could never have carried out such a raid and he claimed that he and the Morelli gang were guilty of the crime. The Morelli brothers were well-known criminals who had carried out similar robberies in the Massachusetts area.

Once again the hopes of the Defence Committee were high. Surely this would mean Bart and Nick would at last be set free? But any hope was quickly dashed when the authorities refused to investigate this confession, arguing against the credibility of Madeiros.

Trando looked up at the notice board above his desk. That last decision had produced an outcry from many leading writers and artists from America and abroad and he had cut out all the newspapers articles he could find. Other cuttings had been sent to him by Mrs Evans.

The Defence Committee now had world-wide support in their campaign for a new trial, with famous names that included Edna St. Vincent Millay, Dorothy Parker, George Bernard Shaw and H G Wells. Trando hadn't heard of most of these people but he had looked them up in the library and was especially impressed by the fact that the great author Anatole France, veteran of the campaign for Alfred Dreyfus, had written an article with the title, *'An Appeal to the American People!'*

The likelihood of death sentences for Sacco and Vanzetti will make martyrs of them both and cover you with shame. You are a great people. You ought to be a just people.'

Trando remembered thinking at the time that surely the country would take notice of that? But it seemed not. Later he had written this out in large red letters and stuck it on his board as a constant reminder of what they were fighting for.

The next entry was a particularly interesting quote and he thought it worth making a note of it -

'Judge Thayer, after delivering yet another blow to the Sacco and Vanzetti cause, went on holiday, where it was widely reputed he said, 'Did you see what I did to those anarchistic bastards? I guess that will hold them for a while. Let them go to the Supreme Court now and see what they can get out of them.'

Trando again consulted his notes and wrote on the paper in

front of him,

The Appeal to the Supreme Judicial Court. January 1926

The defence appealed Judge Thayer's denial of their motions. Both sides presented their arguments over the two days before five judges.

On May 12th 1926, the Supreme Judicial Court returned a unanimous verdict upholding Judge Thayer's decisions. The Court pointed out that they did not have to do more than review the trial record as a whole, or to judge the fairness of the case. Instead the judges only considered whether Thayer had abused his discretion in the course of the trial.

Wearily he put down his pen and thought grimly that it wasn't only the Dagos who had stuck together, the Judges certainly had. It had been heartening to see that Thayer's behaviour, both inside the courtroom and outside of it, had become something of a scandal and was now a public issue. Frank Sibley, one of the reporters Thayer had shouted at in the Dedham Inn, had written an article in the Boston Globe which generally condemned Judge Thayer's blatant bias throughout the trial.

Flexing his hand which had become stiff from writing he stood up taking down another article that had been sent to him, this time one from the 'New York World'. It had attacked Thayer as an *'agitated little man looking for publicity and utterly impervious to the ethical standard one has the right to expect of a man presiding in a capital case.'* He stared at it and sighed, reflecting bitterly that none of this had helped their cause. They were just words, words, words. Behind all these words lay seven years of the most appalling suffering which he couldn't bear to imagine or to dwell on. Action for him was the only answer now.

Carefully he placed these articles along with his notebook and the notes he had just written, in a large folder. Taking down a suitcase from the top of the cupboard, he opened it up and put in the notebook, the folder, some clothes and various other things he thought he might need over the next few weeks. Then, closing the lid he sat for a while wondering what it would be like in his new home in the hotel on Boston Common and whether they could at last make some progress to prove the innocence of Bart and Nick.

Little did he realise then that the next few weeks would turn into months, or that these months would certainly be the most important and traumatic time of his entire life.

CHAPTER 17

Two days later, on another bitterly cold January day, Trando arrived at the small hotel on Beacon Street overlooking Boston Common, which the Defence Committee now used as their headquarters. It was a long street full of elegant houses and the Common, which was covered in snow, looked beautiful. He stared down at the lake and he could see people skating on the ice. It was a peaceful scene but today there was no time for him to linger. Walking through the main entrance and into the lobby he had a feeling of growing excitement. At long last he would be able to do something positive in the fight to free Bart and Nick.

The hotel lobby was a good deal smaller than the premises in Rollins Street which had been the domain of the extravagant Fred Moore, but the atmosphere must have been very similar. There was that cacophony of sound, of people talking and shouting and stenographers tapping away at their machines on large desks covered in clutter and over the whole room was a general air of bustle and excitement.

Trando stood with his bag and violin case suddenly feeling shy and awkward. There appeared to be nobody here he recognised at all and for what seemed a long time wasn't sure what to do. Then at last out of the sea of faces he saw Mrs Evans coming towards him. It was a relief to see a familiar face and although it had been six years since he had last seen her she really hadn't changed at all, except maybe a little stouter with touches of grey in her hair. Trando smiled to himself as he also noted that she was still very smartly dressed. Today she was draped in a long fox fur.

"You have to be Trando!" she exclaimed as she reached him a little out of breath. Then stopping in front of him gave him a thorough examination. "I suppose it would be annoying of me

145

to say that in the seven years since last I saw you, Trando the boy has changed into Trando the man?" Without waiting for a response she continued, "But you have, you certainly have. Of course I knew you would have grown up but I wasn't at all sure I would recognise you again. What a stupid woman I am. I should have realised you would still have those Italian good looks. You seem to have inherited your father's build and your mother's features, an excellent combination!"

Trando must have looked uncomfortable because she gave a laugh, "I know dear boy, I am embarrassing you. I'm afraid it is what older women do!"

He smiled and would have liked to tell her that he didn't consider her old at all but instead he said, "It is good of you to have made all these arrangements for me Mrs Evans."

"Nonsense," she replied briskly, "we are just pleased that you could join us. There is so much to do here we need every bit of help we can get and you couldn't possibly help us without being here on the spot as it were. It seemed the logical step to have you with us and I am particularly glad to have you here and do please call me Elizabeth; we are all on first name terms here."

Once more Trando felt awkward and rather at a loss. Mrs Evans noticed the flushed face and embarrassed expression so she quickly changed the subject. "I have a letter for you, from Bart."

Trando was greatly surprised by this wondering why it hadn't been sent to his home address, because he certainly hadn't told Bart about his move to Boston. As if reading his mind Mrs Evans explained, "I took it upon myself to tell him you were joining us," here she chuckled, "he didn't approve I'm afraid and he'll probably say so in the letter. He thinks you have done enough. But I told him firmly it was your choice." She looked at him. "I don't think I forced you into it did I?" Again without waiting for him to answer she continued, "Well on my last visit, a few days ago, the dear man seemed to have accepted it and gave me a letter to give to you for when you arrived."

A thought came to him. "Will I be able to visit him now I

am here?" He was excited at the prospect, but Mrs Evans immediately frowned and shook her head. "I'm afraid that is highly unlikely. They are extremely strict on visitors for both Bart and Nick and only allow relations. For some reason, probably because Bart has no family here, I seem to be privileged and they have given me permission for short visits, but this doesn't happen often, and it is always difficult and time consuming to arrange."

She guided him across the lobby towards the stairs. "First I will show you to your room and let you settle in. Then you can come down, I will make the introductions and we can set you to work." She paused and looked at him. "It is very good to have you with us Trando."

He followed her up the stairs to the first floor and she led him into a small room with a window that looked out over the Common.

Mrs Evans sounded apologetic. "It's a little small I'm afraid. We have so many people staying here it has been quite a difficult task squeezing everyone in." She waved her hand airily. "There is a bathroom just down the corridor."

"This is fine," Trando assured her, adding tactfully, "it's about the same size as my room at home."

Mrs Evans smiled at this and then took out an envelope from her pocket and handed it to him. "I can't tell you how many letters Bart has written while in prison. I have to send him new supplies of paper almost every week!" She moved towards the door. "Come down when you're ready Trando. There's work to be done."

And with that she was gone.

*

Trando looked around him and decided the room suited him just fine. There was a narrow bed in one corner and above it a picture of an old print and when he peered at it he presumed it was of Boston Common. It was the only picture there was. Otherwise the walls were bare and painted in a faded duck-egg blue. He was pleased there was a small table opposite the bed which he could use as a desk and it had a chair beside it. There was also a chest of drawers. Behind the door was a hook, where he now hung his coat and scarf. He paused again and then carefully putting his violin case down by the table he unpacked his bag. His few clothes went into the chest of drawers and the file of papers he put on the desk. This done he sat on the bed and gathered his thoughts. The room would be a good base and he was rather relieved not to be sharing. It was obvious there was work for him to do here so he would not be in his room a great deal. The thought occurred to him that he might have to send home for some more clothes. He had brought very little, not wanting to give his parents the impression he was going to be away for a long time. Grimly he recollected the long row over his departure, his mother tearful and panicked, his father trying to understand his reasons, then his mother screaming at his father for not insisting he stay. It had been difficult to leave Suosso Lane but now he was here he was very glad he had not given in to the pleas of his mother. Mrs Evans had said they needed all the help they could get, well at last he could do something positive to help his friend.

Taking Bart's letter from his pocket he started to read.

Dear Trando,
I received the picture of you last week from your mother. It makes me happy when I see what a fine young man you have become. And now you tell me you belong to the Musicians' Union for 2 years and you are to go to famous Harvard University. This is the best news I have received in all the time I am here. You are too modest. Your mother tells me in her letter you graduated from high school with an honorary record. And you conduct a youth orchestra and teach violin to 11 pupils in Plymouth. I am so proud, 'A magnifico son of the people.'

Trando felt a momentary pang of guilt at the mention of the orchestra and his pupils. The decision to come to Boston meant he'd had to abandon them for the moment. To his surprise they had been most understanding, although he hadn't given them the real reason, just told them he had to go away for a while. He thought ruefully that the musicians had been rather more understanding than his parents. His actual leaving was made even worse by his little sister Inez who had sobbed her heart out.

He sighed, returned to the letter and read it slowly. *'Dear boy, it brings tears to my eyes when I remember the day at my trial when you testified for me. You kept that stand for 3 hours and never once wavered and only a boy of 13 years but now you have done enough Trando. You have an important life ahead of you. And you see how things are with me. Six years on and we have succeeded in nothing. The lawyers have tried everything, there have been five motions for re-trial, all denied.*

William Thompson, the lawyer who replaced Moore, is a good man and believes in our innocence, but no-one will listen to him now. The Defence Committee and our supporters all over the world have tried for justice. But I see plainly we are the enemy and they are determined to make an example of two poor Italian workers. Even when Madeiros admitted to the crime and said we are innocent they do not believe him. He goes to the chair anyway so they think, what does he have to lose by making a confession?

So I say to you Trando, we must accept what the fates decree. I know you have remained faithful to my cause Trando. Your mother tells me you are always active and keep in touch with the Defence Committee and work tirelessly on my behalf. Now Mrs Evans tells me you are coming up to Boston to work with them. I say to you no! Now I say to you seriously Trando, <u>you must give up</u>. Stay in Plymouth and get on with your life, which is a good one. It is enough for me that you believe in my innocence. You can do no more. No matter what happens, you will always have the love and friendship of your true friend, Bartolomeo Vanzetti'

Trando remained lost in thought for a while. Then putting the letter on the table he left the room and walked down the stairs to the lobby.

CHAPTER 18

A commanding voice greeted him.

"Ah Trando, there you are! Come over here, there is someone I want you to meet."

Obediently Trando crossed the room. Beside Mrs Evans was a tall, frail woman, whom he reckoned must have been in her early thirties, except for the fact that her hair was completely white. She wore it parted in the middle and drawn back to be fastened neatly at the nape of the neck. Her clothes and shoes were elegant and all in shades of cream, with a striking cameo brooch fastening the high collar of her lace blouse. The whole effect was ethereal and rather beautiful. She was certainly different from anyone he'd ever seen before.

Mrs Evans said, "Trando, meet Katherine Anne Porter. You arrive just at the right moment. I was telling her all about you."

Trando took the elegant hand that was held out towards him. Katherine Anne Porter was smiling at him and when she spoke it was in a slow, drawly voice, "Well I sure am glad to meet you Trando Brini. Elizabeth here has been telling me what a hero you were at the first trial and that you are the one person who knows more about this case than anyone else."

Trando felt himself blushing and said quickly, "I wouldn't say that. It has been difficult for me to keep up with things properly from a distance so I have a good deal of catching up to do now. Until today I was living with my parents in Plymouth but I am hoping I can be of some help around here."

Katherine laughed. "There is no doubting that. I'm quite sure you'll be a great asset." She looked at her watch. "Heck is that the time? Forgive me Elizabeth, I have to go. I am lunching with the formidable Lola Ridge. Bye for now. Be sure to see me later Trando."

He watched her go, fascinated that someone could appear so terribly frail and yet have such extraordinary energy at the same time.

"Quite something isn't she?" Mrs Evans remarked and then looked at him, "Why, you poor boy you must be starved. How stupid of me. Come along, we will have luncheon together. The rest of the introductions can wait until after you've been fed."

*

Although it was a small hotel, the dining room gave the impression of a kind of faded grandeur with its heavy embossed ceiling, the thick pile carpet and large potted palms placed at strategic positions around the room. The old waiter jumped to attention as they entered. Trando could tell that Mrs Evans was a person of some importance in the place. She waved an imperious arm and they were quickly led to a table in a secluded corner by the window.

Once the food had been ordered Mrs Evans settled back and said, "Let me tell you about Katherine Anne Porter because she is a woman of some importance. You should know that Katherine is a quite extraordinary person apart from being an exceptionally gifted writer. It is such a great asset to have her here with us." Trando tried to look suitably impressed as Mrs Evans continued "Her presence here is proving to be extremely useful. "

"Useful?" Trando queried.

"Oh yes my dear, very useful indeed." Mrs Evans nodded proudly. "She has attracted many of our leading writers and artists to the cause and all this is making the 'Sacco and Vanzetti case' better known, not just in this country, we now have interest from people all over the world. A flood of mail comes in to us every day."

"But how does that actually help?" Trando asked.

Mrs Evans spoke with great emphasis. "You have to understand that public opinion is vital to us Trando. I cannot over-estimate this. The Massachusetts authorities become very nervous when public opinion is roused. This is exactly how we managed to get the previous motions heard. Even the government in Washington has now been forced to take notice and this is entirely due to the fact that we have such an enormous amount of coverage in the international press. When those motions for a new trial were refused in July last year, we at once had an article written for the newspapers and issued the pamphlets, circulating them world-wide. Immediately there were demonstrations that followed in over sixty Italian cities and several other European capitals. The American Embassy in Paris was bombarded by protest. That, my boy, is when governments take notice." She leant back, exhausted but triumphant.

"And Katherine helps with all this?"

"She does indeed," Mrs Evans replied. "It is impossible to over-estimate the impact she has had. This is now not just a Boston case, but a case for the whole of America and beyond." She waved an arm in a circular gesture as if to imply the rest of the world.

Privately Trando thought it was unlikely one woman had that much influence but he didn't want to appear rude so merely said, "Katherine has a rather strange voice."

Mrs Evans smiled. "That is her Texan drawl. It's very distinctive and a little odd to us here."

He nodded, then feeling he had exhausted the topic of Katherine Anne Porter he asked, "How did the Defence Committee come about? I mean, who organises it all?"

"Ah, now that was the brainchild of Aldino Felicani…"

"I've met him" Trando broke in, "a long time ago. It was before the second trial."

Mrs Evans nodded. "Well, that's useful, the more people you know the better, although Aldino now devotes most of his time entirely with the legal department in their offices and we hardly see him back here at the hotel." She sighed. "I really don't know what we would all do without Aldino driving us on."

Trando had been curious about Aldino Felicani ever since their first meeting. "How did he become involved?"

"Aldino was in it from start," Mrs Evans replied. "I think it all really began for him when that poor man Salseda threw himself onto the sidewalk..." Trando shuddered, remembering that incident only too well. "You see Aldino had been the printer for all the literature and pamphlets for the Boston anarchist group and because of this had come to know Bart very well. They were great friends. It was therefore understandable that immediately after the arrest of the two men, Aldino took on the task of starting the Sacco-Vanzetti Defence Fund and later formed the Committee. In addition to printing a paper which was devoted entirely to the news of the trial and subsequent events, he also acted as its chief publicist and treasurer, working tirelessly to raise money," she paused and smiled, "which is where I came in. I was happy to contribute and Aldino and I have done many, many fundraising events together. The dear man works so very hard and is the driving force behind everything."

There was a moments lull in the conversation as she looked at Trando as if considering something and then she said, "I think I am going to put you together with Mary Donovan. You two should get on well and you will like her. She originally started here because of her friendship with Aldino. He put her in charge of the press office, a huge task, but we have been lucky enough to recruit Gardner Jackson, a 'Boston Globe' reporter. He assists her with all the press and publicity and again it was Aldino who found him for us. Jackson is vital to have around because he bridges the gap between the radical and social elite..."

All this information was rather bewildering to Trando but he felt it was best not to interrupt and ask for clarification. No doubt he would be able to find his way around things and maybe this Mary Donovan would help him. He concentrated as Mrs Evans continued,

"The press side of things is vital to us Trando. I cannot stress how important it is to have someone act as a mediator between the hard set anarchists and the growing number of supporters with more liberal political views." She waved an airy hand. "There is a major difference between each group which needs to be recognised, so it has to be handled carefully. Seeing he was looking puzzled she smiled. "These new supporters can be anyone from socialites to lawyers and intellectuals, even anarchists from beyond Boston. It doesn't matter who they are, we just want as many as possible to join us."

Trando said sadly, "I don't think Bart was ever really an anarchist. He just wanted justice for the workers."

Mrs Evans looked at him and then spoke in dry tones, "I am afraid Trando, that to your average American, it is difficult to tell the difference." She added briskly, "Of course the situation is not helped by the fact that Judge Thayer is on a one man crusade to destroy 'the Reds in Massachusetts' and he doesn't seem to mind how he does it. All along it had perplexed me why Judge Thayer saw fit to continue what seemed to me like a solemn farce. But I had underestimated the dreadful man. Dear Jerry McArney, who is now a judge himself, told me that he felt he was up against a brick wall from the first day of the trial. Thayer was determined to find Nick and Bart guilty." Her face took on a grim expression. "The man has the stupidity and the mistaken conviction that this makes him a great patriot. Our job is to make people see that whatever the circumstances, justice must always prevail. "

She almost shouted the last words and then rose majestically to her feet declaring rather dramatically, "Come my dear, there is vital work to be done."

Throwing her fox fur around her shoulders, she strode from the room with Trando following obediently behind.

*

On their arrival back in the lobby Trando was quickly found a small table beside the desk of Mary Donovan and the introductions were made. As he began to work closely with her it didn't take him long to like and admire her enormously. In their long conversations he discovered she had been a labour leader and a Sinn Fein organiser and no doubt as a result of all this activity it had left her brisk, efficient and hard working. She certainly didn't tolerate shirkers and would reprimand those wasting time in her pronounced Irish accent. 'One of the many Boston Irish,' Mrs Evans had informed him.

He started to make a close study of her. In her general appearance he considered Mary rather plain, except for a mop of startling red hair which she wore in an untamed mass of curls. He couldn't help noticing that among the red curls there were just beginning to be little streaks of grey. One day Mary laughingly remarked to him that by the end of all this, her hair would be as white as Katherine Anne Porter's! She had a large personality and a big heart and on the whole people liked and respected her.

The other occupant in their part of the room was Gardner Jackson, the reporter. He was a waspish, short tempered man. From the outset he was given to handing out verbal lashings and gave the impression he was surrounded by unprofessional incompetence. Trando could see he was bristling with hostility and found him a little daunting. For this reason if he had any query he would always take it to Mary and not bother Gardner Jackson.

Quite soon after his arrival he renewed his acquaintance with Aldino Felicani who looked at Trando and remarked drily, "The change in your appearance my dear boy, makes me realise just how long we have been working on this case!" Otherwise he was very pleasant and enquired kindly after his parents and asked to be remembered to them. However, after this first encounter their paths didn't seem to cross much. Mrs Evans had been right. Felicani now spent most of his time in the legal offices where the lawyers were extremely busy preparing a last and final appeal to the Supreme Judicial Court.

Another important member of the Committee who Trando met during his first days at the hotel, was a Mrs Henderson. She was rather similar to Mrs Evans in that she was a smart, wealthy Boston lady, but in his opinion not quite as formidable or commanding and she didn't speak so loudly, dramatically, or so fast. Mrs Henderson had been in a long correspondence with Bart and she showed him some of the letters he had written to her over the course of the last two years. In one of them Bart had made reference to Trando and in that now familiar scrawl he read;

*'I am angry that it is reported that my lawyers at the Plymouth trial wanted me to take the stand but I refused and sent a boy of 13 years to talk for me by speaking a lesson learnt by heart. A greater wrong than this was never done to truth and to an innocent man as I am. I was **advised** not to take the stand and how can the Governor not believe in Beltrando and all my truthful witnesses? How can he believe that a 13 year old boy could have perjured himself and resisted three hours of cross-examination by Katzmann? Even now Beltrando tells of his positiveness of my innocence and still he is not believed.'*

Trando smiled inwardly at the rather peculiar grammar and handed the letter back to Mrs Henderson and told her, "What he says is true. It wasn't Bart who refused to take the stand at his trial it was the defence lawyers who advised him not to. I now think it was wrong just to rely on my evidence. Katzmann found it easy to sway the Jury and make them believe I had learned it, which of course I hadn't. But they never had a chance to hear Bart's evidence and I believe that was a fatal mistake." He looked at Mrs Henderson and said angrily, "I never trusted his lawyer Mr Vahey and nor did my father. It was Vahey who advised Bart not to be cross examined and I strongly suspect he was influenced in that advice by J J Hughes, the Pinkerton man."

Mrs Henderson smiled at him and told him that she didn't disagree with this, but added that when you considered it, huge mistakes had been made by the defence team in both trials and probably the engagement of Fred Moore was the greatest blunder of them all. She then added in rather brisk tones that there was no point wasting time by indulging in regrets. Now was the time to put the wrongs right, and to see that justice was done at last. She sounded very positive.

Trando was not so sure. There had been so many occasions over the last six years when his hopes had been dashed. He now found it almost impossible to be optimistic. As he saw it, the only objective left to them was to work as hard as they could and hope that in this last push they would win the fight and finally prove Bart and Nick's innocence. Surely, with so many famous people involved, they should have a chance? But the doubts had a way of creeping back in.

*

The time passed quickly and he worked long hours. There was a routine to the days that he'd found easy to slip into. He liked working next to Mary. Every morning she would hand him a file with a list of the things she required him to do. He carried out the work conscientiously, hoping that what he was doing would really make a difference, although it was hard to tell. Occasionally he would be sent out on errands or told to take messages over to the legal desk or give Felicani documents to print. Trando became accustomed to the sounds of the lobby, the low murmurings of conversation and the tapping of the machines. He grew used to fetching Mary endless cups of coffee and emptying the mountain of cigarette butts that piled up in a dish beside her.

Occasionally Mrs Evans would come over to see him, asking if he was all right and if he was eating properly. Once reassured she would bustle off again, with her booming voice over-riding all the other conversation in the room. He once asked her if she had seen Bart again, or had heard from him. She shook her head saying that the authorities were proving even more difficult than usual but that she would inform him if she did. With that he had to be content.

Each night Trando would fall on his bed completely exhausted, only to rise the next morning to start all over again. He hadn't even had the time to take out his violin and the case lay beside the table unopened, where he had put it on the very first day. It felt like a kind of limbo that they were all in, as if waiting for something to happen.

*

Then, about three weeks later a chance meeting occurred

which resulted in Trando's routine in that Boston hotel changing in the most unexpected way.

CHAPTER 19

March 19th 1927 had started like any other morning. After his usual rushed breakfast Trando reached the lobby intending to go straight to his table and resume working. But on this particular day he was stopped in his tracks by a wave from Katherine Anne Porter, beckoning him to join her. This rather surprised him because he had seen little of her since their first introduction. She was a woman who always appeared to be rushing out to meet someone and that someone was usually a person of political importance or distinction in the literary world. He had recognised from the start that she moved in a completely different world to him so was quite relieved that their paths hardly ever crossed.

He now made his way across the room to where she was standing. At her side was a slim young girl, casually dressed, pretty but rather boyish in appearance, with short, cropped fair hair. He looked at her and decided she must be about the same age as him, which would make them the two youngest people in the room.

Katherine was smiling at him in a rather odd way. "Well," she said in her slow drawl, "how about this? I can't believe you two are meeting again in this room for the first time after all these years."

Trando was confused. He looked at the girl in some puzzlement and asked, "Have we met before? I'm sorry I don't seem to remember you."

The girl smiled back at him and said, "You don't? I'm Ella Feenan." She gave a laugh.

"You still have my handkerchief, remember?"

Trando was completely taken aback but managed to say, "You're Ella? The Ella who went to live in New York?"

"I am, the very same." She seemed to be enjoying this.

Katherine looked at them both and then made a move, "I'm gonna leave you two to get re-acquainted. I'll see you later Ella." And with a wave of her hand she was gone.

Trando stood routed to the spot quite unable to think of anything to say. Ella said laughingly, "Well get you Trando Brini, with your film star looks! You seem to be quite the most popular person around here."

He felt a flash of annoyance. It wasn't just the slightly mocking remark about his appearance, it was also that somehow Ella seemed to exude a confidence and sophistication which he knew he didn't have. For the first time since his arrival he felt unsure and uneasy. He hesitated and then suggested they went for a cup of coffee and she readily agreed.

*

Sitting amidst the palm trees in the now empty dining room Ella quickly made it known that she had heard all about him from Mrs Evans, even down to the music concerts, the orchestra position and his place at Harvard.

He felt another flash of annoyance but tried not to show it. "So what about you?" he asked quickly to forestall any further discussion about himself. "How was New York?"

Ella shrugged. "It was all right. I mean I guess it's an exciting place to grow up in, but my parents had a divorce that seemed to go on forever and I was a bit messed up for a while." There was a hesitation before she went on more cheerfully, "then I went to college and began to take an interest in journalism. It was during that time I discovered the writings of Katherine Anne Porter." She looked at Trando and her face suddenly lit up. "Isn't she the most amazing person?"

Trando felt compelled to nod in agreement, although he didn't feel he knew Katherine Anne Porter well enough to make a judgment and if truth were told he felt rather in awe of her and had been content to keep out of her way.

Ella continued, "I was told she had gone to Boston to join the

Defence Committee for the Sacco and Vanzetti case. Of course, I knew all about the case from those days in Plymouth and your connection with it. My father and I had continued to follow the endless reports in the papers. He's a lawyer and he explained each situation to me, so I know how awful it must have been for you with the endless setbacks." Trando nodded again, this time rather grimly, but he let Ella go on. It seemed rude to interrupt. "After last Christmas I decided to give up my studies for a while and come up here to see if I could help." She gave a shrug, "My parents don't seem to care what I do so I had no problem leaving New York."

Trando studied her. She had suddenly lost that confident air and looked almost vulnerable, especially now she had fallen silent. Her face had a sad, closed expression and she sat hunched and waif-like. He wanted to ask her more about her life in New York but felt this might be intrusive so he merely said, "After your parents divorced, which parent did you go and live with?"

Ella shrugged again. It was obviously the gesture she used to show the world that nothing affected her and that she didn't care how other people behaved towards her. She now spoke in a flat unemotional way, as if she were reporting an incident. "It depended. My mother had been an alcoholic for a long time so she had her good days and her very bad days. When things became too awful I just left and went back to my father's. But he had a new wife who's a real bitch and she really didn't like me." Here she gave a mirthless laugh. "Believe me, the feeling was mutual." She paused. "I talked to Katherine about it and she was so sympathetic. She told me that her childhood had been messed up rather like that."

Trando felt a little shocked by all this especially her confiding in Katherine. Why had she imparted all this information when Katherine was almost a stranger?

"We talked for hours last night," Ella continued, "she told me all about her early life. She was born in Texas. Her family tree can be traced back to the American frontiersman, Daniel Boone." She looked at him with shining eyes and although he really didn't want to hear any more it was clear that Ella was not to be stopped now.

"Unlike mine, her mother died just after the birth of her younger sister and Katherine was brought up by her grandmother who she clearly adored." She broke off, "I didn't have a grandmother living, so I was left to the care of my mother." Here she made a face indicating clearly what she felt about that. "Katherine then lost her grandmother too when she was only eleven and because she didn't get on with her father she left home before she was sixteen."

She paused and Trando wondered if that was to be the end of this account but it clearly wasn't because Ella leant across the table and said in slightly hushed tones, "She rushed into a terrible marriage and the man was physically abusive to her" She leant back again. "She managed to escape from him and went to Chicago to work as an actress and a singer. Poor Katherine, a year later she was diagnosed with tuberculosis and spent two years in a sanatorium." She looked at him and announced dramatically, "It was at that time she decided to become a writer and she attracted attention almost at once. But her poor health suffered again when she nearly died in the 'flu epidemic of 1918. She went totally bald and when her hair finally grew back it was completely white, as it is now."

"I was wondering about that," Trando said, at last feeling he could interrupt, "because otherwise she looks so young."

"She's very striking isn't she? You always notice her in a crowd, quite apart from the elegant way she dresses." There was admiration in her voice. He found this annoying as well but Ella was not to be stopped. "She told me that once she had fully recovered and her health was good enough, she moved to Greenwich village in New York and became a full-time writer. It was also at this point that she developed an interest in politics which were definitely on the radical side so it was only natural that this case should have attracted her attention and she came here to get involved. Isn't that an incredible story? I am so glad I have met her. I feel I have known her all my life."

Trando tried to suppress his irritation at Ella's seeming obsession with Katherine Anne Porter. Instinctively he realised that Ella's childhood had been a difficult and unhappy one, but was there really a parallel to Katherine's? It was obvious that it appealed to her to be like this woman who had so quickly become her idol. Ella now wanted to be identified with her in some way and their unhappy childhoods was the catalyst. A memory suddenly came back to him of her saying on their last meeting that she wished she had belonged to an Italian family because they were all so nice to each other. He'd thought this a strange remark at the time, but now it began to make sense.

"Mrs Evans says she will be very useful to the cause" he said, feeling he had to add something, and then quickly decided to change the subject. "When did you arrive and where are you staying?"

She gave a laugh, relaxing once more. "What a lot of questions!" Her answers came out in a rush. "I arrived yesterday evening and I am here in the hotel on the second floor. I think my timing was quite lucky, as someone had just vacated my room that morning. I gather the place is packed full, but Katherine made all the arrangements for me. Wasn't that just wonderful of her? I had written to her, out of the blue, never expecting an answer back, telling her I was interested in liberal causes and all that sort of thing, especially this case, and that I wanted to be a journalist. To my huge surprise I had a letter back a couple of days later, suggesting I come up to Boston to join the Committee. So here I am."

"So here you are," echoed Trando and they both laughed.

He looked up at the clock on the wall. "I ought to be getting back to my post. I'm on the press desk," and he added quickly, not wanting to sound too grand, "in a minor role of course. What task have you been given?"

Ella smiled. "Not an important one like you. For the moment I will be helping to sort out all the letters that pour in. There are mountains of them. You wouldn't believe how many. Apparently they are coming in from all over the world. Katherine told me it would be a temporary job but I think I will find it interesting and quite honestly I don't really mind what I do."

She looked at him and for the first time he noticed she still had her freckles in spite of it being winter, which was probably the reason they were less noticeable. Suddenly Ella jumped up. It wasn't until later that he became used to these impulsive moves. "Why don't we meet up for lunch and then you can bring me up to date with what is going on?"

Before Trando had time to agree she had started back to the lobby.

*

He sat at his desk, a little shaken by this encounter. Ella had obviously made quite an impression on people already, certainly with Katherine Porter and Mrs Evans. It was ridiculous of him he knew, but he felt slightly resentful at the way she had moved in so quickly on something that was so personal to him. And his first impression had not been a good one. In fact, he had thought he was going to dislike her intensely with her New York sophisticated ways and her air of self-confidence. But once she started talking in a personal way to him alone, she had seemed a bit lost, even sad. It was evident that her life had not been easy and it was hard to dislike or resent someone who had gone through the sort of ordeal she had. For him that was unsettling as well, because he couldn't help feeling sorry for her and he didn't want to have those sorts of feelings, at least, not at this moment. He had enough problems sorting out his own worries over Bart.

Glancing up at the clock he thought crossly that she had taken up quite enough of his morning already and putting her firmly from his mind he went back to work.

*

Promptly at one o'clock, Ella appeared at his table. "Coming for lunch?" she asked. He was just about to say that he needed another half hour, when Mary looked up from her desk, smiled and said, "You go Trando, I can finish whatever it is you are doing."

164

They had reached the door when he noticed that the sun was shining, so he suggested they go for a short walk, telling her that there was a pond on the Common and a kiosk fairly close by where they could get hot chocolate. There was also a cafe by the bandstand where they could get some food.

"Suits me." she said.

They crossed the road and stood at the top of the hill above the pond. He pointed, "There's a bench by Frog Pond where we can sit and eat."

"Frog Pond!" she burst out laughing, "Where do they get these names!"

Her laughter was infectious and Trando found himself laughing as well.

"The ice has only just thawed" he told her. "Until last week there were lots of skaters you could have watched." They sat watching the cascade of water coming from the pool's fountains as the sun shone through giving it a rainbow effect.

"It's very pretty here," she said. "And I like Beacon Street with its elegant houses. It's more intimate than New York, although Central Park is bigger than this."

"Well there isn't just the Common," he told her. "If you cross over Charles Street there are the Gardens on the other side, more formal and grand with a big statue of George Washington on his horse."

They were silent again and then she asked him to tell her more about Bart.

Trando thought for a moment. "Well," he began, speaking slowly and choosing his words carefully, "I didn't know much about him before he came to live with us in Suosso Lane, except that he was born in Italy and came to America when he was about twenty. From all that he told me I think he was immediately shocked by the way the working class Italian immigrants were treated by the Americans and this led him into politics. He started going to union meetings and they happened to be full of anarchists and that is where he met Nick Sacco." He broke off and she waited. "Bart was never like them." Trando spoke more passionately now. "He was an anarchist in his views but he was never a violent man. His only interest in going to those meetings was in getting justice for the workers. He never thought of himself only of his fellow comrades. Bart is a good, gentle and kind man." He suddenly couldn't go on. "It's all such a mess." he muttered.

They were again silent for a while. The sun had gone in and Ella shivered. Although it was nearly March the air was still cold.

"Do you want my coat?" Trando asked. She shook her head and jumped up. It was another impulsive move. "We'd better get back. I know you have a lot to do" and added "you can tell me more tonight."

Trando thought a little crossly that this was typical of her. She just presumed they would meet up that evening. But Ella was already striding on ahead and by the time he caught up with her it seemed too late to make any objection.

So that evening she came to his room. Trando sat on the bed, propped up by pillows and Ella sat opposite him in the chair. On her instruction he then told her everything he could remember about Bart, from the moment he had arrived to live with them, right up until the day of his arrest. He explained that from that moment on he had become an eavesdropper. The only way he'd been able to find out what was happening was by listening at doors. And there had been the continual struggle to be allowed to go to Court, except of course when he was giving evidence. Ella listened quietly, totally absorbed in what he was saying. Only occasionally did she interrupt with a question.

"Tell me more about what happened at Court when you were cross-examined?"

So he told her about that as well and about the days at the second trial. Finally he got to the day when the guilty verdicts were given.

"That must have been terrible." she whispered, shocked by his narrative.

Trando nodded and said bitterly, "The worst day of my life."

She looked at him for a moment and then smiled. "You seem

to have lived a lot in your short life haven't you Trando Brini?" Standing up she caught sight of the violin case lying unopened on the floor. He followed her gaze and said rather sheepishly, "I haven't had a moment to practice since I arrived. I don't really know why I brought it with me."

"You must practice," she said firmly. "You must make time for it. In any case, you need a break from all that tension downstairs," and she laughed. "Quite apart from anything else, I want to hear you play again." She walked to the door and gave one of her grins, "but not tonight. The violin performance will have to wait for another day. I'm tired out and you must be too." She paused and said quietly, "Thank you for telling me all that. Good night Trando."

She had closed the door before he also said "Good night."

He slowly got undressed, thinking about this new encounter. It was strange that Ella should have turned up here after all these years. But was it a good thing? He wasn't at all sure. Somehow he felt she might prove to be a distraction just at the time all his energies needed to be concentrated on Bart. He climbed wearily into bed, turned out the light and lay back, thinking it might be an idea to find a tactful way to distance himself a little. But before he could work out how he was to do that he had fallen into a deep sleep.

CHAPTER 20

With Ella's arrival Trando's life took on a rather different routine. At the start of each day they would meet over breakfast and this became a more leisurely meal than he'd been used to. They often shared the lunch break unless called to other duties, and they were almost always together in the evenings. In spite of his best intentions, the effort to distance himself had failed. All his spare time was now spent with Ella, even though he still had rather ambivalent feelings towards her. Sometimes he found she could be quite overbearing, even dominating, especially when they were with Katherine or Elizabeth Evans. This was surprising given her elfin looks, but he soon realised that under that frail exterior there was a real toughness. Ella certainly had strong opinions and wasn't afraid of airing them and when she monopolised the conversation Trando was left feeling resentful and inadequate. It wasn't that he wished to be in the limelight, but he didn't like the way she would just take over. Once or twice he had been tempted to mention it, but he hated confrontation and to be honest, there didn't seem much point. Instinctively he knew that this was how Ella had learned to behave. It was a protective mechanism. She'd obviously had to develop a tough skin in order to survive her unhappy childhood. Her forthright manner came out of this. So he did his best to be understanding.

After a couple of weeks, although he was reluctant to admit it, he realised Ella had become an important part of his life. When they were alone together he enjoyed her company and admired her quick understanding of all the complex issues, although he still found her worship of Katherine Porter more than a little annoying. Yet somehow he managed to put this irritation to one side and to the amusement of others in the room they were now looked on as a couple. Maybe it was inevitable. She was the only person of his age around and whereas before he had kept to himself, now he had a companion and he found that far from distancing himself they had become almost inseparable.

At one point during that first week he had given in to her many requests, taken out his violin and played to her, finishing with "Old Black Joe". This last piece was more for his sake than hers, and he hadn't told her beforehand that it was the tune that Bart so loved. It was only when he put the violin down he noticed that there were tears in her eyes, in the same way as there always had been with Bart. He was moved by this. It was just one more thing that made him feel differently about her.

*

"A whole lot of new people have arrived," she told him over breakfast, talking as usual with her mouth full. "It's difficult to keep up with them all. I am only just putting names to the faces of the people who were here when I first arrived. I'm not like you. I'm no good at remembering names. Faces are good. Names are bad."

Trando laughed at this protesting, "I honestly don't know everyone. There are so many different groups that are arriving now, what with the communists, the journalists, union representatives, foreigners.." he paused and then added, "not to mention the liberal riff-raff like you."

She gave him a shove. "You're so rude Trando Brini! Anyway I am happy to be put in the same category as the Boston Biddies."

He looked at her quizzically, "The Boston Biddies? Who on earth are they?"

"It's my name for Mrs Henderson and Mrs Evans," and she laughed.

Trando joined in her laughter but then his expression changed, "On a more serious note, all these different factions that are arriving are not always an asset. They seem to have their own agendas. It can get to be like war's been declared in there. I also get the feeling that the communists see this case as ripe for manipulation, to use it for their own ends." She nodded in agreement as he went on, "In any case everybody seems to have different views on how to proceed. The communists disagree with the liberals, the journalists disagree with the lawyers and sometimes I wonder if they remember what we're actually fighting for, or the fact that our time is about to run out."

Ella gave him a long look but said nothing. They were both aware that the final decision from the Supreme Court was due any day now. If their lawyers were turned down this time, Bart and Nick would be sentenced and there would be nothing more they could do. She also knew how devastating this would be for all of them, especially Trando.

*

It was Mrs Evans who broke the news to them. They had returned from their usual lunchtime walk on the Common, but as they entered the lobby they noticed at once a decided change in the atmosphere. It was eerily quiet and the people who were standing around, or seated at their desks, were looking shocked and upset. Mrs Evans was sitting very upright in a chair by the window, staring out at the Common, as if lost in thought. Then she turned, saw them and beckoned them over.

Ella and Trando crossed the room and sat down opposite her. Ella took her hand as she looked at them and said gravely, "It's bad news I'm afraid my dears, the very worst, the moment we have all been dreading." For a moment she seemed unable to go on and there were tears in her eyes. Looking straight at Trando she said, "The lawyers have just sent the news through. In reply to our latest motions, the Massachusetts Supreme Court has given their final ruling. It states very clearly that no errors of law or abuses of discretion had been committed in this case and so this leaves Judge Thayer free to pass sentence." Her voice broke and she took away her hand to search for a handkerchief. "I fully expect that the sentencing will take place in Court next week. I believe they have already mentioned April 9th. She addressed Trando directly, "My dear boy, I am so sorry, so very sorry."

He held her gaze for a moment then looked away as he and Ella sat in silence, absorbing the news. Finally Trando asked, "Do we have any options left?"

She shook her head. "No. None. We will now have to wait for the sentences to be passed and then see if we can make a direct appeal to the Governor against those." She paused, choosing her words carefully, "Mr Thompson has warned us that the sentences will definitely be the death penalty." Both Ella and Trando gave a gasp at this. Mrs Evans nodded, speaking more firmly now, "I am sure, indeed I know, this will be seen as an outrage by all fair minded people in the civilised world. Mr Thompson is convinced of their innocence. From the first he said of Bart that he was a radical yes, but not a man capable of a hold-up and murder. They had simply arrested the wrong people but refused to admit it. It is a tragedy."

Trando stood up. He looked in shock and had gone very pale, "Thank you for letting us know. If you will excuse me, I must let my parents have the news at once, as they will want to be in Court next week."

With this he abruptly left and went upstairs. Mrs Evans looked at Ella and sighed. "That poor boy, it is going to hit him harder than any of us," and she patted Ella's hand. "I am just glad you can be with him at this time my dear. It is a great relief to me that he has someone of his own age to talk to, rather than leaving it to the older women."

Ella nodded and tried to smile. Mrs Evans was looking visibly upset and in need of support herself, but Ella found that she had no words of comfort. Inwardly her heart sank as she thought with dread about the next six days. They were going to be a terrible ordeal, not just for Trando, but for everyone on the Committee who had worked tirelessly for so long, only to be given this decision as their reward. It was cruel and unjust and there was nothing any of them could do about it. She felt an angry impotence and knew that Trando felt the same way.

*

As the day of sentencing drew near, Trando informed Ella that he would be sitting with his parents in the Court Room and not with her. She was neither surprised nor hurt by this. In truth he had been in a strange mood ever since Mrs Evans had broken the news to them. Most of the time he would be silent but then there would be the occasional angry outburst, more often than not aimed at himself. She felt quite unable to help him and decided it was best to leave him on his own unless he specifically asked for her company. Rejection was something she was used to and she had long ago learned how to cope with it. In any case even more letters were now pouring into the Defence Committee, so there was more than enough work to keep her fully occupied.

On April 9th, as they made the journey to the Dedham Court House, Mrs Evans asked Ella if she would like to join them in Court as she would be sitting with Mrs Henderson, Mary and Aldino Felicani. Ella had politely declined this invitation, feeling she would prefer to be by herself at the back.

It was a beautiful spring day and once again the crowds stood outside on the sidewalks and spilled over onto the lawns on either side of the entrance. Ella caught sight of Trando, sitting with his parents on a bench under a tree. She didn't wave but made her way straight into the lobby, waiting for the proceedings to begin.

*

Alfonsine Brini had been doing her best to hold her emotions in check but was obviously finding this very difficult. Trando couldn't look at her but sat white-faced and silent wrapped up in his own thoughts. His father had warned him about what was to happen that afternoon, and he knew the effect the final sentence would have on them all, particularly his mother and poor Rosina too, who would be sitting right behind the prisoner's cage. His mother had spoken to him about how she recently had found herself questioning God as to why these terrible unjust things should be happening to all the people she loved the most, and of course she had received no answer. She'd also told him that her faith, always so important to her, was really being tested and her priest had been no help at all. He just kept telling her they were all in God's hands and His will would be done. What good was that? It had left her feeling abandoned, desperate and lost. Trando knew how important her faith had always been, the one thing she had always relied on in the past. Now that support had gone. He thought sadly that as her son he couldn't help her either. He couldn't help her, or his father, or Ella or Mrs Evans. Most of all he hadn't been able to help Bart. He sat on feeling nothing but a desperate, impotent anger.

*

Anticipating the huge crowds this case would attract, the authorities had issued tickets. Trando had organised passes for the three of them and they'd had to push their way with some difficulty into the Court Room to find their seats which were near the front. He learned later that the crush to get into Court was so great that at first Aldino Felicani, Mrs Evans, Mrs Henderson and Mary Donovan had been refused entry and were only allowed in when the State Police identified Mrs Evans.

There was the usual murmur of conversation in the room, but today it was a good deal more subdued than on previous occasions. Trando stared ahead and waited.

Suddenly a silence fell as Bart and Nick were led into the room and locked in the central cage. Neither of the men glanced around but stared straight ahead. Trando thought how ill and old Bart looked, Nick too looked tired, thin and haggard. He watched his mother choke back the tears. His father gave her hand a squeeze and she gave him a brave smile. Neither of them looked at him.

Judge Thayer entered and everyone stood up. Trando gave a shudder. The man seemed like a withered old skeleton in his long black silk robes. All his edges looked sharp and brittle he thought, with his thin, beak noise, pointed chin and beady eyes hooded by thick, bushy eyebrows. He's like a vicious little animal. How he hated him.

The Judge now sank back into his seat and they all sat quietly, waiting for the proceedings to start. The District Attorney, Winfield Wilbur, gave a short summary of the case and then turned to the Clerk of the Court who called out,

"Nicola Sacco, stand up."

Nick got to his feet and the Clerk continued, "Nicola Sacco, have you anything to say why sentence of death should not be passed upon you?"

Nick paused and then he said, "Yes Sir. I am not an orator and it is not very familiar with me the English language. My comrade Vanzetti will speak for longer. But I do say that I never knew, never heard, or even read in history anything so cruel as this Court. After seven years prosecuting they still consider us guilty. I am of the oppressed class and you are the oppressor. You know it Judge..."

Trando stared at Judge Thayer, who merely looked bored and indifferent.

Nick now looked directly at him."...for seven years you have been persecuting me and my poor wife and you will today sentence me to death. You forget all the peoples and the comrades and big legion of intellectual people who know we are innocent. But what is the use? As I said before Judge Thayer, you know that I have never been guilty - never, not yesterday, or today, not ever."

He collapsed back into his chair and Judge Thayer, unmoved and ignoring Rosina's sobs, gave a curt nod to the Clerk who called out,

"Bartolomeo Vanzetti, stand up."

Bart stood and Trando looked across to his parents. Alfonsine gave him an anxious glance but he turned away. All his concentration must now be on Bart.

"Bartolomeo Vanzetti, have you anything to say why sentence of death should not be passed upon you?"

Bart turned round and looked straight at Trando holding his gaze for a moment. Then he turned back and in spite of his physical frailty he spoke in firm, strong tones.

"Yes. What I say is that I am innocent, not only of the

Braintree crime, but also of the Bridgewater crime. Not only am I innocent of these two crimes, but I have never stolen, never killed and never spilled blood. I have struggled all my life, since I began to reason, to eliminate crime from the earth. Everybody that knows me knows very well that I did not need to kill a man to make money. Although innocent, for seven years we are in jail. What we have suffered during these seven years nobody can imagine. Not even a dog should have been found guilty by an American Jury with the lack of evidence that the Commonwealth has produced against us. I say that not even a leprous dog should have had his appeal refused so many times by the Supreme Court of Massachusetts. I am not guilty, but am suffering because I am a radical. "

Bart talked on. It was a long speech, but given with great dignity. In it he explained his ideals and the plight of the Italian workers. He also mentioned the betrayals from his lawyers particularly Mr Vahey who he said had sold him out like a Judas. He then came to his finishing words, "I am suffering also because I am an Italian. But I am so convinced of my innocence that if you executed me two times, and if I was reborn two times, I would live my life again in the same way. I am finished. Thank you."

He sat down and Trando noticed that many in the courtroom like him had been moved to tears by Bart's words. But not the Judge. He now rose to his feet and spoke defiantly,

"Under the law of Massachusetts, the jury says whether a defendant is guilty or innocent. During the trial of this case many exceptions were taken. Those exceptions were taken to the Supreme Judicial Court. That Court, after examining the entire record, after examining all the exceptions - that Court in its final judgement said, 'The verdict of the jury should stand; exceptions overruled.' That being true there is only one thing this Court can do. It is not a matter of discretion. It is a matter of statutory requirement. There is only one duty that now devolves upon this Court and that is to pronounce sentences."

He gave another curt nod to the Clerk who said, "The prisoners will stand."

Judge Thayer waited for them to stand and then continued, "It is considered and ordered by the Court that you, Nicola Sacco will suffer punishment of death by the passage of a current of electricity through your body."

The muffled sounds of sobbing grew louder. Nick shouted out,

"You know I am innocent. That is the same words I pronounced seven years ago. You condemn an innocent man. You condemn two innocent men."

The Judge angrily rapped out, "You will be silent!"

He then turned towards Bart. "Bartolomeo Vanzetti, you will suffer the punishment of death by the passage of a current of electricity through your body. This is the sentence of law."

Having passed the sentences he waited no longer but abruptly left the Court without the usual final sentence of "May God have mercy on your souls."

The door slammed behind him.

There was a stunned silence and then the shouting and screaming broke out. The guards started to put the handcuffs on the prisoners again. Mrs Evans hobbled up close enough to call out, "There's a lot to hope for yet." As Bart turned towards her there were tears in his eyes. Mary Donovan also pushed forward her cheeks wet and Bart told her not to cry but to keep up a brave front. Trando stood still, rigid with shock. He could not speak, he could scarcely breathe. Bart looked anxiously across at him and spoke in clear, calm tones. "You must not be sad Trando. Be brave my friend. Be brave for me."

Others now shouted out words of encouragement but the guards moved either side of the two men roughly pushing people aside. They were then led away out of the court room. As they left a lone voice from the back of the room shouted out, "Tell us the names of your accomplices!" There was a shocked silence as people tried to see who had spoken out. Then the babble of general noise began again.

Rosina had by this time become completely hysterical and Alfonsine and Vincenza moved quickly over to be with her. Mrs Evans and Felicani had gone over to talk to the lawyer

Thompson. Trando searched the room for Ella. She was standing at the back with her eyes fastened on him. He beckoned her over and as she reached him he said, "Ella I can't be with you now. I must wait for my parents. You go on back to the hotel and I will see you later." And he added, looking at her anxiously, "Will you be all right?"

She gave him a reassuring nod. "Yes. I will go back with Mary and Mrs Evans ."

"That is good," he said, "you need to be with someone at this time. I may be back late so I probably won't see you until tomorrow."

She hesitated; lightly touched his hand, and left.

Trando remained for a moment lost in thought. Then he walked slowly across the room to join his parents and Rosina Sacco.

CHAPTER 21

Those returning that day from the Dedham Court House now noticed a marked change in those who worked in the hotel lobby. Gone was that general air of hope and optimism. They still continued to work quietly, but many had a look of despair combined with a kind of grim determination. For a few days many seemed uncertain of what to do next and meetings were held in various corners of the room to try to work out some course of action. Eventually ways were found and the long hours started again. Apart from anything else the letters were pouring in as news of the Sacco and Vanzetti sentencing spread around the world.

Ella was kept busy, not only dealing with the mail but also working with a group led by Katherine, organising demonstrations in the City. They told her it was vital that the Massachusetts public was kept informed of the terrible injustice that had been done and the Committee's great hope was that these demonstrations would put pressure on the Governor to grant clemency. It was Governor Fuller who now held the men's destiny in his hands.

Added to this the legal department was also working flat out, organising a series of appeals. Attorney Thompson had already anticipated the adverse decision of the Courts and had asked the greatly respected Episcopal Bishop of Massachusetts to write to the Governor on their behalf and this he had done. Mrs Evans told Trando that Bart was in the process of writing to the Governor a long appeal for clemency in which he again stated his innocence and also explained his doctrines and beliefs. He was convinced these were the reason that the jury was so prejudiced against him and had found him guilty. Trando was not so sure that Bart's doctrines and beliefs would in any way sway the Governor's opinion, indeed it could have the opposite effect, but he kept these feelings to himself.

What soon became very clear to everyone working in the room was that there was now a major fight for the possession of public opinion, however that might be managed. In consequence those at the press desk were working day and night to exploit anything to their advantage and win victories in any way they could.

In general these activities kept Trando fully occupied, but Ella was not the only person to be worried about him. Mrs Evans drew her aside the day after they returned from the Court House, telling her to keep a close watch on him now that the death sentences had been given.

So Ella watched him, but it soon became apparent that there was little she could do and her concern increased. Trando hardly spoke to anyone now but kept to his desk during the day desperately working on anything he could find. At night he would shun her company and shut himself away.

*

At last, there was some good news and a reward for all their efforts. After a month of frantic work, it seemed that the endeavours of the Committee had achieved a result. In the face of mounting criticism of the legal proceedings and the impending death sentences, Governor Fuller was finally forced into appointing a Committee to review the whole case, under the chairmanship of Professor Lowell, President of Harvard University. This Committee was also to advise the Governor on the issue of clemency.

"Well, at least that is some sort of progress," Ella remarked to Trando over a rare lunch, "and apart from this Committee there have been thousands of petitions for clemency coming in, not just here in Massachusetts, but from all over the world. Surely Governor Fuller has to take notice of that?"

Trando gave a scowl then shook his head. "I no longer feel hopeful about anything. Mr Thomson tells me this Lowell

Committee is full of men who are completely biased. As for Governor Fuller, he is known to be both narrow-minded and politically ambitious. He won't want to jeopardise his career by showing clemency to two Dagos, no matter how many petitions for clemency he gets." Ella looked at him sadly. She had no words of comfort left. All they could do now was to play the waiting game once more, while this Committee made its decision as to whether the trials had been conducted fairly and if there were grounds for clemency.

*

When alone in his room Trando spent much of his time trying to compose a letter to Bart but he was struggling to get it done. What could he say to this man he knew to be innocent and who had now been unjustly condemned to death? He had no message of comfort. Nor did he want to raise false hopes with all the appeals for clemency that had gone in to the Governor, or the fact that the Lowell Committee were once again examining the fairness of the trials. Maybe instead he should tell Bart about Ella? But this was not a solution either. What could he possibly say to Bart about her? That he thought he had fallen in love with a girl and was now ashamed because he was shutting her out of his life? He knew he was hurting Ella by his coldness and detachment. She was suffering too, and yet he had no words of comfort for her either. It was selfish of him to behave like this and Bart would rightly have reproved him for it, but he just couldn't help himself and this began to frighten him. His behaviour wasn't normal, he was well aware of that. The days were bad enough because he found it almost impossible to talk to anyone, even Ella. But the night times were even worse. Once he finally managed to sleep it wouldn't be long before he was jerked awake quite suddenly, trembling and in a cold sweat, as the terrible realisation would sweep over him that they were going to murder Bart. At these times further sleep was impossible. He would get up, sit at his desk and try again to put some words down on paper.

Finally, after one particularly bad night, he decided not to go down to the lobby but stay in his room all day if necessary, until he had finished that letter to Bart.

Halfway through the morning there was a knock at his door. Trando paid no attention to this. There was another knock, and this time Ella opened the door and let herself in. She glanced around the room and at once took in the unmade bed, the clothes on the floor and Trando's wild, dishevelled look. Crossing the room she pulled up the covers and quietly tidied up. Then she looked at the figure hunched over the desk and asked, "Are you writing to Bart?"

He didn't look up but just nodded.

It was at this moment something snapped and she lost her temper. "For God's sake Trando! Do you think you're the only one who is suffering? We are all feeling it, Mary, Elizabeth, all of us. Yes, and in case you haven't noticed, me as well. You're behaving as if it was only happening to you. It's bloody selfish. Is that what Bart would want? Do you really think that is how Bart would want you to behave?"

She stopped, quite out of breath, and then she noticed that Trando's shoulders, bowed over the desk, were shaking. Crossing the room she kneeled down beside him and pulled him round to face her. "Trando, I know it is a terrible, terrible thing that has happened, but you are making yourself ill. You don't eat, you don't sleep, you are completely exhausted. Bart wouldn't want you to suffer like this. He told you to be brave, to be brave for him. You heard him. I heard him."

There was silence. Then Trando threw himself into her arms and began to sob loudly and violently like a small child. Ella watched him sadly realising that he was at last letting go of all the pent-up emotion, sadness and frustration of the previous months and now that he had started he was finding it hard to stop. So she held on to him tightly until the tears began to subside. When he finally looked at her it was with such a look of desperation she could hardly bear to hold his gaze.

"I'm so sorry, so sorry," he finally gasped. "I don't know

what to do Ella, I feel powerless. I don't know how to help Bart. I don't know what to do next. I can't even manage to write him a letter."

She stood up and decided the best course of action was to sound positive. "I know how hard it is for you Trando but you can't give up now. None of us can. We *are* beginning to get results, I promise you. These sentences have shocked the entire world. I know, I read the letters..."

Trando replied bitterly, "How can world opinion help now? It's all too late."

"No," she said firmly, "The Governor must be feeling the pressure. Everybody says so."

Trando shook his head. "What you have to realise Ella is that he had pressure from the other side as well and that will be the side he is more inclined to listen to. You've heard them shouting, 'Give them the juice!' 'Let them fry if they're guilty!'" He looked up at her. "Only yesterday I read an article in the paper saying that America was getting tired of foreigners, of the radicals and anarchists, coming over here and telling them what to do, threatening danger to true Americans. *That* is the voice Governor Fuller will listen to."

Ella was lost in thought for a moment. "What about a petition from *you* for clemency, then he'd have to go over your evidence. If, after that, he doesn't believe your evidence, well, he ought to have you arrested for perjury. After all the man can't have it both ways."

Trando looked at her suddenly alert. "What was that you just said?"

"I said the Governor should be presented with a petition from you for clemency..."

"No, no!" Trando interrupted her impatiently, "that bit about perjury."

Ella said slowly, "Well, I said he either had to *believe* your evidence, or have you arrested for perjury."

Trando leapt to his feet. "That's it! That's it!" He shouted at the top of his voice. Ella stared at him in astonishment, finding it hard to believe the sudden transformation that had come over him. He was now laughing for the first time in days, "Ella Feenan you are brilliant! You have found the solution and I could hug you."

"Feel free." she said, not knowing what she had done but feeling very relieved.

He pulled her to him and then kissed her. It wasn't long or passionate but it was somehow significant because in that short moment they both realised that a line had been crossed between friendship and something much deeper. They stood staring at each other in silence, until Trando finally broke the moment and began to talk very fast.

"Don't you see Ella? This is just the break-through I was searching for. You are right of course, it *has* to be perjury. If they don't believe I was telling the truth, then they have to admit I was committing perjury. Even Governor Fuller can't get around that! I must find Thompson at once. He can get me an appointment to see the Governor. I'll go over to Thompson's office right away."

"You can't go looking like that," Ella protested adding firmly, "First you must have a shave, change your clothes and then at least have some breakfast." She paused. "And as it was my brainwave Trando Brini, I will be going with you."

CHAPTER 22

Trando and Ella reached the Hanover Street offices of the lawyers in the early afternoon. Ella had agreed to sit outside the room, while Trando talked to Mr Thompson and Aldino Felicani, who was also with him. She could see him through the glass door talking excitedly and she prayed that at last this might be the break-through that was so badly needed. After a while she saw Trando sit down and Mr Thompson pick up the telephone. What followed seemed to be a long conversation. When he had finished, he talked again to Trando who finally stood up and shook hands with the lawyer.

As he re-joined Ella he looked excited and grabbing her hand he said, "Come on. Let's get back to the Common. I can tell you everything there."

*

They ran down the slope to the pond and it didn't take long for him to tell her the main piece of news, which was that Thompson had managed to make an appointment for him to see Governor Fuller the following day.

"Well that's just great," Ella said not only surprised, but impressed. "Now you really can put your case directly to him. He must have seen the need to meet you if it has been arranged so quickly."

Trando nodded. "I think so too. The repetition of my evidence must be making them nervous. However, Mr Thompson kept saying I wasn't to expect too much from the Governor. He described Fuller as a self-made business man, very wealthy and above all an ambitious politician. He's also a Baptist, a Republican and a Mason. Oh, and he is a member of the Patriotic

Society of Massachusetts." Here Trando made a face, "None of which is exactly going to endear him to our cause, or to me. Thompson also told me that Fuller had said to Gardner Jackson there was no proof that Vanzetti sold eels. Can you believe that? When Jackson reminded him there had been eighteen witnesses swearing they had bought eels from Bart, Fuller just laughed and said that those witnesses were all Italians. So you see what I'm up against." He gave a defiant shrug. "It doesn't put me off. Both men agreed that I had a valid point which should be made to the Governor if I was willing to take the risk."

"Risk?" Ella echoed and looked at him now worried.

Trando was scornful. "Well yes a risk. Obviously if he is convinced I committed perjury I could be sent to prison. As you yourself said they can't have it both ways." Ella was quiet for a moment taking all this in, but Trando was now frowning. "I just don't know how involved this Governor is with the case. My guess is it wouldn't interest him at all if he wasn't being influenced by public opinion. Apparently he only asked for the Sacco and Vanzetti records two weeks after the sentences had been handed down and that was probably only because he took fright at the amount of appeals for clemency that were pouring in." Here Trando gave a smile, "I also had the impression from Thompson that the Governor is not the brightest of men. Aldino Felicani was of a similar opinion and said that when Fuller was asked what he thought of the Pinkerton report, he asked what the Pinkerton report was! How could the man be so stupid? I can see I am going to have to make my points very clearly and precisely." Trando looked at Ella and laughed. "That shouldn't be difficult. All I have to say is, either believe me, or lock me up for perjury!"

Ella felt a rising sense of panic but said nothing because she noticed Trando pulling some papers out of his pocket. "They gave me a copy of Bart's petition for freedom which he had sent to the Governor's office. I'll read it later because it might be helpful to know exactly what Bart has written."

*

Once they were back at the Hotel, Trando left Ella working at the mail desk and went upstairs to his room. He was especially keen to read the long testimony that Bart had penned to the Governor. Sitting on the bed he took the papers out and peered down at the scrawled writing. Would Fuller really have bothered to read such a difficult document? He doubted it. Some of the words were barely legible and even he had difficulty in deciphering them. He carefully spread the pages out in order and began to read.

The first section dealt with the evidence that was already on record and Trando made a few notes of one or two of the more important points. In one part Bart had written...

'The only way to find us guilty is to make up your mind not to believe our witnesses. To believe that Beltrando Brini, a boy of thirteen can resist four hours of cross examination of Katzmann, telling a false story, is absurd. If you do not believe the Brini boy, then you do not want to believe all the other of my witnesses. If such is the case, all the Plymouth defence witnesses should be indicted as perjurers.'

Trando leapt up and punched the air, shouting "Yes! Yes! Yes!" This was exactly his point and Bart had seen it as well. Returning again to the petition he found another paragraph of particular interest. This one dealt with why Bart had lied when he was first arrested. It was an area that had worried him from the beginning. It was so out of character for Bart to lie. Now Bart wrote...

'When I was arrested I did not know that I could have refused to speak with the policemen. And besides that, they questioned me with a big stick at their side, one by one, and I know of the third degree and am frightened. I remember the fate of poor Salseda in New York. He was tortured until he did give up names. I thought we would have the same and I would be forced to betray my comrades. If it had not been for that, I would not have told a lie.'

Trando felt a great relief sweep over him. Of course Bart had been frightened, not for himself but of what he might have been persuaded to say, of betraying his comrades under torture. It was only natural in these circumstances for Bart to lie. He well remembered the day when he had heard Bart speaking to his mother in their front room and how terrified he had sounded at that time. How much more terrifying was it for him to be in the police station being threatened with violence.

After this entry there were some long rambling pages devoted to the ideas of many men obviously with similar ideas to Bart, citing such writers as Jefferson, Thomas Payne, Ralph Waldo Emerson, Shelley and Tolstoy. Trando was greatly impressed by all Bart's knowledge but wasn't sure this would actually help his cause. From what he had gleaned from Thompson and Aldino Felicani, it wasn't something that Governor Fuller would be the slightest bit interested in and certainly wouldn't affect his thinking on the case.

The final paragraph was more of a passionate declaration. *'Everything is against me, my race, my opinions and my humble occupation. I did not commit either of these crimes. I abhor violence. I am with Garibaldi. Only the slaves have the right to violence in order to free themselves. Only the violence that frees from slavery is legitimate. I lived in this country 12 years before my arrest and worked industriously and honestly, without any act of violence. The only violence that has been committed here, is the violence practiced against us.'*

Trando considered all this for a while and then carefully placed the document in the folder on his desk. After this he went downstairs to the lobby and sought out Mrs Evans thinking it was very possible she might be able to give him further information on Governor Fuller.

*

He caught sight of her sitting at a small table in the far corner with playing cards spread out in front of her. She looked up as he walked towards her and gave a smile of relief.

"Oh my dear, I did hope I'd see you today," and gathering up the cards on the table she murmured apologetically, "I have to do something to occupy my time at the moment, so I play endless games of Patience. It is the only way I know of keeping my mind off unhappier things." She patted the seat beside her and Trando obediently sat down. "I met Ella earlier," she said, "and she told me you had every intention of going to see Governor Fuller."

Trando saw that Mrs Evans had an expression that was not only one of interest but also of concern. She had always been so kind to him he felt he now owed it to her to explain what had happened. So he described his meeting with Thompson that morning and how an appointment had been arranged for him to see Governor Fuller the following day. When he had finished telling her she didn't say anything for a while but slowly put the cards back in their case. When she finally did speak her voice sounded grave.

"You are a very brave young man Trando and I know how passionate you are about saving Bart." She paused, "but I want you to think very seriously about what you are about to do. You tell me your intention is to visit the Governor of Massachusetts tomorrow and to put him on the spot. As I understand it you are going to say to him, 'Believe the evidence I gave at the trial, or convict me for perjury'. Do I have that right?"

Trando nodded. Elizabeth Evans thought for a moment as if considering how to continue and when she did she gave special emphasis to her words.

"I can tell you now that this is a dangerous move on your part, because he won't like it. He won't like it one little bit and you will make an immediate enemy." Trando waited as she paused again. "Do you know that wild animals, when they are cornered, turn vicious and go on the attack?" Trando felt puzzled and wondered where all this was leading. Mrs Evans went on, "Well, I'm very much afraid this is what Governor Fuller will do. I know the man quite well. He is a simple soul with a small intellect." Here she gave a wry smile and then sighed, "Oh he has done well enough for himself and should be admired for that. It's the usual tale of a self-made man making his way to the top from poor and humble beginnings. He has struggled to get to where he has, but you must understand Trando, this means he will do *nothing* that would jeopardise his position. On the contrary he will do anything he can to protect it." She gave a smile. "Normally he is harmless enough, but this action of yours could turn him into something of a bully and a nasty one at that. I really do fear he could make life exceedingly uncomfortable for you."

Trando shifted in his seat not knowing how to react to this. He knew all that she said was true, but his mind was made up so it made no difference. Mrs Evans looked at him and sighed. "I know, you will say I'm a fussy old woman, but you must know how fond I am of you and I am pleading with you to think about yourself for once. It is what Bart would want me to do and apart from anything else I do feel it incumbent on me to give you this warning as your parents are not around to do so."

Trando smiled and made an effort to allay her fears without sounding rude. "I don't think you are being fussy at all but I would point out that I am twenty years old now and am really very capable of making decisions without my parents." He added quickly, "But please believe me, I am grateful for your concern and I promise you I take very seriously everything you say. Aldino Felicani and Mr Thompson said much the same thing to me. But in the end it comes down to what I feel I must do. I am only going to tell Governor Fuller the truth and that is all. I don't see how he can find fault with that."

Mrs Evans had lost her serious expression and was smiling again. "Then my dear boy, there is nothing more for me to do other than wish you good luck, and please let me know what happens the moment you return." She added drily, "That is always presuming they don't take you away and lock you up."

CHAPTER 23

The next morning Trando set out in good time for the Governor's office. At Ella's insistence he was wearing his best suit and a tie, something he was now beginning to regret because the July sun was extremely hot and bouncing off the sidewalk. To add to his troubles he took a wrong turning which meant he had to run the last two blocks, arriving not late but very out of breath.

A smart female receptionist looked him up and down as he panted out, "My name is Beltrando Brini. I have an appointment to see Governor Fuller."

She looked a little surprised and Trando thought to himself that she had obviously been expecting somebody quite different, but in spite of this she said politely, "Please take a seat Mr Brini. The Governor will be out in a minute. He has booked a table for lunch."

Trando was amazed and stammered out, "For lunch?"

The receptionist noticing his look of shock now smiled and repeated, "Yes, for lunch. I'll just let him know you are here."

This was a really unexpected turn of events and Trando sat on the elegant gilt chair, trying to work out why he was being given such special treatment. Maybe that call from Mr Thompson had made the Governor realise just how serious this was. If that were the case, a great deal now rested on his shoulders and he started going over again all the things he ought to say.

Fifteen minutes went by and then the central door burst open and Governor Fuller walked over to him, profuse with apologies. Trando said politely that it was no problem, adding that it was good of the Governor to make time to see him as he knew how busy he was.

Governor Fuller was a man with smooth good looks and a certain rugged charm. The short walk to the restaurant passed

190

pleasantly enough and the restaurant itself turned out to be one of Boston's finest. Trando was immediately awed by the grandeur of the place and he was now rather relieved he had taken Ella's advice and worn a suit. The huge room was full of noisy diners, all of whom seemed to be men, and most of them seemed to know Governor Fuller, so that their progress to the table took some time. Trando inwardly smiled as he thought that they were all probably trying to work out why on earth the Governor was lunching with him.

Once settled into the meal Governor Fuller started to address him and it sounded to Trando like a prepared speech which he was now delivering in rather patronising tones. He began by praising him, "I've heard a lot about you young man and I'm happy to say that all of it good. My great friend Mrs Glendower Evans speaks very highly of you..."

This line of flattery went on for some time and Trando began to feel uncomfortable. Then suddenly the Governor's voice changed and it wasn't nearly so pleasant. Trando had a momentary vision of that cornered animal.

"I have assured Mr Thompson, for whom I have the highest regard, and I now assure you Beltrando, that I *have* read all the files, and studied *all* the evidence. I have interviewed many of the witnesses, as indeed I am doing with you now…"

Trando could hold back no longer and he burst out, "Then surely you must see sir, that Bart Vanzetti has an alibi."

That was a mistake. There was a long silence. Governor Fuller wiped the sides of his mouth with the linen napkin and then placed it carefully on the table. He looked long and hard at Trando and now, when he spoke, his words were chosen very carefully indeed.

"You are obviously an intelligent boy Beltrando, so please do me the courtesy of listening to what I have to say to you without interruption. As I said, I have read all your evidence and I have gone over the transcript of your cross examination and I admire the way, as a youngster of thirteen, you stood up to Katzmann and answered the questions..."

"Because I was speaking the truth!" Trando in his frustration almost shouted out the words. Governor Fuller held up his hand and his look was stern, almost menacing.

"Don't interrupt me boy." He paused, obviously trying to keep his temper in check and when he spoke again it was slowly and firmly. "I repeat, I have read the relevant file on your cross examination and after long and careful consideration I have come to the same conclusion as the Commonwealth and the Jury." He paused and then said, "I came to the same conclusion, that you had learned your evidence by heart." He added almost casually, "There is not even anything in the documents I read to prove that Vanzetti sold eels."

Trando couldn't believe what he was hearing, but before he could say anything to contradict that last statement, the Governor continued, with a note of sympathy in his voice, which made it even more sinister.

"Nobody is blaming you son. Probably by the time you had repeated it that many times you came to believe your story *was true.*" By now the Governor wasn't giving him time to interrupt as he went on in more measured tones, "Now, I say to you that the sensible option here and one you should consider carefully, the *sensible* option as I'm sure you can see, would be for you to retract your evidence."

Trando felt as if he had been shot. "What?" he shouted. "I can't do that!"

"Oh I think you can son. No-one will think any the worse of you. In fact they will admire your courage for the fact that you spoke out for your friend in Court."

This was too much for Trando. "I didn't speak out because Bart was my friend," he said hotly, a note of desperation creeping into his voice. "I spoke out because it was the truth. *It is* the truth. I was with him on the morning of the robbery. "

There was another long pause while Fuller studied him. Trando realised then that he had lost this battle. Fuller was not going to change his mind. He had made the decision even before they came out. So why had he bothered with the lunch?

The answer to this soon became apparent when the

conversation took a new and sinister turn. Governor Fuller leant across the table, "I am told you are an outstanding musician. Violin isn't it?" Trando nodded. "Well then Beltrando, you now have to consider *your* future. What is it you have planned? I think you are destined for Harvard yes? And after that one of the big orchestras?"

Trando was surprised that the Governor should know so much about him, but replied politely, "Yes sir. I am actually hoping it will be the Boston Symphony Orchestra."

Fuller now leaned even further forward his voice now low and menacing. "Let me make this absolutely plain to you boy. Let there be no mistake. Unless you retract your evidence, there is no way you are going to make it into any major orchestra in the land." Trando gasped in shock and Fuller went on, obviously pleased his words were having the desired effect. "Think boy, think. Do you imagine anyone will employ the person who testified for a murderer?" He pointed his finger violently at Trando. "Do you? Do you? Because that is how you are going to be known. You will always be known as the 'Brini Boy', the one who defended a murderer and an anarchist. The Brini Boy who did great harm to his adopted country. Do you think one of our finest colleges, Harvard, will want you after that? Think boy think. You have intelligence. Work it out for yourself." He finished with a statement that sounded final. "I urge you to consider carefully about your future Beltrando Brini. It is entirely in your hands."

The meal was over. Trando sat in shock and no more was said.

Once outside the restaurant they shook hands and the Governor walked briskly away back to his office, obviously satisfied with the way things had gone. Trando lent against a wall and realised he was shaking. So this is what he had been warned about, that Governor Fuller would turn nasty, but nobody had told him the Governor would resort to this kind of blackmail.

The only small consolation was that Fuller was obviously worried that he still remained a threat. Why otherwise would he have bothered with the lunch or with the threats?

*

Trando returned to the hotel, dragged Ella out of the lobby and marched her over to the Common. They sat by the bandstand and she watched him, her heart sinking, as he angrily tore off his jacket and tie. She could tell by his expression the interview had not gone well. He was looking angry and upset.

"My God Ella," he burst out, "The man is a complete bastard. He's an absolute monster!"

She put her hand on his and could tell he was shaking. "Calm down Trando. Why don't you just tell me what happened? Start at the beginning."

So he gave her the whole account of the morning's events and when he finished he could see she was as shocked as he had been. "And do you know the worst part?" he added. "The very worst part is that I am certain he knows I was telling the truth. He must know that I couldn't have learned all that evidence by heart and stood up to over three hours cross examination. Not at the age of thirteen. So if he knows I was telling the truth, as I am sure he does, it's a huge dilemma for him. Because if that is the case, he also knows he will be sending an innocent man to the electric chair. He's definitely rattled, which is why he resorted to the bullying tactics and finally to blackmail."

The sun went behind a cloud, giving them momentary respite from the afternoon heat. Ella sat lost in thought until she looked up in panic, "But Trando what about all those threats? What about Harvard and your music? You have to take that seriously. He's threatening your future."

"Well of course I take it seriously," he said almost irritably. "But I can't worry about that now." He stopped and looked at her pleadingly, "Please Ella, don't tell anyone about the threats, especially not Elizabeth Evans. She would want to tell Bart and he must never know about it." He suddenly leapt up. "My God, Bart! I must go and see him and tell him what has happened. Not about the threats, but about Fuller not believing me."

Ella stood up as well. "Trando, he is on death row. They'll never let you in."

Trando thought about this. "Elizabeth Evans, she's the answer. I know she's made friends with the Warden and she'd told me that he is sympathetic. I am sure she will find a way to get me in to see Bart. She just has to."

CHAPTER 24

Events now moved fast. The Lovell Committee submitted their findings on July 27th. After two weeks of hearing witnesses and reviewing the evidence, they determined yet again that the trial had been fair and a new trial was not warranted. They therefore advised Governor Fuller against clemency. This was a terrible and seemingly final blow to the Defence Committee, but to Felicani and Thompson it didn't really come as a surprise. They explained that the three man Committee had never been likely to reach a different conclusion, simply because they were not lawyers and therefore not capable of seriously re-examining the legal case, which was the task the Governor had set them. To give the men their due, there was never any doubt that they had been thorough and conscientious, but a great deal of the specialist legal evidence had been quite beyond them and they actually ignored exculpatory material that the defence had discovered since the trial. The only small satisfaction was that in their final report there was some criticism of Judge Thayer's indiscretions outside the Court Room, but in spite of this, they were unanimous in praising his actual conduct of the Trial.

"How could they still ignore my evidence?" Trando asked Mrs Evans, "These are meant to be learned men. They can't have believed that a thirteen year old boy was cross examined for over three hours and had learned the whole thing by heart. I just don't understand it."

She replied drily that nothing surprised her any more. Apparently, Thompson had also again tackled Governor Fuller about the fact that Vanzetti was selling eels on December 24th, which gave him a cast iron alibi. Fuller had snapped back that he found no proof of this.

"But my evidence was the truth and the proof he needed. He

continues to ignore that!" Trando shouted in his frustration.

Mrs Evans nodded in sympathy. "I know my dear. But you have to realise you are up against a very obstinate man in Fuller. His reasoning, however misguided, is that there isn't a single document he can find proving that Vanzetti sold eels. There is only the word of all his Italian friends in the neighbourhood and that, my dear Trando, I'm afraid includes you."

"That is ridiculous." Trando protested, adding, "And he knows it."

Mrs Evans looked at him and said sadly, "Indeed it is ridiculous as you rightly say my dear boy. Indeed it is. But the man is obviously not to be moved and we have to accept it as one more monstrous injustice that has been the story of this case all along."

*

On August 3rd the news spread that there was to be a mid-day announcement when the Governor would finally make a statement on the Sacco and Vanzetti case. Members of the Defence Committee and a group of reporters arrived in the Governor's office and waited. By late afternoon there was still no statement and the small crowd was becoming restless and angry. There were mounting shouts from the reporters of, 'What the heck is taking so long? 'We've been here all day'. Fearing they might have a riot on their hands, the Governor's officials hastily provided chairs. Ella and Trando sat side by side, silent and tense.

After almost five hours, the Governor's secretary Herman appeared, looking extremely nervous. "Gentlemen, I have here the Governor's statement, which I will now give to you."

He cleared his throat and started to read.

'The task of this review has been a laborious one and I am proud to be associated in this public service with clear-eyed witnesses unafraid to tell the truth, and with the jurors who discharged their obligations in accordance with their convictions and oaths. As a result of my investigation, I believe, with the jury, that these men, Sacco

and Vanzetti were guilty, and that they had a fair trial. I furthermore believe that there is no justifiable reason for giving them a new trial. The death sentence stands.'

"That is all gentlemen." He gave a little bow and then left as quickly as he could.

The reporters raced out of the room to tell the news to their editors. Trando grabbed Ella's hand and ran with her all the way back to the hotel, neither of them uttering a word. Outside the main doors they stopped, both out of breath. She clung to him as he kissed her and wiped away her tears as she finally gave in and started to cry.

"Elizabeth has managed to persuade them to let me see Bart," he told her. "It is all the more important now in view of this announcement. I will go the day after tomorrow. There is little else any of us can do now." He added angrily, "They seem absolutely determined to murder Bart and Nick."

*

The newspaper headlines the next morning confirmed this in large bold print,

"SACCO AND VANZETTI TO DIE.
SACCO AND VANZETTI MUST DIE, SAYS FULLER
SACCO AND VANZETTI GUILTY AND WILL DIE."

The reaction was immediate and worldwide. Trando and Ella sifted through the press cuttings together. Demonstrations had broken out in South America and in many European cities. Even The Vatican had sent a message of hope that an appeal for clemency would be answered.

"You'd think they'd listen to the Pope." Ella said. "Even Mussolini has asked for them to be saved from execution."

Trando just shrugged at this and commented, "They won't take notice of anyone now. What will affect us more is that here in America they have announced immediate precautions. I gather public meetings have been prohibited in all States and Boston has refused demonstrations of any kind, especially on the Common. If anyone does so they would be put in prison."

Ella nodded. "Katherine tells me it's because of the bombings in New York and Chicago."

Trando said a little sarcastically, "And I'm sure Katherine would know."

Ella decided to ignore this. She had realised for quite a while that Trando didn't share her admiration of Katherine Anne Porter, so she merely said, "There's still things we can do. The Committee is planning a stream of appeals to President Coolidge," and she added defiantly, "and in spite of the stupid ban, people are still demonstrating on the Common and there are picket lines outside the Court House and what they are calling a 'death watch' at the State Prison."

Trando said nothing to this. All his thoughts were now taken up with his visit to Bart.

*

The news of the execution date was broken to the prisoners by Felicani and Thompson. Thompson told Trando that they both took it calmly and with resignation. Nick and Bart were now moved from the Prison to the Death House and this is where Trando made his way a day later. The arrangements for his visit had been secured, albeit with some difficulty, by Mrs Evans and on giving his name at the door Trando was allowed to enter. He was carrying his violin case and after inspecting it a guard immediately led him to a dark corridor containing the death cells. Trando reckoned there were about five in all. The floor of the corridor was of white tiles with a black line running down the middle about six feet from the cells. There was little light, just one lamp outside each cell and the whole place was pervaded with a terrible smell, a mixture of sweat, vomit and urine.

Trando put down his violin case and peered into the dark room that he was told was Bart's. The guard fetched him a chair. "Don't go over that line boy," he warned and returned to sit on his own chair at the end of the corridor.

Trando tried to adjust his eyes to the gloom. He could make out a narrow bed, a bucket in one corner, a chair and a small table. Bart was sitting at the table writing with his back to him.

"Bart!" he called out, his voice giving out a strange echo in that cavernous place.

Bart looked around and then slowly walked to the bars. "Trando!" he gasped out. "What are you doing here? This hell-hole is no place for you."

Trando looked at him and a great sadness overwhelmed him. Here was a man, old before his time, frail, tired and with suffering etched in every line of his face.

"I had to see you Bart," he explained. "I wanted to tell you that I went to see the Governor."

Bart held on tightly to the bars. His voice was weary but Trando could tell he was angry as he said, "I know you did, Rosina Sacco told me. She also tried. The Governor would not listen to her either. Not to you, not to Rosina, not to the lawyers, not to me." He gave a hollow laugh and now spoke bitterly. "He told Rosina that you got the time wrong. He thinks while you looked for your rubber shoes, I travelled twenty miles, did the shooting and then came back to sell fish!"

Trando leapt to his feet in anger and the Guard shouted, "Siddown kid. You gotta siddown!"

Trando resumed his seat and tried to stay calm as he said, "That's crazy. How could you possibly do all that in half an hour? I'll go and see the Governor again."

At this Bart seemed to gather up all the strength he had left and almost shouted, "No Trando no! I forbid it. It is no good anymore. They are determined we should die." And then he added more gently. "Do not worry about me. I am ready. It is time. I have no wish to endure more of this terrible life. Nick also is ready. We will die as anarchists and comrades should."

This last exertion had taken its toll and he staggered a little, clinging onto the bars in the effort to keep upright. Trando became alarmed. "Bart, you are ill. Let me call someone. You look so ill..." He turned towards the guard but Bart stopped him.

"No, no, it is nothing. I have not eaten for two days since Governor Fuller's verdict. Nick has been on hunger strike for longer. He is very weak." He looked directly at Trando. "Please, you must not be unhappy for me Trando. I meet my fate calmly. I am at peace," adding, "although I do have anger in my heart for some." He paused, "Do you remember John Vahey?"

Trando remembered him only too well. "Of course I do. He was your lawyer in the first trial."

Bart now spoke with real anger. "He was a traitor! A Judas!" He spat out the last words. "He deliberately told me not to go on the witness stand. He knew very well because of this I would be found guilty. He did not tell me this thing, so I fell into his trap. And can you believe this Trando? Two years later he joined the firm of the enemy lawyer Katzmann. Reward for his great treachery." He paused, regaining his breath. "Then there was Moore, a terrible man, who was only in it for money and fame." He shook his head sadly. "There were so many betrayals Trando. So many mistakes were made and so many unanswered questions remain. Where are the other men who they say did this thing? Where is the stolen money? There were thousands of dollars. Where? Have they found it? No! No! And if we were guilty, why do they think we walk around like free men? Why didn't we run away like Boda, Coacci. Why?"

Trando had no answers to this but said sadly. "It was those guns Bart. If only you hadn't been a known anarchist and most important of all, if only you hadn't been found with all those weapons on you at the time of arrest."

Bart shook his head. "I know but I tell you again I was only getting rid of the stuff for my comrades. I was given the responsibility of protecting the others. It is important to me that you believe that Trando."

Trando nodded. "I do believe you Bart. You know I do."

Bart's energies were nearly spent. "I am tired, tired, tired, but I am going to say to you now, what I said to a reporter some days ago and I want you to remember this always Trando. It is what you must remember about this time above everything else and you may find it of comfort in the days that are to come." He now spoke with a sudden vigour. Even through the gloom Trando could see that the burning zeal of old had returned, if only for a brief moment. Vanzetti now spoke with passion.

"If it had not been for these events my friend, I might have lived out my life, talking at street corners to scorning men. I might have died unmarked, unknown. A failure. But now I am not a failure. This is my career and my triumph. Never in my life could I have hoped to do such work for tolerance, for justice, for man's understanding of man, as now I do by my death. My words, my life, my pain, *nothing!* The *taking* of my life, the life of a poor fish-peddler - that is all! The last moment belongs to me. In that agony is my triumph."

This last effort had completely drained him and he leant his head against the bars as if he were about to faint. It was then he caught sight of the violin case on the floor beside Trando's chair.

"You bring your violin with you? Will you play for Bart one more time?"

Trando nodded and took the violin out of its case and after a moments tuning, he started to play "Old Black Joe." The guard stood up and was about to make a move to stop him, but then deciding against it, sat down and listened. As Trando played the other prisoners moved toward the bars of their doors. The dark corridor gave the music an eerie echo which somehow added to its poignancy. Long after it had finished nobody moved.

Then Bart spoke in a voice shaking with emotion. "Your beautiful music and your friendship have been the most valuable part of my life Trando. Now you must forget all the dark things you have witnessed over these seven long years and live out the good life I have always known you would have. You must know you could not have done more for me and I am grateful from the bottom of my heart for that and for the music I hear for one last time. As I tell you so many time. The sentiment makes me both happy and sad." He paused and then with one last effort he said, "You must go now. It is time. Goodbye my very dear, dear friend."

With that he turned, walked slowly away and sank down on the bed.

CHAPTER 25

Trando and Ella were now inseparable, both needing the other for comfort and strength to see them through. They spent every waking hour together and this was generally noticed, and affectionately commented on by members of the Defence Committee. Katherine Porter called them 'the little lovebirds', which would have made Trando furious had he known. Only Mrs Evans watched them with a sad and heavy heart, knowing that this was not a conventional love affair and could well be crushed by the momentous events they all now had to endure.

On returning from the visit to Bart, Trando immediately sought out Ella who had been anxiously waiting for him. They walked to the Common to be out of earshot of the lobby and once seated on their usual bench he reported on his visit. He looked down at the brown and dusty area that a few months ago had been so green and thought that even the grass had given up.

"You wouldn't believe how thin and weak he was Ella. He could hardly stand and had to cling to the bars. The place was terrible, suitable only for rats. What sort of human beings are we to keep a man locked up in that sewer?"

She looked shocked. "Didn't the warden tell Mrs Evans that he was giving up the hunger strike?"

Trando nodded. "She did and I am sure he will now. He wouldn't want to face the horrible ordeal of being force fed like Nick. Anyway he'd already told the warden there was little point and I think he's too tired to withstand further pain." He turned to her. "I can't bear it Ella. He's been shut away for seven years for a crime he didn't do. Bart, who loved life, animals, plants. As a child he taught me all the names of the plants when we went on walks together, and the names of the stars and the planets..."

He broke off lost in thought for a moment and then he suddenly said, "Will you be joining the picket line tomorrow?"

She was surprised at this, "Yes of course, won't you?"

He shook his head. "Yes, at the beginning anyway but then I'll leave. I've decided I am going to try to see the Governor one last time."

This was worrying news, but one glance at his expression told her that he was determined and she knew it would be futile to even try to argue him out of it.

They started walking back and she asked a little nervously, "What more can you tell the Governor that would make a difference now?"

"I am going to put it in a letter," Trando said, "about the perjury. If he thinks he can bully me in person maybe he will take notice of something in print. I could even threaten to send it to the newspapers."

Although she admired his courage Ella couldn't help feeling alarmed by this latest development.

*

The following morning they stood in the lobby with Mrs Evans, as people gathered ready to join the picket lines. Placards were being handed out with various slogans painted in large black lettering.

GOVERNOR FULLER! IF YOUR CONSCIENCE IS CLEAR WHY DO YOU KEEP YOUR INVESTIGATIONS SECRET?

IF THEY ARE NOT INNOCENT, WHY ARE YOU AFRAID OF A NEW TRIAL?

GOVERNOR FULLER! WHY DO YOU CALL ALL OUR WITNESSES LIERS?

DON'T LET TWO INNOCENT MEN DIE!

JUSTICE AND FREEDOM FOR SACCO AND VANZETTI

While they were waiting and on impulse, Ella turned to Elizabeth Evans and told her about Trando's plan. She could see that this annoyed Trando but it had worried her all night and she had slept little. Now she said bluntly that she didn't really see what good it would do seeing the Governor again. She hoped Mrs Evans might use her influence to stop him from going. Disregarding the black looks from Trando she said,

"Honestly Elizabeth, I just don't see it can do any good. The Governor seems to be even more prejudiced than Judge Thayer."

Mrs Evans shook her head vigorously, "Oh no my dear. You are quite wrong about that. Never forget that it was Judge Thayer who turned to his companion while playing golf and said quite clearly, 'Did you see what I did to those anarchistic bastards?' Oh yes. It was truly shocking. There should be another trial on that alone." She sighed. "I can assure you that the Governor is not similarly biased, but he's an ambitious politician and as such I'm afraid he will do whatever is necessary to make sure he gets re-elected." She looked at Trando. "What is it that you are going to say to the Governor this time?"

Giving Ella a glare he told her about the letter he had written which stated that if the story he had told at the Plymouth Trial was fiction, they should arrest him for perjury. "I'm also going to threaten to send the letter to the papers," he added defiantly.

Mrs Evans picked up a placard and handed it to Trando, before taking one herself.

"My dear boy, I do so admire your courage, but I fear it will do you little good."

It was all she said and Ella thought sadly that this last try had failed. She feared what they might do to Trando but there was nothing more she could do to prevent him from going.

They went to join the others and Mrs Evans turned to them. "Did you know that Bart's sister Luigia is arriving tomorrow?

Mary Donovan told me. Apparently she is bringing yet another written plea from Mussolini begging for clemency. But between you and me my dears, I think we're all beginning to lose hope, even though those lawyers continue to work day and night."

Trando glanced at her and thought to himself that the poor woman looked completely worn out as well. The strain was beginning to take its toll on all of them. Katherine Porter joined them and she too looked drained, her face even paler than usual but, as always, she was elegantly dressed and today wearing a large sunhat. It was one of the hottest days of the summer.

They set out for the Court House.

A great stream of people, carrying placards, had already gathered and were marching in an orderly fashion around the square. On the sidewalk opposite there was a smaller gathering of people who were making a considerable noise. Shouts of abuse were being hurled at the silent marchers, shouts of, 'Let the Dago Bastards fry' 'Down with the Reds!' 'Dagos go home!' 'Lynch the lot of them!'

Mrs Evans spoke quietly, "Take no notice of them my dears." She paused and then asked, "Have you noticed that the police have a routine now? They let us march round twice and then they move in for the arrests."

Ella nodded. "I've become quite friendly with one of them and he told me yesterday he was sick of the whole thing."

Katherine Porter drew level with them. "Everyone's weary," she said. "Even the other side have quit yelling quite so much. And this God-awful heat doesn't help."

"No indeed it doesn't." Mrs Evans had slowed down. "I'm afraid my dears I can only manage one circuit today."

Trando looked at Ella and handed her his placard. "I'll see you later," he said and without another word turned back towards the Governor's Office.

*

He made his way across town and half an hour later was back in the familiar room, hot and out of breath. It was now crowded with reporters, detectives and what he presumed to be secret service men, all standing around in various groups. A male secretary was sitting behind a large desk looking extremely harassed. Trando crossed to him and finally managed to get his attention, telling him it was urgent that a letter was delivered to the Governor and in person. The secretary told him, not very politely, that this would not be possible. There was something in his tone that made Trando burst out angrily, "Don't you understand? I have brought a letter for the Governor which he needs to read at once. It is very urgent. The letter states that as I still refuse to retract my evidence, he will have no option but to arrest me for perjury. So he has to see it."

The secretary leant across his desk and said with equal anger, "And I have told you sir, it is not possible for anything to be given to the Governor right now and I must ask you to leave."

Trando thumped his fist on the desk. "I will not leave until my letter has been delivered."

The secretary looked across to two security men and gave a nod. The men, both large and menacing, came over and manhandled Trando into a small adjoining room, where he was thrown onto a chair. The situation had suddenly turned frightening. The two men stood either side of him, having first carefully checked he wasn't carrying a weapon. They held him down and it was obvious they were waiting for developments. After a few minutes, another man entered who Trando realised at once to be someone far more sinister, probably Secret Service. Even at this moment when he knew he was liable to be arrested or worse, he felt some satisfaction that they had sent in the big guns to deal with him.

The man looked extremely annoyed as he drew up a chair and sat down opposite Trando. "All right kid. Let's have it. Who sent you here?"

"Nobody," Trando replied, trying to stay calm. "I came here of my own accord, to deliver a letter to the Governor." He wrenched his arm free and removed the letter from his pocket.

The man took it from him and asked, "Is this some kind of publicity stunt?"

Trando shook his head. "No it is not. I have been told that the Governor thinks Bart Vanzetti did the robbery in the short time I left him to go back to my house for my rubber shoes. That is an absolute impossibility. Fetching those shoes only took me half an hour at the most, as I said on oath. So Vanzetti's alibi stands and this proves his innocence." He could tell he had the secret service man's attention so he continued, "I have written this letter to the Governor making it very simple. Either he believes my evidence, or, if he thinks I am lying, he should arrest me for perjury. He can't have it both ways."

The man snapped back at him, "Who told you what the Governor thinks about Vanzetti's alibi?"

Trando was silent. He didn't want to make trouble for Rosina, or Bart?

His interrogator now lent back in his chair and said wearily. "Listen to me kid and listen carefully, this is doing you no good and it is going to hurt you far more than it can help either Sacco or Vanzetti. They will go to the electric chair. By the end of this week they will both be dead and there is nothing you or anyone else can do about it."

Trando became desperate and shouted, "But Vanzetti has an alibi. Does Governor Fuller want to be responsible for sending an innocent man to the electric chair? Bart Vanzetti has an alibi! How many more times do I have to tell you?"

The guy stood up. "No more times. Your time is up. If you want to make speeches, the place for that is the picket lines, or on the Common."

"I tried that yesterday and I was stopped." Trando said angrily. But he knew they were beginning to lose patience with him. The two security men pulled him to his feet as the secret service man said, "My advice to you son is to go home. Don't be a hero. It won't wash. The whole country wants 'em dead and they ain't going to listen to you, or the sobbing sister or the hysterical wife along with the kids. It's over. Go home."

He opened the door and rather than allow himself to be thrown out Trando walked past him with as much dignity as he could muster and out of the building. The man was right. It was all over. There was nothing more he could do now to save Bart. They seemed absolutely determined to murder him.

As he mulled over all that had happened, a sudden realisation struck him. In killing Bart in this way they were somehow fulfilling his greatest wish. He now understood that Bart was determined to die as a working-class hero. He had made that very plain to Trando in his last passionate speech in the prison. Maybe there was some small comfort to be drawn from this. At least Bart would achieve his aim in that.

*

Back at the hotel he was told that Ella had fainted while on the picket line and had been taken to a prison cell with Katherine. Frantic with worry he was about to set out to find her when she and Katherine walked through the door. On seeing him they parted company and Katherine went upstairs. Trando grabbed her by the arm. "What happened to you? Are you all right?"

She gave him a wan smile. "I'm fine. I'll tell you all about it, but let's go out of here."

*

They sat on their usual seat by the pond. Ella watched Trando anxiously. From the grim look on his face it was obvious his further meeting with the Governor had not gone well. She was just thankful that he was back, so tactfully she didn't question him but embarked on the account of her own adventure.

"It was all a bit stupid," she told him and gave a shrug as if to indicate its non-importance. "I think the heat got to me and I fainted."

"Start from when I left you," Trando said firmly. "What happened after that?"

Ella made a study of him. She didn't want to cause him worry but knew someone would tell Trando what had happened if she didn't, so she took a deep breath and dived in.

"Just after you left, that police officer came up and started walking beside me and insisted on making conversation. He asked me where the boyfriend was. Well I didn't bother to reply to that. Then he said why didn't I quit as I was doing no good. That really riled me so I told him that all we wanted was to be listened to and for the men to be given a fair trial. He got annoyed at this point and told me that the picket line wouldn't make the slightest difference, or give us another trial, and that folks were getting mad at us and looked on us as law-breakers. This made me so angry. I told him that we were serious-minded people unlike the noisy rabble on the other side of the square, so why didn't he arrest them? He just shrugged and said they weren't the ones picketing and that I knew the rules. If I continued to picket he would have to arrest me." She hesitated.

Trando looked at her defiant expression. "Is that when he carted you off to prison?"

"Not immediately," she replied and hesitated again. "He was obviously hot and irritated by the whole thing because he suddenly blurted out that he was thankful it would be all be over in a few days. I asked him what he meant by that and that was when he told me…" Her voice faltered.

"What did he tell you?" Trando almost shouted.

Ella was close to tears. "He was almost gloating as he told me, as if he relished the news. It made it worse somehow." She took a deep breath. "He told me that the executioner had arrived along with the official witnesses, so it wouldn't be long now. Bart and Nick would be having their heads shaved ready for the chair…" Trando stared at her in shock so she tried to steady her voice. "I think it was this news, plus the heat… well, next thing I knew I had fainted and everyone was crowding round me. The officer looked a little contrite and kept asking me if I was all right. I burst into angry sobbing and kept moaning that I couldn't bear it. It was stupid of me to become so hysterical. I just somehow lost control."

Trando nodded grimly. "What happened then?"

"Katherine and Mrs Evans came over. The officer told them it was the usual practice to arrest the first forty pickets, having given them a seven-minute warning first. Then they would be taken to jail. Those were his orders and he had a problem with me because I was halfway down the picket line. Mrs Evans then took charge and told him firmly to arrest me first, without a warning, because I needed a couple of hours in the cells to recover. He seemed almost relieved to be told what to do. I remember Katherine then suggested Mrs Evans should give up and go back to the hotel as she had done enough. Katherine then came with me and the officer. It wasn't a long walk to Joy Street Jail but I felt very odd and wasn't sure I would make it. Katherine kept talking to me the whole way. She told me that hundreds were joining the picket line all the time and she had caught a glimpse of Dorothy Parker and Edna Vincent St Millay with reporters swarming all around them, so that would be in the papers tomorrow. She said a whole lot more that I can't really remember. I was just in a daze you see. It was all like a dream," and she added, "or more like a nightmare."

She paused for a moment. Trando felt a sudden pang of guilt. He should have been with her, looking after her, not Katherine. Why did it have to be her? As if to compound these thoughts Ella went on, "Katherine was brilliant. I was so glad she was with me. We were put in a small prison cell on our own which at least was cool. Katherine told me that the officer must have taken a shine to me because usually she was thrown in with everyone else. She'd also persuaded the officer to get me a glass of water and she made me drink it. I did start to feel a bit better then and quite frankly felt a bit foolish. I told her what the officer had said about the executioner arriving and about the shaved heads. This started me crying again but I think this time it was because I was so worried about how you would take this news and I said so to Katherine." She broke off. "You'll never believe what happened next…" Trando shook his head trying his best not to be irritated by the constant references to Katherine. "She offered me a cigarette. I told her I didn't smoke but she said it would calm my nerves. I remember that as she lit two cigarettes her hand was shaking and I thought, we are all affected by this, even Katherine who I thought was so strong. While I was trying to get used to smoking she talked to me again and I know she was somehow trying to comfort me. She said she was sure you would manage all right as you had great inner strength. We were all somehow going to have to try and get through the next few days by calling on our reserves in the best way we could, but she added she was particularly worried about Elizabeth..." Ella looked at Trando. "Katherine's right. We must keep an eye on her. I thought she was looking very frail as we set out."

Trando nodded but deliberately tried to keep things light. "How did the cigarette smoking go?"

Ella laughed. "Not very well. I kept coughing and spluttering while Katherine blew the smoke out slowly in rings. But she was right, it did make me feel calmer. She remarked that it was strange how differently everyone was reacting to the death sentences. She, like me, felt the full horror of it. Mrs Evans and Mrs Henderson had a kind of moral outrage and she felt most for you Trando because you had a desperate feeling you should have done more, which we both agreed you couldn't possibly have done." Trando said nothing to this but waited for her to go on as Ella gave a grin. "She really lashed into the bloody communists. She asked me if I knew Rosa Baron, who I didn't by name but I recognised the description, a short stroppy woman with an angry expression. You must have seen her too?" Trando nodded. "Well this horrible woman actually asked Katherine what would be the point of saving Bart and Nick? What earthly good would they be to the cause if they were allowed to live?"

Trando said grimly, "There are many who think like that."

"Katherine says that we have to face the fact that they look on us as bourgeois liberals and probably think the same about Dorothy Parker and all the other great writers and artists who are giving their support. The hardliners *want* Sacco and Vanzetti to go the chair because they want martyrs for their cause."

"I'm afraid that's true." Trando said and then he asked, "How long were you left in the cell?"

"It must have been a couple of hours. Katherine asked me what I was going to do once all this was over. I told her I didn't really know but told her I would return to New York and would like to try my hand at writing, maybe even journalism. She was so nice about this and told me we could travel back together and she would give me some introductions to get me started. Wasn't that great of her?"

Trando didn't comment but sat looking hunched and his face had a mulish expression.

"She asked about your future as well," Ella said quickly, "I just said things were uncertain after all the Governor's threats and it might not be possible for you to go to Harvard and join a big orchestra." She dropped her head in her hands, "Oh God Trando. This is all such a mess."

He took her hand and held on to it. They sat on in silence each lost in their own thoughts. Her words had left Trando with mixed emotions. He felt wretched that it was to Katherine she once again turned and it was with Katherine she had been discussing her future. He had presumed they would be together after all this was over. Was she accepting that they had no future together? Ella was the first girl he had fallen in love with. He suspected that there might have been a few men in her past, but they had never discussed it. From the little she had told him he gathered there had been years when she had been quite wild. Maybe she'd had the odd affair just to annoy her mother. She was angry and wilful enough to do that. He just didn't know. It was obvious this present situation had thrown them together in a strange way, but was their relationship love? He was confident it was for him, but Ella? Katherine had far more to offer her than he ever could and she seemed fascinated by the damned women.

Abruptly he stood up. "We'd better be getting back."

"What happened at the Governor's Office?" she asked.

"Nothing," he said angrily. "They threw me out. There's nothing I can do now. They just don't want to know. For them it's a matter of getting the whole thing over and done with as quickly as possible. We finally have to accept that we have lost."

CHAPTER 26

That evening Mary Donovan stood in front of the assembled Committee members in the lobby and waved a piece of paper.

"My friends, this is a letter sent to the Committee from Nick Sacco and Bart Vanzetti, which they wished me to read to you."

She put on her glasses and started reading in her soft Irish accent,

'We know we have lost. Therefore, at this time, we decided to write this letter to you to express our gratitude and admiration for all you have done in our defence during these seven years, four months, and eleven days of struggle. The fact that we lost and have to die does not diminish our appreciation and gratitude for your great solidarity with us and our families.

Friends and comrades, now that the tragedy of this trial is at an end, let all of us be of one heart. Only two of us will die. Our ideals, you, our comrades, will live on. We have won. We are not vanquished. Remember our suffering, our sorrow, our mistakes, our defeats, our passion for future battles and for the great emancipation. We embrace you and bid you goodbye with our hearts filled with love and affection, now and forever. Long life to you all, Yours in death. Nicola Sacco and Bartolomeo Vanzetti.' "

She folded the letter and looked round the room, seemingly unable to add anything further. People silently shuffled back to their various places and resumed whatever work they could find, knowing it to be useless.

*

Ella now turned all her attention to Trando.

"There's a final rally tonight at some big hall," he told her. "I feel I ought to attend, but you don't have to."

She shook her head. "No, I want to be there."

Trando added, "I went to see Thompson this morning. He's a good man and I think he feels as distressed as all of us. Apparently on his last visit to the prison, he'd told Bart that although he had always believed in his innocence, he wanted that reassurance one more time, at this moment when he was about to meet his death. I can understand that. I suppose he thought this might be the opportunity for Bart to make a last minute confession if he'd actually been guilty. Well, apparently Bart looked at him straight in the eyes and gave a solemn vow that he was innocent of both crimes. Thompson said he spoke these words with calmness and great feeling and he knew it was the truth." He broke off, "Of course I am the one person who never doubted Bart's innocence for a minute because I had the actual proof. I suppose it was different for Thompson, he just had to rely on Bart's word and his instinct, so this was really important to him. He said it was a peaceful last meeting for them both. Bart's final words were that he wanted the lawyers to do everything they could to clear his name. That was his final instruction, to clear his name."

"Will they ever be able to do that?" Ella asked.

Trando nodded. "I hope so, one day. I will certainly continue to work for that." He then gave a wry smile. "I don't know whether Thomson was trying to comfort me, but he told me that he thought Bart was a man of the highest ideals who had a completely unselfish character, and that he was facing his death with dignity and great bravery. I was pleased to hear him say that. I like and trust the man." He broke off and was quiet for a moment. Ella waited for him to speak again and could see he was struggling. "I did ask Thomson how Bart would occupy his final hours and he told me he was busy writing letters to his sister, Rosina Sacco and also to her son Dante, so the boy could read about his father in the future. That is typical of him, thoughtful and kind to the last."

Trando was finally overcome with emotion and close to tears

he walked quickly away. Ella didn't see him again until they met that evening.

*

The hall where the rally was taking place was a bleak building, already stifling in the heat, with a vast and noisy crowd crammed into it. Trando and Ella stood at the back waiting for Rosina Sacco and Luigia Vanzetti, Bart's sister, to make their appearance and be led into the hall. The noise was deafening but the place fell suddenly silent as the two women threaded their way towards the platform.

As they walked up the steps a great deal of shouting broke out, both in Italian and English, some expressing anger at the injustice of their fate, others giving encouragement to the women. Trando stared at Luigia trying to find some resemblance to Bart in her gaunt and bony appearance but could find none, except perhaps in the darkness of the eyes. Both she and Rosina now looked completely overwhelmed as they stared out over the noisy crowd. Rosina put her hands over her face and started to sob and this made the crowd rage all the more.

Trando turned to Ella, "I can't stand this anymore. Let's get out of here."

*

They walked slowly back to the hotel and found the lobby completely deserted, presumably because everyone else had gone to the rally. Boxes of letters and telegrams were piled high on the trestle table. These had trebled in volume as soon as the day of the execution had been confirmed. Ella idly picked out a few.

"There must be thousands of them here. They're from all over the world."

"What good can they do now?" Trando sounded bitter and flung himself into a chair. "Tomorrow night it will all be over and I will have failed."

Ella looked at him sadly, "Bart wouldn't want you to think like that. You know what he said, 'in my death is my triumph'. That is what he wants people to think, you most of all."

He shook his head, "I know, but I can't think like Bart. It's not just the fact that I couldn't make anyone believe me. It's, well..." he hesitated and then burst out, "it's that I can't believe in American justice anymore."

He stood up and said abruptly. "I am going out. I need to be on my own." Crossing the room he stood in front of her. "I'm sorry Ella. I know I am failing you too."

She shook her head. "You're not failing anyone Trando. I understand, truly I do."

He looked such a lonely and forlorn figure as he left the hotel. She desperately wished there was something she could do to comfort him, but instinctively knew that he needed to have his own private vigil outside the Death House, alone with his thoughts of Bart.

August 22nd 1927

The account leading up to the executions was given to Trando by Mrs Evans, who in her turn had been given all the details by her friend the Warden of the Prison. He then repeated it to Ella.

In the afternoon Luigia and Rosina Sacco had visited Death Row, as he had done, and were led into the cells. They were not permitted to embrace the prisoners, but could only stretch their hands through the bars while they murmured their tearful farewells.

Bart later told the Warden that for him this was the worst ordeal of all. Luigia was all that was left of his family and now he had brought upon her this great suffering. What comfort could he give her except to assure her of his innocence? By the end of the visit Bart was out of strength and it was almost a relief when the guards came to take the women away. He heard Nick tell his wife he would always love her and she had replied through her tears that she would be dying with him. It then took two men to drag the screaming Rosina down the long corridor.

*

An hour later the Warden had made the obligatory visit, in order to inform them that they would die that night. Vanzetti replied quietly that they would bow to the inevitable. Both men refused the service of the chaplain.

Mrs Evans added that at all times, in spite of all he had suffered, Bart remained dignified and calm.

*

Now it was evening and Trando and Ella joined the thousands outside the prison who were gathered behind the ropes put in place by the police. They stared up at the windows. There was no sound, except the wind in the trees as they all stood in silence holding their flickering candles. Trando had been told that every entrance to the Death House was heavily guarded. There were also machine guns on the roof and firemen had been instructed to open power hoses should the need arise. They could see the police river boats as they patrolled the river near the prison and their lights gave an eerie backdrop to the prison walls. They also learned afterwards that these scenes weren't just in Boston. In New York, thousands gathered at Union Square. Similar crowds assembled in Philadelphia, Chicago and San Francisco. All were silent. All were waiting.

Mrs Evans joined Ella and Trando. She leant over and whispered, "I am told the light in the tower will go on and off, according to how many charges of electricity they put through the body."

Ella shuddered and Trando hung on to her tightly as they stood staring out into the gloom, their eyes fastened on the tower.

*

Once again it was later, after Mrs Evans had learned about it from the Warden, that she gave them an account of what had happened in the prison that night.

*

In the execution chamber the chief electrician and the executioner made their last inspection and tests of the equipment. By early evening the officer's club in the prison was filled with reporters. The room had been installed with extra telephones especially for the occasion. About twenty witnesses, including the Warden and the Governor were already sitting in the execution room, staring at the chair through the glass window.

When the clock on the wall arrived at 11.30, the Warden stood up and went to a telephone on the wall. In the officer's club the telephone rang. A guard picked it up and announced to the reporters, "The first prisoner, Nicola Sacco is being taken down now."

Nick was led out of his cell, his head shaved, wearing grey trousers which had slits up the sides in order that the electrodes could be fastened to his legs.

The cry went up, "Dead Man Walking!"

As he went past Bart's cell he raised his fist and shouted, "Viva L'Anarchista!"

He was strapped into the chair and said, "Farewell my wife and children."

The guards fitted the skullcap, slipped as mask over his face and stepped back. The first jolt sent his body violently forward. Minutes later Sacco's lifeless and smouldering body was put on a litter and taken behind the screen.

*

Outside the light in the tower went on and off several times. A gasp ran through the crowd and there was the muffled sound of weeping. Someone started to pray and others followed.

*

In the execution chamber the Warden went to the telephone for a second time. Once again it rang in the officers' club and was answered by the guard who said, "Nicola Sacco was pronounced dead at 12.11. The second prisoner, Bartolomeo

Vanzetti is being taken down."

Bart was now led out of his cell, with shaved head and wearing the same grey trousers. As he reached the doorway of the execution chamber he stopped and spoke to the Warden.

"I wish to say to you that I am innocent. I have never done a crime - some sins maybe - but never any crime. I thank you for everything you have done for me. I am innocent of all crimes, not only this one, but of all. I am an innocent man"

He shook hands with the Warden, then with the doctor and finally with the four guards. He sat in the chair and the guards strapped the electrodes on his legs. His arms were tightly buckled down.

Vanzetti looked at the Warden and spoke gently. "I now wish to forgive *some* people for what they are doing to me."

The Warden understood his meaning and told Mrs Evans that he was deeply moved by this and his eyes filled with tears. The headpiece was placed on Vanzetti's head. He clenched his fists and shouted, "Madre!"

*

Outside the prison, the light in the tower blinked on and off again for the final time. There was a stunned silence for a moment and after that the crowd started to blow out their candles and slowly dispersed. Katherine joined Mary Donovan and putting her arm round her they walked away. Mrs Evans turned to Ella and Trando. She was holding back the tears.

"I am going in to see the Warden," she said. "I will join you back at the hotel and let you know what he can tell me about Bart's last moments."

She moved away towards the prison but Ella and Trando remained rooted to the spot, watching the lights in the prison windows going out one by one.

Unable to bear it any longer, she turned to face him. He gently pulled her to him and they both wept silently in each other's arms.

CHAPTER 27

In the small hours of the morning some of the Committee members gathered back in the lobby. Many faces were tear-stained, and they were a sad, defeated and dispirited group. Some just sat looking stunned. For Mary Donovan the grief she had held back for so long finally overwhelmed her and she was being comforted by Katherine and Mrs Henderson.

Katherine remarked bitterly, "Life feels very grubby and mean, as if we are all of us soiled in some way now."

A man shouted out, "Jesus! I'd like to leave this country."

Another mockingly answered, "Where would you go?"

Someone came through the door with a box full of bottles. "I managed to find a supplier. Bootlegger gin! I thought we might be needing some of the hard stuff."

Nobody took much notice and he put them down on a table near where Ella was sitting on her own by the window. She watched him put down the box and then moved to a chair at the table, opened a bottle and started to drink, taking large gulps. Wasn't this what her mother had always done in times of crisis? Well now she would try it.

Again, nobody noticed what she was doing because at this moment Mrs Evans arrived and took it upon herself to address the room.

"Dear friends, I thought you would like to know that I have just been to see the Warden. He told me that both men died very bravely and with great dignity. Dear Bart protested his innocence to the last..."

"Because he was innocent," Trando shouted angrily.

Mrs Evans nodded in agreement and then continued, "The Warden also told me that just before..." her voice faltered, "just before he died, Bart forgave him. The poor man seemed so upset. I think he had grown very fond of him."

She took out a handkerchief and wiped away a tear and then said with defiance in her voice, "But my friends, the fight must go on. We must never give up until we have finally proved their innocence and shown the world what a great injustice was been done here. That is our duty to these poor dead men who died so bravely tonight."

There were murmurs of agreement and then the room fell silent.

Quite suddenly, the quiet atmosphere was broken by Ella getting to her feet, holding an almost empty bottle of gin in her hand. She started to sing in a raucous voice a song that sounded straight out of an Irish wake, as she marched up and down the room.

"They took the ice from off the corpse and put it in the beer!
Your feyther was a grand old man. Give us a drink!"

Trando looked at her bewildered as she upended the bottle and took another swig. He hardly recognised her. This was a new Ella and one he had never seen before.

Almost at once others followed her example and began to help themselves to the bottles. One man started to sing the "Internationale" and someone else chanted in frenzied Italian, "Giovinezza, giovinezza! Primquavera die bellezza!"

It was as if the alcohol let them finally to give way to all their pent up feelings of anger, frustration and grief which had been building up over those long months of struggle. All the control and discipline they had shown up until now was gone. The room quickly descended into a chaotic rabble with people dancing, singing and shouting. Chairs were knocked over and papers scattered. Mrs Evans, Katherine, Mrs Henderson and Mary retreated to the far end of the room and looked on in bewilderment.

On and on it went. Ella now climbed on the table, and started to shout out "The Battle Hymn of the Republic". In her manic, drunken state she was half singing and half crying, beating out the rhythm with her feet.

"In the beauty of the lilies, Christ was born across the sea..."

A man shouted bitterly, "Jesus! Let's leave Christ out of this!"

"With a glory in His bosom that transfigured you and me!"

She took another swig and waved the bottle wildly. Mrs Evans crossed to Trando and spoke sharply, "Trando this is getting dangerous. You have to stop her."

He didn't move but stared at Ella in horror.

"Trando" Mrs Evans barked, "get her down!"

The last order was rapped out so loudly that Trando was jerked into taking action. He moved to the table and with some difficulty managed to pull Ella down, but before he could stop her, she broke away and ran through the lobby towards the stairs. On the first landing there was a large window which was half open. Ella ran straight up to it and started to climb, as if to throw herself out onto the street. Trando and several men stopped her, pulling her down to the ground, where she lay quite still, strands of her fair hair covering her face. Trando stared down at her, thinking she resembled a frail bird, a little bag of bones. It struck him that this was his fault. It was he who had allowed her to be driven to this state without giving her any words of support or comfort. She had been strong for him all the way through and now she had finally broken and was lying there like a small rag doll.

Mrs Evans once again took charge giving out the orders in a loud firm voice.

"Trando, take Ella up to my room. It is best we use that for her tonight." She beckoned to two men to pick her up. Following Mrs Evans they carried her gently into the room and laid her on the bed. Then they left, leaving Trando and Mrs Evans alone with the girl.

There was now silence from downstairs. The sudden drama had shocked them. Slowly one by one they drifted away. Mary, Katherine and Mrs Henderson picked up the bottles, chairs and papers and then they too went to their rooms.

A clock in the distance chimed three.

Ella lay lifeless on the bed. She had passed out. Trando stood looking down at her feeling bewildered and helpless. He had never seen anyone drunk before, least of all Ella.

Mrs Evans fetched a damp cloth and wiped the girl's brow. "You will have to keep a careful watch on her my dear. She may well start vomiting. You must wake me immediately if she does. That is important. Do you understand Trando?"

He nodded and drawing up a chair he sat by the side of the bed. Mrs Evans went to the chaise longue on the other side of the room and lay down.

"Not many hours now until morning. I am going to try and get some sleep. You must wake me at once Trando if you are worried."

She closed her eyes and almost immediately slept. Trando took a quilt from the end of the bed and carefully laid it over her. In her sleep she suddenly seemed to have become a very old woman. He watched her for a moment and then returned to the chair by the side of the bed and took up his vigil.

He sat on, holding Ella's hand, forcing himself to stay awake and never once taking his eyes off the sleeping girl. His mind went over and over the events of the night. The clock chimed the passing hours until finally, the dawn crept in and the sun's pale light filtered in through the window.

It was only then that there came to him the sad realisation that this would be his very first day without Bart.

CHAPTER 28

It took Ella a day to recover from her alcoholic poisoning. She was pale and listless and didn't seem inclined to talk about what had happened to her, in fact it appeared she remembered little about it. Trando tactfully thought that this was probably for the best. It was just one more terrible event that had taken place on that truly terrible day. The strain had told on everyone in their different ways. They now needed time to recover.

Once he had reassured himself that Ella was going to be all right, he decided to leave her in the care of Mrs Evans and return home for a couple of days. It was a break he knew he desperately needed, especially before the ordeal of the funeral that was to take place the following Sunday. It had been something of a relief that he wasn't involved in any of the arrangements for this. Those were being undertaken by the leading members of the Committee along with the Sacco family.

So on a hot August day he returned once more to Plymouth and Suosso Lane.

*

His parents were kind and tactful, giving Trando the space he needed and allowing him to be alone. He spoke very little and slept a good deal of the time.

On the day before he was due to return he joined his father in the gardens, helping him pick the vegetables. When finished they sat down on the usual bench in the shade of the tree and his father fetched some lemonade. It brought back a memory of a similar time, seven years back and yet now that memory seemed to Trando a lifetime ago.

They drank the cool lemonade in silence until his father

turned to him and said a little awkwardly, "Trando, I need to ask you something. I find it hard to discuss these things with your mother you understand because she gets so upset." He hesitated as if trying to work out what to say. Then he plunged in, bursting out, "I need you to tell me, truthfully and honestly. Deep down in your heart, do you believe that Bart was innocent?"

Trando looked at the distress etched on his face. His father was a man of action, not of words and Trando was well aware that this kind of conversation did not come easily to him. He therefore took his father's question seriously and took great care over his reply.

"Deep down in my heart Papa, I know that Bart was innocent," he paused before adding, "but I think he died to protect others. Maybe he also wanted to be a martyr, to make his case for justice for the workers. I believe that's what he felt he had achieved in the end."

Vincenzo nodded. "What you say is a great relief to me. I could not bear to think that you, and all of us, had gone through such terrible times and made so many sacrifices, without a good reason." He hesitated again. "I heard some things which I never told you before, because I never knew for certain. They were things about Nick Sacco." Trando waited as his father looked anxiously at him. "You see, I heard something from someone who was drunk on the bootlegger gin. When he was drunk this man said that Sacco was in the car. He didn't think Nick did the killings, but he did say he was in the bandit car. And I thought to myself that even if Bart knew this thing, he would never have betrayed him." He looked at Trando. "I heard it said that Bart was told he would have a better chance to be free if he stood on his own without Nick. But Bart had always said, 'Save Nick. He has the wife and children'."

Trando had been watching his father while he had been speaking and thought sadly that all these difficult years had taken its toll on him as well. What he said was true. He knew Bart had tried to protect not only Nick but all the comrades, just as his father had tried to protect him and his mother. They were

226

both good men. One day in the future, there would be time for a proper discussion, but not at this moment. It was still all too raw. For now he simply said,

"That is interesting Papa. I didn't know that about Nick but it could well be true. All I ever knew for certain was that Bart was innocent and that the American justice system let him down."

They were quiet for a while after that until his father again said a little awkwardly, "We are proud of you Trando, of what you did for Bart. You could not have done anything more, but now we are relieved and happy that you can get on with the rest of your life with a clear conscience. "He looked at the boy and said firmly, "You have the college and the big orchestra to look forward to, yes? Bart would have liked that. He was the first person to tell us about your great talent for music."

Trando nodded and smiled, touched by his father's words. He decided that this was not the moment to mention the Governor's threats.

They sat on, father and son, in the peace of the garden, lost in their thoughts, each thinking back over those years and the events that had changed them all.

When he remembered this moment in later years Trando thought he had never been closer to his father than he had been on that day.

*

A day later he was back at the hotel and he went straight up to his room. Nobody was around when he arrived and he couldn't help wondering how it would be between him and Ella. It might be awkward seeing her again after that traumatic night. Things had been left up in the air between them but on the whole he felt it best to try and pick up from where they had left off, without resorting to post mortems.

He unpacked his things and then, for the first time since his visit to the death cell, he felt the urge to take out his violin. Almost without thinking he started to play "Old Black Joe".

*

Looking back on it, he never really understood what happened next. All he knew was that it was as if something finally snapped inside him. He never reached the end of the piece but on a sudden impulse, stood up and violently smashed the instrument against the wall until it lay on the floor in small pieces. He flung down the bow and sat on the bed, out of breath and staring wildly, as if he were in some trance-like state.

An hour went by and still he hadn't moved.

There was a knock on the door and Ella came into the room. She looked at him a little shyly and said, "I heard you were back. I hope it's all right to come in."

He said nothing, and then she noticed the smashed violin on the floor.

She burst out, "Trando, what on earth have you done?" She knelt down gathering up all the pieces, carefully putting them on the table and then stared down at the broken bits of violin. Should she put the pieces in a bin? It wasn't as if they could be put back together. The bow at least lay unbroken so she placed it carefully in the case and shut the lid.

Trando still hadn't moved.

Ella hesitated and then sat beside him putting her arm around him rocking him gently as if he were a small child. After a while she turned his face to hers and kissed him. He suddenly responded, at first tentatively, and then kissing her more urgently, giving in to mounting passion. They started to tear at each other's clothes, stripping them off, until they were both naked on the bed.

The love-making that followed was a strange almost primitive act; part love, part grief, violent, yet gentle at the same time.

When it was over, Ella fell asleep in his arms, while Trando lay, not daring to move, holding her as carefully as he would have done a fluttering moth.

The day of the funeral started overcast and gloomy. It seemed that the mad, scorching summer was finally over. Over the course of the morning the skies went dark and the mist turned into a monumental thunder storm. This was followed by rain and by the start of the procession there was a torrential downpour. Mary Donovan immediately declared in her Irish way that this was an Act of God. Wasn't it certain sure that the Almighty was showing his anger for the evil deeds that had been done? Most people were of a more practical frame of mind and went searching for large umbrellas.

Act of God or no, the pouring rain did not deter the vast crowds that gathered along the entire route. Indeed, the crush was so great it was rumoured that some people had been pushed back through the shop windows in Hanover Street.

In anticipation of the large numbers, there had been some argument in the preceding days between the Police and the Committee about the size of the procession, but the Committee had remained adamant, insisting that all who wished to march should be able to do so. Reluctantly the authorities, afraid of yet more bad publicity, had finally agreed to this and a permit was granted. They now braced themselves for what was to come.

The Committee had been busy all week organising this day, but even they hadn't anticipated the vast numbers in the crowd. It was reported that up to two hundred and fifty thousand people lined the route. Red armbands had been given out, to be worn by all Committee members in the procession and these were embossed in black print;

"Remember Justice Crucified August 22nd 1927".

Mrs Evans, Mary Donovan, Mrs Henderson and Katherine

with Ella, had been instructed to travel in the second car, and this would follow Rosina Sacco, her children and Luigia Vanzetti. These cars were immediately behind the two hearses.

*

And so the procession set out from the Langone Funeral Home in Hanover Street.

Trando, carrying a large laurel wreath, walked with Aldino Felicani and Carlo Tresca in the first line of the procession. Behind Trando came six men carrying an eight foot high floral piece showing photographs of Sacco and Vanzetti. The marchers walked in ranks of eight. Vincenzo Brini took his place some rows behind them, along with other men from Suosso Lane and the Plymouth area. Fifty thousand people followed after and more marchers kept joining the procession all along the route. The men wore black neckties and had red carnations in their buttonholes. They walked slowly in the pouring rain, silently following the hearse, the cars with the mourners and the six open topped cars filled with red flowers.

They walked down Tremont Street and then at Scollay Square there was a scuffle with the mounted police who tried to turn back the procession. Some were lost, but the majority walked on, down Columbus Avenue, along Washington Street, into Forest Hill Street and finally into Forest Hills Avenue. Every inch of the sidewalk was filled with people under black umbrellas, watching with bowed heads as the procession went past. A line of mounted police hemmed them in on either side. On, on they marched until they reached the Forest Hills Cemetery, where lines of police blocked the way in order to stop the thousands of people who were trying to get in. The hearses and the cars were allowed to pass through, followed by the first group of mourners. The rest, who had walked the eight miles in the pouring rain, were cordoned off and forced to wait outside.

*

Inside the small chapel the two coffins were placed side by side on a dais in the centre, which was again covered in red flowers. Ella held on to Trando's hand as they both stared straight ahead. Sitting beside them was Mrs Evans elegant in black and wearing a large hat with a veil, but it was Mary Donovan who stepped forward to give the oration. She began to speak in clear tones, first turning towards the two coffins.

"Nicola Sacco and Bartolomeo Vanzetti.

You came to America as workers, searching for liberty and equal opportunities and now America has killed you, murdering you because of your beliefs. "

Trando saw Luigia Vanzetti bow her head in grief and Rosina Sacco put a comforting arm round her as they both silently started to weep.

Mary Donovan continued with anger in her voice. "For more than seven years they had every chance to know the truth about you but they refused to listen and allowed the bitter prejudice of class, position and self-interest to close their eyes."

Then she spoke in gentler tones, "Your long years of torture and last hours of supreme agony are the living banner under which we will march to accomplish that better world for which you both died. In *your* martyrdom we will fight on and conquer."

And then she made her final plea, turning back to mourners as she raised her voice and called out; "Remember, Justice Crucified, August 22nd 1927! Remember!"

There were murmurs of 'we will remember' as she returned to her place and there was a silence broken only by the sounds of muffled weeping from Rosina Sacco and Luigia Vanzetti.

After some minutes Mrs Evans turned and gave a nod. Twelve men stood up and walked to either side of the two coffins ready to carry them out to the crematory. Everyone stood as the coffins were lifted and borne shoulder high out of the little chapel. Then, from the back, someone started to clap, and then another person, and soon everyone was clapping and they heard the sound of it outside and the thousands standing in the rain started clapping as well and then they began to cheer and they kept cheering and clapping until the coffins finally disappeared from view.

*

It was over. The years of fighting for justice, the years of momentary successes and hours of dark despair had finally come to an end in this small chapel on a hill above Boston. Yet, as Trando returned to the hotel, there came into his heart a strange feeling of hope. He felt a lightness, almost a feeling of optimism. Something extraordinary had happened that day he was sure of it. Bart had been right. Out of the deaths of those two poor Italian immigrants, changes would come to their adopted country and this would mean that their sacrifice had not been made in vain. Even if their case was never resolved, even if they never managed to clear their names, it was through their actions, their endurance and their pain, that American Justice had also been put on trial, not just in this country but around the world, and it had been found wanting. That fact alone was something to be proud of. The battle may have been lost, but the victory remained. Things would now change, he was certain of it, and he, Trando Brini, felt a sense of pride, at having taken his small part in it.

*

Back in the hotel lobby a few people were sitting around talking quietly, but most of the Committee had now left and returned to their homes after the Funeral had ended. Trando noticed Ella on the far side of the room in deep conversation with Katherine Porter. He decided not to interrupt. He had no real wish to talk to Katherine. After today he would have Ella to himself because Katherine had already told him she was leaving for New York in the morning. Mrs Henderson, who had been sitting with Mrs Evans, now crossed the room. She took Trando's hands in hers and looked emotional as she said, "I am not going to say goodbye to you Trando as I know you will keep in touch with me. God keep you safe and happy dear boy." She kissed his forehead and left. Looking round the room he could see that Katherine and Ella were still talking. Then he caught sight of Mrs Evans. She seemed such a lonely figure. As always she sat very upright, still elegant in her black funeral clothes, but now there was a look of frailty about her, and great sadness. He crossed over and sat beside her.

What followed was a strange and emotional outpouring from the old lady, which he found hard to follow and put down to the strain of the last few months, especially the stress of the day. It went on for some time and he didn't interrupt her. As he kissed her goodnight he noticed that they were the only two people left in the room. Ella and Katherine had obviously slipped away to their rooms. He reached the foot of the stairs and looked back. Mrs Evans was still sitting in the same position, alone with her thoughts in that empty lobby.

CHAPTER 30

Trando slept deeply that night and woke rather later than usual. He didn't get dressed immediately, but lingered in bed for a moment, anticipating with pleasure the day ahead. He and Ella could now spend time together, without all the cares or worries. The stress and pain of the last few months was at last behind them. It was time for a fresh start. They could get to know each other properly, slowly, without any outside pressures. Maybe even enjoy the carefree and happy life that he knew had been going on around them and which he had steadfastly neglected. Of course he'd been vaguely aware of the music of Louis Armstrong and George Gershwin and the frenetic dancing with the Charleston and Black Bottom. It had all seemed a world way. Now at last he and Ella could join in the general spree.

He looked across at the window. The storms of yesterday had completely cleared and now the sun was streaming in.

His thoughts then turned to the evening before, remembering the long conversation he'd had with Mrs Evans. She had been such in a strange mood and kept repeating that he was to be sure to let her know how he was and how he must always come to her if he needed help, and that he must know he was like a son to her. Then, when he finally stood up to say goodnight she'd clung to him and kept repeating, 'Dear boy, dear boy. You must be brave. Whatever happens now you must be brave.' He thought she'd never let him go. It was very unlike her to be so tearful and over-emotional. Perhaps he shouldn't have left her alone but seen her to her room. On the other hand, his instinct had told him that she needed to be on her own, holding a private vigil for the two men she had so valiantly fought for.

It was then that Trando noticed the envelope which must have been pushed under his door during the night. He crossed the room and picked it up. His name was written on the front in large letters and it was not in a hand he recognised. Ripping it open the he took out a sheet of paper and read,

"Trando,

I am a coward and I hate goodbyes, so I hope you will forgive me for just writing to you instead. I am catching the early morning train back to New York.

I know this will be a shock but I have thought about this a great deal and know it is for the best. Don't try to stop me as my mind is made up and please Trando, don't be sad or angry. We had reached the zenith - there is nowhere else for us to go.

I will never forget you and you will always be in my heart. Ella"

Trando dropped the letter on the floor and looked at the pocket watch his father had given him which he kept beside the bed. Throwing on his clothes he left the room, leapt down the stairs three at a time, and arrived in the lobby. Frantically looking around for someone who could help him he saw Mary Donovan hard at work, packing up boxes. He crossed the room in seconds and asked if she knew the time of the morning train to New York. She looked up at the clock and said, "Well I doubt you'll make it now Trando. It leaves at 9.30."

Without another word he left the lobby and started running. He ran without stopping, his heart pounding, his breath coming in short gasps. He ran until he reached the station, with just two minutes to spare.

The platform was crowded with people and luggage as he began a desperate search for Ella among the sea of faces, his panic growing greater with every second. Then at last he saw Katherine Porter's white hair and there was Ella standing beside her. It looked as if they were getting ready to board the train.

He started running again, up the platform, calling out her name. At last she heard him and turned, and as he drew level with her he could see there was a look of dismay on her face. Katherine gave a quick glance from one to the other and taking in the situation she said,

"I'll go get us a seat Ella, the train is about to leave." She then looked at Trando and said, "Goodbye Trando and good luck," but he gave no reply, never taking his eyes off Ella.

She hung her head and said sadly, "You shouldn't have come Trando. I told you, I am no good at goodbyes."

He took her by the shoulders and shook her. "Why, Ella why? You can't leave just like this? We have to talk. There's our whole future ahead. What about us?"

Ella shook her head sadly. "There is no 'us' Trando. You have to understand, there could never be 'us'. This whole thing has just been too big, too momentous. Don't you see? If I stayed with you I would always be a reminder of what happened, and you would always remind *me*. We could never survive that."

Trando was close to tears. "Please Ella. I love you. I can't bear to lose Bart, my music *and* you."

Ella held him close. "My lovely Trando. Please understand. I know in my heart it could never work. I'm sorry, so sorry," and she whispered in his ear. "Bart was right. You are a 'magnifico son of the people'. You and your music will go on to great things. He knew it. I know it. But that can't happen with me. We'd only hold each other back."

Trando was crying now and Ella took out a handkerchief and as she handed it to him she gave a smile, "This is becoming a habit Trando Brini. You can keep this one as well. Add it to the collection."

Behind her the train doors were slamming and then a whistle blew. Katherine called out "Ella!"

Ella tore herself from Trando's grasp, grabbed her bag and leapt onto the train as it started to move. She pulled down the window and called out,

"Trando, I will always love you and I will always remember..."

He stood rooted to the spot as the train pulled out of sight and he could see her no more. Then he turned, made his way slowly out of the station and started making his way back to the hotel. As he walked his feelings of anger and bitterness increased. Why had she done this to him? It must be Katherine's influence. He had never trusted her and now she had taken Ella away from him. It meant he had lost everything, including the two people he loved most in the world, Bart and Ella. All along he had tried to do the right thing and to tell the truth, in spite of the insults and the threats. He had stood his ground, held on to his beliefs and now, at the end of it all, this was his reward. He was left with nothing. Nothing!

He slammed through the lobby doors and Mary Donovan looked up. "Did you miss the train?" she asked. He gave a curt nod and walked to the stairs. She called after him, "Oh Trando, a package arrived for you, a very large box. I had it sent up to your room." Again he said nothing but ran up the stairs. Mary shrugged and went back to her work.

He went into the bedroom and leant against the door. After a while and feeling calmer, he noticed the large package Mary had mentioned and which had been placed on the bed. Crossing the room he looked down at the label which was typed and addressed to "Mr Beltrando Brini". This gave no clue as to where, or who, it was from. He ripped open the wrapping and took the lid off the box, then stood back and gasped. There before him lay a beautiful violin.

He stood for a moment just gazing at it. Then he gingerly took it out and gently plucked the strings. It was a far better instrument than the one he had smashed against the wall. In fact it was far more expensive than any violin he could ever have hoped to buy. He searched through the wrapping paper in the box. Again, there was no message to be found, but by now he knew instinctively that it had to be from Mrs Evans. He thought back to their strange conversation of the night before. Ella must have told her about his broken violin. She had also probably told Mrs Evans that she was leaving him as well. That repeated message of 'Be brave' now made sense to him.

He tucked the violin under his chin and gave it a quick tune. Then he picked up his old bow out of the case, tightened it and started to play. He played as he had never played before. He went through his entire repertoire. As soon as he finished one piece he started another, and as he played he began to be filled with a new serenity and calm. It was as if he was once more free to experience that old joy, that joy that his music had always given to him.

Down below in the lobby Mary stood up for a moment, rubbed her aching back and listened to the music. Then she smiled and continued with her work.

*

Sometime later Trando packed his bag, and carefully wrapping his new violin in a cloth, he placed it in his old case and shut the lid. Then he looked around the room one last time. What a lifetime of experiences he'd had in this room which had been his home for the last few months. When his glance finally reached the bed he instinctively closed his eyes, shutting out the memories that were still too raw and painful for him to think about. That life was over. Ella was gone. Those memories were to be locked away forever.

He quickly picked up his bag and his violin case and walked out of the room and down the stairs. For the first time that day he noticed that the lobby had been transformed overnight. It was a completely different place, unfamiliar and cold. Apart from Mary's last few boxes it had been returned to what he presumed must have been its previous state, before the Defence Committee had taken it over. Now it merely looked like a hotel lobby and a hotel lobby with a sad and gentile shabbiness. Gone were the trestle tables piled high with papers and files. Gone were the telephones ringing and the stenographers tapping away. Gone was the noise and the clatter. Gone were all the people, so many friends and colleagues. Nothing remained except a few boxes piled high by the main door and the ones that Mary was struggling with in the far corner. It reminded him of that play he had once seen, where the last act was about a house being packed up and all the residents were leaving to go to their new lives. Only Mary, like the aged retainer remained as she went through the last of the papers and packed them away.

She looked up as she saw him standing there with his suitcase and violin and she laughed. "My oh my Trando Brini. Isn't that just how you looked when you first arrived here way back in January?" She straightened up and gave her back a rub. "Are you off now?"

He nodded and she said, "Well, come over here and give me a hug."

Crossing over to her she squeezed him so tightly he could hardly breathe. When she finally let him go he asked if Mrs Evans was still in the hotel.

"Lord bless us no. Her chauffeur arrived first thing and took her away poor soul. She looked completely exhausted. I hope she gets the good long rest she so richly deserves."

She rubbed her back again. "By all the saints, it's what we all need! I'm looking forward to a rest myself."

Trando looked at her. She did indeed look tired out and he noticed the many new grey streaks in her mop of red hair.

He hesitated and then said shyly, "I want to thank you Mary, for all the help you gave me and to all of us. It was a great privilege for me to work with you. "

She looked close to tears as she said, "Oh, be off with you! What nonsense you do talk. Go on now! Be off with you. Some of us still have work to do you know!"

Trando smiled and picked up his cases as she called out after him, "Good luck to you Trando Brini. Mind you have a great life now."

He stepped outside into the sunlight and the heavy lobby door slammed shut behind him. It seemed significant somehow.

CONCLUSION

Fifty years after Sacco and Vanzetti were sent to the electric chair, on August 23rd 1977, Governor Dukakis issued a proclamation, which ended with the words...

WHEREAS: The trial and execution of Sacco and Vanzetti should serve to remind all civilized people of the constant need to guard against our susceptibility to prejudice, our intolerance of unorthodox ideas, and our failure to defend the rights of persons who are looked upon as strangers in our midst; and,

WHEREAS: Simple decency and compassion, as well as respect for truth and an enduring commitment to our nation's highest ideals, require that the fate of Nicola Sacco and Bartolomeo Vanzetti be-pondered by all who cherish tolerance, justice and human understanding:

NOW,THEREFORE,I, Michael S. Dukakis, Governor of the Commonwealth of Massachusetts, by virtue of the authority conferred upon me as Supreme Executive Magistrate by the Constitution of the Commonwealth of Massachusetts, and by all other authority vested in me, do hereby proclaim Tuesday, August 23rd, 1977, "NICOLA SACCO AND BARTOLOMEO VANZETTI MEMORIAL DAY"; and declare further, than any stigma and disgrace should be forever removed from the names of Nicola Sacco and Bartolomeo Vanzetti, from the names of their families and descendants, and so, from the name of the Commonwealth of Massachusetts: and I hereby call upon all the people of Massachusetts to pause in their daily endeavours to reflect upon these tragic events, and draw from their historic lessons the resolve to prevent the forces of intolerance, fear, and hatred from ever again uniting to overcome rationality, wisdom and fairness to which our legal system aspires."

*

Sadly Mrs Glendower Evans would not have lived to read these words, but it was something that would have greatly pleased Trando Brini, who by that time was seventy years old. Although this Proclamation didn't proclaim their innocence, it would have been seen as a great achievement by Bart Vanzetti and exactly what he would have wished to accomplish by his death.

*

As for Trando, Governor Fuller had been proved right when he made all those threats. The 'Brini Boy' never did go to Harvard, nor did he join a major orchestra. But thanks to a scholarship and an anonymous donation, he was able to go to Boston University and study music. He then went on to play the violin, conduct orchestras, teach music and become a school principal. He retired, a highly respected member of the community, never leaving the Plymouth area but living in a beautiful cottage just a short distance from the sand dunes and the ocean which he so loved. He also had a long and happy marriage.

When he was 84, he was interviewed about his experiences of the years between the trials and the execution chamber. He was asked about Vanzetti and what kind of man he was. This was his reply.

"He was a wonderful man, like a father to me. He was quiet and gentle. We went for long walks in the country together. Once, I found a sick cat and Bart nursed him back to health. Another day we encountered a group of boys coming home with May flowers they had picked. Bart bought the flowers. Later he told me it was good the boys should earn something for their efforts. Before we reached home he dispersed most of the flowers. He didn't care about his money - ever. He would love to listen to me as I played the violin."

The interviewer then asked if he had been afraid to give evidence as so many of the Italian community were. Beltrando Brini shook his head, "I was never afraid to tell the truth. Even in later years, even in those years of appeals and finally when I presented myself to the Governor after the appeals were denied and I related the story again. I was not afraid because I was telling the truth. I asked the Governor why he was not arresting me for perjury if they thought that I had not told the truth. I always told the truth about my evidence. Every single word was true."

He finished the interview by saying that he thought of those 'Vanzetti years' almost every day of his life and remained convinced of Vanzetti's innocence to the very end.

Beltrando Brini died in 2004, aged 97.

The last word must go to Bartolomeo Vanzetti;

If has not been for this thing I might have lived out my life talking at street corners to scorning men. I might have died unmarked, unknown, a failure.

Now we are not a failure. This is our career and our triumph. Never in our full life can we hope to do such work for tolerance, for justice, for man's understanding of man, as now we do by accident. Our words, our pains – nothing.

The taking of our lives, lives of a good shoemaker and a poor fish peddler, all that moment belongs to us.

That agony is our triumph.

ACKNOWLEDGMENTS

There are many who have helped me in this project, but among those I must mention are: the late Robert H. Montgomery Jr who gave me all the transcripts of the trial and encouraged me to start on this journey. I am grateful to Dr Frank M. D'Alessandro who gave me permission to use the extracts from the interview with Beltrando Brini when he was 84 years old. I am also indebted to Kimberly Reynolds at the Boston Public Library for allowing me to see the Aldino Felicani Archive of Sacco and Vanzetti, which provided me with such a volume of interesting material, including the original death masks. This was a moving and inspiring experience.

Especial thanks are also due to Dr Stephen Carver for his detailed report and helpful advice.

Finally, huge gratitude goes to my family and friends for their interest and encouragement during the process of writing this book.

21502639R00144

Printed in Great Britain
by Amazon